The Bigot List - Book 1

"[The Bigot List]" is a mystery thriller from S. D. Skye ... hard to put down for lovers of spy fiction, highly recommended.—Carl Logan, Midwest Book Review (April 2013)

"Thick with layers, [The Bigot List] is filled with strife, deceit, lust, pain, mystery, and humor."— OOSA Online Book Club

FBI Special Agent J.J. McCall and her co-case agent, Tony Donato, are drawn into an unsanctioned mole hunt when a Russian intelligence officer, working for the FBI, is murdered and they suspect a traitor burrowed deep inside the U.S. Intelligence Community is responsible.

Situation Critical - Book 2

2014 Next Generation Indie Book Award for Multicultural Fiction

★ ★ ★ ★ ★

"If you like a brilliantly executed, thrilling, and addictive suspense novel, SON OF A ITCH is for you. S. D. Skye can flat write her butt off, I was sold, and tagged. This is a great series and J.J. is Jack Ryan with a [lady part]."—Sebella Blue

The award-winning follow up to *The Bigot List* which takes J.J. and her counterintelligence task force on the hunt for Russian moles who breached the nerve center of U.S. national security.

THE SHADOW SYNDICATE

THE FBI SPYCATCHER SERIES (BOOK 3)

(Previously Published As A No Good Itch)

S.D. SKYE

FRANKIE V BOOKS

AN IMPRINT OF LADYLIT PRESS

For Frankie V

Acknowledgments

To my son, William, who is one of my biggest fans and supporters. You are my manager/agent/assistant/bag carrier/anything mom needs, and I appreciate everything you do to help me do what I love.

Lisa and Becky, my Beta Readers. Every year you go through the drudgery of reading my first drafts. I couldn't do this without your support. Thanks for taking time out of your busy schedules to help me make my work better for the fans.

To Mike Lance, thank you so much for taking a chance to tell me something I didn't want to hear. Your feedback has been invaluable to helping me make my work shine, and I appreciate you for it!

To the readers and fans of the J.J. McCall series, thank you for spending time with J.J. and the crew. A lot of people thought I was nuts for attempting this series, but each year I pick up more and more fans who are also crazy enough to believe this is a story worth telling…and reading.

Thank you, Ella Curry for all of your PR efforts, sharing your knowledge, encouragement, and always going the extra mile. It does not go unnoticed or unappreciated.

Thank you to the "real" J.J. McCall—for being such an inspiration to me, even though you never knew it. You're a role model every girl can aspire to be—a consummate professional, an intelligent thinker, a hard worker, and a badass FBI Special Agent.

S.D. Skye

A No Good Itch (A J.J. McCall Novel)

Key FBI Espionage Series Characters (Books 1 and 2)
Federal Bureau of Investigation (Current)
Russell Freeman – Director
John Nixon – Assistant Director of Counterintelligence
J.J. McCall – FBI Special Agent/Russian Operations
Antonio "Tony" Donato – FBI Special Agent/Russian Operations

Former Characters
Naomi Jones McCall (Killed in the Line of Duty) – FBI Special
Agent/Counterintelligence and J.J. McCall's mother.
Lana Michaels/Svetlana Mikhaylova (deceased) – former FBI Special
Agent/Russian Operations; Russian Intelligence Deep Cover Agent also known as the
ICE (Intelligence Community)Phantom.
Jack Sabinski (forcibly retired) – Former Supervisory Special Agent/Russian Opera-
tions
Christopher Johnson (Jailed) – FBI Special Agent/Russian Operations – Served as
cut-out for Lana Michaels' operations.
James "Jim" Cartwright (deceased) – former FBI Assistant Director of Counterin-
telligence, blackmailed and killed by Lana Michaels.

FBI Washington Field Office
SAC MacDonald – Special Agent in Charge of the field office
Kyle Oliver – FBI Supervisory Special Agent/Russian Operations
Hopper Mack – FBI Supervisory Special Agent/Russian Operations

Russian Embassy Personnel
Andrei Komarov – SVR Resident – Responsible for intelligence operations conducted
from Washington Embassy. Comparable to the CIA Chief of Station.
Aleksey Dmitriyev – Security Officer – Most senior counterintelligence officer.
Yuriy Filchenko – Counterintelligence Line Chief – Responsible for supporting
operations that involve recruiting American government personnel to spy for Russia.
Boris Gusin – Signals Officer – Responsible for listening device operation targeting the
White House
Igor Sonin – Counterintelligence Officer – Sent by Golikov to spy on Embassy
Personnel
Vasiliy Turov – Counterintelligence Officer – Sent by Golikov to spy on Embassy
Personnel

SVR Headquarters (The Center)
General Anatoliy Golikov – Counterintelligence Directorate Chief – Oversees all
Russian counterintelligence operations in U.S.-based embassies.
Pavlov Mashkov – Russian organized crime associate – conducts "off-the-books"
operations and murders as ordered by Golikov.

Key Terms

AD – Assistant Director

ATF – Bureau of Alcohol, Tobacco, and Firearms

COINTEL – Counterintelligence

COINTELPRO – Counterintelligence Program

Cut-Out – Operational intermediary. Facilitates the exchange of information between agents.

DEA – Drug Enforcement Agency

Dead Drop - Method of espionage tradecraft used to pass items between two individuals using a secret location and thus does not require them to meet in person.

Exfiltrate (Exfil) - The process of removing personnel when it is considered imperative that they be immediately relocated out of a hostile environment and taken to a secure area.

FSB – Russian Federal Security Service – roughly analogous to the FBI.

Goomar – Mistress

HUMINT – Human Intelligence

ICE Phantom – Intelligence Community Phantom

IED – Improvised Explosive Device

MVD – Ministry of Internal Affairs security forces

NOC – Non Official Cover officer – works undercover with no diplomatic immunity

RAPTURE – A Russian intelligence bugging operation targeting the White House.

SAC – Special Agent in Charge; heads FBI field offices.

SVR – Russian Foreign Intelligence Service – roughly analogous to the CIA.

SIGINT – Signals Intelligence

TAC Team – FBI Tactical Team

TMZ – Gossip Magazine and TV Show

VTC – Video Teleconferencing

WFO – FBI Washington Field Office

Prologue

"THE SUPREME ART OF WAR IS TO SUBDUE THE ENEMY WITHOUT FIGHTING." ~ SUN TZU

Fear, failure, and the fear of failure turned enemies into friends like nothing else in the convoluted world of intelligence and spying. This is no doubt the reason FBI representatives had been summoned to the Russian Embassy in Washington following Lana Michaels' death.

The Minister of Foreign Affairs reeled after a reported "heated discussion" with the U.S. Secretary of State; she promised harsh and swift diplomatic sanctions following the successive wave of embarrassing Russian intelligence blunders that resulted in FBI and Secret Service agent arrests. The tense political situation had outraged the Russians' now tight-lipped government contacts in Washington and New York, drying up critical sources of American intel. The stone silence threatened to paralyze the SVR's intelligence collection across the United States unless they quelled America's fury. Thus, the come-to-Jesus meeting called by the SVR Resident was inevitable and necessary.

FBI Special Agent J.J. McCall marveled at the embassy's ornate grand lobby. Rich white and dark European marbles accented by cardinal red carpet runners, stately winding staircase crowned in gold, and paintings of lush landscapes brightening the halls and sitting areas, J.J. placed it among the most beautiful embassies she'd visited. The sight was impressive and a stark reminder of the country's willingness to spare no expense when it came to putting up deceiving fronts and paying American traitors.

"We'll need a dump truck for the bullshit about to be heaped on us today," J.J. whispered to her co-case agent, Tony Donato. As the lead case agent behind the ruckus, she'd been ordered to attend the meeting, listen, and respond to nothing.

"Shhh," Tony whispered in reply. "The walls have ears."

Resident Andrei Komarov, the Russian equivalent to the CIA Station Chief in Moscow, led J.J., Tony, and Assistant Director of Counterintelligence John Nixon through the hallowed embassy halls until they reached a well-appointed conference room. It contained mahogany-paneled walls, large, open armchairs, and an oversized table large enough to seat Komarov's ego and attitude, both massive in her past experience.

The group, all dressed in their services' uniforms—pin-sharp, woolen suits in late-fall hues concealed under beige all-weather overcoats—was met by the only other declared SVR officer in the Russian Embassy, Security Officer Aleksey Dmitriyev.

Jolted by his presence, J.J. avoided his gaze, kept their handshake and greeting brief. The last time they met, he was not working for her. Now, he was—and the only other person in the group aware of his status was Tony. Butterflies rolled in her stomach as everyone took their seats, and the meeting began. She forced a poker expression and prepared herself for the barrage of lies.

Komarov settled in at the head of the table, his face reddened and contorted. It was as if every word he was about to speak, no doubt carefully selected by the Foreign Minister, would sear his throat and exit his lips like sharpened razors carving him from the inside.

"We've all met before and are quite familiar with one another," Komarov began, shooting a slicing glare through J.J. "So, I'll feel free to dispense with the pleasantries. We all understand why we are here today." Her aggressive targeting of SVR officers for recruitment was legendary...or infamous, depending on which side of the table you sat. She suppressed the awe she felt. The personification of the Russian James Bond in looks and dress, he was devoid of any semblance of an accent.

J.J., Tony, and Nixon exchanged strained glances before she took a deep breath to brace herself. Komarov was about to progress through the four steps of surviving a massive operational failure.

Step 1: Admit nothing.

"There has been a spate of unfortunate and seemingly unfounded reports regarding the activities of our foreign intelligence service inside the United States," he began.

Her birthright, her gift, the ability to detect lies, sent the sensation of an army of crawling ants through her fingertips and up the length of both arms. She clenched her teeth and prepared for *Step 2: Deny Everything.*

"We have no information to substantiate the many reports circulating in the media nor can we speak to the involvement of any of our staff. However, I can assure you that if such activity occurred it was orchestrated by rogue officers conducting unsanctioned operations. If ever discovered, they will be dealt with accordingly. This brings me to my next point..."

As the lies continued, the annoying sensations intensified. The itch stretched through her back and up into her neck. She shifted in her seat and tensed her body to suppress it.

A moment of relief would come with *Step 3: Demand Proof.*

"If your Secretary of State persists in her current path and continues to threaten sanctions against our diplomatic corps, we must require access to the evidence used to justify these unfounded accusations against our government or we will be forced to reciprocate and target the American in Moscow."

They always demanded proof because they knew the FBI couldn't provide the most critical elements, at least not so early in the investigations. Such provisions risked revealing FBI sources and methods, potentially compromising the Russian Embassy recruit sitting across the table from J.J. It would also expose the FBI's knowledge of the listening device found in the White House Situation Room, an announcement the President had postponed for reasons unbeknownst to her.

Nixon cleared his throat. "It's forthcoming," are the only two words he offered, which was two too many in J.J.'s estimation. He said, "Continue with your little speech, please," in his typical condescending way.

From the pinched expression on Komarov's face, he took the comment in the spirit in which it was intended, just as J.J. would've. This certainly contributed to *Step 4: Make counter-accusations.*

"And if your government should bring forth any evidence against the Service, we may be required to present our own proof that these arrests are merely a provocation to discredit Russia and increase hostilities within the international community given U.S. opposition to our security operations in the Ukraine."

Bullshit. But J.J. gave credit where it was due—the guy was good.

"We're not here to debate the validity of your political and military agenda," Nixon replied. "The FBI's primary concern is securing the homeland from terrorists and spies. So, if we could cut to the chase, why have you requested our presence here today?"

J.J.'s eyebrow arched. She'd never known Nixon to be a man with backbone. He usually preyed on the weak rather stand up to the strong.

"Ahhh, yes," Komarov said, relaxing his tone and posture, he leaned his back against the chair. "We brought you here to extend an olive branch, if you will. I've been asked to assure you that the Service is not controlling any operations targeting citizens inside the United States. Negotiations regarding the specifics of the new plans are underway within our executive channels and will demonstrate our proposed new era of cooperation. We would like to collaborate on issues, such as terrorism, which would be mutually beneficial to both our countries."

By now, the itching sensation had permeated J.J.'s entire being. If the human body contained over a billion nerves, every one of hers had been stimulated in the worst way. She clenched her legs together and strained not to dissolve into a scratching frenzy.

But, finally, the truth had been revealed. The Russians wanted to purchase conciliation with terrorism intelligence. J.J. felt relieved. With FBI Director Russell Freeman at the helm, U.S. national security could never be bought at so cheap a price.

Chapter 1

Monday Afternoon — Alexandria Jail

The U.S. Attorney's Office had stacked so many charges against Maddix Cooper, the next time he set foot outside of prison would be to take the pine box dive into a six-foot pit. Mandatory sentences for espionage, conspiracy, first-degree murder, and obstruction of justice. The list of traitorous offenses had left FBI Special Agents J.J. McCall and Tony Donato in a major predicament: How to convince a man with zero motivation to divulge information contrary to his best interest – without the use of torture? This question plagued J.J. as she and Tony crossed through the barbed-wire fence into the detention facility. Within a few minutes, they'd be face-to-face with the lowest form of human in existence; the answer wasn't coming fast enough.

The stench of confinement, an unsettling combination of despair and delinquency, permeated the cushy looking fortress on the outskirts of Northern Virginia and turned J.J.'s stomach. She'd spent more time in this hell hole over the past month than in her entire career, and she didn't care if she never saw it again.

Her last visit was at the behest of her then jailed boss, Supervisory Special Agent Jack Sabinski. Framed for committing espionage by his Jezebel, the dead Lana Michaels, Jack summoned J.J. and pled for her help in proving his innocence, a feat she accomplished despite her longstanding contempt for his mistreatment of her.

Now, J.J. focused her mind on interrogating the newest offender—Maddix Cooper, who, to her delight, was on the verge of becoming some inmate's bitch. He'd already ratted out Gary Mosin as the second member of Lana Michaels' Russian sleeper agent network during their showdown on the Devil's Rest. He also spilled that Mosin had disappeared off the grid and was fleeing to Moscow—but left out the details of Mosin's travel route, facts they needed to know in order to intercept him.

Never had an interrogation been so pointless from J.J.'s vantage point. No way in hell would Maddix divulge the details of Mosin's escape plans. The only reason he confessed their connection in the first place was to escape the bullet from J.J.'s gun. Now, tucked behind the bars of Virginia's premier correctional facility for newly arrested spies, he awaited a conviction that would guarantee if he died twice and came back to life, he'd still have to serve forty years. As far as he knew, a plea bargain might do little more than eliminate only one of his many life sentences. He had no viable reason to reveal another word. Certainly not out of the goodness of the cavernous pit where his heart was supposed to be.

The Sheriffs walked J.J. and Tony through a series of security doors until they reached the interrogation room. They left their overcoats with their escorts and tugged their suit jackets straight before entering. The sight of Kendell Phillips' murderer shrouded in orange and shackled at the hands and feet gave J.J. a burst of pleasure she hadn't felt since her early morning romp with Tony. A reddish-blue bruise circled his eye and spread to the cap of his jaw. His gaze disintegrated under the weight of her glare and fell to his twiddling thumbs. She prepared to speak when an overwhelming scent jarred her senses—the smell of contemptible swine.

"Figured you two would show up sooner or later," Maddix said, his arrogance soaking up the little-remaining tolerable air in the room. It was a small box with dirty white cinderblock walls and a two-way mirror on the back side. He scratched the five o'clock scruff seeping from his square jawline. Red cracks peppered Maddix's penetrating steel gray eyes, and Lipton-sized bags bubbled from beneath them. His first few nights behind bars had left him sleepless and worn, an inconsequential justice for a scumbag who offed his fiancé to ensure the survival of his spy ring.

He locked his eyes on J.J. and all but ignored Tony. "Hope you enjoy the view because I've got nothing to say to you…or your little partner here." He jutted his chin toward Tony.

"My, my, my," J.J. said to Maddix. "What an ugly fall from grace. Too bad they don't make an Armani perp suit. You used to wear him so well."

Positioned across from Maddix, Tony scanned the rat's face and looked at him with a pained expression. "Rough night, eh? Did they forget to put you in solitary? Looks like you've been mingling with the locals."

"Nothing I can't handle," he said with a shrug. Then he leaned back, spread his knees wide, and placed his hands in his lap. "So, this is the reason you came all the way to Shangri-La? To gloat?"

J.J. savored his misery and then vexed him with a tight smile. "We're here to discuss your comrade in arms, Hawk—Gary Mosin."

The usual good cop/bad cop routine would have zero impact on Maddix, the former Secret Service agent. For him, the routine would be a day at the office. The puppet show held no mystery. The little information he'd dribbled to date wouldn't help a dog find bone. Even with the odds stacked against her, taking down Mosin before he found comforting shelter in the eager, waiting hands of Russia's FSB was an imperative, not an option. He'd hatched what appeared to be a foolproof escape plan before defecting to Russia, but even the best-laid plans had vulnerabilities ripe for exploiting.

"Newsflash, doll." Maddix forced out a grating laugh, overplaying his weak position just a smidge. "You get nothing from me, not without a deal. I want immunity."

"Immunity?" J.J. blinked in rapid motion. After rolling her neck and eyes, she folded her arms over her stomach, lifted a single eyebrow, and prepared to kill any dream he'd concocted of shaking his bid. She'd arrived with the intent to take the path of least resistance, but his crassness suggested he sought the off-road experience. "First of all, my name is J.J. or Agent McCall, not doll. Secondly, if you ever deign to—," she started. Tony rested his arm on hers to stop her rant and signal he'd take over. He understood better than anyone that the bees-to-honey approach went out the door with the word "doll."

"Listen, you ain't gotta make this difficult. We didn't come here to pick a fight. Give us the information we need, and you can go back to counting the tiles on the ceiling . . . or whatever it is you do on the inside." Tony contrived a calm demeanor as he reached into his pant pocket and pulled out a pack of Marlboro 100s and a book of matches. He slid them to the middle of the table until they stopped beside a plastic ashtray. "Our treat. Enjoy. But if you choose to stay on the difficult route, we can reverse course any time."

Maddix cupped his hands and with no show of gratitude, pulled the offerings to the table's edge, his shackles jangling with his every move. He folded back the foil on the corner of the pack and knocked the open end against his wrist until a cigarette emerged. Then his brow drew together, furrowed in confusion. "You don't have a clue, do you?" His gaze ping-ponged between J.J. and Tony before he shook his head. *"That's* why you're here. You don't know!" With a slight air of cockiness, the corners of his mouth edged upward in a sneer; he eased back against the chair. "At the rate you're going, *The Washington Post* will get the scoop before you do."

"The fuck you talkin' about?" Tony's gruff New York attitude released like the Kraken. His face reddened as the sound of his grinding teeth emitted a low hum. Maddix's arrogance stoked his anger, affecting Tony as easily as J.J.'s. "What part of 'you ain't gotta make this difficult' did you not understand? You're already testin' my patience. I promise you that's not a smart move, not for someone in your position…which in…"—he glanced down at his watch—"about an hour will be bent over for some booty bandit."

Maddix took a slow drag from his cigarette and allowed the smoke to swirl around his lips before resting the cancer stick in the ashtray. He again shifted his cocky gaze between the two. "The great and powerful J.J. McCall. Just as ignorant as he is, huh? Man, I should tell both of you to go screw yourselves. I don't need *you.* You need *me.*"

J.J. caught a glance of Tony's fist which had curled into a tense ball. She pressed her hand to his arm to dissuade him from any impulsive actions. Like an electric current coursing through her brain, the touch sparked an epiphany, brought to light the answer to the question she posed to herself earlier. The solution to her Maddix predicament was simple. How do you make a man divulge information against his best interest?

You don't.

Chapter 2

Standing at his seventh-floor window, Assistant Director John Nixon stared down into the stone-paved courtyard in the heart of the J. Edgar Hoover building. The personified bronze figures representing Fidelity, Bravery, and Integrity glowed like beacons of justice in the fluorescent up-lighting. They shone a stark light on his glory . . . and his shame. While his mind should have been focused on overseeing the operations to hunt down fugitive traitor Gary Mosin and Task Force Phantom Hunter's efforts to shut down the illegals network, his thoughts centered on more selfish concerns—ending his career in humiliating disgrace.

Jack Sabinski had warned him days ago that J.J. had started asking questions neither he nor Jack ever expected to answer. They struck a deal; they buried the truth...until now. What were the chances the daughter of FBI Special Agent Naomi Jones would follow directly in her mother's footsteps and position herself as one of the top agents in the counterintelligence program?

His stomach curled at the thought of J.J. discovering the truth. She'd supplanted her mother as the bane of his Bureau existence and posed a dangerous threat to the life he held dear. Jack should've eliminated the risk when he had the chance. Now, the more success she experienced, the better her chances of discovering the secret and the greater the effort required to contain her.

Leaving the important task of concealing the Black Panther Party investigation to the likes of his inept friend demonstrated poor judgment, at best, unbridled stupidity at worst. Nixon realized he should've dealt with the situation in his own way. Now with the burn of his deception flaming at the nape of his neck, he would make damn certain he succeeded where Jack failed. He'd use his power in the way Jack never displayed the balls to do.

Serving as acting director in Freeman's absence while he recovered from his mild "episode," Nixon planned his first step: Obtain the file holding the key to his and Jack's collective fates. He'd ensure the damning document disappeared forever. Tying the missing documents to him would prove an almost impossible feat. He'd claim they were gone before he received the file.

Nixon released a groan and, in a swift motion, turned to his desk and hit the intercom button.

"Get Jack Sabinski on line one," John barked to his secretary. "I need to speak with him now."

"Yes, sir. Right away," Luisa Sanchez replied.

The decision to hijack the documents rested on his shoulders, but keeping the lies consistent was both of their responsibilities.

A few moments later, a buzz jarred him out of his thoughts. "Jack Sabinski on Line 1," Luisa said.

"Johnny Johnny Johnny!" Jack bellowed. His words slurred as if he pulled them from the bottom of a liquor bottle. Rumor had it Jack filled the empty first weeks of his retirement swimming in a pool of Jack Daniels, to Nixon's dismay. All available evidence had proved the gossip was grounded in fact.

"Jack, long time, no hear from," Nixon said, the tone in his voice measured. "Heard you skipped the interview I set up for you last week. Wasted a lot of pulled strings."

"Johnny, come on," he said. "I'm a thirty-plus year FBI vet. You can't expect me to take a job as a glorified security officer. Makes me appear desperate."

"No, it would've made you appear employed. Stopped you from drowning your sorrows…and your liver."

Jack sighed. "If I wanted a guilt trip, I woulda called my mother. You're wastin' your breath. So, what's goin' on?"

"As a matter of fact," he replied. "I called for a more important reason. Have you been keeping up with recent events?"

"You mean, J.J.?" Jack said. "Her position is strengthening with every success. If Freeman concedes and gives her access, that'll set off a shitstorm from here to Houston. In hindsight, advising her to ask her father about what happened may not have done us any favors, either. She caught me off guard."

"You listen to me, Jack. Your days of being off-guard are over. If you don't pull your act together, Houston's going to be the least of your concerns."

"Agreed," Jack said. "I guess I should've dealt with her while I had the chance. Funny, she believes the root of our dissension revolves around her race. She hadn't even scratched the surface. Playing racist didn't distract her; it added fuel to an out-of-control blaze. She's more determined than ever to discover the truth. You and I both understand what must happen to make this go away, but I couldn't get into headquarters now if Jesus escorted me."

"I'm on top of it. I've already put in a call to Devin Fitzpatrick in New York. He owes me a big favor. If we can't stop her, at least we'll slow her down. In the meantime, I'll recover the documents and make them disappear."

"How? The Chief File Inspector or whatever he is, is anal and OCD to a fault when it comes to tracking the ins and outs of the files."

"Yes, the files, not the documents. Once I get my hands on them, this entire nightmare will be over. By the time she returns from New York, she can kiss goodbye any hope of finding out what happened to her mother. The story will live and die with you and me."

"Well, not quite. Don't forget about Max McCall. He knows."

"Yeah, but he's got more to lose than either one of us if the truth gets out."

"What's that?" Jack asked.

"His daughter."

Chapter 3

Monday Evening — Alexandria Jail

J.J. stood up and circled the interrogation cell, throwing her hands in the air for dramatic effect. "Caught me red-handed, Maddix," J.J. said. "You're right. If you don't cough up the 4-1-1 on Mosin, we face major, if not insurmountable, challenges. Score one for you. But, uh, I came bearing news that might be of interest to you. We've contacted an attorney on your behalf. He'll be here shortly to discuss the latest twist in your case."

"What? I told you I already understand my charges. I'm not ready to talk to some shit public defender."

"Public defender? With all the money you …" she paused. "Wait, he cleaned you out, didn't he?" Of course, Mosin took the money and ran to Moscow, she thought. The question she had was why Maddix would still protect him.

He cut his eyes at her and drew another long drag from his cigarette.

J.J. offered a cocky smile. "Hate to add insult to injury, but there's been a new development. Justice is filing capital charges."

He jerked his head back. "They wanna give me the death penalty? Bullshit!" His brow furrowed in confusion which transformed into anger. Then he laughed. "You two should become an act. What do you take me for? Get a new routine. I invented this one. Now, could you zip this farce along so I can return to counting ceiling tiles? Go ahead. I'm listening…cooperate with the FBI or blah blah blah…vain pointless threat…blah blah blah. Same old shit."

Maddix's split-second of shock did not escape J.J's notice. She'd spotted the chink in his armor despite his bravado and committed to digging in until he fessed up the truth.

J.J. gave a half-shrug as the corners of her lips curled up into a smirk. "Is that what you were saying when you got cracked in the skull last night? Blah, blah, blah. What your bunk buddies do to your ass in prison is nothing compared to the stench of burning flesh after you spend seven minutes in the hot seat. And right now, *two* people stand between you and a, shall we say, shocking finale. I'll give you one guess as to who they are. Go ahead. I'm listening."

Maddix paused and rolled his eyes up to the ceiling, ditching his poker face. "There's no fucking way you've got the evidence to make capital charges stick. I'm law enforcement, remember? I didn't contribute to the death of a covert agent, nor did I give information to aid and abet our enemies in a time of war. So you can take your piece of shit threats and stick 'em where the sun don't shine. Then pound sand back to FBI headquarters. I've got nothing left to say." He tamped his cigarette in the ashtray. With a smug grin, he said, "Except one thing…thanks for the smokes. Guard! I'm ready."

"Au contraire, mon frère." J.J. sat back in her seat. "You can return to your quarters, but take this with you. We've got you on tape. You confessed your participation in a spy network responsible for the deaths of not one but two of my sources—Mikhail Polyakov and Kostya Belikov. Both covert agents. Dead. You may not have loaded the gun, but your prints are all over the trigger."

He shook his head in feverish motions. "No, no, you're making this up," Maddix said. The arrogance drained from his face along with the color, leaving him pale and sapped. J.J. figured he hadn't considered this new angle.

"Trust me. I'm not a good actress. Justice plans to make an example of you to discourage your little treasonous alliance from further illegal activities." Her voice was soft but convincing. "They want to send a strong message to the network and to the Russians. Since you're the only member of Lana's organization in custody…well…you're the man, so to speak."

"No, no. Justice will never take this to court. The government won't risk releasing classified information to the public."

"Ah, but you forget. My sources are dead, and the Russians are aware of their identities. They've already conducted a damage assessment to determine each and every piece of compromised intel. My guess is the Russians fed them bad information to pass to us anyway. I no longer need to protect them or their data," J.J. lied. "Besides, you yourself suggested Mosin's going to the press. Once he goes public with the information, our worries about disclosing classified intelligence in court are over. Any bargaining chip in your hand will dissipate the second Mosin's safe in Moscow."

Maddix's face turned flush; the little bit of life remaining drained from his eyes. He leaned forward on his elbows and cupped his head with both hands, pressing his fingers into his scalp until the tips whitened.

"Funny how things worked out, huh? Seems no one needs the FBI to find Mosin more than you," Tony said, handing him a new cigarette. "Here. Light this and take an after-sex puff…because you've royally screwed yourself."

Maddix sat soundless, all motion frozen. He didn't turn or glance up. Just stewed there, his mug as grim as death, shackled to the table and his lies. His deception had ricocheted and exploded in his face like a scum-seeking missile. At once, his body trembled; he released a burst of sniffles and descended into intermittent weeps. "You don't understand. Look at my face. You see this?" He pointed to his bruises. "The network—Russian mafia associates—they're as thick as roaches on the inside. They'll kill me if I talk."

"I've got news for you—they're ruthless. You're dead either way…" J.J. said. "Without our help, no prison has walls strong enough to protect you. Cooperating will ensure you're placed where you can serve out your sentence without getting shanked to death. That'll depend on the value and reliability of the information you provide."

He grudgingly sat upright in his seat and scooted his chair closer to the table, his eyes inflamed. "Fine. What do you want?"

"Mosin's location and a detailed accounting of the information he stole from the White House," Tony replied.

After letting out a long hard breath, he said, "He's meeting with some doctor. Why? I don't have a clue. Then he's taking a passenger freighter . . . to St. Petersburg. He didn't tell me the shipping line. From there, he's on a train to Moscow. Understand, this guy's fucking paranoid like no one you've ever seen. Doesn't trust anyone he can't kill. Not in Moscow, not anywhere. He's scared half the Russian Security Services are working for the U.S. or our allies. So he's planning to walk in."

"Walk-in where?" J.J. said.

"Lubyanka Square."

"Wait…FSB Headquarters?" Tony asked.

Maddix nodded as J.J. and Tony exchanged strained glances.

Tony sat up straight. "And what intelligence is he trading?"

"The man masterminded the operation to bug the Situation Room—the fucking Fort Knox of intel," Maddix said, his expression incredulous. "Isn't it obvious?"

Tony pinched his lips together and released a heavy sigh. Through clenched teeth he growled, "This ain't Blue's Clues. You've got thirty seconds to spill before I crack your skull open."

J.J. turned to Maddix and glared in silence. Her twisted expression sending a strong message: If he didn't offer an explanation soon, he wouldn't live long enough to receive the death penalty.

"Must I spell out everything for you?" Maddix said. "He's got recordings. The President, National Security Council, Joint Staff, CIA. Maybe years' worth. Every meeting that took place in that conference room. Every word spoken. Plans. Strategies. Damaging high-level discussions about our enemies…and our allies. I mean you gotta figure the batteries couldn't last forever, but they probably lasted long enough."

"Jesus, Mary, and Joseph!" J.J. swallowed hard and tried to control her breathing which had become more labored. The thought of this information getting to the FSB or SVR sickened J.J.'s stomach, forced her morning coffee to the back of her throat like acidic bile. Any disclosure would cause untold damage to U.S. national security. "How could he…there's no way. No way."

"Voice activated recorder with extended battery reserve. This system's designed to serve as the back-up he would deliver to the Russians in the event the bug failed. He installed them at the same time. Must've removed it the night the fire alarm sounded in the Sit Room, and he took it with him when he defected," Maddix said.

"How…how do you know the recorder was there? And that it's missing?"

"He told me. Had me by the saggy bags. No way I'd rat him out. Mashkov's people would chop me up like last night's sushi. I searched for it during the fire alarm that emptied the White House after you found the listening device. Came up empty."

"Dammit!"

Maddix continued, "I don't need to tell you what's gonna happen if that gets into the hands of the Russians."

"Not to mention the press." J.J. clenched her eyes shut for a second. "They'll massacre the president…even more than usual. We've got to report this to the director now. As for you," J.J. said, slicing Maddix with a machete sharp glare. "You better pray we find Mosin before the FSB does or you've just committed suicide. I swear if you don't die in prison, I'll take you out myself."

13

Chapter 4

Wendell Hinkley had spent the better part of the morning preparing the mail cart for his staff's file deliveries when he heard the clack of heavy footsteps padding toward his office. He peered through the door's window panel and noticed a man with a hard expression bustling toward the Special File Room.

John Nixon? he mumbled under his breath. The Assistant Director rang the bell on the counter and stared at the door as if telepathically summoning someone to respond. The sight struck Wendell as unusual, an agent of Nixon's stature descending from on high. In most instances, their secretaries handled such administrivia on their behalf—or they received briefings on the contents from more junior agents or analysts. His eyes narrowed with suspicion.

Sporting his favorite slacks, button down, and bow-tie in hopes of impressing Sunnie, Wendell's curiosity piqued. He emerged from the back room with his lop-sided afro and glasses weighed forward on the bridge of his nose.

"Yes, can I help you?" he asked before acknowledging the AD's identity. "Ohhh, Mr. Nixon. What brings you down here? Luisa always takes care of your file requests."

"Well, yes," he responded, "but Luisa is handling another matter, so I decided to process this request myself. Uh, here's my file request form."

Wendell took the slip of paper from his hand and scanned it. Given his encyclopedic knowledge of most key cases in the storage area, archived or otherwise, he recognized case number and his mistrust mushroomed. He typed the number into the computer sitting on the counter.

"Sorry," he said, jutting the paper back to its owner. "I can't let you review that file. Under strict orders from Director Freeman, no one can access it without his expressed permission, and your name does not appear on the list of authorized reviewers."

"Check again," Nixon ordered.

"Whatever you say," Wendell replied.

Two weeks prior, Director Freeman had restricted access to several groups of files, and Nixon's inquiry was among them. Wendell found Freeman's interest odd and Nixon's even more so. No one had requested access to any of the records in over two decades. He typed the case number and waited for the rejection message to appear then shook his head no.

Nixon shot a condescending glare at the identification badge dangling from the clerk's neck. "Excuse me, Wendell is it?" He puffed out his chest. "I'm acting in the director's stead while he recovers from his episode. I'm sure his instructions do not apply to me."

Wendell traced the words on the screen with his index finger and pretended to read them again. "The instructions do not say 'me or a party authorized to act on my behalf.' They say 'without my expressed permission.' Period."

John's face reddened and jaw clenched no doubt stunned at the audacity of what he considered the two-year-old file clerk denying his majesty's request. Wendell read the spurn in his every expression. Nixon barked. "Get the supervisor, now! I will not stand for such disrespect…from the likes of *you*."

Wendell jerked his head back and paused. Nixon grew incensed and had garnered an infamous reputation for bullying to get his way rather than using common courtesy and consideration. In a calm voice, Wendell replied, "Give me just one moment." Then he disappeared into the back room. He peeked past the sheathing to watch Nixon without his notice, before leaving to grab his lunch.

Ten minutes later when he returned, Nixon still paced the floor, grunting and mumbling under his breath, again and again, his glance flitting between the back door and his watch. In the midst of his fury, Sunnie walked in and took a seat on the guest chair behind him, eyeing Nixon with her brows drawn in.

Wendell bounded through the door with half of a sandwich in his hands and smiled, "Oh Sunnie! I'll be right with you."

Nixon glowered at Wendell. His eyes narrowed; his nostrils flared.

"Afternoon, Mr. Nixon. Don't think we've met. I'm Wendell Hinkley, the Chief Supervisor of the Special File Room. As you've suggested,

I've conferred with management. If the director provides his authorization by signature or phone, I will be happy to deliver the files to you myself. Until then, please see yourself out. I'd like to finish my lunch."

Nixon pinched his lips and growled between gritted teeth. "You won't get away with this. You're going to wish you'd never seen my face." He stormed out, slamming the door behind him.

"Too late," Wendell mumbled. Nixon's threats had no impact on him whatsoever. He understood as well as any government employee that Nixon would spend the better part of three years navigating a web of bureaucratic red human resource tape to fire him. And, in the process, he'd be forced to reveal the reason for the urgency of his request, which Wendell suspected he'd never do.

He took another bite of his sandwich while eyeing Sunnie's sexy ensemble. He loved the curve of her wide hips, thick thighs, and ample breasts spilling from her V-neck tops. He even loved the colorful streaks in her black hair that used to cause a stir amongst Bureau conservatives but now were little more than routine. Maybe that's why she'd quit wearing them. The new suits were classy, but he liked it more when her wardrobe accented her charismatic personality. She'd stopped into his office, which meant she needed him. He loved those days…even if he could only offer access to files.

Sunnie covered her mouth in shock. "Uh, Wendell? You recognized his face, didn't you?"

"Of course," Wendell said. "Assistant Director of the Douche Bag Division."

"He seemed pretty fired up at you. What the heck was all the fuss about?"

"He wanted access to a restricted file but the director didn't give him authorization."

"Authorization? What'd he want to see? Hoover's file?"

"No, which is the strange part. The case started during the Hoover-era. One of those old COINTEL cases. The FBI agent was Naomi Jones. Never seen one of these with so many restrictions."

"I'm sorry. Did you say 'Naomi *Jones*'?" she asked, holding her hand against her chest, her mouth hanging open. "Did he explain the urgency?"

"No, also kinda strange. I remember she was one of the first black female agents, killed in the line of duty. Went undercover in the Black Panthers or something. The Bureau released most of those files through

Freedom of Information Act requests but for some reason this one remains restricted."

Sunnie exhaled and sprang toward the door. "Uhhh…well. I've got to run," she said without even bothering to look back.

"But…but what did you need?" Wendell called out to Sunnie's vapors.

"I'll be back," she replied from half way down the hall. "I've got an important phone call to make."

Wendell took a moment to consider the implication of Nixon's visit and Sunnie's hasty departure. Something was amiss and, to his knowledge, he had one option to prevent the worst from happening. So, he gulped down the last bite of his sandwich and headed to the storage area for a long afternoon. He had a lot of work to do.

Chapter 5

Tuesday Afternoon — U.S. Embassy, Moscow

Six dreaded the thirteen-hour flight back to Moscow, as he downed the Smirnov with a gulp and pulled a blanket over his shoulders. His mind weighed down with thoughts of the woman he'd left behind, rather than the challenges that lay ahead. Watching J.J. and Tony squabble over Hershey Bars and peanut brittle gave him the shred of hope he wished to exploit for his own good. At least this was before he received a call indicating the CIA Director had fingered him to support a mission in the one place in the world he vowed never to return again.

This was not to say the city had not been kind to him even with its bi-polar charm. Sprawling modern skyscrapers juxtaposed against white communist-era tower blocks. Bright, multicolored cathedral onion domes against the Kremlin's towered fortress. Not unlike D.C. in many ways with the beauty of its monuments interspersed with its monolithic government headquarters. But deep inside Moscow was the heart of its people. Even during the frigid winters, and under the watchful eyes of the security services, one could always find pockets of warmth where borsch ran cold and the vodka ran deep.

Only after receiving the hand of J.J.'s source in the mail did Six feel pressed to leave. The gruesome dose of Russian intelligence "hospitality" sent him scrambling for American shores.

Before he left Langley, Director Lance Miller's orders were clear, un-wavering. The mission: Impossible.

"You can thank General Ronaldson for this, always giving me shit. He convinced the council to overrule me," he said, taking a seat behind the desk in his seventh-floor suite. He was a muscular, broad-shouldered man whose immaculate suit and spit-shined shoes harkened back to his Army past. "Been a bug up my ass since they created the Director of National Intelligence position," he said. "Mosin is officially a DIA HVT

– high-value target—subject to kill or capture orders—which is code for Kill-on-Sight. Stupid son of bitch doesn't even know what he stole."

Six jerked his head back. "What *did* he steal?"

Director Miller invited Six to take a seat across from him on the couch and leaned in. "We have every reason to believe covert plans for the European Missile Defense may have been revealed in a conversation on those recordings. If the information gets out, it'll leave the U.S. in a political and military shit storm so thick, fresh air will be a distant memory for years to come."

"Jesus." Six felt a brain spasm; the migraine came on like gangbusters.

"A military special ops team is on its way to Moscow. Your job is to get to him first and keep him alive—we must recover the intelligence. We can't risk it getting into the hands of Russian intelligence."

"I understand, sir. But how? I'm a declared CIA security officer for goddsakes. They know who I am. How the hell can I operate from the Embassy?"

"We've hired you some help. You'll get the details when you arrive at the Station. Our contractor operates one of our black sites outside of Moscow—Ghost Man. He's got a head start, and you have the intelligence from Task Force Phantom Hunter that the DIA team isn't privy to. I've got to warn you…if Ghost gets wind of the special ops team, he may turn on us."

For the first time in years, Six felt almost impotent. A thousand factors lay outside his control. If he dropped the ball, the country would suffer for it. He couldn't let that happen.

"Say what you have to say, do whatever you have to do. Keep him alive and recover that intel at all costs. You are not to return to Langley without it."

"So, what happens if…when I recover the intel?"

"You're the best exfil specialist we've got. Extract him, and we'll turn him over to the FBI. I've got Congressional oversight breathing down my neck like a horny teenager. I'd like to come out on the other side of this one on the high road and with my hands clean."

"And if he doesn't turn it over…if I don't recover it."

"Simple," Miller said. "Kill him."

•••

Not two hours after landing in Sheremetyevo Airport, Bart Russell, the Moscow Station duty officer, whisked Six into the Embassy to attend a case briefing with Mark Levin, the CIA Chief of Station. The U.S. Embassy complex, America's soil in the heart of Moscow, was enclosed on all sides by bricked and gated barriers. Moscow station operated inside an architecturally indistinct 12-story block of steel-reinforced concrete and blue-green glass. Though its environs were distinctly Muscovite, with one side facing the Russian White House, the interior workspace design was distinctly American, down to the open floors, big-wig offices, worker-bee cubicles, gray industrial carpeting, and left-facing doorknobs.

A bathroom stop and a bag of chips later, Six entered the secure facility conference room and took a seat at the head of the table, adjacent to Mark, where he belonged. Six noticed Mark's attire had gone from stylish to shabby with his silk tie loosened, collar unbuttoned, and sleeves rolled to the elbow. His close-cropped black hair was now scraggly, and his smooth-shaven jaw now sported a five-o'clock shadow. The piercing blue eyes which weakened the knees of most women in the station were now bleary and cracked red from late nights and early mornings. The political instability and spy games had taken their toll and Mark's Adonis reputation paid a hefty price.

"Back so soon," Mark said, joking given that Six had left Moscow a little more than a month before.

"What can I say? Couldn't stay away," Six replied. "So, who's on first and what's on second?"

"Stanislav Vorobyev," Mark replied. He launched into an in-depth briefing on the former Washington Residency security chief and now fugitive. He'd killed his allegedly depraved Directorate Chief and absconded from SVR Headquarters, the Center, with enough secret documents to start a Russian intelligence archive.

"Hear he's dead," Six said with a wink and a scampish smile. "Or didn't you receive the memo?"

"Yes, and we're trying to keep him that way. But he'll rise like Lazarus if we don't develop an airtight plan to get him out of here." Mark scratched his head. "While J.J.'s plan is this side of genius, we have yet to produce a body; there's been no meeting with the family to return the remains, and this guy's got other issues too."

Six studied the pained expression on Mark's face. "Oh, hell, what's the problem?"

"Let's just say that while he's a good handler when it comes to running agents, he's not good at *being* handled. He's giving us shit at every turn. We put him in a guarded safe house, and one of our trusted assets checks in on him every so often. Despite our explicit instructions, he does whatever the hell he pleases. Refuses to stay in disguise, damn Russian pride. Even worse, he refuses to turn over the documents. Says he'll reveal where he stashed them once he's inside the embassy."

"Well, shit. Who's controlling whom?" Six asked. "If he doesn't cough them up, we cut him loose."

"Easier said than done. We need the intel, and it's worth more than the cost of abandoning the idiot who can hand it to us, no matter how careless he is."

Six shrugged.

"And don't forget our President killed him, so-to-speak, even if he did it through a channel they shouldn't have been listening to. If they find out he's alive, due to our screw-up, how many sources do you think will trust us in the future? Zero." His fingers formed a circle.

Six understood that while the op was not easy, whatever bullshit the Agency had to endure to get him to safety would be well worth the trouble. The intelligence cache might bring down not only the illegal spy ring, but put a screeching halt to all Russian operations targeting the United States at home and abroad.

"Let's not forget we've still got a high-ranking source working in place at the Center. We stand to lose a whole lot more than this intel if the Russians gut Moscow Station."

Six nodded. The big picture kept his concerns about Stan's carelessness in perspective. "So, is he safe?"

"For the moment. He's holed up not far from our safe house in the Biryulevo area. Our most significant problem now is one of logistics. We've got to get him inside the embassy or out of the country and under close scrutiny. We could walk from Moscow to Washington on the surveillance bodies the FSB is using to cover us."

"Why can't we just put him in a trunk?"

"Increased random militia checkpoints throughout the city, at least fifty of them. They're also on high alert for a terrorist threat. Our personnel are stopped daily. We can't explain away an undead SVR officer hiding in the trunk. We can't risk it. So you're going to have to come up with something a little more creative."

Six palmed his forehead. "Yeah…creativity is my middle name. So, let's move on to the second."

"Gary Mosin," Mark said. "Son of a bitch arrived here on a freighter three days ago. He's been lying low ever since. Good news is we're ninety-nine percent certain he hasn't passed the intel to FSB yet. On the flip side, we can't contain him under grid for much longer. Once the Russians get a hold of him, he's as golden as that other piece of shit, sleaze ball who shall remain nameless."

The notion sparked a well of fury in Six's gut. He'd dedicated almost every moment of his professional life to protecting his country, a patriot until the end. He characterized any American who put U.S. national security at risk as an enemy of the state subject to trial and imprisonment. And he expected Mosin's capture to result in a lifetime in Supermax once they turned him over to the FBI. His eyes squeezed into slits. "One thing American history has proven—from Al Capone to Osama bin Laden—nobody who betrays the U.S. is untouchable. When you're on the list, there's two ways to get off it—both of them end in justice. Mosin can't hide forever…neither can the other one," Six snapped. He slipped off of his soapbox and relaxed his tone.

"Agreed," Mark said. "But I'm not certain justice is the goal this time. I'll be honest. We've been thrust between two dissenting camps in our executive political leadership. To put a fine point on the issue, both sides want to see Mosin in hell. One side wants to send him there by the end of the week. They think we need to send a message to anyone who considers selling U.S. secrets. If we don't get the point across successfully, more damaging compromises are ahead."

Six shrugged. "Well…something to consider, I suppose."

"And some of the black bag operatives want him dead whether we recover the intel or not—hard to determine which camp they fall in."

"So, we got a location on Mosin?"

"Three days ago, I got headquarter's approval to enlist some support. A Marine, former Force Recon special ops. One of the contractors I told you about. He's on the case because we can't risk using anyone from the Station. Leads a team coordinating black bag ops across Russia and the Republics for the Agency. His father's a Russian Jew. Immigrated to the U.S. 35 years ago but he's still got some legit but sketchy connections. Works in our favor as long as nobody finds out he's CIA operated and owned."

"A Marine, huh? You trust him?"

Mark nodded. "With my life. I wouldn't be standing here today without his help. Saved my ass twice in the first Iraq war."

"So what's his deal?"

"Loose Russian mafia ties. Some of his mob connections are also tied to shady Russian intel officers who'd give up their mothers and first born for crisp new hundred dollar bills. But he's the real deal. And we've scheduled a meeting between you and him…tonight."

"Tonight? You need to lay off the vodka because you are drunk if you think I'm going anywhere except to bed."

"Yes, I do need to lay off the booze…but you still must go."

"If I leave the embassy in the open, the FSB will be on me like honey on a bee's ass. I'm declared, remember? And thanks to Ames, they're well aware that I'm exfil. They've got to be wondering what's brought me back to paradise so soon."

"You'll be concealed."

Six grimaced and rolled his eyes. "My life's been moving a thousand miles a minute for the last two weeks. I'm jet-lagged, starving, and craving the comfort of meager accommodations, hard pillows, and listening devices, and you expect me to pull a tuck-and-roll out of my ass tonight? You must've bumped your head."

"Listen, we could wrap Mosin up any minute now and our Marine contractor tends to follow his own orders without adult supervision, if you get my point. He's that kind of Marine. Your role is to make certain his methods don't drag us into a murky mess we can't get out of. We need Mosin alive…until we want him dead."

Six let out a deep sigh. The Director ordered him not to return to Langley without the intel, and he planned to fulfill the mission at all costs.

"Guess I'll be on trunk duty tonight."

"Time is short and every second counts. In less than two weeks, we're on desk duty for the next three months, so we need to wrap this up. I'm not ashamed to say I hope he leaves in a body bag."

Chapter 6

Tuesday Morning — J.J.'s Condo

> *Turn your lights down low*
> *And pull your window curtain…*

J.J. McCall drank in the magnificence of Tony Donato, the love of her life, as he plunged between her legs slowly grinding to Bob Marley's rhythm. His eyes spoke with the softness of an angel's breath. Yet, his chiseled body curved with the glory and power of Roman gods. His bulging pecks propped him above J.J. as he penetrated her with a passion too delicious to contain. She gripped his hips and slowed his hungry strokes to a gentle paint-drying drag, intensifying his moans and strengthening her groans. He called out her name and vowed his everlasting devotion in loving whispers, his adoring gaze, and his tender touch. Tony's arms trembled with weakness from pleasure's pain when she pulled his soaking body to hers. He pushed his hand underneath her taut bottom and gripped her ass as she wound her hips with a churning speed that drove them to heavenly peaks. They lay together in a silent embrace until their panting slowed. Nothing could be heard except the sound of Bob Marley humming from her iPod, and rain pattering against the window after a winter downpour.

"Mmmm, the best ever," Tony said, purring like a man who'd tasted chocolate for the first time. He rocked to his side, propped himself up on his elbow, and stared at her with awed appreciation. "Damn, babe. You're tryin' to kill me, aren't you?"

"Me gwine kill yuh wit a smile 'pon your face," J.J. said in her Jamaican patois. She learned it from years of listening to reggae…and an ex-college boyfriend of two years who spoke in his native tongue whenever trying to conceal information from her.

"Ooh, sexy. Sound like you're straight out of Flatbush," he said. "A woman of many…talents."

"Baby, you don't know the half of it." She brushed her palm against his cheeks, and the corners of her mouth turned downward, coloring her face with the melancholy pout. Gloom hovered over their coming days and weighed heavy on her heart. "Wish we could stay here forever."

He forced a smile but shifted his eyes from hers. "Someday we will, make no mistake about it. For now, duty calls." He wrapped his arm around J.J.'s waist as she tried to escape. "You finished packing yet?"

"Yeah. The sooner we wrap up this case, the better. I'm limiting my luggage to two suitcases…in a vain attempt to will my wish into reality. If I need any more clothes than that, I'll shop when I get to New York." She kissed his fingers and pushed his hand back before slipping out of bed to start the shower. "Anything new from the home front? How's your brother doing?"

"Same. Vitals are stable, but he's still in critical condition. Hasn't regained consciousness. Even if he recovers, the doctors aren't sure he'll walk again." She brought him a warm washcloth and sat beside him on the bed.

"I've never met him but your blood's running through him, so I have no doubt he's a fighter. The Russians better come with more than a couple of bullets to keep him down."

Tony's smile was tenuous. "Listen. I should warn you up front. My family, they're not going to welcome you with open arms…at first."

"You mean, the way my dad welcomed you? Inviting Six, of all people, to breakfast?"

"It's not the same. They can be real drama queens. I'm talkin' Susan Lucci drama. My sister Dree, ugh, she's a bitch on wheels. You think I'm exaggeratin' but we grew up together. She's a troublemaker, for sure."

"You mean, like my father?" she said with a chuckle. "You're trying to make a point here, so cut to the headline."

He grabbed her hand and caressed her fingers, avoiding her hardened glare. "I think it's best…that we don't tell them…about us…at least not right away. Give me some time to ease them into the idea."

"Ease them? Hmph," she snapped. "Perhaps on the way to New York we should take a side trip to OZ so we can ask the Wizard to give you some courage."

"J.J., listen—"

"Ummm, no. My father's not any happier about our relationship than yours will be, as evidenced by his effort to hook you up with a deranged killer. But, guess what? I told him; he got over it. Well, he's getting over it, but you get the point," J.J. growled, grabbing her lingerie from the drawer. She stomped into the bathroom before slamming the door shut. "I'll bet if my name were Gia Campioni you'd have no problem introducing me to your family."

After a few moments of silence, she heard the locked doorknob wiggle.

"Really, J.J.?" His voice sounded muffled as she brushed her teeth. "Listen, I understand your frustration, babe. I do. Trust me, if I had the close relationship with my family that you do with yours, I'd tell 'em in a heartbeat," Tony said. "My relationship with them is strained to the point of breaking. We should be pulling together not tearing apart. Dealing with you and me, the death threats, Dante's condition, and God forbid, his death? For Christ's sakes, a man can only take so much and dumping this on them isn't fair, either."

J.J. stared in the mirror and tried to empathize, get past her own selfish desires and be supportive. Truth be told, he had a good point, several of them. Dante's health trumped any efforts she might engage in to ingratiate herself to his family. But the moment he turned the corner, and she believed he would, Tony better 'fess up, or their relationship was over. She wouldn't allow him to hide her like some family shame, loved under the cover of night like a side-chick as Six had done. He could put that in his bank and smoke it.

She cracked open the bathroom door, and his face met hers, nose to nose once he bent forward. He slipped his hand through the crack and caressed her cheek, flashed half a smile, and pecked her on the lips. "Okay, Tony. We'll do it your way…for now. Not forever, but for the time being I'm silent on the matter." She zipped her fingers across her lips.

"Thank you, babe," he said. "Did I ever tell you that you were the best woman in the world?"

J.J. nodded. "How about you show me with diamonds?" She chuckled. He would get the irony of her statement given she didn't wear much jewelry. Just her mother's promise ring and a pair of diamond studs in her ears, a gift from Six.

"So, what time are we leaving?"

She spun around and stepped into the shower. "You drive ahead of me whenever you're ready. I'll meet you at Federal Plaza first thing tomorrow morning. And before your brain starts churning, this has nothing to do with the family issue. I've got to meet Dmitriyev."

"You sure it's not—"

"I'm positive!" she replied before he could finish. Her suggestion had nothing to do with him. One lesson her father had instilled in her from the time her feet could reach the gas pedal is to be responsible for her own transportation. When an argument broke out, a woman should always be able to get home on her own. "Hopper Mack's is going to stand in for me. He'll be Dmitriyev's handler until we return, so I need to give him contact instructions," J.J. said. "Plus, I'd like to get an update on new developments in the New York residency and find out how much he knows about this Troika business."

"So, you don't want me to hang back and meet him with you?"

"No, I've got this covered. You go home, support your family. God forbid the worst should happen; the last thing you want is to live with the regret that you could've been there, but you weren't."

Chapter 7

Tuesday Afternoon — Russian Embassy

"Where do you think you're going?" Yuriy Filchenko barked as Aleksey Dmitriyev made his way to the door. "Our meeting begins in twenty minutes. At such a delicate time, our comrades will question your absence."

Filchenko was the new Counterintelligence operations chief in the Washington Residency and Dmitriyev was his superior in rank and moral fiber. Their entire relationship had been built on mistrust and resentment: Yuriy's for the treacherous turncoat he believed Aleksey to be, and Aleksey for the backstabbing snitch Yuriy had proven himself to be.

Aleksey growled under his breath and rolled his eyes. Filchenko nosed around him and dished heaping servings of grief at every opportunity. Aleksey's saving grace came in the form of the leverage he'd gained from Yuriy revealing his major fuck up to Aleksey. If Aleksey played his trump and revealed the junior officer had, by accident, led the FBI straight into the White House operation, the disclosure would deal a crippling blow to Filchenko's career.

"Tread lightly, little boy," Aleksey snarled. "You don't want to push me too far, not whilst my grip is so firm around the weak bones in your neck."

Filchenko paused and reconsidered his stance before waving Aleksey off.

Dmitriyev exited the main building and headed out for his daily Starbucks run, now more aware of the time. As he pulled out of the gate and neared Wisconsin Avenue, he scanned his rearview and side mirrors for familiar faces from the FBI's surveillance team. He recognized the one he'd met in the park and tipped his hat. They kept their coverage loose, as he expected they would. Aleksey was meeting one of their own.

Distancing himself from the residency liberated his mind, allowing him for the first time in days to absorb the gravity of recent events and his own looming peril. He clenched his eyes shut for a brief moment and shook his head at the disbelief at Svetlana Mikhaylova's death. Her father's grief, which had transformed from sorrow to rage, set him on a path of revenge and destruction, steeled his determination to avenge her murder. Aleksey himself had sunken to the pit of all moral lows—pretending to celebrate the death of his dear friend Stanislav Vorobyev in order to protect his cover and guarantee his future by spying on behalf of the FBI. After defecting from the service, he could leave the duplicitous life behind and live out the rest of his days in peace. Until then, he'd be forced to work in place; he'd crossed over the line too far to turn back now.

With this sobering realization, Aleksey understood he must muddle through his days and sidestep Filchenko's attempts to out him. Mikhaylov's impetuous gaffe in turning over the identity of Svetlana's killer to Golikov might cost the residency dearly. He ordered Mashkov's people to gun down the Italian in New York and may have set in motion the chain of events that'd prove to be Aleksey's and the Residency's undoing. The faster J.J. McCall shut down Svetlana's band of spies and neutralized Mashkov's people, the sooner their lives would return to semblance of normal.

Aleksey grabbed his coffee and made two quick cover stops on the bustling stretch of Wisconsin Avenue to verify that his own colleagues hadn't followed him. Then he made his way down Van Ness Street to Connecticut Avenue where he'd connect with J.J.

He drove into the parking garage adjacent to the University of the District of Columbia, an ideal location. McCall was nothing if not smart and security conscious. The location was one of the few with one entrance and two exits, the second just off of residential side street leading to a cut-through route to Wisconsin. He'd leave from one side, and she from the other. The interlude must be kept brief because the longer he stayed away, the more Filthchenko would scrutinize his every move. Despite his disdain for the cretin, Yuriy had made a valid point. Any activity out of the ordinary would be examined through a skeptical, microscopic lens.

When Aleksey reached the lower level, he spotted J.J.'s black Challenger with tinted windows parked near the stairway exit. He parked in a spot adjacent to hers and slipped into her passenger seat. She refused to sit in his vehicle, insisting Filthchenko or someone else from the counter-intelligence line would dust for fingerprints and identify hers if suspicions of a mole in the Embassy reached critical mass.

"Long time no see," J.J. said facetiously. She extended a hand to him. "We've got a pretty big mess on our hands."

"It's good to see you well, Agent McCall," he began, "however, I must cut this meeting short. They've scheduled a conference this morning. I'll draw suspicion if I don't return in time."

"Filchenko and the rest of the Golikov's crew still giving you a difficult time?"

"*Filthchenko* is an asshole, but I can keep him contained," he said. "Golikov ordered Vasiliy and Igor to New York. They're supporting Mashkov's people. In what capacity, I'm not certain. They left on the heels of Mikhaylova's death... at her father's request."

"Mashkov? You aren't suggesting the residency orchestrated the Bonanno hit?" she asked.

"Orchestrate? No. Involved? Yes. Mikhaylov begged Golikov to avenge his daughter's death. Now he's in bed with the devil." Aleksey glanced at his wrist to check the time. "Idiots. They shot the wrong man, a mistake egregious enough to not only implicate the Residency but cripple the younger brother's organized crime operations; the elder is furious, flying into New York to deal with the fallout himself. No telling how he'll punish those who made the mistake."

J.J. gave him the side-eye. "Pavlov Mashkov? He's on our No-Fly list."

"And? He's got the best counterfeit passport money can buy and uses it to travel to the United States once a year. He comes to oversee operations but, with the increased potential for conflict between his people and the Italians, you can be certain the reason for this visit is not to make peace."

"I'd love to roll him up, but more important than eliminating Mashkov is finding a way to penetrate Troika. I'm convinced that's the key to neutralizing the network. Money is the root of all Mikhaylova's evil. Kill the root; kill the weed."

"I must implore you to keep your distance. Mashkov will kill you and throw your dismembered body into the river. Then he'll fly back to Russia on his fake passport like a ghost who was never here," Aleksey warned, his expression grim, his voice urgent. "Troika Technologies is almost impossible to breach. Mashkov relies on a small cadre of trusted associates; only they have access to the facility and information you would need to shut them down—and those people are not only well controlled under threats of violence, but also well-paid to keep them quiet."

J.J. shook her head in disbelief. "I don't buy it. The Mashkov's are assholes. Anytime assholes run anything, unhappy people with axes to grind almost always lay low until they're positioned to strike. Someone in Troika wants out. Any ideas? Who's the weakest link?"

Aleksey bit his bottom lip and rubbed the fuzz on his chin. "There's one person I've heard rumors about, and that's the accountant. They refer to him as The Sparrow. No one in the Washington Residency knows his true name. The only reason he's working with Mashkov is because he's afraid not to. Elicit his support, and you may have a chance at dismantling the organization. All roads to taking down Troika lead through the money. But getting to him will be next to impossible."

"Believe it or not, I find comfort in that statement," J.J. said.

He appeared confused. "What do you mean?"

"Impossible situations are my specialty…if you hadn't figured that out by now."

He chuckled and nodded in respect.

"I'm leaving for New York in the morning," J.J. said, "but I'm placing your safety in the capable hands of a most trusted colleague. Hopper Mack." Trusted yes. Most trusted? If Aleksey survived until she returned, then yes. "Usually, there'd be a formal hand-off during which I'd introduce you two, but we don't have time for formalities."

"Name sounds familiar. He's the young agent who met with Mikhaylov in the sandwich shop, if my memory serves me correctly?" Aleksey asked. Hopper had pulled off a gutsy operation which allowed the FBI to get a GPS on Mikhaylov's car and track him to his daughter.

She nodded with a chuckle. "Infamous already, huh? I believe it was his debut."

"I never forget a name. Sounds like quite the character." He checked his watch again. "Shit. I must hurry back. If I'm late…" he sliced his index finger across his throat.

She handed him a slip of paper. "These are your communication instructions. He will monitor our signal sites until I return. To report problems or pass vital information, reach out to him, and he will contact me."

"One thing before I leave," Aleksey said. "The Italian, the one who shot Svetlana… a reliable source informed me that the Mashkovs put a bounty on his head. If they catch him, he's dead."

J.J.'s thoughts shifted to the love of her life; she let out a hard breath. Santino was Tony's family and had saved both from an executioner's bullet. She'd warn him and press Santino to lay low until this conflict blew over. Another hit on the Donatos at this critical juncture would heat the simmering tensions between the organized crime factions to a quick boil, with mayhem spilling into the streets of New York.

As Aleksey exited, and she pulled away, her cell rang. She looked down the lit screen. Sunnie again. Something was going on. Must be very right…or very wrong.

Chapter 8

Tuesday Afternoon — New York City

Santino Castellano's eyes dampened as he peered into the hospital room and watched his uncle grieve for his son's condition. "Shoulda been me," he repeated in his mind over and again, as if his thoughts could turn back time and change the bullet's course. In his mind, enduring the wound would've been more bearable than suffering the guilt of knowing the two shots fired had his name etched in them.

Sal stood next to Dante's bed, flanked by "family" soldiers packing enough heat to arm a police precinct. Usually lion-like with his tall, thick frame, prowling stride, strong jaw, and thick mane of gray-streaked hair, he looked permeable, vulnerable somehow, as he gazed upon his son's weakened body. Some New York Feds had warned them that the Russians wanted a do-over on the Santino job and to finish off Dante for good measure. So the family upped the level of protection and planned to punish the Russians for entertaining the thought. The family rejected support from the cops; they never offered anything without a bunch of strings attached. And after an FBI mole came close to destroying the Bonanno family, which took years to rebuild, Sal refused to risk even the slightest chance the Feds would ever infiltrate them again, at least not under his watchful eye.

Santino and his cousin Dante partnered in crime way back before they could comprehend the lives of wise guys, before either realized their genetic lineage had set them on a course veering toward death and dysfunction. He chuckled as he remembered their first criminal enterprise, selling stolen candy bars out of the elementary school lockers at PS 102. Dante was always the more fearless of the two. He wasn't so tall, but he had the kind of presence that drew respect at the mere sight of him. Took after his father, for sure. To see him connected to these wires with tubes running in and out of him, Santino slumped over as if he'd just taken an unguarded uppercut which left him gasping for air.

Santino glanced at the U.S. Marshalls escorting his Uncle and offered a nod. They were on the Bonanno payroll and gave him and Uncle Sal the space they needed to discuss family business before he returned to the federal corrections half-way house in Scranton. Santino drifted over to Dante's bed and with all his might resisted the urge to pat Uncle Sal on the back. Unc had never been a touchy feely guy. Santino motioned his head toward the other side of the room, and Sal followed him there.

Sal pulled a handkerchief from his pant pocket and wiped his eyes and nose. "Find out who's responsible for doing this to my son."

"Feds say the Russians did it. Somebody hooked up with the mafia," he said and lowered his head. "Dante wasn't the intended target."

Sal's brow furrowed. "Is 'at right? Then who did they mistake him for?"

Santino's downcast eyes told Sal everything he needed to know.

"You? Why would they come after—what'd you do?"

"Unc, this ain't got nothin' to do with family business. I was layin' low in D.C., tryin' to earn enough money to pay back Nicky Mumbles and I started messin' with this broad. Turned out she was Russian, but you couldn't even tell. No accent. She was planning to make me take the rap for killing a couple of Feds...one of which was Tony."

"What?"

"She paid me to hit somebody. I refused to go through with it when I found out he was the target. Did what I had to do. She musta found out who I was, snoopin' around in my shit. I dunno."

"Ummm, hmmm. You dunno," Sal said with a raised eyebrow and pursed lips.

"I didn't tell her much. The Russians ordered a hit, came after me, and the cocksucker had a bad aim."

He nodded and patted Santino on the shoulder. "You and Nicky talk to Swifty and arrange a sit-down with those Russian fucks. Swifty's hooked up tight with them in some money laundering shit. He'll arrange everything."

"Sure thing, Unc. I'll take care of that tomorrow."

"No, you'll call tonight." Sal jabbed Santino's chest with his index finger. "Listen, you also need to call Stevie Pics." Sal considered Stevie a loyal member of the family, and he had more sources on the street than the *New York Times*. "Tell him to find out the name of the shooter the minute I'm outta here, you unda'stand? You better have a name and a location for the son of a bitch who did this tomorrow. You don't get the information, and I'm takin' it out on botha yous! Whoever he is, he's gonna die in excruciating agony if it's the last thing I do. I'll fill his body with a piece of hot lead for every day my son lies in this fucking hospital bed. We clear?"

Santino threw his hands up in the air. "We're clear, Unc; we're clear. But, uh, there's somethin' else I should tell you."

"What now?"

"Ton's on the way to New York. He's working the Russian thing for the Feds. Spoke with him a couple days ago."

He snatched up Santino by the shirt, snorting hard breaths through his nose. "I told you never to speak to that fucking rat. Now, you disobey my orders?"

"I know...I know." He tried to loosen his uncle's fist from his shirt. "But there's something you gotta unda'stand."

Sal tightened his grip. "What's he comin' here for? I warned him to stay away from me and my family. The only reason he's still walking this earth is because I ordered it. But I can rescind that order if he thinks he gonna come around snitching to his bosses about my business. So what do I need to understand!"

"On my mother's grave, the only reason that I'm standing in front of you right now is because of Tony; he saved my life. Kept me from takin' a bullet." Sal jerked his head back; the surprise was visible. "And get this—after I whacked the Russian cunt who tried to turn on me, he let me walk. Scot-free."

Sal's eyes widened, and his shoulders relaxed. He released Santino's shirt, confused for a moment. He took a step back and leaned his hand on a nearby chair.

"Yeah, my sentiments exactly. The family's been through a lot, and things went to shit before he skipped town. But here's what my gut tells me—what he did for me *is not* the act of a rat."

Sal pinched his lips and rubbed his chin. Santino could almost see the gears in his head churning; he recognized the look, felt the same sense of confusion when he left Irving Street, his place in D.C.

"Think about this. Why would a man who ratted out his family compromise his entire career by letting me walk? For all he knew, I coulda called the Feds and told them he let me walk," Santino said. "When Dante got shot, he had every reason to stay in D.C. You already issued the order. Nobody can hit him. He ain't working no cases associated with the family. Hasn't so much as *flown over* New York in almost ten years. So why come here? Why not turn his back on me and let me get pinched?"

"He nodded you off, huh?"

"Yeah…no strings. Didn't ask for nothing. Didn't even ask what I was doing. And there was some fine mooley with 'im too. Another agent. She made the suggestion. It was her idea as I think about it. But he went along with it."

Sal nodded and half-smiled. "Okay, I'm convinced but the next obvious problem becomes—if Tony didn't drop the dime on Jimmy Toots, we still got a rat in the family."

"Yeah…so who do you suppose had the most to gain from Jimmy Toots gettin' pinched?"

Sal thought about it and narrowed his eyes. "Get Stevie on this one, too. When he gets back to me with the information, we'll make our next move. Until, then—nothing. You understand me? As far as our little friend is concerned, we got no problem with him. That cocksucker will *mumble* no more if he set up my son to make a power play on me."

Chapter 9

From a young age, J.J. hated the smell of sterility permeating hospital halls. Her chest rose and fell in dramatic heaves as she paced toward his room, struggling to catch her breath and push the haunting memories to the back of her mind. The attacks didn't often come or endure for long. It'd been four years since her last. But they lingered on her soul like a scar. A sense of hopelessness pervaded her core every time she crossed the threshold, but this was one visit she couldn't avoid.

In his delirious state before he was admitted, Director Freeman tried to warn her about Nixon—and before she headed to New York. She wanted answers. Answers about Nixon and her mother.

"You're sitting up!" J.J. said to Director Freeman as she poked her head inside his private hospital room. Every surface spilled over with cards, flowers, and cheesy Mylar balloons. His tired eyes drooped, worn and heavy, but the corners of his mouth lifted when she appeared.

"Didn't think you'd get a chance to stop by before you headed to New York, Agent McCall."

"Well, I had to make certain you'd be around to tighten the leash on me when I get out of hand. How're you feeling?"

"Like 10,000 pounds of shit in a two-pound bag, but making progress. Been up pacing the halls in this drafty gown. My nurse says walking is the fastest way to secure my release. I can't begin to express how ready I am to get the hell out of here."

"Well, my mother always used to say, 'baby steps are still steps forward.'"

"Wise woman."

"She was…is. She's with me, you know. Present in everything I—" she paused to stop the tears. The mere thought of her mother set loose the flood always dammed just behind the wall she'd constructed to keep them secure. She swallowed hard to choke them down. "Anyway…"

"Well." He flashed an empathetic smile. "You couldn't have timed your visit better. The President called with some good news this morning. Well…most is good." His expression flattened with the last words.

"Ugh." J.J. grunted and collapsed in the chair next to his bedside table. "Give me the good news first. Better to receive the upper before the downer."

"The good news is, the President is so pleased with our recent White House operation he's authorized us to keep 'our fortuitous find' in place for two weeks."

"Get out!" J.J. beamed.

"Not so fast…"

Light dawns on Marblehead, J.J. thought.

"Ah, let me guess. He's not keeping it active for the Bureau. Our sister agency across the river must've convinced him."

He chuckled. "How'd you guess? They're using the device to conduct disinformation campaigns; however, it'll be available to the task force, if necessary."

"How considerate of the CIA to Bogart, as usual. Especially given that they wouldn't know it existed if an *FBI* task force didn't locate it." J.J. narrowed her eyes to slits and braced herself for the letdown. Judging from the discomfort masking Freeman's face, the next bit of news promised to deliver D.C.-style disappointment. "So what's the bad news?"

The director pushed himself straight up in bed, adjusted the pillow and folded hands in his lap before he spoke. "You're aware that some high-level discussions have taken place in the face of the increased tensions between the U.S. and Russia."

J.J. nodded and smiled. "I catch the news on occasion."

Freeman cleared his throat. "Everyone agrees we must shift the tide of mistrust and resentment to one of cooperation and goodwill."

She rolled her eyes. "I think I just threw up in my mouth."

Director Freeman smirked. "Since the Lana Michaels investigation and Stanislav Vorobyev's death,'" he made quote gestures with his fingers, "they've stonewalled us on terrorism intelligence of vital importance to stopping another Boston attack. So, to cool flared tempers, both sides have agreed to expand counterterrorism cooperation between our two countries. In exchange for critical intel on Chechen terrorist cells operating here and in Russia, each side will observe an operational stand-down, subject to a binding agreement this time. And it applies to their residencies in the U.S. and the CIA stations in Moscow and the Republics."

"Never thought I'd hear those words come from your mouth, sir. Guess the price of U.S. national security is cheaper than I thought."

"That's patently unfair, J.J. We're all under orders. The FSB and FBI, we all must cease offensive operations for a term they're calling a 'cooling off' period. If either side breaks the agreement, all bets are off, the intelligence exchange stops, leaving too many lives at risk. We can't afford to disobey these orders. Not right now."

J.J. sat dumbfounded; she blinked through a blank stare.

"The gears turning in your head are starting to smoke. Consider this an olive branch."

"No, consider this the dagger they're going to jam into our backs the second we give them the benefit of the doubt. I mean…am I the only one who's been working this target for the last decade? You can be certain if they hand us a branch, it's because they're planning to beat us with the rest of the tree."

"I understand your frustration, but the President's decision is final. Now, we must abide by the agreement."

"You agreed with this?"

"J.J., I'm not just the FBI Director of Counterintelligence. I'm in charge of the entire Bureau, and the terrorism information is also within my jurisdiction. I'll take one on the chin to save American lives."

J.J. muffled her grumbles. He'd spoken the truth. She often had to remind herself that the world didn't revolve around her—not yet.

"Don't cut your eye at me, Agent McCall. The President has no misgivings about Putin or his government, okay? He trusts Putin as far as he can throw him. And if he's agreeing to this, you better believe the United States will come out ahead on the tail end. Too many people underestimate him, you know. Just because he accepts a branch doesn't mean he's not wielding a tree of his own."

She let out a long sigh and nodded. "So what does this mean for our cases? The trip to New York? Six's mission in Moscow? Do we abandon plans to take down the financial hub and allow the Russians to catch and kill Stan? We give Gary Mosin a pass and stand by as he hands over the damaging intel to the FSB?"

"Absolutely not. The President bought you ten days—starting *today*. I don't care if you are in the middle of speaking a sentence. When the whistle blows, whatever you're involved in comes to a screeching halt, case closed or not. Are we clear?"

"Yeah, yeah," she said as she collected her purse and coat. "How long will the stand-down last once the clock starts?"

"Unless otherwise directed – ninety days. Desk duty for all."

No two words made her cringe more—desk duty. Even worse, the FBI would be the only agency abiding by the agreement. The Russians never held up their end of the deal.

Powerless, she wondered why she'd fought so hard to stay. Maybe this stand-down presented a fortuitous opportunity to explore her next move, dip her toe in "life" after the Bureau and find out what the world had to offer beyond the halls of the J. Edgar Hoover building. Just before she reached the door, she remembered the reason she came and turned to speak again.

"Uhhh…one last thing. You were a bit delirious during the ambulance ride, but you started to tell me something of great concern to me, to say the least…about Nixon."

Freeman's expression hardened, and he expelled a long hard breath. "I'll handle Nixon…until you can handle Nixon. You're concerned, and you should be. But I need you focused on New York. The Bureau needs you to bring this one home. Many lives and key operations are at stake, and you don't have much time to wrap it up."

"But what if…"

"No ifs. You contact my secretary if you run into walls you can't get around on your own. I'll help where I can…and I have a pretty good record, wouldn't you say? Don't worry about problems outside of your control. Focus on the mission; let me take care of the rest."

"Yes, sir," J.J. said with a salute as she turned to leave. She swung back around and locked her gaze on him. "Listen, about my mother…"

He held up his hand. "Focus on the mission, J.J.! The mission."

She waved goodbye and skulked out of the room like a child shushed by a parent. At least he'd used more tact than her father. Still, she'd grown sick of everyone treating her with kid gloves. She carried a gun for crying out loud, shot people. What information contained in her mother's case could be so volatile that everyone connected was hell bent on concealing it? Her mind began to ruminate on the little she'd been told. Perhaps no one wanted J.J. to discover the truth because her mother was part of the problem, had somehow failed. Maybe she'd gone rogue or broken the law. Doubts circled her mind threatening to destroy every good memory she held so dear. By the second, she grew more determined to discover the truth, and the reason so many sought to hide it.

Her phone rang again. Sunnie was nothing if not persistent. She answered, reluctant to talk while her mind was still fogged by negative thoughts.

"Sunnie! Gotta make it quick. I'm in a hurry. I'll never get to New York on time for the Troika in-briefing if I don't get on the road now."

"Yeah, I'm so sorry to bug you but today in the mailroom. I discovered something."

In the mailroom, she thought. Nothing critical ever happened there. She decided to let the discovery wait.

Chapter 10

Wednesday Morning — FBI New York

J.J.'s yellow cab pulled to the curb in front of Federal Plaza, and her stomach bound into a hardened knot. After handing her turbaned driver a twenty, she stepped out into the brisk late-fall breeze. She used her hand as a visor to shield her eyes from the sun's glare as she inhaled a deep breath. The enormity of Federal Plaza, a towering mass of concrete, steel and reflective glass scraping the sky, was a lot to take in compared to the squat J. Edgar Hoover building which was less than half its height. The FBI New York Office building dwarfed even the tallest structure in D.C. Although she loved Manhattan, how the streets bustled with energy and breathed life into her weary, overworked body, her fears about what lay ahead stalked her.

She brought her gaze back to street level and spotted two dapper-suited G-men eyeing her. One had the caramel skin tone and curly hair of a man of Hispanic decent and the other was a blond-haired blue-eyed—a pretty boy by most standards. She stepped up her pace toward them and extended her hand and a smile.

The caramel-colored gentleman called out, "J.J. McCall?" as she neared them.

She got a positive vibe from this one. "Yes, I'm J.J. I presume you're my escorts?"

"Glad you arrived in one piece. I'm Manuel Vasquez. Everyone calls me Manny. This is Scott Lewis."

Scott gave her the once-over, in a dismissive sense, refusing to greet her or shake her hand. She looked him in the eye, but his gaze shifted left. He had no intention of returning the favor. "We should get going. The rest of the task force is upstairs waiting on you," he said, his voice gruff and brutish. "We'll begin the briefing in a few minutes."

J.J. shot Manny a side-long glance, and he shrugged in response. Scott's voice conveyed all the colors of his attitude, but she dismissed the diss as yet another internal Washington versus New York field office turf battle. Agents became touchy when they perceived outside agents encroaching into their territory, especially when they didn't believe they needed help. Truth was J.J. would take the same protective position if some agents had deigned to trespass on her case, so she didn't take this cold reception to heart…at least not at first.

"So, you settled in? Where'd they put you up?" Manny asked, passing the time as they rode the elevator up twenty-four floors.

"The Plaza."

"Hmph. Fancy digs for the government rate, huh?"

"Yeah. Tony Donato, my co-case agent, knows the head of security, a former agent. He hooked us up with the government rate. I've got a beautiful view of ice skating rink in Central Park."

"How appropriate. Celebrity treatment for the TV star," Scott piped in as the elevator door opened. "But if you're rooming anywhere near Donato, I'd avoid the windows. I'm just sayin'."

"Excuse me?" J.J. snapped her head toward him and growled, "You got something to say? Speak your mind. No better time than the present."

"Don't pay him any mind, J.J.," Manny said, shaking his head. He allowed her to exit first. "He's constipated. Didn't eat his Wheaties this morning."

"No," she said. "If he's got something to share, let's get it on the table now. My English is good, and I know *all* the big words."

"This is New York, not D.C.," Scott barked. "We don't need you or your antics screwing up our investigation, okay? We work by the book in this office. And no one here's getting pimped by the media. You want to get anything accomplished in this office, you play by *our* rules."

J.J. stopped square in her tracks and rested her hand on her hip. "Let's get something straight." She calmed her voice and leveled it just above a whisper. "You don't have to like me, and my sun will continue to rise and set every day if I don't earn your respect. But if you in any way obstruct, hinder, or otherwise get in the way of me doing my job, I'll have you buried so deep in HR complaints, you'll have to dig up thirty-feet just to get back to hell. Anything else?"

She waited for an answer but only received silence in response.

"Good. I believe we're all on the same page now. Manny, you've got the con. You lead; I'll follow."

Manny stifled a laugh at his colleague's expense while J.J. could feel the heat from Scott looking daggers into her back, hot enough to almost burn a hole through her chest.

Manny led them to the meeting room and opened the door for her to enter. Sitting at the large executive-sized conference room table were Gia and Tony. J.J. had thought it best to keep Walter in D.C. with Sunnie to support analysis. Scott made his way to the side of the room opposite J.J., getting as far away from her as possible, while Manny moved toward the whiteboard which ran the length of the front wall. In no surprise to J.J., Gia occupied one of the chairs on either side of Tony. So, J.J. grabbed an open seat in back of the room.

Taped to the wall hung pictures of five Russians written under the title "Troika Technologies," each aligned in a hierarchical structure. She recognized the lone face on the top tier—Levi Mashkov. He was the brother of the infamous Pavlov Mashkov who was responsible for the deaths of at least two of her sources; Pavlov had more than likely masterminded the Dante Donato shooting.

She grabbed a pen from atop the legal pad in front of her and prepared to take notes. Reflecting on her talk with Aleksey before leaving D.C., she was most concerned with finding out about The Sparrow. After short introductions, during which Manny explained he was the lead agent on the case and Scott was supporting, the briefing got underway. From this point forward, the pressure was on, and every second counted. Ten days to solve the case was no time at all.

"We've been investigating Troika Technologies for several years. Their operations are wrapped up tight and we've had difficulty getting confidential informants to report on their activities. If they get caught talking to the Feds they're dead, as evidenced by the mysterious disappearance of five CIs we sent to target them," he said. "Troika is tied to the Russian Mafiya—no question."

Scott added. "Yeah, these guys are ruthless, you hear me? They won't just kill the informant. First, they will murder their wife, kids, the family dog, and make the informer watch as they cut their hearts out, and then they'll torture them, maybe slice off an appendage or two. *Then* they'll kill them. Unlike the Italian mafia, the Russians abide by no codes; there are no boundaries. You get in the way of their money, and you're dead; collateral damage is not only tolerated, it's encouraged."

"So, what've we got on the Mashkov brothers and their New York operations?" Tony asked.

"The Gruesome Twosome," Manny began. "Levi, who is also known as The Duke, is the brains of the operation—he's the money man. Pavlov is the muscle; he's in charge of his henchman. We estimate their criminal enterprises, which involve narcotics, extortion, money laundering, and other activities, rack up about a half a billion a year. They distribute the proceeds among a bunch of shell companies in the United States and across Europe. They may even own some interests in Israel and Southeastern Asia. Multiple reliable sources indicate they're hooked into cocaine suppliers coming out of Afghanistan."

"And it's clear these guys are taking their cues from Russian intel, using some limited classic tradecraft," Scott chirped in. "We don't often observe them talking on office phones or any kind of land-based communication. They conduct business face-to-face, so they're in and out of the country pretty often. We'll catch 'em using payphones in Brooklyn every now and then."

"How are they communicating with their overseas networks?"

"Encrypted email and cell phone communications. Manny theorizes that they've procured some old Russian intel comms equipment from the New York residency in the consulate, but we don't know. We've never been able to get inside the headquarters to check out the set up."

"One other strange item of note. One of the guys we'll discuss in a minute, Max Novikov, has been in frequent communication with a suspected Russian arms dealer, but we can't make heads or tails of the reporting. The names don't mean much to us."

"I can help with the arms angle," Gia said. "I've conducted extensive research into the subject." As the DIA representative in the group, she promised to tap into intelligence from the military attaches posted in Moscow. She scanned the photos and asked, "Which one's Novikov?"

Scott stood up. "This is Max, right here," he said, pointing to a thirtyish Russian gentleman dressed in a pricey suit. He had an arched nose and roguish glare. "He's into the narcotics side of the business as far we can tell. We've seen him meet with some high-ranking members of the Genovese family. We think Novikov is the supplier, and Genovese soldiers do the distributing. Move it on the streets."

Manny pointed at the wall. "This one, Leonid Tenenbaum, serves as the Chief Operating Officer. Mr. Clean. He's the legit face of the business. No criminal records…which doesn't equal no criminal activity. He just doesn't get caught."

"Zory Kozlov is the Accountant." Even with his slight frame and unimposing countenance, J.J. sensed an impish manner in his air, a thought codified by the menacing tattoo on his neck. "We've got one CI on this guy who says Kozlov tighter than a duck's ass. Chatty until you mention business or anything involving his work. The CI's had to use kid gloves with him because the minute he suspects anyone of working with the Feds, he cuts them off. So he remains a challenge."

"This other guy, Matvey Trifonov, he's quiet, low key. Always under the radar. Not often seen outside. We think he's Levi's assistant. He's seen with him most often." Matvey was a dead ringer for Wayne Gretzky with more gray hair and brown eyes.

Dmitriyev's voice flashed through J.J.'s head. He told her the accountant was the key, but she wasn't yet ready to pass on the lead. Doing so would've sparked questions she couldn't answer for Aleksey's safety. As a counterintelligence officer, paranoia was not only standard it was necessary. Fearing Russian moles, even inside the FBI, was considered a healthy caution.

"Any other information on this Kozlov character?" J.J. asked. "He married? Got kids? What's his deal?"

"Yeah, he's married. Got three young kids, all under ten years of age. Wife's a stay-at-home mom. They own a place out in Brooklyn in the Brighton Beach area. Nothing fancy, but not shabby by any means. He's making some sweet cheese, so we think the understated choice is intentional, to avoid drawing attention."

"Sounds reasonable," she said, playing down her interest. "I'd like to get access to anything we've pulled from the wire so the team can conduct reviews and get acquainted with these characters."

"Wire?" Scott laughed as if questioning her sanity. "Hate to break it to ya, but no wire's been authorized."

"What! No wires on the residences or the business?"

Manny shook his head. "Not for a lack of trying. The SAC rejected seven requests for insufficient justification," Manny said. "The IG's been clamping down with all this NSA oversight shit goin' on," he explained. The Justice Department's Inspector General had been lodged in the FBI's ass like Fleet since the Snowjob compromise. J.J. seethed at the notion. The information they'd presented should've been more than sufficient justification. Every time she thought of the piece of shit so-called whistleblower she wanted to scratch his eyes out.

She shook her head in disgust. "Wish I could say I'm surprised but let's call the eighth time a charm. With the information we've collected from Lana Michaels' investigation, the SAC will have to justify *not* approving the request. You got a free body to pull together the paperwork?"

Manny glared at Scott, squinting his eyes.

"I, uh, I think I know who's available," Scott said.

"Good. Between a wire and a national security letter for phone records, we'll have enough data to take the next steps. We've got to get inside the fortress. Given our severe lack of CIs, we need every means necessary."

"I'll start Maggie on this." Scott nodded and shot out the door.

"Meanwhile, I'd like to set up a meet with this lone CI. Perhaps I can persuade him to share what he knows about Kozlov." J.J. knew whether he told the truth or lied, she'd walk away with more knowledge than he ever meant to provide.

"I'll make a few calls, see what I can do," Manny said. "Until then I'll bring in the case files so you can get up to speed and set you up with some desk space. We've got some vacant ones you can use."

Manny stepped up beside her. He shifted his glance between them. "I gotta tell ya I was a little bit skeptical when the S-A-C told us he had agents coming in from D.C. but you seem to be on your game. I look forward to putting this one to bed."

"Thanks, Manny. Me too," she replied as she watched him leave the room.

She turned to Gia. "While you wait on the files, Tony and I are going to step out. We'll be back in a few minutes." They headed out the squad bay door into the hallway just beyond the elevators. Posters of arrested spies lined the walls; they contained messaging designed to deter insider spying, like "Espionage does pay…and Prison is the bank" and mug shots of convicted spies like Hanssen, Ames, and Pitts. A critical reminder to J.J. of why she was still an agent.

"Glad you made it okay. You get checked in?" Tony asked.

"Sure did. Fantastic room. Everywhere we go you've got the hook-up," she said with a chuckle.

"Listen, I need to check on Dante. I'll be back in a couple of hours if you're all set."

J.J. peered over his shoulders and behind her back. "Our friend, he passed some critical information. It's the Mashkovs. They put a contract on Santino," she whispered.

"What?"

"Yeah. In her last act of betrayal, Miss Svetlana sent her father some evidence implicating Santino in her murder. He's dead if he doesn't stay off the streets. After saving our lives, we owe him a warning."

"Shit," he said with a quick nod. "I'll take care of it after I leave the hospital."

"So…you're going alone?" She tried to force a smile. He didn't ask her to tag along which pissed her off. No matter how she or he tried to spin the situation, in her mind, the truth added up to one fact: Tony was ashamed of her. She couldn't mask the disappointment. His actions revealed more than his words ever said or her expression could ever conceal.

"Quit with the sad puppy dog eyes, will ya?" Tony said. He looked as if he wanted to reach out to her, but he couldn't, not on the job. "You told me you understand."

"Unfortunately, I do," she said, her eyes dampening before she shifted her gaze to the floor. Then she pushed through her hurt and shook off the sting. "Listen, whatever, I'll be fine." Her voice hollowed. "The Russians are my biggest problem. Not you. Not your family. Scott hit the nail on the head. Their ruthlessness is equal to our doggedness and— their code is to eliminate all perceived obstacles in the most gruesome ways possible. If we don't figure out how to prevent an all-out war, Santino's life won't be the only one in danger. Go ahead and check on your brother. I'll get a head start for tomorrow. I'll be fine."

"You've said that twice now."

"Well…I meant it the second time."

He jammed one hand into the pocket of his black leather coat and pushed the call button with the other. "A couple of hours, okay?"

"Sure." She offered him a weak wave before he stepped on the elevator, and the door closed.

He left…son of a bitch. Her mouth began to water as she leaned back on the wall for a brief second. Her thoughts drifted to the hotel minibar. How she craved just one shot to soothe her emotional wounds. She snapped her mind to reality and decided to opt for something less detrimental, such as the room service menu. One of everything chocolate.

She pulled in a deep breath, opened her eyes and turned her head. The stairwell door opened, and footsteps clunked toward her.

"Tony? I thought you'd left."

"Get your coat, woman. Let's take a ride."

Chapter 11

Wednesday Afternoon — U.S. Embassy, Moscow

Six's anxiety grew in the night's blackness with his body curled in a fetal position; the trunk space was too constricted to extend his legs beyond a slight bend. After almost two hours of driving, the stench of gas and oil made him dizzy but the fresh air would be his to breathe soon. He held up his hand in front of his face, couldn't even detect the white of his freshly manicured nails. He drew in long deep breaths to achieve calm as the Michelins absorbed successive shocks from the minefield of potholes peppering the street. Twenty years of conducting operations and Six never had quite adjusted to riding in the trunk. After a bumpy ride, made longer by his exhaustion, they'd arrived at the switch car, a Russian-licensed Volga Siber; the trunk was significantly smaller than the Embassy's Camry. It'd be another few miles before he'd kick down the back seat to combat roll onto a deserted side street in Biryulevo (a Moscow warehouse district) in the dark of night.

Mark had scheduled a critical meeting for Six to attend with Ghost Man at the black site. The topic: Mosin. The landing gear had barely touched the runway on his flight from Washington, but Mark forced Six to keep it.

"We clean?" Six asked Bart. "We can't afford to blow this op or this site."

"Yes, sir. Squeaky as a monk's conscience. The location is about a half klick ahead. When I stop, you roll out to the right. Take the worn path into the woods fifty yards. Ghost Man will meet you."

"Into the woods?" Six hated going any place with more trees than asphalt and more grass than concrete.

"Well, we can't exactly pull up to the front entrance, Six. We use the back entrance," he replied as the car rumbled over a span of railroad tracks.

Moments later, Bart slowed to a near stop. "This is it! You've got a thirty minute window then we head back. If we don't return to the grid soon, the watchers in the stationary post outside the embassy will report unusual absences."

Six kicked down the seat as the car came to a halt. He opened the door and rolled out onto the gravel and into the tall grass lining the roadside; the door was a hair from shut before Bart took off. The shock from the severe wind stopped his breath as his body adjusted to the temperature. After the taillights had disappeared into the darkness, he scanned the road to ensure surveillance wasn't behind Bart. He curled into a crouched position, careful to stay behind the stuttering beam of light emanating from the streetlamp, and scuttled into the patch of evergreens.

His feet crunched through the brush as he crept into the darkened brush, his eyes stretched open to the height of alertness, volleying back and forth, monitoring for movement. As he made his way toward the lone light, a twig snapped behind him. His head jerked toward the sound; he sensed the presence of a large body behind him and the stiffness of steel in his back.

"What the fuck are you doing here?" the man asked in perfect Russian.

Six, a Level 3 Russian speaker, understood every word; the dialect was authentic. The man had learned Russian in Moscow, which didn't bode well. Could the FSB be onto him? Bart was the best officer they had in terms of surveillance detection but perhaps the worst had happened. Maybe the Embassy had a mole who had tipped off the Russians before they even left.

He had two choices: Fold and concede or go for broke.

Folding was an option for cowards and fools. Not for Six.

He stiffened his back and in perfect West African French replied, "I don't understand. I'm looking for my chicken. We're taking the train over there to Africa."

They stood in proximity to the railroad tracks, a couple hundred feet away.

The Russian jammed what felt like the muzzle of a gun deeper into his spine, then ordered him to lay the down on the ground and put his hands behind his back.

Six stumbled forward in a drunken gait, wiggling his fingers and yelling, "Here Chickie Chickie. Here, Chickie Chickie," to get a couple of feet of separation. In a lifesaving bum-rush, Six lunged with a wild right hook to the Russian's horrified face before the man jerked back and yelled "Waaaaait!" This time in perfect English.

Six dead-stopped the knockout blow just a whisper from his nose and then his eyes shifted to the USMC baseball cap on his head. "Jesus! It's you."

The man returned the gun to the holster and grunted with disappointment. He stood at Six's height and appeared to be a typical V-shaped Marine—broad shoulders and, from what he could see from the sweater and slacks, no beer gut at the waist. With skin creased around the eyes, he had to be in his late early-to-late 50s. His air had badass written all over it, but he leaned to the side and walked toward Six with a heavy limp. "I'm Ghost Man. Pleased to make your acquaintance."

"Wish I could say the same, man. They told me you were crazy, but are you trying to get yourself killed?" Six chuckled, swiping his forehead in jest before accepting the extended hand.

"That's the question I should be asking you since, I'm the only one between us with a gun," Ghost replied with a smile.

"How'd you learn to speak such perfect Russian?" Six asked.

"My father was a Russian Jew who immigrated to the U.S. My mother was a Southern belle fresh from her family's Atlanta plantation. I'm a mutt. Go figure," he answered. "Follow me this way. We don't have much time."

Ghost Man led him through the thicket and a small cluster of trees to a large aluminum shed-like structure in a desolate area. A dirty-white eight-foot fence contained a man-sized hole which had been carved into the base and concealed by large trees. Appeared as if he'd cut a covert access into the unlit rear. They passed through and paced toward a side door.

A cloud of cigar smoke choked Six as they stepped into the dimly lit structure which was maybe fifteen-hundred square feet. A large wood dining room table and chairs sat on one side, an old roll top desk on the other. At the far end, a windowless caged area, sealed by bars, appeared as if Ghost had conducted more than one creative interrogation inside. Inside the two open doors, he spotted a closet and small bathroom. Thick rope, turned over buckets and a trail of cut zip-tie hand restraints littered the floor. Two aluminum light fixtures dangled overhead, and the lone side window served as the room's sole source of outside ventilation. A smallish window on the far wall had been blacked out.

Six took a seat and grabbed a container of bottled water from the center until he noticed Ghost reaching into the desk.

"So Mark tells me you're a former Army Ranger," Ghost Man asked as he gripped a bottle of Scotch and poured a shot into two short glasses. He handed one to Six who nodded his head in response.

"Yep. 82nd Airborne," Six said.

"You know what ARMY stands for, dontcha?"

Six shook his head no, but he knew where this was going. Marines couldn't be happy unless they were giving shit to members of other branches. He considered himself fortunate he wasn't a sailor or an airman.

"Ain't Ready to be Marines Yet," Ghost said with a hard chuckle.

Six winced in discomfort and let out a strained laugh.

"Okay, bet you can't guess what U.S. ARMY backward stands for?"

After rolling his eyes, Six replied with a flat, "What?"

"Yes, My Retarded Ass Signed Up." Ghost laughed as he poured a second shot and downed it.

"Well, I'd planned join the Marines but I couldn't pass the physical," Six said, his facial expression sullen. "Disgrace of my life."

"Oh, yeah? What was the problem?" He faced Six with an expression of curiosity and concern.

"My head—it wouldn't fit in the jar," Six replied with a hearty laugh; Ghost joined in after an awkward pause. Then Six glanced at his leg. "How'd you get hurt?"

"Served on the Marine Expeditionary Force in Fallujah, Sunni section of western Iraq. We had a sympathizer in our unit who leaked our patrol route to the brother of an Iraqi insurgent. One IED later, my truck was overturned. Almost lost a leg. We lost three men that day. Something in me snapped—I don't much like traitors of any kind."

After a few minutes of discussion about Ghost's service, Six got down to business. "So, do we have eyes on Mosin? I heard he disembarked yesterday."

"Yeah, he's in a rattrap hostel, the 7 Penguin Hotel on Petrovsky Boulevard. Walking distance from Lubyanka Square, about twenty-five klicks from here. My team's got him under close watch, and we're tapped into his cell phone," Ghost Man said. "Made a few calls to unknown subjects, and he's talking in circles but we believe he's planning to walk-in at FSB Headquarters tomorrow. The time for all this tiptoeing bullshit is over. We're gonna take him out before the Russians get to him, or he's in the wind. Gone. And we'll never get our hands on him."

A chill shot through Six's core. "Your orders have changed—I need him alive."

Ghost Man tightened his lips, removed his hat, and scratched his head in frustration. "Your boss explained his position. But the word on the street is General Ronaldson ordered him killed on sight. Now I know General Ronaldson personally. I don't know you or your boss from Adam's housecat. Given what that son of a bitch Mosin is trying to get away with, I'm inclined to side with the military on that one."

Six's eyes bulged. "Listen, you may know Ronaldson, but he's not bankrolling your stay in Moscow. The CIA is."

"Son, if you think I'm doing this for the money then you've really picked the wrong Marine."

Six's mind churned. Ghost seemed impenetrable. There had to be another way to persuade him. "You're right, Ghost. I apologize, but I'm tired and desperate here. There's some critical intel to which you're not privy, and you're my only option. I can't tell you what the intelligence is. But I can tell you that it involves a covert military strategy involving our biggest allies and, if exposed, it could eventually cost the lives of American soldiers—a lot of them. I'm asking you to give me a chance to recover it before disaster strikes."

Ghost man looked at him with a skeptical expression, but Six held his ground. He hadn't lied—much.

"I'm telling you; we've looked. Son of a bitch doesn't have the intel on him. We searched the room, which isn't bigger than a minute, by the way—nothing. I suspect he stashed it somewhere, but we haven't been able to locate any trace of it. If we snatched him without it, the FSB could find it before we do; we'd be no better or worse off if he was dead."

"How the hell could he get rid of it?"

"Got no fucking idea. If I could answer that, I wouldn't be sitting with you in this room right now."

"Give me an option here. We have procedures…and he's an American."

"I don't give a shit if he's the Queen of Sheba. He's an enemy of the state."

Six shuddered inside. If Ghost accomplished his mission, Six would never return to Langley with the intel—and that was not an option.

"Listen," Six implored. "Capture him and give me the chance to recover the intel. One week. If I'm unsuccessful, you take him whether I have the intelligence or not." Six took the gamble of his life. Staked his entire career on his interrogation skills against a lying traitor. He'd never met a man he couldn't make sing canary strong with non-lethal encouragement. His record was impeccable. Director Miller told Six to do whatever he had to do, say what he had to say. But he probably didn't intend for Six to barter with Mosin's life or make returning Langley without the intel an option. Now Six's bargain would be the difference between a commendation and a pink slip.

Ghost looked at Six expressionless, unmoved, as if he's pleas has fallen on deaf ears and a hard head. "The only thing I can promise you is this: Our op's going down early tomorrow morning. I don't care whether he survives it or not."

"Seven days," Six pleaded for the last time.

"Six, I like you. I'm not making any promises, but I'll leave you with this... I'm running the show around here. Now, you can be an observer. You can be a facilitator. But what you won't be is an obstruction. Are we clear?"

"Crystal."

•••

Back at his room in the Embassy's residential wing, Six collapsed on his bed exhausted from the day's events. Ghost Man's declaration hung heavy in his mind. He wanted Mosin caught and brought to justice more than anyone. But he hadn't considered what that meant—in Moscow with rogue Marines contracted to hunt him down and kill him. The endgame haunted his conscience and complicated his mission, but he still held out hope that once caught, Mosin would turn over the intelligence. He refused to entertain the alternative until he had no other choice. At that moment, all he wanted to force himself to do was sleep.

He stripped down to his boxers and T-shirt and slipped under the heavy blankets. The second his lids closed, a ring sounded.

J.J.'s burn phone.

He scrambled from the bed to grab it and glanced at the caller ID before answering.

"Yes? Who am I speaking with?" Six asked.

"I don't have long to talk."

It was Stanislav Vorobyev. Six scrambled to shake the covers from his feet and sit up in bed, his heart now racing. "What's going on?"

"They spotted me. I wore the disguise, well not every time…but…I think an FSB watcher following the American recognized me," he said, his voice panicked, strained. He lowered it to a hush. "I can't be certain. He stared too long for my comfort."

"Shit. What were you doing out of the safe house? We gave you very explicit instructions. Are you following them?"

A lengthy silence preceded a stammered beginning to his speech. "Well…understand, I—"

Six's anger raged to near eruption at the pause. "Goddamnit, Stan. Three simple rules. Stay out of the public. Use the disguises. Don't contact anyone outside of the Agency."

"I know. I know…but…"

"But nothing!" Dealing with Ghost took him to the ledge; Stan nudged him over it. "You're a dead man, remember? If you've got some bullshit macho Russian hang-ups or pride about laying low because you think you're a goddamn hero then you better choke down that testosterone like bad borscht and do as you're told. Get this through your thick head right now—a lot of people are putting their asses on the line for your safety, including the President of the United States…and me. If you so much as set a toe out of line, so help me God I will rent a helicopter and drop your sorry ass in the middle of Lubyanka Square and watch the FSB eat you for dinner. Do you understand me?"

"Okay, okay," he said in a conceding tone. "I swear it will never happen again, but you've got to get me out of here. Move me into the embassy compound or I'll be discovered, spelling the end of my life and a political disaster for the U.S."

"I know," Six replied. Only hours in Moscow, he'd been dragged from one crisis to the next—with no clear plan to resolve either.

Chapter 12

Wednesday Evening — New York City

Sweat secreted between J.J's fingers as she clutched Tony's hand like the butt of her Glock. Her stomach constricted and curled into tight nerve-wrecked knots. Waves of nausea washed over her. She hated the smell of sickness in the air; the scent sparked a bum rush of memories tucked safe and secure behind the wall she'd built to contain the grief of her mother's death. She fought back the mental images of her dying mother as she looked for any excuse to run. She wanted out of this deal she'd worked herself into and in the worst way.

J.J. experienced an emotion she didn't often encounter—pure unadulterated fear. She now had the deepest sense of regret for the puppy dog eyes and the glum demeanor she used to guilt Tony into inviting her to meet his family. She had little appreciation for the dread Tony experienced when she muscled him into meeting her father. Now, she feared she'd fallen victim to the adage, "Be careful of what you ask for."

J.J. locked her eyes on the end of the hall where two olive-skinned mounds of muscle and flesh clad in leather jackets, open-collared shirts, and slacks, stationed outside the hospital room door. The bling from the gold chains around their necks was like a beacon guiding them to Dante's room.

Tony released her hand as they drew closer. Visual aggression masked their faces. He slowed his pace as he eased toward the men, exchanging the strained glares of enemies.

On edge, J.J.'s glare shifted between the two. One sat back in his seat, and his jacket opened to reveal a sliver of the butt of his holstered pistol. It was two against two, and odds were equally in her favor because she was packing just like them. She also had a quick draw, an itchy trigger finger, and a badge.

Tony jutted his chin toward them in greeting and said, "Vin. Richie. Long time."

Tony told her about them, and they behaved like the jackasses Tony described.

Neither replied, just hardened their stares before shifting their attention to the curvaceous nurses pushing IVs into the room next door. Tony had portrayed the tension between him and his father's family with the utmost accuracy. Anyone could see in their cold, detached glares that they looked on him as a stranger. Or worse, a man for whom home was no longer an option. He was a traitor, one that years ago should've been bludgeoned into a ditch, beaten to a pulverized heap of blood, broken bones, and bruises, and abandoned with the ass of a dead rodent stuffed down his throat. To them, he was the rat that couldn't be touched, not without the order. And as the son of the Boss, they'd never get the go-ahead.

J.J. entered the room on Tony's heels to see Dante strung with tubes. They delivered the life-sustaining fluid and oxygen that kept him clinging to his last inch of life. Tony appeared to struggle for air. On one side of Dante's bed, a diminutive, silver-haired woman gripping a rosary lay with her head on Dante's arm. On the other side, a pair of brunettes, both late twentyish, dabbed their mascara-ringed eyes with tissues.

At the sound of Tony's and J.J.'s steps, each bolted to attention and shifted their deadlocked eyes on the entrance.

"Hey, Ma." He paused for a reaction, as if unsure of what to expect from any of them.

"Tony!" the choir called out—minus one. The youngest of the two, who wore thick permed tendrils, rushed to his side, squeezed him as if she hadn't seen him in years. According to Tony, she hadn't. An older woman, a svelte Vogue cut-out with an icy glare, cut her eyes at J.J. and Tony and then rolled them.

"Well, well, well. Look at what the cat drug in," the younger one said. With her brow furrowed and a mischievous half-smile, she gave J.J. a quick once-over. "Uh, who's this?"

"This is my co-case agent, J.J. McCall. J.J., this is my sister, Carla."

"J.J., huh?" she said with a welcoming smile.

"Sorry, we're meeting under these circumstances," she replied.

Carla tightened her lips and lowered her chin. "Me too. Nice to meet you." She spoke with a squeaky accent straight out of Brooklyn. She shook J.J.'s fingertips before returning to her brother's bedside, tugging the thin white blanket until it covered his chest. She grabbed his hand and said, "Dante, Tony's here. He came all the way from D.C. to see you."

Carla studied Dante, waited for him to react, but he never flinched.

The older woman swept up from the bed, into her son's arms, and held him with the thankfulness of a mother grateful for his life and presence. "Antonio!" she sang in a matronly tone before her smile vanished, masked behind a look of fearful concern. "I'm glad you came, but you can't stay."

"Ma…"

"I mean it, Antonio. Your father runs his business, and everybody thinks I'm Miss Clueless in the Kitchen. Don't let these innocent eyes fool you. I've got my spoon deep enough in the sauce to understand you shouldn't be here," she ordered, patting his face with her open palm. She appeared ready to upgrade the show of affection to a full-on slap if he didn't concede.

He gripped her hands in his before saying, "I'm not going anywhere. Not until my brother is out of that bed. So, save your concern for the son who needs it. How're you holding up?"

"Me? Fine. Him? Not so good. Still unconscious." She turned to Dante. "His fingers moved the other day when I sang to him. He hears my voice. He just won't come—I'm sorry," she said turning to J.J. "Look at me. Forgive my rudeness. This must be the partner you told me about. I'm Tony's mother." She shifted her gaze between J.J. and Tony and jutted her chin toward J.J. "So you're the one who steals him from Sunday dinner."

J.J. stomach sunk, and she flashed a sheepish grin. "Not without heaping servings of grief and shame. My dad has the same complaints."

Tony walked beside his other sister. "What's up with you, Dree? It's been ten years. Still got a bug up your ass?"

"Hey! You watch your mouth. I'm still your mother."

Dree leaned back in her seat and met his eyes with a hard cold stare. Then she turned to Carla, "Do you hear someone speaking? The hospital must be haunted."

"Really, Dree? Our brother's laying on his death bed and you're acting like a three-year-old." Carla rolled her eyes. "Tony's got every right to be here. You don't like it? Bergdorf's is havin' a sale. Leave and go buy yourself a clue."

"You want coffee, Ma? I'm going to the cafeteria until the riff-raff leaves."

"The riff-raff will leave when it goes to get Ma a cup of coffee," Carla snapped.

"You two knock it off. No more of this useless bickering. Dree, go. I'll have tea."

She stormed out, bumping into J.J. without the consideration of an excuse me. J.J. fought to keep her cool. If Dree had been related to anyone other than Tony, J.J. would've helped Dree to a dose of manners. She had a high tolerance for BS but the bitch-on-a-stick attitude had to go.

Mrs. Donato shook her head as her daughter stomped off. "I apologize for my daughter's behavior. Wish I could say it's because of the stress." She threw up her hands and turned to Tony. "So, I presume since your partner is here with you, Tony, you two are working on a case?"

Tony glanced at J.J. as if to apologize for what he wasn't going to say. "Yeah… it's J.J.'s case…"

"It's our case," J.J. interjected. "I couldn't do it without Tony."

An awkward silence fell into the room. J.J. thought back to the sound of her voice. The words flowed out with so little hesitation, she feared the tone might've given away more than their work assignment. She felt exposed but no regret.

Tony shifted their attention back to Dante. "So, uh, how's he doing?"

Mrs. Donato shrugged. She tried to speak but choked with emotion. "The doctors…they aren't hopeful—" She began to sob.

Carla walked over and pressed her hands on her mother's shoulders to comfort her. "They hit him twice; both exited his chest. One hit a vein in his rib cage. He lost a lot of blood."

A chill went through J.J. Her mother died in a similar way. Her first ride on an airplane was a trip to her mother's bedside. For that reason, she hated planes more than hospital rooms.

"And the other?"

"Nipped his spinal cord, lots of nerve damage. Internal bleeding. He just…he lost so much blood, possible brain damage. God knows if he's gonna pull through. Only God knows."

"Mother of God," Tony said.

J.J. longed to reach out to him and hold him, but she impotently stood by as Tony took hesitant steps toward his brother's bed. His face weighed down with concern and regret; his breath labored. He patted Dante's arm and whispered, "I'm here. I'm gonna find who did this to you…and I'll make him pay."

Dante went pale as he began to struggle for breath. The steady pulse of the monitoring sped to a frenzied pace. He shook in a full-body convulsion.

"Nurse! Nurse!" Tony yelled as Carla, J.J., and Mrs. Donato stared in abject horror.

J.J. stood frozen, panicked, wanting to help but not knowing what to say or what to do. She was a spy catcher, not a doctor. Not a miracle worker. All she could do for Dante and his family is pray. So she did.

"Noooo, Dante! My baby, my baby," his mother cried, clinging to his arm.

A doctor and four nurses swept in. "He's going into cardiac arrest!" the doctor said. "We need you to leave the room. Now!"

Tony scuttled everyone into the hall as the nurse snatched the defrib paddles from the wall and put them in the doctor's waiting hands. He rubbed them together, pressed them against Dante's chest, and yelled "Clear!"

As Dante's body sprung in reaction to the voltage pulsed through him, Tony blocked the window to obstruct his mother's and sister's view. He turned, gathered them both in his arms, and pulled them close, clenching his eyes. He was powerless to help his brother and the strain aged his face in a fleeting instant.

He embraced them as he locked his eyes on J.J.; hers filled with tears. She mouthed the words "I love you."

He fought back the moisture pushing through his damp, reddened eyes, forced a half smile, and in reply mouthed the words, "I love you too."

A woman's unexpected shrill interrupted the scene. "What the hell's going on here?"

J.J.'s head snapped to her left. Dree. She had returned with her mother's tea in hand and, from the expression on her face, had witnessed the exchange between she and Tony. Their secret was out in the worst way and in the poorest timing.

Dree's gaze volleyed back and forth between the two; her face roiled in revulsion, disgust.

J.J. grunted and closed her eyes, shaking her head in disbelief. Her stomach curled with anxiety. Would Dree tell her mother they were in love with one another?

Chapter 13

Thursday Morning — New York City

Ominous clouds, pushed across the sky by blustery winds, masked the moon's light as J.J. and Tony arrived at the hotel at THREE A.M. Dante's condition had stabilized, but doctors refused to speculate on how long the improvement would last, if at all. Mrs. Donato ordered them to their hotel rooms to steal a few hours of sleep before a new relapse.

The dramatic events had left their emotions hollow to the core and their relationship exposed without warning. But J.J. couldn't stifle the look of doe-eyed Disney wonderment that seized her expression every time she marveled at the Plaza's decadent luxury. The view helped take her mind off the heaviness of the day's events. She remembered, even if for a brief moment, the existence of another realm beyond this world of smoke and mirrors driving her existence from day-to-day. The sight forced to the forefront the dream of a life centered on something other than the empty lies of traitors and the honor they spurned. Success trapped her. She was too good at her job to walk away from those she'd committed to helping. She hoped for more than daily drudgery. For a change, she wanted to have it all.

They'd just stepped onto the elevator platform when a voice screeched, striking J.J.'s nerves with the same effect as the slow and steady drag of nails down a chalkboard. They turned, and Gia had thrust her arm across the sensor of the almost-closed door, her suit still crisp from the day before.

"Late night, huh?" She directed her eyes at Tony. "I waited for you. Wanted to tell you what we found in the files, but judging by the haggard looks on your faces I'll leave you to sleep."

"Hey, Gia." Tony kept his greeting flat and unsmiling. "Why don't you brief us in the morning after we catch some Zs? This day couldn't get any longer."

Gia nodded; the corners of her mouth turned down in disappointment.

"What are you doing up anyway? Figured you'd be knocked out by now," he added.

"I wish," she said with a devilish grin. "I closed down the Champagne Bar and then 5th Avenue called to me. So, I took a stroll. Window shopping."

"In this weather? What were you drinking at the bar, dragon's blood?"

"If her name is Mary, then yes."

J.J. cleared her throat to hint that the time had come to leave Gia to her own devices, preferably something to choke her. Barely out of the hot seat, Tony took the cue with all the seriousness it deserved. "All right. We gotta go."

"Breakfast in the Palm Room? I hear the pastries and desserts are to die for," Gia said to J.J.

"To die for? Hmph. Sounds like reason enough to give it a shot. Maybe I'll get lucky." Her voice disappeared into a mumble. "We'll see you at TEN A.M.." J.J. paused after realizing she'd answered for both she and Tony and made a quick course correction. "I mean if that's okay with Tony."

"Great. We're on," Gia replied, her tone a mix of pompous and glib. Didn't take a genius to figure out what Gia would prefer to eat for breakfast, and the Italian dish she desired was excluded from *her* menu. She would've had Tony as a midnight snack if J.J. hadn't been standing next to him. Who could blame her for trying? After all, Tony was every bit a Roman god in the flesh with genuine soul. Gia's total lack of respect was the egregious error J.J. could never tolerate, nor forgive.

The elevator stopped moments later, and Gia disappeared down the third-floor hallway. Tony spun toward J.J., pressed his body toward hers, and whispered in her ear. "My room or yours?"

The corners of her mouth lifted with her libido. "Why, sir? I do declare. I believe you are trying to sully my downright upright reputation. After all, we are not betrothed," she replied with a laugh. She loved his look. The way his body towered over hers made her feel more protected than carrying a Glock. The way his eyes feasted on her as he drank her in with lust-filled stares. If she didn't break up the tension, she would've had him right there.

"Well, maybe I need to correct that…make an honest woman out of you."

J.J. snapped silent. Her jaw dropped to her chest, and she stared him in the eyes, waiting for a hint of jest. None came. She resolved to treat his words as a joke because to take them with the seriousness in which he spoke them would open a Pandora's box.

"Why, I do declare the long hours have made you delirious," she joked, continuing her Scarlett routine. "Why don't you have a shower and pop around later for some—"

Her cell phone rang; she thanked the stars. She glanced at the screen. Sunnie. What in hell was she doing calling at this time of the morning? For her to be awake at this ungodly hour was a sure sign the message was urgent. She'd tried to deliver it on repeated occasions. An instinct told her the time had come to stop and listen.

"Sunnie! What's going on?" She waved to Tony, gesturing for him to go ahead to his room. Sunnie was long on words and short on silence. The conversation wouldn't end anytime soon.

"J.J., I'm so sorry. I figured you'd turn off your ringer, and I'd leave a message for you."

"No, we're just getting back to the hotel." She slipped the key card into the door slot and entered her suite. "Rough night at the hospital, but Dante pulled through…at least for now."

"Where are you guys staying?"

"The Plaza. And now I'm spoiled for hotels. No other place in the world will measure up. It's divine," she said. "Now, what's this about? You don't keep these hours for mailroom gossip."

"I'm calling about Nixon…and your mother's case files. He attempted to access them."

"What?!"

"Yes! Ran into him at the Special File Room yesterday. He asked to sign them out, but Freeman restricted access. He can't get them without the director's approval."

Freeman told her he'd handle the situation from his end. Nixon must be seething by now, already devising an alternate plan.

"Why in hell would Nixon want old Black Panther files?"

"I can't say," Sunnie answered, "but pissed doesn't quite come close to describing the expression on his face when he walked away empty handed. This may be his first time attempting to access them; you can rest assured it won't be the last."

"I have no doubt," she said, wishing she was standing inside headquarters so she could confront him face-to-face and ask him what he had to hide. Without the director's persistence, no way would this one setback stop him for long. She could ask for more help, but she'd begun to feel as if she'd leaned on that post one time too many already. The next favor she requested better be critical, like approval for the wires and national security letters which were necessary to wrap up the New York case. However, another option occurred to her. She might be able to explore another way—a Wendell way. "It's clear the director realizes Nixon's intent, and the only thing standing between Nixon and the file is Wendell," J.J. said. "How strong is his backbone?"

"To my surprise, he's got some bricks back there. But, as acting director, Nixon will probably find a loophole. It's only a matter of time."

"If I ask, do you think Wendell can make that file disappear? Not forever, but until I return to D.C."

"If *you* ask, maybe," Sunnie said. "If *I* ask, yes."

J.J. sighed with relief. "You're a lifesaver," J.J. said. "What would we do without you?"

"Let's hope you never find out," Sunnie replied before saying, "but I've got more news. The visitor's desk called requesting approval for a visit request. Jack Sabinski is meeting with Nixon, and they wanted to verify that he is allowed in the building."

"Not a surprise. They're buddies from way back, but I'd be lying if I said I'm not concerned," J.J. said. "When two snakes unite, the product of their union will slither. The reptile population is going to explode."

"At least you won't be blindsided," Sunnie said. "Now, I'll let you get some sleep."

"Oh, one more thing," J.J. said. "We've requested a national security letter. I'm going to need analytical support when we receive the numbers in the next day or two."

"Yeah, Walter gave me a heads up yesterday. We've still got access to VECTOR. But with Nixon at the helm, let's just hope the request goes through in time."

Chapter 14

Thursday Morning — U.S. Embassy, Moscow

Through the darkness, Six patted his hand along the nightstand trying to pick up the handset in order to stop the aggravating ringing. After a few unsuccessful attempts, the noise stopped. He perched himself on his elbows and glanced at the clock. FOUR A.M. He'd been asleep for a mere three hours.

He sat up and swung his legs over the edge of the bed.

Memories from the safe house flooded his mind in a moment too quick to stop them. The panicked call from J.J.'s burn phone. Vorobyev's face recognized by watchers. The exfil op he needed to develop in order to save the stubborn son of a bitch's life. And the FSB—a rabid Pit-bull. If they even suspected the CIA had rooked them and Vorobyev was still alive, they'd sink their teeth into the hunt for him and lock their jaws until he choked out his last breath. How in hell would he orchestrate an exfil under microscopic scrutiny?

Before he could even conjure up his mental magic, the phone rang again. He dreaded picking up the handset. He imagined the worst. Was Vorobyev dead? Was the FSB flaunting his mangled body in front of the press? A barrage of worst-case scenarios flooded his mind, and Six didn't want to answer, but he needed to. He grabbed the phone and allowed his body to collapse against the bed.

"Whatever it is, it better be good," Six said, his voice thick with gravel from the sleep deprivation.

"The news. They're reporting an explosion," Bart said. "We're meeting in one hour."

"An explosion? What do you mean?" Six asked, bolting upright in his bed. He was up before he even realized he'd moved. He pressed his fingers in the cracks of his eyes which had dried with grit. They bombed Vorobyev?

"What do you mean what do I mean? Fire, smoke, BOOM!"

"Is he dead?"

"Is who dead?"

"Vorobyev. He's why you're calling, right?" Six shot a twisted expression at the phone as if Bart could see him.

"No. I'm calling about the explosion…on *Petrovsky Boulevard*," Bart replied. "Security services are on the scene, and we've got the fucking disaster of the decade on our hands."

Petrovsky Boulevard. Six turned over the thoughts in his mind. He recalled the name but couldn't remember where he'd heard it. Just as he started to tell Bart he didn't know what the hell he was talking about, the memory rushed in. Ghost Man. Petrovsky Boulevard is the place where he said Mosin was hiding out.

He froze. The son of a bitch killed Mosin, and Six would never fulfill his mission. Ghost hadn't made any promises, but Six held out a thin hope that he'd permeated his thick skull anyway. His anger erupted inside, but he kept his cool despite the rush of emotion.

"Hello? Sorry. Took me a minute to get my head together. Our…uh…*friend* wasn't involved, was he?" Six asked.

"You'll receive a full briefing when you arrive. Move your ass. You can finish your beauty rest later." He found no consolation in Bart's response. His angst just shifted from a bad situation to the worst one. Worse than fearing Mosin was dead—he now dreaded that the FSB would find the missing intel before he did.

He jumped out of bed and scurried through his morning routine, splashing water in the cracks and crevices needing a rinse, including the little-noticed ones trapping the crust around his eyes. In the midst of preparing to handle the chaotic turn of events, he stole a few moments to allow his thoughts to wander to J.J. He slipped into a pair of Dockers, the woolen Christmas sweater she bought for him when they were one, and slid his feet into his Rockports—wishing his body could follow his mind stateside to be with her.

His mind coiled through memories of a thousand mornings when either he or she shot out of bed, stumbling through the dark. The cell phone ringing at all hours while they did the crisis dance into their clothes and out the door after late-night tangles between the sheets. Back then, with her, the CIA was his job, not his life. She was his world, until he made a mess of everything they'd built. He'd ruined their love like new sin in an old soul. Six believed with the fervor of a patriot at war, whatever distractions drew them apart—Stanislav Vorobeyev, Gary Mosin, the Mashkovs, or even Tony Donato—destiny or fate would bind them again.

He vowed with every fiber of his being that however the opportunity presented itself, he would seize it and never again let her go.

He needed J.J. His life made no sense without her. He wanted to be at her side. Not here in this godforsaken country chasing a jackass Benedict Arnold. But Moscow had called him.

Time to get to business.

In ten minutes flat, he'd pressed across the blustery compound, through the razor-sharp gusts, and up the steps to the administrative building until he reached the secured floors at the top. After badging himself into the SCIF, the CIA station's top secret compartment, he made his way to the conference room where Station Chief Mark Levin and Bart stared at the phone as if turning away would cost them their lives.

Six took a seat, folded his hands together, and waited for one of them to speak. With the exception of a customary "Good Morning," neither volunteered a word.

"Uh, any word on Mosin or the blast? You called me here at the crack of dawn. I assumed we'd be doing more than staring at the telephone."

"No fatalities, but two civilians sustained serious injuries. Our sources tell us ambulances transported them to International Medical Center. Ghost Man doesn't have an update."

"So, we have no clue as to whether Mosin's one of the injured, right?" Six asked.

Bart hunched his shoulders. "No idea. The FSB swarmed on that hospital like flies on a dead bunny after the explosion. If he's hurt, getting to him will be harder than trying to rob Fort Knox once he's inside. Whether or not this phone rings could make or break us. If it doesn't ring, we don't have him."

"Shit," Six said, now joining the staring contest. His every ability to recover the intel and accomplish his mission lay in Ghost's hands. The entire station may be dangling on the precipice of an international relations nightmare for the United States sure to last for months, perhaps even years. He tensed every inch of his body trying to will the phone to ring, all to no avail. He settled his nervousness, but one truth was painful and clear.

If this intel got out, the name America is mud.

Five minutes later, he'd had enough.

"Screw this," Six said, breaking the silence. He bolted up from his seat. Between Vorobyev and Mosin, he stood on the brink of insanity, and one wrong move threatened to push him over. He conceded one fact: If he was powerless to solve this problem, at least he could work on the other. "Hate to break up this party, but if I sit here with you guys, I'm gonna go nuts."

"Where are you going?" Mark asked.

"We better step out into the hall. Another situation is brewing that requires your immediate attention."

They made their exit, and Six closed the door behind him, bringing his voice down to a whisper. "Vorobyev called yesterday from the burn phone. He thinks FSB watchers spotted *…and recognized him.*"

Mark's face turned red in an instant. His head all but spun around and popped off like a champagne cork. "What the hell is wrong with this guy? I mean, the man can't stay put for a second. It's as if he has a death wish, and he wants his murder on our heads. How in hell did *this* happen?"

Six shrugged. "Our asset said he's been half-assed about wearing the disguises. I've ordered him to stay inside from this point forward, or I'm gonna drop his ass off at Lubyanka Square myself."

"Jesus. So what's the plan?"

Six looked at him with his head cocked to the side, and his lips pursed. Mark had to realize they didn't have a choice at this stage. The person they needed to contact was a worst-case scenario option, and they'd arrived at the tipping point.

Mark nodded. "Damn, I hate to tap that well. We'd be taking a gargantuan risk." He scraped his fingers through his scalp. "I know you're right. We're at DefCon 1 and a finger's hovering over the red button. We gotta do what we gotta do. Make the call."

"On my way," Six said as he headed down the hall. He badged into a smaller secure area. Inside sat a rectangle-shaped, oak table lined with special ops phones used to contact sources and support covert operatives working outside the embassy. He walked to the last one on the right, picked up the handset, and dialed. After two rings, a dead space filled his ear.

"Hey, I'm on the way out. What is it?" asked Connor Burke, a CIA non-official cover officer—or NOC—running a CIA-backed high-tech front company in Moscow.

"We're requesting your help…we need to get a, uh, *package* inside the embassy. And you're the only one with the experience and cover to deliver it."

"Mm hmm," Connor said. "No way you're calling me to move intel. This should be good. Who is it?"

"Can't pull the wool over your eyes," Six said before reducing his voice to a mumble so contorted he sounded as if he was walking under water. "Stanislav Vorobyev."

The sound went dead again.

"Hello?" he said. "We must have a bad connection. Some crazy fuck interrupted the line and said 'Stanislav Vorobyev'."

"The crazy fuck would be me…and, yes, I did say 'Vorobyev'." Six's voice was weak but his words were clear.

"I'm sorry. I've always known you were nuts but never suspected clinically insane." His voice rose an octave. "The most wanted man in Moscow. The one whose name and pictures are splashed on the front covers of every newspaper from here to Siberia. You must be joking out of your ass."

"I wish," Six said. "He's passing us the entire cache. We've got to get him off the streets and the intel in our hands."

"And you thought eliciting my support was the way to go? I've spent fifteen years building this cover," he said. "You and I shouldn't even be speaking right now…and you want me to do *this?* I'll be catching flies in some dank cell in Lefortovo Prison before this is over."

"Do you think I'd bother subjecting myself to your ridicule if we had any other viable alternatives?" He paused. Six listened to his own heart pound in the silence.

"How?"

"Well…I, uh…haven't figured out the plan yet," he said. "But I'm working it. Just understand, today this is a favor, but one phone call and tomorrow this is an order. The President's neck is on the line. We've got to get Stan into the embassy yesterday or we're all screwed. Your cover will be worth less than used toilet paper if the entire Station is expelled."

"You deliver one hell of a pep speech. Give me a call when you've got your act together. I'm in."

Six breathed out to bring his stress level down a notch. He'd recruited ops support, now he needed a plan to bring the most wanted man in Russia into the U.S. Embassy. Not two seconds after Six hung up, the door burst open. It was Bart…and his face looked surgeon serious.

"Mark needs you in the conference room," he said. "There's been a development."

"A development?" Six replied, not moving an inch.

Bart cocked his head to the side. "Well, your hearing's all right. Let's see if those feet work. Come on."

Six jumped up from his seat and padded behind Bart, anticipating the colossal blunder he'd encounter when returned. From the stoic expression on Bart's face, this announcement had bad news written all over it. The intelligence had vanished, and Mosin was in the hands of the Russians. Six's mind spun in circles. The Russians would first splash the reports all over the media, and begin the painstaking process of expelling the entire station. He took a slight comfort in the fact that he hadn't emptied his suitcases and, despite the mess he'd leave behind, he'd soon be headed home to J.J.

His stomach knotted into a ball as Bart pushed the door open and stepped aside to let Six enter. The look on Mark's face was intense. His eyes were low and crunched together. The mood was bleak, hopeless.

Six stood next to Mark with a pointed expression and asked, "What's going on?"

Mark pulled back a chair and, with his hand, gestured for his colleague to take the adjacent seat. "You'll need to sit down for this one."

Chapter 15

Thursday, Late Morning — New York City, The Plaza

The blackout curtains left the room pitch dark. J.J. stretched out her arms into Tony's side of the bed and felt cold pillows where his warm body lay a little more than a day before. She realized she must've dozed off after her phone call with Sunnie. She looked at the clock. TEN A.M. had just barely come and gone. She never would've slept so late into the morning with Tony at her side. His morning routine always started with a workout. Oversleeping left her unsettled, as if she'd missed something important.

She ran her fingers along her body and touched yesterday's suit. Groping her way through the darkness, she tip-toed to the window and pulled the curtains back to allow the sun's rays inside. They warmed her face as she took in the beautiful Central Park views. A sudden urge to stretch pushed her hands into the air before she expelled a long, loud yawn.

Where's Tony? she thought. *And why hasn't he called?*

Then she remembered Gia's last words from the night before. J.J. had a hunch about where he might be.

After dialing his room once, his cellphone twice, and getting no answer, she hurried through her shower and dress routine. Within minutes, she was at the door and on her way to the Palm Room. J.J. had a sneaking suspicion the Sicilian bombshell wouldn't be far behind Tony. Her mind began to spin out of control with visions of them huddled together over coffee while Tony's eyes stayed peeled on Gia's excessive cleavage as they exchanged flirtatious glances. The mere thoughts made her want to hurl . . . both of them out of her seventh-floor window.

Anger bubbled in her gut as she snatched her purse strap from the edge of the chair and fingered her holster to ensure her Glock was secure and at the ready. She jerked the door open, when her heart collided against her rib cage.

"Good Morning, Sunshine!" Tony said, his face bearing a wide grin. He carried a cardboard tote with two steaming cups of java in one hand. The other paper bag contained some kind of warm carbohydrates judging from the potent aroma jarring her senses and making her stomach growl. "I let you sleep in for a few hours since we had such a late night," he said.

Her confused expression mimicked his own.

"Uhhh, can I come in or are you gonna make me eat the bagels out here in the hall?"

J.J. shook her head to snap out of her surprise at his presence. She'd convinced herself Tony was up to no good and, once again, the green-eyed monster had led her astray. She'd devolved into a high school psycho in a matter of minutes, the speed of which frightened her. "Oh, yeah. I'm sorry. Come in." She stepped aside to let him pass. He headed straight for the sitting area and rested the morning goodies on the coffee table.

"What's up with you?" Tony asked, fixing a suspicious glare on her. "Why are you gawkin' at me as if you're surprised I'm here? We're together now, remember? Or do you have someone hiding in the bathroom?" he said, playfully jumping up to inspect it.

His quick move made her laugh. "Don't be ridiculous. Denzel just left. You missed him by seconds." Her mind resettled back into reality. "No, I've been calling since I woke up, and when you didn't answer, I, uh .... well, you're here now. Nothing else matters."

Tony's face contorted into a confused expression, and he patted down his coat until he retrieved his cell phone. He glanced at the screen. "Two missed calls. I'm sorry babe, the volume's set on silent. Forgot to turn it back up when I woke up this morning. Where'd you think I was?"

"Don't ask." She took a sip of the coffee and removed a cinnamon raisin bagel from the bag. "Sunnie called me last night. Nixon's on the prowl."

"What's he up to now?"

"My mother's case files. He's trying to get access to them."

"What is the issue with this case? It's like the biggest secret in the FBI since Hoover's love of couture."

"It's complicated…at least that's the bullshit story everyone keeps shoveling. Lana's case has consumed every ounce of my energy for these past few weeks; I've hardly had time to string together two seconds to think about it. Just when I got the courage to ask the director, he had a heart attack. I'm beginning to believe the universe is conspiring to keep me from finding out the truth."

"Well, then the universe doesn't have a clue about who it's messing with," Tony said. "Otherwise, it would realize trying to stop you is an exercise in futility. The question we should be asking is what do all these people have to lose?"

"We?" she smiled and touched his hand. For the first time, she didn't feel alone. "You're reading my mind. What in the hell would Nixon have to lose…unless he was somehow involved."

Tony started shaking his finger as if he'd had an epiphany. "Wait a minute. Didn't you tell me Jack met your mother?"

"Yeah," J.J. said with a nod.

"Well, weren't Jack and Nixon buddies from the Academy?"

About to take bite of her bagel, J.J. stopped an inch before it reached her lips. "You know, you're right. They've been tight for years, and both have specialized in counterintelligence for their entire careers. They had to be involved in COINTELPRO," J.J. said, referring to Hoover's counterintelligence program targeting The Black Panther Party and other black liberation organizations. "If they played a part in the death of an FBI agent, a part requiring a cover-up, then they indeed stood to lose a lot more than their reputations."

Tony tightened his lips, and his eyebrows arched.

"I've got to get inside the file, come hell or high water. I'm hoping the answers I need are inside. The sooner we put this Troika business to bed and ease the hostilities, the faster I can return to Washington and figure out this puzzle. Anyway, enough about my drama. What's going on with your father's . . . family?"

"I'm not sure, but I'll find out later. I'm headin' to Brooklyn to see Santino this morning."

J.J. turned to him, her expression one of fear and concern. "Is that safe? Do you want me to go with you?"

Tony shook his head. "No, I'm in charge of dealing with family business. You focus on Troika. Submit the wiretap requests so we can go home."

"Speaking of wiretaps, I hope we got Fitzpatrick's approval for the emergency request," she said, referring to the Russian Organized Crime squad supervisor—Devin Fitzpatrick. "Without that, neither the SAC nor Nixon will sign off. And without the court order we're screwed."

•••

"What do you mean Fitzpatrick rejected the wiretap request?" J.J. barked at Scott, who seemed to take some personal pleasure in the denial. He gloated because the case remained stalled despite her storied reputation. Manny's frustration, on the other hand, teetered on the edge of eruption like hers. But J.J. was too stubborn to give Scott the satisfaction of knowing he'd ruffled her feathers. "He couldn't have conducted a serious review of the new information."

"Yes, he did…and he killed it, anyway. Just as he's done to every request we've submitted to him in the past year. Said there's insufficient evidence of criminal activity and intent."

"Are you fucking kidding me?" Didn't take a genius to figure out something else was afoot, given the case's clear and undisputed connection to Lana Michaels—a known Russian sleeper agent.

"I wish we were kidding," Manny said. "We've been banging our heads against this same brick wall for over a year."

He'd hamstrung the entire case. She developed two theories about the reasons for Fitzpatrick's rejection, and neither of them was a legitimate excuse. Either one threatened to land him in a lot of hot water someday. The first was that he didn't even bother to read the full request—or he was taking orders from on high, engaged in a deliberate campaign to obstruct her investigation. Wouldn't be the first time. She had no choice but to devise a plan to get the information another way until she worked out that snag. As far as J.J. could determine, she had only one option.

"Oh, yeah? Well, the banging stops today. I've got a couple of phone calls to make but in the meantime,"—J.J. turned to Manny— "arrange a meet with the CI."

If the accountant, The Sparrow, was the key to striking at the heart of the Troika organization, and they couldn't get a tap into the phones, then they would tap into his associates.

"To which CI are you referring?" Scott asked.

"The one connected to Zory Kozlov—the accountant. I want to talk to whomever it is to find out whether Kozlov's got any vulnerability we can exploit. If he's the accountant connected to The Duke, the one linked to Levi Mashkov, then we can use him to track the money and then freeze the accounts."

Manny nodded in agreement. "Okay, but you gotta understand, this guy's skittish right now, and he may not agree to meet with you. You gotta figure if Mashkov's people will hit the son of a Bonanno boss then they won't think twice about taking him out if they found out he talked to the Feds. And he understands, like us, the Mashkovs won't stop at him. They'll slaughter his entire family."

"I realize this is a longshot, but we've got to try," J.J. said. "The wiretap has fallen through for now. This is our final option."

"Agreed." Manny stood up and headed to the door. "The guy's in Brooklyn and doesn't like to use phones. Give me a couple of hours. We'll pitch the idea to him and tell you how it goes."

"Can I ride along?" J.J. asked.

Scott shook his head. "He doesn't even trust *us*. We've got to allow him to dip his toe in the shallow end first."

"All right. Two hours and I'll see what I can do about this wiretap."

J.J. watched them walk away, picked up her cell phone, and scanned for Mrs. Whitehouse's phone number. The director told J.J. to call his secretary if she had any emergencies. She had planned to pull the Director card with caution; Fitzpatrick had now given her just cause to leverage it. The success of the entire Troika investigation rested on their ability to obtain the wiretaps. Even more, their ability to wrap up the entire illegals network depended on taking down the financial hub.

The phone rang twice before she answered. "Hello, Mrs. Whitehouse? It's J.J. McCall. I have an emergency. Need you to get a message to Director Freeman…"

Chapter 16

Thursday Afternoon — Washington D.C.

Santino Castellano and his captain, Nicolas "Nicky Mumbles" Muzzatto, had been standing outside Swifty's goomar's apartment for so long, Kentucky bluegrass grew under their feet. Santino wanted to hurry and get the meet over with. To find out who tried to clip Dante, he needed Nicky to arrange a sit-down with the Russians. Swifty, the conduit between the five families and the Russians, was the man Uncle Sal had told them could get the job done.

Five minutes after they started knocking, Swifty plodded across the floor like a stuffed elephant and opened the door.

"Nicky! Santino! Long time," Swifty said, greeting them both with affectionate hugs and pecks on the cheek. "Come in. Come in. Take a load off." He shuffled toward the kitchen, lumbering like a snail on valium. They headed for the living room.

Frank "Swifty" Zanetti, a paranoid loyal-for-the-moment capo in the Genovese family, got his nickname because he moved as slow as an iceberg. He was built like one, too. Whatever the task at hand, the words "rush" or "quick" didn't exist in his vocabulary. Connected guys found it hilarious that he talked and ate as if on fast forward. Words shot out of his mouth at a hundred miles per hour and food went in just as fast. But the only time he picked up his walking pace was to turn down the fire on the Sunday sauce. This explains why he took five minutes to open the freakin' door after Nicky and Santino knocked.

"Frankie Z! How's life?" Nicky asked. As a Bonanno capo, he led the conversation. For the most part, on Sal's orders, Santino's job was to listen, observe, and analyze in case Nicky had questions after. Speak when spoken to. "Still eatin' good, I see."

"Life's good. Never seen a plate of macaron' I didn't like. Isabella's got some beer and a nice proscuit' in the fridge if you want somethin' to eat," he offered. They replied with no thank yous, eager to get to business.

Swifty turned toward Santino bearing a somber expression; his mouth curved downward, but he averted his gaze to the door. "Santino, how's Dante doin'?"

Santino paused, combed his fingers across his scalp. Anguish ripped through his stomach and dampened his mood. "Not so good," he said. "Doctors are saying he may not make it."

"Bullshit. Screw those butchers, you hear me?" Swifty remarked, pointing his sausage-sized fingers. "Your cousin's a fuckin' bull. Stubborn as one, too. He ain't goin' nowhere until he's good and goddamn ready. Don't you worry about Dante. He'll come out stronger than when he went in."

Santino nodded. "God willing. Appreciate it, Frankie."

Nicky waited for a comfortable pause and then proceeded. "We want to let you enjoy the rest of your day, so let's get down to business."

Swifty pored over the room, the corners, the phone, out the windows. Felt like twenty minutes passed by the time he started speaking.

"The fuck you think you got? X-ray vision? I mean, c'mon," Nicky said. "If the Feds planted a wire in here, you sure as hell ain't gonna find it by gawkin' from your seat."

"Fuckin' Feds. They'd wire my balls if they weren't hanging between my legs. You can never trust 'em. Let's step out on the veranda."

Frankie's place was on the top floor with nothing overhead except blue horizon. If the Feds ever figured out how to wire the sky, they'd all be in trouble. Swifty was a new capo in his family and refused to be the weakest link. His paranoiac behavior, constant checking, refusal to have conversations in any place his people hadn't swept for bugs at least twice a week, kept him off the Fed's radar…or so he thought. "You need a sit-down with the Russians."

"Yeah," Nicky Mumbles said. "It's out of our deepest respect for your business interests that I'm askin' before we make a move."

The concern on Swifty's face was obvious. "Listen, I understand your issue. Under any other circumstances, if those Russkiy cocksuckers hit one of us, someone in our family? Heads would be rolling all over Brighton Beach. But every single family is drawing water from this well, including yours, and the Russians control the supply end," Swifty said. "You've got a legitimate beef, but we need to keep the peace for the time being. Any move would bring a lot of heat from the Feds. We can't afford any more indictments. We got millions tied up in business with those jerkoffs, and we can't rock the boat."

"Rock the boat?" Santino questioned, his simmering anger coming to a quick boil. "With all due respect, Frankie, this is my cousin we're talkin' about here. My family…*mia famiglia.*"

Nicky Mumbles glared at Santino. His look said, *Shut your fucking yappin'. You're talkin' out of school.*

"You know me and your uncle go away back, Santino. But we can't step over dollars to pick up dimes here," Swifty said. "If we were talkin' chump change, I'd take 'em out myself."

"If not chump change, then what are we talkin' here?" Nicky replied.

"Millions," he said. "A hundred of 'em."

Santino glanced at Nicky. The response had taken aback both of them. With so much money on the line, forget about allegiance from the other families. Santino would have to avenge Dante's shooting and ask for forgiveness later. Forget about permission. Wasn't happenin'. Not then, not ever.

Santino seethed at Nicky, sitting there like a dead stump of wood, not giving two shits about his own boss's son. Not until Santino checked his phone did Nicky speak up as if he had some skin in the game. "You grew up in the neighborhood, Frankie. There is no way in hell we can let this shit go. No way. And the pennies we earn from our little piece-of-shit cut, we can earn elsewhere, hai capito? The question is no longer whether we hit; it's how and when."

Swifty took a seat in his steel-enforced lawn chair and leaned back. "Nobody involved would have a problem with you roughin' them up a little bit—injure 'em, cripple 'em, but you don't kill 'em. It's not like they're gonna run to the cops, but we can't afford a street fight right now. With the Feds handing out indictments like two-cent candy, we gotta keep earning for the lean times, which are coming. I can feel it in my bones. So therein lies the compromise," Swifty said.

The remark almost brought Santino to laughter. He didn't know Swifty had bones.

"In the meantime, I'll arrange a sit down with Russians. They'll cough up the shooter. We don't want a war, but they don't know that. We'll work something out to our mutual benefit. A larger cut maybe."

Nicky smiled and nodded.

At that moment, Nicky's motivation became clear. He didn't give a shit about Dante, but planned to use Dante's shooting to get a bigger share of the Russians' narcotics business.

Santino's anger warmed him to the core; he thought a thousand words he dared not say. Nicky's performance was pathetic. No loyalty to the boss, even with his nephew sitting next to him. His only concern was lining his pockets. Whatever front Nicky was putting up, Santino understood his true feelings and intentions. Until he got the order from Uncle Sal, he had to proceed with the sham, business as usual.

Before Santino spoke another word, his cell phone rang. His cousin Dree's number flashed on the screen. He excused himself and stepped inside to the kitchen. "What's goin' on?" Santino whispered, his voice panicked. He asked Dree not to call unless Dante was about breathe his last. "I just left there a few hours ago. Is he okay?"

"He took a bad turn, but he pulled out of it," she said. "That's not what I'm calling you about, though. We got a visitor today. Blast from the past."

"Who?"

"Tony," she snarled. "Fuckin' rat showed up here. Walkin' in the room like the Lone fucking Ranger with some black chick. Large and in charge as if he gives a shit about what happens to this family."

Santino let out a long sigh. Dree could hold a grudge longer and harder than any wise guy he'd ever tangled with.

"Listen," she continued. "Dante survived the day, but you oughta pay another visit soon. He only made it through by the skin of his teeth. I…I don't know if he's gonna pull it off a second time." Her voice cracked.

"You'll be okay, Dree. Try to keep it together. I'll be back as soon as I can. Tomorrow."

"It's not fair that he's lying here, fighting for his life, Santino. The cops called earlier. They got no idea who did this." She sobbed, spilling over with emotion. "Find out who's responsible, Santino. The son of a bitch has to pay for what he did to my baby brother."

"Stop crying, Dree," Santino said. "If you don't believe anything else in his life, believe this: Whoever did this is gonna pay, if it's the last thing I do."

By the time Santino returned, Frankie and Nicky were shooting the breeze about the good ole days. Santino made his excuses and said his goodbyes.

Once inside his Mustang, he promptly dialed Tony's phone number. He understood why Tony felt obligated to come to New York, but he had to warn him. He couldn't stay. If Nicky got word that Tony came to town, there'd be little Santino or Uncle Sal could do to keep him safe, unless they took out Nicky Mumbles. And with the state of disarray following crippling drug busts and Uncle Sal moving to the halfway house, a hit from inside the family might deal a blow too powerful to recover from.

As the phone rang, he thought about ways to convince the world's third most stubborn person (after Uncle Sal and himself) to leave the city when the mere suggestion was diametrically the opposite of anything he stood for.

After three rings, an empty space followed by noise in the background filled his ears.

"Hello?" Santino said.

No one spoke at first…and then a voice sounded. "Hey, Santino. I was just gettin' ready to call you. I've got something important to tell you. Hold on and let me step to where it's quiet."

Santino waited…now he was on edge. What the hell did Tony have to say?

"Listen, I got some news today…about your, uhh, health."

Santino jerked his head back and then cocked it to the side. "*My* health?"

"Yeah, meaning you might want to stay off the streets. Some people are looking for you. From the east."

Santino cursed to himself. "Where'd you hear that?"

"Don't worry about where I heard it. Just keep a low profile until I can get over to visit so we can talk. You still at pop's place?"

"Yeah, but you can't go there. It ain't exactly Disney World around here for you, either. If anyone sees you here, it's gonna cause major problems…for both of us."

"Nobody even knows I'm in New York except you and pop's people watching Dante. I'll get with you tomorrow."

"But, Ton'…you can't—"

The rumble of his Mustang's engine droned in Santino ear. He hung up the phone cursed Svetlana Mikhaylova, the dead leader of the Russian spy ring who'd introduced herself to him as Katherine. "I shouldn't have trusted that cunt." Falling into her trap was a mistake for which he very well might pay…with his life.

Chapter 17

Friday Afternoon — New York City

Tony blasted his radio as he cruised down the Bay Ridge Parkway through Bensonhurst, remembering his times in the old neighborhood. It was vastly different from D.C. where distinct lines had been drawn between residential and commercial streets. In New York, mom and pop shops weaved through the blocks like threads holding things together when community broke down. Grocery stores. Dry cleaners. Restaurants. Everything located on your street or around the corner. The thought made him nostalgic for his favorite pizza joint. Decided to stop by Originals for a slice before heading back to the city.

The brownstone where Santino was staying had been in the Donato family for over fifty years. His father inherited it from his grandfather, may he rest in peace; Santino would bunk there, at least until the hospital released Dante. Helped cut down the drive from Jersey in case of an emergency.

Thinking about his old stomping grounds brought back a rush of memories of him, Santino, and Dante—the Three Musketeers—playing stickball in the alleyways, sitting on the stoop talking smack about being wise guys, and riding their Schwinn Stingrays to Third Ave and 85th to look at the Verrazano Bridge and buy Italian ice from the old man who operated the pushcart. A nostalgic smile edged the corners of his mouth upward.

Tony checked his rearview mirror out of habit, but the last two times, he noticed a familiar car. An older silver Mustang with local plates. A dick on wheels, the car was hard to forget He suspected the guy driving had followed him. Tony noticed the man from the minute he pulled out of the Plaza parking lot but blew off his suspicion as paranoia.. He remembered the look of the guy at the stoplight. With his thick, wavy mane, the pinky ring glimmering in the sunlight during a stop in the city, and a two-hundred dollar pair of Ray Bans. The light bulb went off. Tony recognized him from his past.

One of his father's buttons—Ricky the Razor, a hit man whose mantra was "Life is short. Death is long." He was more heavyset back in the day. He'd gotten the name for the gruesome way he slaughtered the family "rats" and other miscreants, wounding them to an inch of death and then slicing off their fingernails with a razor. Tony looked down at his fingers and shuddered at the thought.

He made a hard right at a do-not-turn-on-red light around 68th, and the guy followed him, turn-for-turn in a complete 360 to the parkway.

"Son of a bitch," Tony said as he circled back to where he started. He checked his rearview mirror again for the fiftieth time in the last thirty minutes. He was still there. Same Mustang still clinging to his bumper. Same streak of silver that had tailed him through the city, across the Brooklyn Bridge and now a dozen blocks from Santino's place.

The surveillance detection run had served its purpose. Tony confirmed his father's hit man had trailed him; he no longer had any doubts. Before the day ended he'd come face to face with somebody's death— maybe his own.

He felt an empty pit in his stomach and his heart palpitated.

He glanced down at his phone. The only voice he wanted to hear was J.J.'s. Tony wished he could tell her he loved her, that he'd never discovered the best version of himself until he met her. He wanted to share his wish that his first son be blessed with her courage, her heart, and her eyes. The life he'd planned for them slipped away the moment his car hit 5th Avenue. He refused to go out like some spineless chump. If Ricky wanted to whack him, he'd have to work for it and he'd better hope Tony didn't get to him first.

Tony calculated a few scenarios before he devised a strategy to save his life. Even though nobody would ever accuse the Razor of stealth, he'd had experience in stalking his prey before going in for the kill.

Tony slowed his speed, doing 15 in a 45, and Rick mirrored his movements. Yet another confirmation that his presence behind Tony's vehicle was no fluke. In true New York fashion, a barrage of horns blared and expletives flew alongside flipped birds as Tony maneuvered to become the hunter instead of the hunted.

He reached a cut-through at an alley off 86th Street and, in screeching halts, hooked successive right-hand turns until he wheeled into a parking space. When the Razor's car passed, he backed out and made a quick right, checking his rearview mirror which revealed nothing but his own fumes. Seconds later, back on 4th Ave, he sped around scanning the area, trying to catch the Razor from behind. With all the turns, Tony expected to be on his bumper within a minute or two. But after ten minutes of circling, his target was nowhere to be found. Not ahead of him. Not behind him. Not anywhere.

Tony breathed sigh of relief, believing he had shaken his tail, but the moment of comfort did not last long. Ricky knew Tony was staying at the Plaza. He feared the possibility of the Razor showing up to take him out with J.J. lying next to him.

His anxiety mushroomed.

He parked on the main thoroughfare and waited to see if the silver Mustang reappeared but it never did. Tony smacked himself in the head with the heel of his palm and slammed his hands against the steering wheel before heading to Santino's place.

A few minutes later, he arrived on 74th. He decided to park a couple blocks away and enter through the back of the house to avoid nosy neighbors and any of Pop's people who might be monitoring out front. He whipped his car into the parking space and paused for a moment. As he checked the side mirror before opening the door into traffic, he spotted it.

The Razor's silver Mustang.

Parked two cars down and across the street from his. He could tell it was the same car from the decal on the front left side of the windshield—a kid wearing a Yankee hat pissing on a Red Sox logo.

Tony's mind raced, and he padded full speed to the alley behind Santino's. The Razor wasn't in the car. Where had he gone? He couldn't have predicted Tony would park two streets away. Either he was visiting someone else in the neighborhood (the possibility of which was slim and none)—or maybe the Razor had planned to use Santino as bait, lying in wait for Tony to show up.

Tony decided to bust in, barrels loaded and then his heart sank. Chances were Santino was already dead anyway.

Chapter 18

Friday Night — U.S. Embassy, Moscow

Six took the seat Mark offered him and braced himself for news on the explosion near the hotel where Mosin was staying.

"Ghost Man can't find Mosin. He's not in the hospital, but he's nowhere to be found—including dead."

Six scanned the room, taking in all the glum expressions. The implications did not escape him. Without Mosin in custody, he'd never return with the intel, and the threat of its disclosure would loom over the administration for the days and years to come. And if he eventually turned up dead, killing Mosin without recovering the intel would eventually be viewed as an epic failure by all involved.

"No sight of the cache either, huh?" he asked, standing up to pace around the room.

Mark and Bart both shook their heads. "Nothing."

"Damn," Six said, throwing up his hands. That son of bitch slithered from between their fingers. He scrubbed his hands over his face and collapsed back into a chair wondering how the situation could go so far to the left so fast. He needed to talk to Ghost and confirm what the hell happened.

Then one of the admins poked her head inside the door. "Six, you've got a call out here. Line 3."

His eyebrow scrunched wondering who in hell would be calling him from the main line. Maybe it was J.J. with news about the investigation. Part of him hoped he was wrong; she'd go ballistic when she found out Mosin was back in the wind.

He pressed his way to the admin's desk, grabbed the handset, and said, "Hello?"

"Yeah, this is Ghost."

"Speak of the devil."

"I need you at the safe house and don't tell anyone you're coming. Bought you seven days. Your clock starts now!"

•••

The drive to the barren structure just outside of Moscow proper felt shorter this time. The shock from the potholes more tolerable, the trunk less cramped. Perhaps because his mind strayed ahead in anticipation of what lay in front of him.

The brakes squealed and Bart, his driver, signaled that they'd arrived and the coast was clear. Six rolled out of his trunk, crept into the wood's edge, and crouched into the darkness of the brush as he watched the car's taillights disappear into the distance.

He waited, listening for the crackle of rubber against broken asphalt from an FSB watcher's car. There was no movement, no sound. Just the harsh fluorescent glare of a distant street light. He turned and trekked through the woods, his eyes following a trail of worn grass to his destination. Once he reached the fence, he heard the thunk of wood against wood and muffled grunts as he made his way around to the front and approached the entry. It struck him how thin the walls must be.

When he stepped up to the landing, a dark figure startled him.

"Jesus!" Six said, holding his chest.

Ghost appeared out of the shadows. His face drew into a sour scowl, sweat beaded on his forehead, and he dressed from head-to-toe in black except for the sleeves rolled to his elbows.

"Were you followed?" Ghost barked. His voice was gravelly and his attitude gruff.

"Bart is one of the best in the business. We would've aborted the op if the FSB was onto us. Then I'd be sitting in the Embassy right now, not looking at you. Let's get inside. We need to talk," Six said, padding up the steps.

"Wait," Ghost said, shoving his palm into Six's chest. "It ain't pretty in there."

In a flash, Six's face transformed, an animalistic glare shifted from Ghost's hand, to his eyes. His chest hulked and fingers rolled up into his palms.

"Put your hands on me again, and it won't be pretty out here, either."

Ghost snatched his hand back to his side and glanced back at the door when thumping and mumbling emanated from the inside.

"He's inside?"

Ghost nodded.

"What the—wait. What did you do to him?"

Chapter 19

Friday Afternoon — New York City

When Tony arrived at the back of his father's house, he noticed the door was ajar. Santino would never leave it open, even in Bay Ridge which housed Brooklyn's upper middle crust. He imagined the worst. The Razor had already put a bullet in Santino's chest and was watching him bleed out as he peeled his nails from his hands. Tony clamped his eyes shut to press the image out of his mind and tip-toed inside, keeping his footsteps cotton-soft. He slipped the Glock from the holster and crept through the laundry room, listening for Santino's screams.

He heard nothing except a couple of voices whispering as he eased into the kitchen, holding his breath as the sound of his heartbeat thumped in his ears. Following the faint voices into his father's office, he spotted Santino sitting behind the desk waving his arms in the air as if the Razor had held him up. The Razor's back faced Tony; he stood with one hand in front of his body as if he was holding something. Tony concluded it must be a gun.

Tony kicked the office door in and yelled, "Santino! Get out!" He gripped his pistol with both hands and tightened his fingers around the handle. With his arms extended, he levered one in the chamber and rushed inside.

"Are you fucking kidding me?" Santino yelled.

The Razor turned and spotted Tony. "Holy fuck!" he yelled, his hands shot up in the air.

Chickenshit didn't even fight back.

"Ton', for chrissakes put the gun away!" Santino barked.

Tony growled through his teeth, adrenaline coursing. He walked over to the guy, who by then was one log deep in his pants, and pushed the muzzle of his Glock into the Razor's temple. "Why the fuck did you trail me here? You fuckin' prick!" He'd snapped under the stress and forgot everything except that some douche bag threatened his life and the blood of warriors coursed in his veins.

Santino walked over to Tony and pushed his hand against his chest trying to urge him to back up. "Tony, this is Ricky. He's a stand-up guy who'd take a bullet for Uncle Sal." Santino turned to Ricky, who was sweatin' like a Hebrew slave. Tony backed up, his face red hot from volcanic anger. "Go sit over there and calm your ass down," Santino growled.

"Ricky, this is my infamous cousin, Tony Donato. Who shouldn't even be here, by the way."

"Nobody saw me…except *him*," Tony said, jutting his head in the Razor's direction. "Why the hell are you havin' me followed?"

"Uncle Sal's orders. Not mine."

Ricky nodded. "Nicky Mumbles got word you're in town. One of the guys in Monty Fazello's crew is monitoring the hospital." Monty was Nicky's right-hand man. "Nicky ordered me to break an egg, if you know what I'm sayin'. Make you disappear upstate. He doesn't know our history." Ricky shifted his glance toward Santino. "Sal saved my life. That's why I stay close to Nicky, to keep an eye on him. Make sure he doesn't pull any bullshit like he's trying now."

"Jerkoff," Santino said. "Uncle Sal ordered that no one was to blink in your direction without his say so."

"Well, Nicky ordered otherwise. Said Tony's death better be headline news by the end of the week or my wife would be filing a missing person's report, and my body would never be recovered in one piece."

Tony returned his gun to the holster and took a seat in one of the two empty chairs in front of his pop's desk. Ricky followed suit.

"I'm not surprised. Told you that motherfucker was dirty."

"He's been making a move on the family this whole time. The only thing I'm confused about is why he picked *you* as a target. You're a Fed, for chrissakes, living in D.C.; what kind of threat are you?"

Tony pinched his lips together and rubbed the back of his neck. Nicky Mumbles masterminded the hit on him from the jump. He had no doubt Santino was right, and so was his intuition. Nicky set him up to take the fall for ratting out Uncle Sal's underboss, Jimmy Toots. What Tony didn't understand is why no one else in the family had figured out his plan until now. Maybe because the notion of someone being so moronic as to frame the boss's kid was just beyond the bounds of belief.

It was a risk nobody thought Nicky was power-hungry enough to take. A boneheaded move. Getting whacked for framing the boss's son to get a promotion seemed like a stretch.

"What do you want me to do?" Ricky asked Santino. "Whatever you need, just tell me."

Santino walked out of the room and returned a minute later with a stack of cash, a torn sheet of paper and two keys. "Here, take this and lay low for a few weeks until we get this shit handled." He handed over the items and patted Ricky on the shoulder. "Stay in. Order delivery. Don't fuckin' budge, don't call anyone until I give you the okay. Don't forget, we got more than one reason you need to stay off the radar. Be smart. You got me?"

Ricky nodded in affirmation and headed for the door. "Yeah, I got it. Just call me Jimmy Hoffa. You gonna have a, *ahem*, sit-down with Nicky?"

Santino hunched his shoulders, exhaled, and sucked in his bottom lip, before saying, "I dunno. Gotta talk to Uncle Sal. The family's taking a lot of hits now. There's only so much more we can survive before our crews start questioning their loyalty to this family and look elsewhere. Until we squash this shit with the Russians, he's not gonna stir the pot."

"I hear you," Ricky said as he walked down the hall. "I'll wait for your call, and, Tony, sorry for the mix-up."

"No problem," Tony replied, watching him leave.

After Ricky disappeared from sight and the door clicked shut, Tony turned his attention back to Santino.

"So, what the hell are you still doing in New York? I told you not to come."

"You know why I'm here," Tony said, one marked man to the other. "I hadda make sure you understood the threat on the streets right now. These Russians, they don't play. Let the FBI handle them. You lay low."

Santino pursed his lips and in a sarcastic tone said, "Anything else, *Godfather*?"

"Hardy har har. You're a real Goumba Johnny. Fuckin' wise ass," he said. "I need you to be honest. Is the family plannin' to go to war with the Russians?"

"Honest, huh?" Santino said. "Guess that all depends on who I'm talkin' to. Am I talking to my cousin or a Fed? Because if it's the latter, then you can walk your ass back to your car and go to the Plaza."

Tony paused for a moment and considered his answer. For the first time since he left for Quantico, his role seemed unclear. A Fed would seek an arrest at any cost, and "the family" would seek retribution at any cost. With a pledge to protect his country, and Santino, Dante, and his Pops lives in as much danger as his own, he could be either—or neither. All of a sudden, the answer didn't seem so complicated at all.

"I want justice," he said. "My brother is hanging onto life by a thin thread. What? I'm gonna sit back and let that crazy Russian fuck slaughter him, my father, or—," he paused and looked at Santino, "whatever I gotta do, I'm gonna get 'em off the streets before this family loses another ounce of blood. For my mother and sisters . . . for myself."

"And you expect me to cough up what?"

"I need you to listen, Santino. I'd sooner pinch you than visit you in the bed next to Dante, you understand me? Your respect is optional— your cooperation isn't."

"Heh. Who says you can't take the Brooklyn out of the boy?"

"I'm after the Russians, not the family. So what can you tell me about the Mashkovs."

Santino took a moment to consider his response. He grabbed a beer out of the mini-fridge and took a long swig.

"To give you the straight truth, Nicky doesn't want to go to war with 'em. He's content to let this ride. Some of the crews loyal to Uncle Sal are ready to crack heads. The family's split."

Tony eyed Santino and furrowed his brow. "Let 'em ride?" As long as Tony had lived in Jersey and New York, he never heard any shit like that. He was positive the order hadn't come from his father. Being in the mob, it was very similar to intelligence—all smoke and mirrors with heavier artillery and more dangerous moves. Nicky was making moves. Tony wouldn't be surprised if Nicky had a relationship with the Russians or was trying to build one to strengthen his position with more money, more power. Santino and his father treaded in deep water, with open wounds, and sharks circling them at every turn.

Tony pursed his lips and rolled his eyes.

"What? He says it's business."

"Yeah, business may be part of it. But I'm puttin' two and two together and this shit just isn't adding up."

"What do you mean?"

"Think about it. Nicky used Jimmy Toots to get rid of me. He never thought I'd have the balls to come back here. The Russians hit Dante and, like magic, Nicky's their fuckin' third cousin, and he doesn't want to go after them? Don't you see? Now, the Russians have a legit excuse to come after you and Pop. Nicky reaps the benefits, gets protection from the Russians, takes over my father's business interests and gives the Russians a distribution partner. It all makes sense."

Santino soundlessly chewed on his thoughts. The expression on his face spoke volumes above the silence. Nicky would exploit this Russian beef and step over the dead Donatos to climb up the family ladder and become Boss. "I hear you, okay? Loud and clear." Santino growled and mumbled under his breath, his words searing with the bitterness of a man who'd been played like the fifth movement of a Beethoven symphony. "All I know right now is a sit-down is being scheduled with some Russian. Swifty's setting up the meet with some guy Max Novikov."

Tony bolted up and sat at attention. He remembered Max's name and his ties to Troika, the narcotics leader. He now had a direct link between Troika and Russian organized crime. If they could get a wire on Novikov's car or house, it might yield the information needed to stop the Russians and put Nicky Mumbles behind bars before any violence erupted.

"Swifty and Nicky told me I'm not invited because it's leadership to leadership, but let me make a few calls. If I can find out anything more, I'll let you know."

"Hmmm…interesting. I'm surprised they didn't ask you to be there. Seems like the perfect opportunity to ambush you. From this point forward, you keep your eyes and ears open. Any changes in plans, any mention of you meeting with this Novikov guy or any Russians, and you don't have to guess what's gonna to happen next."

•••

Santino's path ahead was clear—confirm the depth of Nicky Mumbles betrayal and deliver the news to Uncle Sal. He needed to run any proposed resolution by the other families and take care of this traitor once and for all. It suddenly struck Santino; he hadn't received a phone call from Stevie Pics. He looked at his watch. It'd been more than 24 hours since he told that jerkoff to call him back whether he found out Nicky had ratted out Jimmy or not. Stevie's muzzled silence set Santino's suspicions in full drive, made him consider whether or not Nicky's knowledge of Tony's arrival and the planned hit were indeed coincidental. Maybe Stevie, one of Uncle Sal's so-called most loyal soldiers, couldn't be trusted after all.

Santino decided to pay him a house call instead of a phone call.

Stevie had some explaining to do.

Chapter 20

Friday Night — Moscow Safe House

Six's gaze clouded; he turned away to collect his thoughts. Based on the noise erupting from inside the safe house, Ghost had definitely caught Mosin. The question troubling Six's mind was why he tried to prevent Six from going inside. If you put a Marine and a detained enemy of the state in the same room, two things were certain: one person was going to wind up tortured — and it wouldn't be the Marine.

Ghost just stood in silence staring back Six like a stump. "I'll ask again, what did you do to him? You promised me seven days."

"Listen, Six," Ghost began, "I convinced my team to bring him in. My methods may have put you in a bind but, in all honesty, I don't give a shit. It's not my job to worry about your binds; it was my responsibility as a patriot to kill the belligerent son of a bitch, but I kept him alive for you. I've spent some time with him, and I'm telling you if you want to complete your mission, you better get okay with what's going on in there damn fast. Report this and he disappears along with any hope of finding the intelligence."

Six took a deep breath to center his thoughts and pushed past Ghost, bumping him at the shoulder and daring him to speak a word. He thundered into the room and zeroed on a sight that sent shivers through him like Moscow's frostbitten winter wind. He audibly gasped. He turned to Ghost horror stricken.

Ragged and lethargic, Mosin had been stripped down to his tidy whities. His entire body shook in endless trembles. His hairy arms were strapped to wooden kitchen chair arms from wrist to elbow. A soiled white cloth, stained with the fresh blood dripping down the blackened skin around his eyes and nose, gagged his mouth. He struggled to sip air through his mouth causing him to snort through his nostrils. At the sound of footsteps moving closer, his head bobbled and he struggled to lift it before growing tired and locking his weary eyes on his detainers. Six searched for life in his eyes but found little.

As Mosin chattered, he drew enough energy to grunt and direct Six's glare his to his hands. Needles protruded from beneath all ten fingernails, and his feet were bound at the ankle and immersed in ice water almost halfway up his calf. He was free to remove them, but two large steel buckets containing hot coals sat on either side. Burn or be frostbitten, there was no in between. Resting on the floor was stage two – a sledge-hammer and a pair of pliers with red rubber grips.

"This?" Six whispered, staring at Mosin's gagged face. He wanted to say more, but the words lodged in his throat. No sound would come, except "Jesus H. Christ!" He covered his mouth and turned to Ghost, who was now standing next to him. "Let's step outside for a sec."

Six paced to the door with the crazy Marine in tow. He was no stranger to interrogations. He'd led a few harsh ones himself, and he knew a lot of guys he worked with could turn away with zero guilt and forget. Whatever bravado he masked himself with from day-to-day, his sense of right had cut him from a different cloth. Even if naturalized, Mosin was still an American—and there were laws and rules and an Intelligence Oversight Committee Chairman itching to drag the director through the mud once the report came out. And he'd have to write one at some point—to account for finding Mosin and the intel, if they found it.

It was Day 1. If he could stop it now—he'd have to nothing to say. But Ghost was ornery with a head of granite, and he'd set his strategy. Six put on his armor and decided to go head-to-head, Goliath to Goliath. While Ghost may not respond to reason, he would have to respect moxie. Six strode out into the cold and stepped aside as Ghost followed and closed the door.

Six stood in silence and stared down at Ghost in outrage. "This is step ten, not step one! You gave me seven days."

Ghost's eyes shrunk to slits, and his nostrils flared. "Don't you look at me with your self-righteous indignation. Inside here," he pointed at the door, "this is my world! He's an enemy of the state. By my calculation, you only have six more days to find the intel before you and your high ideals return stateside and this motherfucker's dead," Ghost said. "How did you think this worked, huh? What'd you want me to do, hug him?

Invite him in for a cup of tea and ask him play nice and tell us where the fuck the President's information is? Because if that's what you believed you picked the wrong goddamn Marine."

"Outside here is my world," Six said, pointing to the floor. "He's still a goddamn U.S. citizen and he's got the right to be charged and tried. This is torture—and out here … you and me? We die in prison for shit like this."

"You listen to me, Son. We're at war, and the war ain't out here. It's in there. You ain't no preacher in a pulpit. You ain't no butcher, baker or candlestick maker. You are a C-I-A Counterintelligence Officer." He jutted his accusatory finger toward Mosin. "And that son of a bitch has committed treason against your country. And my country. The one we took an oath to protect, the one we put our lives on the front lines to fight for every goddamned day. We're at war, son. This shit isn't James Bond fun and games; it's war.

"You have a job and a responsibility and a right by the very oath that brought your sorry ass to Moscow to return the intel to our President, our Commander in Chief, and ensure this asshole doesn't find his way to the welcoming arms of the FSB. You have a duty to make this son of a bitch pay for his treachery—with his life. And if you're not here to do your job, the least you can do is stand the fuck out of the way and quit giving me shit while I do mine. Capiche?"

Treason. Oath. Responsibility. War. Every word Ghost spoke resonated like a sword to his armor of reason, slicing every shred to pieces. More than Mosin, Six loathed Ghost Man at that moment, hated him for the truth he'd spoken. Detested him for reminding him of one simple truth: while he might not fight the enemy over battle lines, every day he went to war for his country, to keep it safe from harm from enemies foreign and domestic—and Mosin was both. Six had never lost a battle, and he hadn't planned to start now.

Six carved his fingers through his hair, rubbed his neck and exhaled a long breath, the warmth fogging in the cold air. He didn't say a word, just walked back inside and took a seat in front of the interrogation area. Ghost stood next to him and crossed his arms over his chest.

"So, what now?" Ghost asked.

"Remove his gag," Six said, avoiding Ghost's gaze at all costs.

"I'm warning you; he's a real piece of work," Ghost said, his steps thundering toward Mosin's seat. He pushed Mosin's head forward to untie the gag at the back and removed his feet from the bucket and into a dry towel. "If he'd been the slightest bit cooperative do you think he would be sitting here like this? No, I'd be out locating the intel."

With the rag in Ghost's hand, Mosin stretched his lips and glared at Six as if *he* was the one under interrogation. His glower confirmed what Ghost had said.

"Listen, Hawk is it?" Six asked, waiting for a response. Hawk was the name they called Mosin when he worked in the White House. He took the name of a bird of prey—seemed fitting. Mosin stared at him with unyielding, empty eyes.

"I think you understand that there's two ways out of here—both are life sentences; however, one will sting a lot more than the other. The faster you confess your sins, the faster you get water, food, and a one-way ticket to justice. So, are you ready to talk?"

Hawk's lips quivered as he struggled to speak, and his words staggered. "I will get out of here…and I will cut the hearts … from the bodies of … everyone …you love …and fry them…and serve them to you … for breakfast … including that whore…FBI agent…J.J. M-M-McCall."

Six snapped at the sound of her name spewing from his mouth like poison. Six didn't know how his hand locked tight around Mosin's neck. Or when his face turned blue. He just bared his teeth and snarled, "Not if I eat yours first."

Then Six released him and revealed tight smile. He turned to Ghost Man and said, "Well, two things are for certain."

"What's that?" Ghost Man replied.

"First, we're going to need to find another way to find the intel."

"And two?"

"With that mouth, he's without question a Russian," Six said. "Did you find anything with him?"

"Yeah, his clothes and a duffle bag are in the closet by the front door. Nothing in there but some clothes, travel documents, and a book."

A book?

Ghost grabbed the bag from the closet and riffled through his belongings. Travel documents. His wallet. A receipt from a tattoo parlor. A hotel claim check. A prescription. And a book wrapped in a Fruit of the Loom T-shirt with a rubber band stretched along the outside. He removed the shirt to view the title.

The Commandant's Daughter.

Odd. They'd found the same title at the home of Lana Michaels, the sleeper agent posing as an FBI agent at headquarters. It contained the numbers for her illicit accounts.

Six unwrapped the book and found it—a possible answer to their problem.

The book wasn't a book at all. He'd crafted the cover to appear genuine, even the pages flipped. But inside, he'd carved a space large enough to secure what appeared to be a ten-inch Netbook.

"Bingo!" Six muttered aloud. Ghost was at his side seconds later. He lifted the lid and hit the power button. "I'll be taking this with me."

He grabbed his coat and headed toward the door.

"What do you want me to do about our friend here?" Ghost asked.

Six glared at Mosin, turned his back, and walked out the door to the sound of Mosin's muffled screams.

Chapter 21

Friday Evening — New York City

With the wiretap request tanked, and nothing left but a skittish confidential informant remaining their last immediate hope for penetrating Troika, the team headed to Brooklyn for a discussion with the mystery man. The single human source with a connection on the inside of Troika Technologies. The only one with direct access to the accountant.

Right now, he was their biggest—and sole hope.
Without him, the chances of shutting down the financial hub before their ten-day deadline, which was now seven days away, was slim and none.

J.J., Tony, and Gia piled into a black government-issued SUV, and Manny took the wheel with Gia riding shotgun. Seated in the back seat beside Tony, J.J. stared out of the window knowing the interview was a long shot. Scott and Manny pressed her to understand their informant was scared shitless with good reason. If the Russians would pick a fight with one of the most powerful crime families in the country, shooting the son of a boss, they'd think little of smashing this CI like a twice-boiled potato. She ran through each question in her mind, designing each to find out whether the CI was a liar and what kind of liar he was. There were degrees.

They pulled up to an apartment building on the edge of Brooklyn, not far from Emmons Street on Sheepshead Bay's main drag. Manny told them that in the Sheepshead area, Russian gangsters guzzled vodka, clubbed until dawn, and extorted local businessmen for protection money while their wannabe-brigades patrolled the stoops keeping trouble close and their enemies in line. The meet took place at a safe house. The informant was so paranoid he'd refused to be seen on the streets, at his home, where he worked, anywhere without security access. So the Bureau rented a dive safe house, which doubled as a lookout post. There, the

Bureau could eyeball the streets for shady Russian characters wandering in and out. The most dangerous bad guys concocted schemes from indoors, but when they came outside to play, they played hard, and in full view of the FBI.

When they buzzed inside and entered the apartment, J.J. and Gia followed Manny inside; Tony paced a step behind. Her eyes locked on a bubble-headed man sitting with his back facing the front door. The greasy dark hair with limp curls looked familiar to her, and his voice strummed an odd pitchy chord she'd recognized. She'd definitely heard it before. Her eyebrow furrowed as she elbowed Tony and glanced at him. When Tony's face reflected her thoughts, she knew his identity, the way you know milk is bad. Everything around them soured.

Manny announced, "We're here," and the slug turned to face them, confirming her suspicions.

"Misha?" Tony and J.J. yelled in unison.

"Oh shit!" Misha snapped his head toward Scott. He jumped up and backed toward the nearest wall like a trapped rat. "You didn't tell me they were Washington agents."

"What the fuck's goin' on here?" Manny said.

"Wait, wait. You know this guy?" Scott's eyes volleyed between the three until locking in a scowl on Misha's duplicitous mug.

Gia stood frozen like a stump; she had no idea what to do.

Misha's eyes grew saucer wide, and his jaw slammed into his lap.

"So *this* is where you disappeared to. Couldn't fucking stop while you were behind, could you?" Tony asked. He and J.J. stormed over and snatched him onto the couch. He sat dead center, and they took up seats on either side. His breathing sped up, and he gulped hard. His lip quivered as much as his hands as he leaned forward to stand. "I gotta go to the bathroom."

J.J. and Tony grabbed him by each shoulder and pressed him deep into the cushion. "Hold it!" Tony barked.

"Don't you know agents are like brothers and sisters, Misha," she said. "You've been playing my family for fools again. I warned you. The last time was the last time." J.J. shifted her gaze to Manny. She refused to acknowledge Scott any more than she had to. "He's a fraud. They call him the Magic CI. Been bilking the Bureau out of thousands of dollars for years, selling half-accurate intel. New identity for every field office. Seattle, San Francisco, Miami, D.C., and now New York."

"Yeah, now you understand why he insists on all the security," Tony added in. "He's not paranoid or even conscientious. He's afraid to get caught. What name's he going by today?"

"Vanya," Manny replied.

"Fucking douche bag. Wastin' our time." The revelation threw Scott for a loop. The confusion took him off his game, left him looking to J.J. and Tony for answers he didn't have.

"Misha, you've gotten yourself in a real pickle. These New York agents, they have anger issues." J.J. looked at Scott until her eyes met his. She shifted hers toward the second exit from the room, the window. Scott looked over his shoulder. She hoped he got the hint. "What kind of tail-chasing bullshit have you been feeding to my brothers here, Misha? Tell me so I can calculate how many charges I can tack on to your *existing* obstruction warrant. Feeding false information to an agent during a federal investigation?"

Scott grunted and growled and snatched Misha up like a rag doll, dragged him to the window and pressed Misha's face against it until his neck almost bent backward. "What games are you playing? Spit it out or I swear to God I'll bury you so far down, the Earth's core will burn a hole in your ass."

"L-l-l-l-listen," he stammered. "You…you got this all wrong. I never bilked the Bureau outta anything. I love you guys... I'm not playing games."

"I dunno, Misha…or Vanya…or whatever the hell you're going by," Tony said. "Cough up some information of value or you're not gonna make it. That's a long drop. Scott doesn't look happy, and I'm not gonna stop him."

"Me either," J.J. added.

Misha laughed. "He's not gonna throw me out the window."

"You're right," Scott said, snatching his gun from his holster and pressing the barrel against his head. "But I will shoot you. And, as I look around the room, I don't see any witnesses."

Each one mumbled. "Nope…no witnesses here."

Then J.J. stood next to him. "No, no, Scott. I can't let you do this. Tarnish an honorable career on this piece of shit? No, we can book him today, and he's doing five years minimum in federal prison," she locked eyes with Misha. "Should be a fun bid when we put him in a cell sur-rounded by Bonannos and tell them you're the Russian responsible for trying to clip the boss's son. You'll be shanked before the number dries on your jumpsuit."

"That's a lie!"

"One good lie deserves another…wouldn't you say?" She signaled Scott to release him, and he sunk to the ground. "Get up!"

Misha scrambled to his feet, breathing hard as he looked into her eye. "J.J., you and me we go way back. Don't do this. I swear. I can explain."

J.J. pursed her lips. "No, you didn't play the 'we go way back' card. You've got two minutes. Start 'splaining."

Yes, their relationship went way back but not to any place she wanted to go. Misha befriended a number of intel personnel from the Washington Residency. He helped her spot and assess Kostya Belikov, her first recruitment target. She considered Misha a reliable source until he disappeared, and Kostya was recalled to the Center out of the blue. While she'd always attributed his compromise to the ICE Phantom, now known as Lana Michaels, something about him always left her feeling uneasy, as if he could sense the precise amount of truth he needed to tell. He rarely made her itch, but she didn't trust him as far as she could throw him.

"This isn't a con. I-I do have access to information on Troika. It's just not…*direct*."

J.J. waited to feel a sensation, but none came. He'd started with the truth, but she doubted he'd end with one. Tony and the others grabbed chairs to sit and listen to his tale of woe. "Okay. If you don't have direct access, then who's your source?"

"My cousin, Dani. He's Levi Mashkov's driver."

J.J.'s eyebrow arched. No sensation. No lie . . . which meant they had found another way to get into Troika. The question was how they'd use him. "Is that right?"

"Yes. Mashkov holds a lot of his meetings in his limo, so my cousin overhears conversations. He listens to their problems. He tells me. I tell you. He and I—we split money," he said. "Our family in Russia, they're poor. We send home money."

"Heartwarming story," Scott interrupted, "but in a year of reporting, the only thing you've managed to find out is the accountant has a beef with Mashkov."

"I must be careful of what I say…to protect Dani. He's my only family in America. If they find out he speaks to me about Troika business, they'll kill him. They'll slaughter everyone in Russia like pigs. And when I'm in my darkest hour of pain, they will come for me. I had to take special care. When the agents push too hard for my source, I leave, move. But I want to help."

"I'm still missing something here. Why even bother? What's in this for you?" Tony said.

"Pavlov Mashkov, the brother in Russia, he killed my uncle…over a five-hundred dollar gambling debt. Five-hundred dollars." He emphasized each syllable with sweeping hand movements. "What's that? He wipes his ass with that much every morning. Why kill people for it? Americans, you spend that much money on shoes. His life wasn't even worth the cost of a pair of shoes. I want to help you. You tell me, how can I support you without getting my cousin killed?"

"Do you think he'd help us wire the car?"

He thought for a minute and shook his head no. "Mashkov is very paranoid. Dani said they use the scanners on everything. The building. The cars. At least once a week. They check him every day."

J.J. exhaled in frustration. It was worth a try, but she'd heard similar rumors about the Mashkovs herself. Maybe he'd offer some assistance with the money man. "What more can you share with us regarding the accountant?"

"Ahhh, yes, Zory Kozlov. Trust me when I tell you he hates the Mashkov's as much as anyone, but he can't quit. The only way he leaves Troika is in a casket or five separate trash bags. He knows too much…although it seems maybe not enough," he said.

"What do you mean by that?" Scott asked.

"Well, yesterday my cousin told me Mashkov and Zory argued in his car. Zory complained about never having all the information he needed to process the transactions. Said the baby was coming this Monday but he couldn't attend the delivery. Something like that."

"Hmmm. Strange." Manny glanced at J.J.

"My cousin thought so. He's seen their wives. Neither one is pregnant."

"Sounds like code for something. Maybe drugs or money—or both."

"Man, if we could get our hands on a shipment and tie it to Troika," Tony said, "we'd have enough evidence to put *this baby* to bed."

J.J. stood into a stretch and patted Misha on the shoulder. "I think I've got everything I need for now. Let's go." The gears in her head turned. She'd worked with Misha enough times to know the team needed to quit while they were ahead. "Glad you decided to come clean. But we need you to ask your cousin to find out where Zory hangs out. Where does he go drinking or to the grocery store? Any place away from Troika? And I want to know if there's any way we can get inside. When I contact you, I want an answer."

He offered quick, successive nods. "So, you're not going to arrest me?"

"Not today, Misha. Maybe tomorrow," she said with a wry smile.

•••

J.J. stewed in her thoughts on the way back to the office, wondering how she could leverage Misha's cousin without getting him killed. Lord knows, she'd put too many families through too much suffering already. Six would tell her to screw the families, do her job, and figure out a way to bully him into cooperating, but her conscience was her own. There had to be another way to get some insight into that company, to find out more about the shipment. Just as the thoughts flitted through J.J.'s mind, a text came through her cell phone. It was Sunnie's number.

> National Security Letter approved.
> I have Troika's phone records.
> Walter and I are working on the analysis.
> Initial results tomorrow.

"Yes! Hallelujah!"

Every head in the car turned toward her.

"What is it?" Tony asked.

"We got 'em. No wire yet but we've got the phone records. Sunnie and Walter are conducting the analysis now. We're gonna nail these sons of bitches."

"Or die trying," Tony added.

Chapter 22

Saturday — Russian Embassy, Washington D.C.

Aleksey Dmitriyev had finished typing up a report when the daily thirst hit him. He glanced at his Invicta, the time said coffee, but he knew from the date that he needed to check the signal. J.J.'s communication instructions indicated he must mark it to let her know if he had an emergency and needed to meet. The embassy had been in a period of relative peace since the celebrations over Stanislav's death ended. Komarov stood down most operations, except the RAPTURE operation at the White House, which they still monitored, even more so than usual. The intelligence they'd pulled from the listening device had begun to change in quality if not quantity, but Dmitriyev was careful not to say so, at least not until J.J. returned. Eventually, he'd be forced to identify the degradation in intelligence quality to Komarov—or Filthchenko. That snitch would no doubt fly into Komarov's office like a sniveling tattle if he even for a moment suspected Dmitriyev had provided an inaccurate assessment regarding its value.

Aleksey locked his computer screen and strode down the stairwell to make his coffee run. No sooner than he put his hand on the doorknob did a hollow cold noise emanate from behind him.

"Where do you think you're going?" Filthchenko snapped; his voice twisted like a knife in Aleksey's spleen. He'd never held such deep-seated contempt for another human being in his life. Intensified in all likelihood by the fact that Filchenko served, honored, and obeyed the most despicable man in the Service—Anatoliy Golikov, whose father was responsible for the torture of his own. Filchenko, a parasite, latched onto Golikov, leeched the diabolic blood from his being and absorbed them into every crevice of his own cells until they became woven into his own DNA. Now the two were indistinguishable from one another, in almost every way. Standing in his presence was like being hosed from head to toe with pond sludge.

"Why? Would you care to take a ride with me? I have someplace where I'd like to drop you off," Aleksey remarked, still pressing ahead down the steps toward his car while Filchenko followed behind.

"Ahhh, then you haven't heard today's news out of the Center," he said.

Dmitriyev stopped midway down the flight and spun around toward his nemesis. "What news?"

"Stanislav Vorobyev—he's still alive."

Dmitriyev held his poker face as long as he could and then exploded with false laughter. He shook his index finger at Filchenko and said, "You are a funny man, Yuriy Vasilyevich. But don't quit your day job."

When he turned away, he concealed his bulged eyes and stunned expression, struggling to catch his breath. His face tightened along with his throat as he thought, *Mother of God. What has Stan done now?*

"I've no doubt he's holed up in Moscow."

"By what evidence?" Aleksey said. "You expect me to believe a trained operative who is supposed to be dead would be seen strolling along Gorky Street? Give me a break. You've been watching too much television. Mistaken identity."

"Oh, you think so, yes?" Filchenko asked. "Do you not find it odd the Americans have not turned over the body to the family? Our watchers in Vienna observed no signs of a grieving family."

"We're Russian. How can you tell? My mother didn't laugh or cry until I graduated from the institute and then it was after four celebratory shots of vodka."

Filchenko sucked his tongue and rolled his eyes as if Aleksey was a simpleton. "The watchers? They've seen someone who favors him in the company of an American."

"An *American* intelligence officer?"

"Well...no."

"Then what we are we discussing here? In poor lighting and with a little vodka in their systems, the watchers could walk the streets of Moscow and pluck fifteen people from the crowds who favor me and twenty who look like you."

"I suppose time will tell." Filchenko shrugged, still unconvinced. "The implications for you would be much greater if he is found alive, tried, and imprisoned, wouldn't you say? It is fortunate the FSB won't give up until they've verified one way or the other. And if what they suspect is true, heads will roll. I, for one, hope one belongs to you."

As Filchenko stopped in his tracks, Aleksey continued down the steps to the bottom level and pressed the exit bar on the door. "The feeling is quite mutual. Now, if you'll excuse me, Starbucks awaits."

Aleksey high-tailed it to his car, glancing down at his watch. The time for leaving an emergency signal had passed. Even if he marked it today, they wouldn't meet for two days which might be too late. If he was going to warn J.J., he had to do so now—and there was only one way to do so safely.

• • •

FBI Special Agent Hopper Mack was flying high and riding easy down Connecticut Avenue in Upper Northwest D.C., on his way to check Aleksey's signal in J.J.'s absence. His supervisor at Washington Field had now trusted him with more responsibility. His addition to the bigot list afforded him access to the identity and reporting on J.J. McCall's very trusted source in the Russian Embassy and now he must keep him alive for two weeks, which wouldn't be an easy feat based on her briefing about him. According to J.J., he had a big mouth, quick temper, and a persistent enemy in the embassy looking for every opportunity to take advantage of both.

As Hopper approached the 4000 block where the signal mailbox was located and slowed his speed; some dumbass blocked the side where the mark was supposed to be placed and didn't appear to ready to budge anytime soon. Hopper shifted his eyes back and forth to scan the area, looking for a bus stop or something to indicate why the slug was stand-ing there, in that spot. Nothing came to mind. He craned his neck as he passed the man trying to see around him and, for some reason, his eyes drew up to the gentleman's face.

Hopper gasped and did a double take. "What the hell?" Dmitriyev was the slug blocking the mark. When Hopper turned forward, a car had stopped in front of him. He slammed on the break and skidded within an inch of the bumper in front of him. His heart raced and not just because of the accident. Dmitriyev had shown up in person and hadn't marked the signal as instructed. Something must be *very* wrong.

Hopper circled back at the next light, making an illegal U-turn when the coast cleared. By the time he arrived at the mailbox again, Dmitriyev had vanished.

"Damn!" he yelled. Then he noticed Dmitriyev padding down the sidewalk along Tilden street which was accessible by a one-way east-bound road. He made a left-hand turn onto the adjacent westbound lane and pushed his pedal to the floor, looking for a place to park. Anywhere. Four blocks down he found a spot. Hopper put on a skull cap and sunglasses, jumped out, and ran at top speed to catch up with Aleksey.

As he huffed and puffed, every breath fogged. He reached Aleksey a couple minutes later; he was leaning against a lamp post along a sleepy residential street. Hopper studied his expression, waiting with his guard up until Aleksey signaled it was okay to approach. Then he walked forward, with his hands in his pockets and, head down, trying to recall the parole J.J. told him to speak so Aleksey could verify Hopper's identity as a friendly. Something about the Redskins. The words failed him, so he winged it.

Aleksey bowed his head forward, giving a nod to Hopper's approach.

"Ummm…how about those Redskins?" he asked, his face crumpled with discomfort.

Aleksey gave him the side-eye.

"Sorry, I'm not prepared. Thought this was a drive-by."

"It's okay. I'll be leaving soon. You must pass an urgent message to Agent McCall."

"What's going on?"

"Moscow. They remain unconvinced of the reports suggesting Stanislav Vorobyev is dead."

Hopper stepped back, and his eyes widened. "Damn," he said, catching himself. "Why? How?"

"His family is being watched. No remains have been turned over to the wife, and they don't appear to be grieving. Although this is subjective. They are Russians, after all."

Hopper exhaled and tightened his lips. "Well, it's only been a few days. I'm certain the Agency has some logistics to work out. Anything else?"

"Watchers report seeing someone who resembles him in the company of an American. I sense they will intensify surveillance until they determine one way or the other whether their suspicions are valid. If the Agency is going to make a move, now is the time."

"Okay. I'll tell her right away," Hopper said. "You all right otherwise?"

"Don't worry about me. Get this information to her. The implications don't only impact Stan. If they find out he's alive, they will have no doubts RAPTURE has been compromised. With Golikov's thugs lurking about, the time it takes to point the finger at me will take what you call…a New York minute."

Chapter 23

Saturday morning arrived on the heels of a heavy rain. Grayish wisps skipped across the morning sky as J.J. prepared for Sunnie's briefing on the Troika phone records. She questioned whether the analysis would reveal information she needed to solve the case. Then her mind clouded with Misha's reports about babies being delivered on Monday. What could that mean?

The office was as quiet as the city, J.J. noticed as she gazed out of the window and peered down to the street; she eyed workers fidgeting with festive holiday wreaths dangling from light posts. Somewhere in the Big Apple, she imagined there was a woman around her age rolling out of bed, thinking about shopping. Or the Christmas bauble that would adorn the tree-top. Or—Do *these shoes go with that dress?* Or—*Can Paulo squeeze me in for a Brazilian at the salon?*

J.J. envied that woman wherever she was.

Most days she woke up from her slumber devising plans to keep sources from dying and putting bad guys in jail. All the while trying to stay alive in the midst of the conflict. The contrast was stark, jarring, part of her inner conflict. Was she the kind of woman who could ever think shoes and dresses before national security, even if she had the mental space to do so? Or was the fleeting moment of uncertainty a matter of the proverbial green grass in the neighbor's yard?

Through the streams of thought, she heard a voice call. "J.J.? J.J.? Earth calling J.J."

She shook loose the jealous thoughts and turned to spot Scott standing behind her; his demeanor was relaxed in an uncharacteristic way, which may be why she didn't recognize him at first. She struck the heel of her palm against her forehead. "Scott…sorry. My mind drifted off again." She grabbed her notebook and pen from the otherwise empty desk, leaving the room and her reflections behind. She glimpsed the time. "Sunnie on the VTC yet?"

"Yeah, she just called in, but the sound's not working. The tech is working on it," he said. "Listen, I gave you a hard time, but I figured, to be fair, I should tell you that you did all right yesterday, with Vanya—or Misha. Whatever the hell his name is."

She bowed her head in acknowledgment. Took a lot of backbone to choke those words out given he'd been a douche bag toward her since the minute she arrived. "Thanks, but Misha's not a hard ass…from what I can tell. If you understand his pressure points and when to push them, any agent could've made him talk…even you," she said in jest with an accompanying smile. "With that said, Misha isn't to be trusted. Ever."

As J.J. looked around she couldn't help but compare New York's squad bay to Washington Field's which had undergone a major renovation and New York's was in need of one with its tall, closed-in cubicles, ancient wooden desks, and carpeting that had seen better days.

He chuckled as they rounded the corner and approached the conference room door. "Only six days left. You think we can get this done?"

"I've got to tell you, Scott, this situation's not looking good. Between Misha and Sunnie, I'm praying we get a breakthrough. If we don't wrap this up before the deadline, we may never get the momentum or a shot at the evidence again," she replied. "With that said, we've both been at the Bureau long enough to understand one thing about the FBI: You can count us down, but never out."

They entered the conference room where the video teleconferencing equipment was installed and a picture of one of the VTC rooms at headquarters appeared on screen. Accompanied by and a twenty-something, studious looking Asian woman with long hair and a smart pantsuit, Sunnie was conservatively dressed. Even her hair was coiffed in a manner more consistent with the Bureau uniform. Walter sagged in his seat along with his suit. Looked a few cups of coffee short of alert. Must've been a long night.

J.J. scanned the room and noticed Tony eyeing her with a sheepish expression, no doubt because Gia had taken the lone seat to his right. He was posted at the table's end. J.J. opted not to sweat it and sat on the side opposite him between Scott and Manny. "Good to see you, Sunnie," J.J. said, making introductions around the room. "Who's with you?"

"Thanks, J.J. This is Amie Chang, an Intelligence Operations Specialist from the Organized Crime/Drugs Section downstairs. She's supporting a joint FBI, ATF, DEA task force and provided some intel that's pretty vital to understanding the expansiveness of this network."

"ATF and DEA? Sheesh. Sounds messy."

"Believe me, it is, so we should probably get started," Sunni began. "Yesterday, we received the phone records for six office lines at Troika technology—five business lines, one fax machine. We assess five are used by the executives and administrative staff."

"Have you noted anything of interest?" Tony asked.

"Yes. What's interesting is they rarely use the office lines to make calls. Classic criminal/intelligence tradecraft, a huge red flag given this is supposed to be a legitimate business. Most of the calls made were international, so we asked NSA to run the numbers through VECTOR. Ten minutes later we got a hit, several in fact. A fax machine linked to a company called VolgaTeK Investment Group, headed by Jov Rakov, a former FSB officer with ties to Rusvorzheny."

Hmmm…a former FSB officer, J.J. thought. The report came as no surprise her. After the fall of the Soviet Union and break-up of the KGB, many intelligence officers ditched public service for criminal enterprises, leveraging their international contacts, networks of networks, to support some of the most insidious mafia enterprises operating today. The line between Russian intelligence and organized crime was often a murky one, and Jov Rakov was but one example of that.

Gia sat at attention. "Wait, Rusvorzheny is the state arms company. All Russian arms transactions are conducted through this company, both above and under the table. The Russians have been engaging in major military upgrades over the past few years. Some get sold; some get stolen and then sold. That's an interesting connection." She folded her arm across her chest. "So NSA had already initiated a SIGINT op targeting VolgaTeK because of this drug investigation; it's not intelligence related, correct?"

"Yes. A joint DEA-ATF investigation targeted Rakov's narcotics and arms trade network operating throughout Russia and the Republics. DEA traced parts into Latin America. The reporting is languishing in NSA's dissemination channels; they've not been released yet. Amie's going to explain more about the network."

"Thanks, Sunnie," Amie began, her posture as stiff as her voice. "Based on available intelligence, we assess that Rakov leverages his ties with Rusvorzheny to illegally obtain and sell older military-grade Russian arms to South American drug cartels in exchange for narcotics, heroin and cocaine. Max Novikov's people, we'll get to him in a minute, sell the narcotics throughout Russia, the Republics, and inside the United States. They get top dollar for the drugs in the American market, amassing millions more in sales than if the cartels paid them in cash for the weapons' value."

"Arms for narcotics. Do we have proof?" Tony asked. "How strong is the intel?"

"Rock solid," Amie said. "DEA has CIs who help move the arms and drugs between Russia to South America. A complex web of narcotics traffickers and Russian organized crime figures."

"So, I don't understand how Troika fits this equation," J.J. said.

"Based on what Amie and I discussed," Sunnie chimed in, "we assess Max Novikov from Troika is the New York *krysha*—a roof or cover for Russian mob narcotics operations on the east coast. He's the big boss."

"Exactly," Amie added. "Drugs are transported from South America and into Miami using Russian-made Narco subs—DEA intercepted two off the coast of Bogotá in joint operations with the Colombians. Miami-based Russian mob networks pay for their cut of heroin and cocaine which they sell on the streets; the remaining cash proceeds and drugs are transported to the New York area where they are sold up and down the east coast. Huge market. Lots of cash."

"And when the drugs are sold," Sunnie said. "Troika launders the money. They pay big cash to live high on the hog so to speak—cars, money, women—the usual suspects. They convert the remaining proceeds into small bank deposits, less than 10K so they stay below Treasury's radar and disperse them into multiple accounts. The remaining money is shipped overseas on pallets containing millions of dollars in hundred-dollar bills. One account belongs to Lana Michaels' illegal network which we discovered last week; it's now frozen. A second account is new and still active—we think this is the new account the SVR setup to pay off the Russian illegals. The third account is the unnamed Russian company I had identified last week—we've now determined it is VolgaTeK."

Walter piped in. "If I may, NSA intercepted fax transmissions from Troika to VolgaTeK—phony purchase orders and requisitions for technologies and building supplies. Troika pays the fake invoices and transfers the cash to VolgaTeK. Rakov uses money from the money laundering account to buy the illegal arms…and the cycle begins again."

"How is ATF involved in all of this?" Manny asked.

"The Latin American cartels are taking the guns they buy from the Russians and supplying them to their U.S.-based smuggling networks, putting some heavy firepower on American streets. It's a problem at the border and for law enforcement. ATF confiscated several weapons from a cache used to hit U.S. Border Patrol agents in an attack last week. Three wounded in a shootout, but our agents got the best of them."

"Jesus, this is bigger than I thought. There's a lot at stake here." J.J. expelled a hard breath. She stood up and paced to the back of the room, scribbling some boxes onto a small whiteboard. Once completed, she had arranged boxes representing the networks into a circle as Sunnie and her team had described. "Sorry, I needed to wrap my head around this. It's the freakin' Circle of Life…an organized crime syndicate operating in the shadows of the intelligence world. And it starts with Jov Rakov. Keeping in mind we're on a tight deadline, we have few ways to penetrate this network. Either we get inside Troika, which is looking more and more impossible. Or somehow get our hands on a shipment—the money, the vehicle, or the driver with Troika. Or wait…Wasn't MCM Construction a part of this network—Gary Mosin's company?"

"Yes, MCM Construction bank accounts were linked to Lana's accounts but now both are frozen," Sunnie said. "If we had Mosin in custody, he might be able to provide the proof we need to demonstrate that Troika and the Mashkov's are financing illegal arms deals, narcotics, and intelligence operations—the criminal trifecta. But what are the chances we could catch him, right? He's hidden in Podunk, Moscow, by now."

"You're right," J.J. said, once again deflated. The U.S. had as much hope of catching Mosin as she did in joining a convent.

"I'm glad you said that, J.J. because there's more," Sunnie said.

"Jesus, Sunnie. You trying to solve the case all by yourself?"

She chuckled and pulled out a short stack of papers. "In a few of these faxes, we found multiple references to the delivery of a baby. The next baby is coming on Defender of the Fatherland Day and Victory Day. I Googled the dates—the first is February 23rd, the latter is May 9th. What's strange is the same days are mentioned in multiple months, including *this* month, and they're discussing the deliveries as if they are urgent or imminent. We believe it's code for something, maybe deliveries? We don't have enough intel to confirm it at this time."

J.J., Scott, and Manny exchanged knowing looks. Misha had just reported the same thing.

"This language is pretty typical in the criminal world," Amie said. "We have information from validated sources across the criminal spectrum indicating terrorists discuss 'weddings' before operation or bombing. We feel certain this terminology is along the same vein."

J.J. pulled out her cell phone and looked at her calendar. "Hmm. The 23rd is on Monday." She turned to Manny and Scott. "The date is consistent with Misha's information. If the discussions on these so-called baby deliveries have taken place in multiple months, I doubt they are referring to the actual holiday, rather they're referencing a day of the month, time of day—or both."

"I dunno," Gia said as if someone asked her for her opinion. "Sounds too straightforward to me. Russian intel codes are much more complicated and require more math."

"That statement may be true of Russian intelligence," Sunnie said, "but for the Russian Mafiya? I doubt the low-level support network is as sophisticated or as well educated as intel officers."

"I agree," Amie said. "Troika's leadership may have ties to Russian intel, but the guys in the trenches aren't geniuses. They'd keep the schedules and terminology simple for couriers, smugglers, dealers and the like. They won't trust just anyone with more complex codes because they don't want botched shipments. People die for mistakes in the narcotics trade."

"Without an address and time, we need 24-7 surveillance on the Troika execs. There's no other way to find or intercept the shipment."

Scott tightened his lips and shook his head. "No way will Fitzpatrick authorize those kinds of resources for this investigation. No way."

"Why not? We've got two independent sources corroborating the possibility of a multimillion dollar shipment of drugs and cash, which may help shut down the Mashkovs. He'd be crazy not to."

"Hmph. You gonna pitch to him? 'Cause I'm not," Scott said, still unsold on the op.

"Hate to ruin your weekend, Sunnie, but I'm gonna need you and Amie to keep running the phone records through VECTOR and call us the minute anything comes up suggesting a time and place for the Monday shipment. In the meantime, Manny and I will pitch Fitzpatrick. Nothing beats a failure like a try."

•••

As Tony and Scott waited outside, J.J. and Manny walked out of Fitzpatrick's office, their expressions stony and shoulders slumped.

"No, go, huh?" Tony asked, eyeing J.J. with more tenderness than he perhaps was aware of. J.J. noticed and appreciated it.

She shook her head no.

"That was a fail," Manny kicked in.

"An epic fail," J.J. added. "It wasn't just a no; it was a hell no. He wants more evidence. Another source. An address. A time. Something more than a hunch and a prayer, which is all we can offer. He thinks we have shit for intel. Unless by some miracle an answer falls in our laps, we're screwed."

Chapter 24

Saturday Night Dinner — The Donatos

J.J.'s stomach had commenced a Riverdance of twists, turns, and thumps as the group approached the Brooklyn brownstone where Santino and Tony's mother were staying. Not only had her entire case just gone to shit, she'd been roped into dinner with the Donatos.

Her nervousness about being held hostage with his family for hours was compounded by her desire to roast Tony's ass on a spit for inviting Gia. She gave him some lame sob story about depression and her dead father's birthday. He thought J.J., of all people, could empathize, and that would be true…with any other human being on the planet except Gia.

J.J. had accepted an invitation to Saturday's dinner which now appeared to be a mistake from the moment the word "yes" slipped from her mouth. With the family still in turmoil from Dante's shooting and his father Sal's recent release to the halfway house, emotions ran high. Putting herself in the midst of the volatile situation would bring out the best of the Donatos…or the worst. And she feared, if the latter, both sides may say things that neither could retract, leaving J.J.'s and Tony's relationship D-O-A.

On a brighter side, Santino and Tony were on the road to mending fences. They realized they had common enemies—but not each other.

Tony knocked on the door, and the ball-busting Dree flung it open with a massive chip on her shoulder. She then left it ajar and stomped away without so much as a hello.

"Hello to you, too," Tony said, allowing Gia to proceed first. He tugged J.J.'s arm and whispered in her ear. "Remember how much I love you. Whatever Dree says today, and trust me she will say something, she doesn't know me, you, or my heart. You understand me?"

J.J. nodded, casting a glance over his shoulder at Gia, who was dripping in jealousy green while admiring the photos lining the foyer walls.

Dree hated J.J. and made no attempt to hide her contempt. With each scornful glare, every cut of the eye and icy Italian sneer, J.J. told herself over and again this was only two hours out of her long life, but the short span now seemed a lifetime too long. That's why she insisted on bringing her own car. Catching a cab while black was as impossible as finding a parking space in New York.

Once they stepped inside and the door shut, Tony said, "Here, let me take your coats. Follow the smell of Sunday sauce back to the kitchen," which she discovered was spaghetti sauce, the red kind.

J.J. crawled along the wood-paneled hallway, taking in her surroundings. She somehow felt comfortable there. The home reminded her of Grandmother's place. The living room, to the right, had a similar brown velour sofa covered in three-ply plastic, which also ran the length of the carpet from the front door to the kitchen. And like her grandmother's place, it looked like the un-living space, not a speck of dust in the room and not a table or knick-knack out of place. It was clear nobody was allowed to sit in there. All the real living was probably done in the kitchen and the family room.

Stalling the inevitable, she looked at each school picture of Tony, his brother, and sisters lining the walls, waiting for him to catch up. She wouldn't approach the lion's den without him. In a moment too quick to take a breath, his mother's voice boomed. "Well, aren't you lovely?" Then, in Italian, she asked Gia if she was Sicilian. J.J. remembered the question from when Tony had asked her the same only weeks ago.

Of course, Gia responded likewise, her voice happy, demure, and innocent. J.J. fought the urge to stick her finger down her throat and fake hurl.

"How wonderful! Come. Have a seat right here."

"I'm Carla, his sister. Dree's in the family room sulking…as usual. This is our cousin, Santino."

Couldn't have escaped Gia how much Santino and Tony resembled one another. Certainly hadn't escaped J.J. She hoped Gia might transfer her affections to him instead, but Gia didn't bat an eye. Perhaps she preferred the law-abiding type.

"Nice to meet you all," she said.

J.J. rolled her eyes at Tony and tightened her lips before she crossed the threshold into the kitchen. He shrugged with an uncomfortable expression. He clearly understood how it pained J.J. to endure Gia and his family in one dose, but he had to know the only reason she stayed was because she loved him.

At least when Six showed up at her father's house, she had not invited him, and she gave Six the blues the entire time he stayed. Gia had already formed alliances, and Tony would not be taking the same aggressive posture.

J.J. greeted everyone in the warmest tone she could muster. "Thank you for having me…us over. I realize you have so much going on right now."

His mother offered a sincere smile in return. "Forget about it. We must keep up our strength. Sit down, please. Make yourself at home," she said with a welcoming pat on J.J.'s hand. The sincerity and warmth in her demeanor reminded J.J. of her mother a bit. Mrs. Donato had an air of peace and serenity J.J. hadn't sensed from a woman outside her family in years. At this moment, she thought she might survive the day. She had no idea what fate had in store.

"So," Tony began, "what's on the menu, Ma?"

"Ahhh," she said. "A little antipasto in the fridge. Carla, take the tray out." She motioned to her daughter, flipping her hands. "I've got macaroni and sauce. And then your favorite—melanzana!"

Everyone in the kitchen froze and hesitated as they turned to J.J., their expressions somewhere between shocked and embarrassed. She'd said eggplant in front of a black woman, God forbid.

J.J.'s gaze shifted from face to face, confused by the hush that had fallen over the room. "What? It's my favorite, too. Or do you guys consider that cannibalism?"

J.J. had almost forgotten her gift for attempting uncomfortably funny jokes at awkward moments. A strained silence continued to fill the air and then they each, one after the other, broke into raucous laughter. J.J. chuckled and relaxed, swiping her forehead with the back of her hand which intensified the guffaws. This was a good time for vodka, but she'd settle for something lighter. "I could sure use a glass of wine if you have some?" J.J. asked Mrs. Donato with a crooked smile.

Tony's mother, who had almost laughed herself to tears, patted J.J. on the cheek. "You are funny, dear. You can have anything you want. Tony, get some wine from the basement," she ordered.

After supper had ended, his mother shooed everyone from the kitchen. Tony and Santino made their way to the TV in a basement man cave.

College ball was on, and for a change, he had a little spare time to watch. With no resources and no case, she couldn't use work as an excuse to make her escape back to the Plaza. So she stood there trying to devise a way out. Once Gia disappeared into the bathroom, and Carla trotted upstairs to take a phone call in private, Dree and J.J. were left alone in the pristine living room.

As J.J. feigned excessive interest in the family photos, Dree crept up behind her hand said, "You're not fooling anyone with this act. Helen Keller can see what's going on between you and my brother."

J.J. cranked her neck toward Dree, the motion oozing with attitude. "Oh, he's your brother, now," J.J. snapped back. She spun around in slow motion, crossed her arms, and pursed her lips. She didn't want any trouble with Dree, but since Dree brought it to her doorstep, she had to answer. "Hard to tell. You've been treating him like crap since you laid eyes on him."

Dree gave her the once-over. "Let me give you a little warning about Italian men. They may date and play around with people like you. Have their little fun, get their rocks off. He might like you. He might even love you. But he ain't never gonna marry you. Ever. So you can keep up this sham of a relationship all you want. When it's all said and done, he'll walk down the aisle with a woman who looks nothing like you…and everything like her," she spat, directing her eyes to Gia, who had emerged from the bathroom and appeared clueless as to why she was now the center of attention.

J.J. wanted to bite back. She wanted to scream. She wanted to yell and tell Dree where she could shove her opinions, but the words choked in her throat. Deep down she believed Dree was right. Tony was the greatest hope of her life, yet the searing words had bought to the fore-front her worst fear. Tony hadn't lived under the cloud of racism and prejudice and ill-informed perceptions. But she had known it first-hand. To spend their entire relationship wondering if he'd ever cross the finish line with her, she now seriously questioned whether he was a risk she was willing to take with her heart.

She soundlessly walked away and found Tony in the basement. Unable to contain the hurt and disappointment on her face, he turned to her, his expression filled with concern. "What's wrong? Did she say something? Tell me the truth."

J.J. shifted her eyes to the floor and prepared to lie. Their family was going through enough without her adding to the drama. Besides, no matter how hurtful, Dree had not said anything J.J. hadn't already considered. "No, I'm okay. Your mother's cooking was so delicious I think I gorged myself, overdid it. I'm gonna head back to the hotel and lay down."

"Okay, then…let's go," he said, preparing to stand to leave.

"No, no. You stay. Enjoy your family. We're in separate cars, anyway. I'll be fine." She turned to leave. "Nice to see you again, Santino."

"Hey! Look at me," Tony called out to her as she ascended the stairs. She turned to face him, and he mouthed the words. "You're my family."

She smiled and waved goodbye. If she only could believe that was true, she thought. If only she could believe…

Chapter 25

Early Sunday Morning — New York City

Reconnecting with Tony after Saturday's dinner convinced Santino more than ever his cousin was no rat. The certainty steeled his determination to verify what he already knew in his mind to be true—Nicky Mumbles framed Tony for getting Jimmy Toots pinched. And one person would confess the truth—whether he wanted to or not.

Santino wheeled into a parking space in front of Stevie Pic's house, which sat on a tree-lined street framed by red-brick single family homes east of 76th Street in Bensonhurst. He reconned the area and spotted Stevie's car half way up the block; he was still home. Time to make the call. He dialed the douche bag's number and, just before the voicemail picked up, Stevie answered with a shaky, "Hello?"

"*Paesano*! What's happening?"

"Santino! Hey man, nothing much. Been under the weather, so I haven't been able to dig up the information you asked me about."

"Ohhh, okay," Santino replied, his tone nonchalant. "Wondered what happened to ya. Think you'll dig up some info for me soon?"

"Yeah, yeah. I'll get on it today. Tomorrow for sure."

"Good, good, good. Listen, I have a little business proposition for you. Mind if I stop by and talk to you. I'm in the Bronx, so it's gonna take me a half hour, forty-five minutes to get to you."

"Sure, stop by. I'll be here."

Santino hung up, sucked his teeth, and shook his head. He'd been smarter than a fifth grader since the second grade. Stevie couldn't pull one over on him. He tightened his lips and shoved the cell back in his pocket. Then stepped out the of his car and scanned the area for nosy neighbors before opening the black, wrought-iron front gate and proceeded up the steps to Stevie's brick duplex.

Without knocking, he stood and stared at the door, knowing he wouldn't have to wait long before the fuckhead arrived. Minutes later, quick footsteps padded down the stairs. The door swung open and surprise, surprise—Stevie Pics—as expected. About to scatter like a guilty rat. Santino scanned him from head to toe and fixed his eyes on Stevie's hand wrapped around the smoking gun—a carry-on bag with a backpack bungee-corded to the expandable handle.

The bitch was trying to run.

His attempt to haul ass meant one thing to Santino—Stevie P's alliances had shifted from Uncle Sal, and he was now working for a dead man.

There they stood eye to eye, Stevie huffing as if losing the ability to inhale. Like a chameleon signaling danger, his color phased from white to red. He went rigid and his mouth fell open wide; his lips trembled and a tendon thumped in his neck.

"Stevie!" Santino said, baring his teeth through an angry Pit bull's smile. "The fuck you think you're goin'?"

Stevie struggled to collect his words. "I was just going to the corner store to get me a taste. Been a rough week."

"Corner store my ass with your fuckin' luggage. Plan on moving in? Get back inside before I bash your head in, ya moron."

Stevie backed into the foyer far enough for Santino to step in and shut the door behind him. "You think you've had a rough week until now? You ain't seen nothing yet. Put that shit down."

"You…you're making a mistake, Santino." He stammered, releasing the luggage handles.

"A mistake, huh? Let's go somewhere where we can chat. You can enlighten me."

Stevie put his hands in the air, striking a perp pose. Then he turned around with care and directed his steps toward the living room.

"No! Where's the basement? I don't want your nosy neighbors in my business." Santino cocked the pistol, the quick clicks echoing like the clock ticking down on Stevie's life. It was an unspoken warning to Stevie not to do anything funny.

Santino followed Stevie down the hall and through a door leading downstairs. When he looked at the landing at the bottom of the enclosed staircase, he glimpsed the painted concrete floor. He wondered what or who lay on the other side of the wall but didn't worry much. The Beretta was firm in his hands and his fingers were tight to the trigger. From his vantage point, the space appeared unfinished and smelled of must and paint fumes.

When they reached the last step, Stevie flipped on the light. His head shifted from left to right in nervous jerks. He sprang past the wall to the right and returned with a bat in a movement too quick for Santino to react. Fear jolted Stevie's nuts loose, made him determined to draw blood before Santino did. He wasn't going down without a fight.

Before Santino could get off a shot, the bat careened toward his head. In a reflexive move, his arms flew up to block the slicing blow and a crushing pain radiated through his arm…and emptied his hand. The gun had slid across the slick gray floor.

As Stevie pulled back the barrel to take another swing, Santino dove for the weapon, missing the grip by inches. Stevie slammed the bat into his spine, and Santino screamed in pain. Before Stevie could land his third blow, Santino thrust his body forward, palmed the gun handle, and flipped to his back. He fired two quick shots into Stevie's leg—one in the knee and another just above it. Stevie tumbled to the ground clutching his left leg and releasing an ear-piercing shriek.

"Make one wrong move, and I'll splatter your fuckin' brains across this basement. You hear me?" Santino scrambled to his feet, grunting all the while, then hulked over Stevie, aiming the muzzle with both hands. Reeling from the crushing blows, he noticed an old dusty couch that had seen better days and took a seat to ease the ache. He stared down at Stevie, still laying in the floor, with a cold, narrow-eyed glare.

Crimson fluid oozed through the cracks of Stevie's fingers as he gripped his bloody knee cap. He rocked back and forth, writhing in pain, pleading for his life. "I'll do whatever you want, just don't kill me. I'll do whatever you want."

"Now we're getting somewhere," Santino said. "Answer my questions truthfully and I'll let you skip town for a few months until things cool off. On the other hand, I'll fire a slug in you for every lie you tell…starting with your other one." He pivoted his aim to the right leg. "We clear on the ground rules?"

Stevie nodded; his face wrenched as he struggled to sit upright. He clenched his eyes, trying to suppress the burning as he waited for Santino's first question.

"Who snitched on Jimmy Toots? And remember the consequences."

"Santino, listen to me! How would I—"

"Wrong answer!" Santino snapped the trigger, and an explosive crack broke the brief silence.

"Ahhhhh!" Stevie screamed, cursing Santino in quick successive beats.

"What part of 'I'll fire a slug in you for every lie you tell' did you not understand?" Santino paused to wait for the new round of squalling to stop.

"You're gonna kill me if I tell you," Stevie cried.

"If you don't, I'll kill you so slowly you'll be eligible for retirement by the time I'm through with you."

Stevie peered up, his eyes flush as though he'd just received his death sentence. His face trembled as he choked out the words, "I...I did it," he stammered. "I called in a tip to the Feds."

"You?" Santino said, giving him a side-eye glance. "You son of a bitch. Uncle Sal trusted you. On whose order?"

When Stevie hesitated, Santino cocked the gun, eyed his balls, and aimed his arm to prepare for a shot. The motion loosened Stevie's tongue.

"Nicky...Nicky Mumbles." He strained to get the words past his pain and fear. "He wanted to make Captain. Said he'd be first in line...to become Underboss...and when the time is right—Boss."

Santino's blood brewed to a quick boil. His anger heated his body from his hair to his toenails. "Why'd he set up Tony? Why not somebody else in the family? Or in another family."

Stevie stammered again with a short hesitation before he spit out the answer. He knew what was coming if he didn't. "He...he was planning a coup...Eliminate you, Dante, and Sal. Take over the family." He took gasping breaths between each sentence. "He was scared Tony would come at him...and with the FBI behind him. Tony was a threat...he couldn't afford. Now...he's planning to hit Sal."

"Son of a bitch!" Santino's mind churned over Nicky's plot to take over. The douche bag had ripped both of Santino's families apart. No way would he walk Scot-free after this betrayal.

"Swear to God...that's everything, Santino. Everything," Stevie pleaded, whimpering from the pain. "Please, let me go. I need help."

"Sure, sure," Santino rose from the couch and walked over to Stevie. Through clenched teeth he growled, "But first I'm gonna *give you* an anonymous tip."

He narrowed his eyes and fired—one shot into his groin. Stevie howled and cursed.

One shot to his chest. Blood oozed from the pit, and the screams trailed off.

Two final shots to the head.

Stevie was silent; he would rat no more.

Santino spat at the corpse and headed up the steps, pulling his cell phone from his pocket. He called his right hand—Giancarlo "Knuckles" Brancati.

"Knuckles."

"Santino, where are you? Been trying to reach you all morning. Nicky called and said he wants you to attend some meeting with the Russians."

"Oh, he did, did he? No, problem. I'll take care of that. First I have a situation. Send a crew to Stevie Pics. I need a clean-up on aisle six."

"Jesus! What happened?"

"Let's just say he engaged in discussions detrimental to family interests and…skinned his knees."

"We'll be right over."

•••

Santino drove two hours to talk his uncle in Scranton. He couldn't share Stevie's confession on a phone call. The Feds monitored everything. The news was too urgent to sit on. Under the guise of being distraught over Dante, Santino fast-talked himself into an unscheduled visit.

Standing outside in the cold, smoking cigars because neither trusted the house wasn't bugged, Santino walked his uncle through the events of the past few days, including the latest revelation that Nicky set up Tony to take the fall for ratting out Jimmy Toots.

"Nicky's always been a backstabbing son of a bitch, but I never thought he'd stoop this low. Guess what goes around, huh?" Sal took a long drag and blew out the smoke. "When I think about what coulda happened if I didn't show restraint…that cocksucker's gonna pay. And big."

Santino nodded. "Yeah, well, he's down one stooge. Stevie won't be phonin' in anymore anonymous tips. He's as silent as a lamb."

"Good riddance to bad trash. Never liked that kid anyway," Sal said before leaning forward and lowering his voice. "But we can't afford to put his pimp on ice right now. The order…it can't come from me. I'll think of something. Just gotta be creative."

"Swear to God when Stevie told me that shit, I almost fucking exploded. If Nicky had been standing within a foot of me, I'd have strangled him with my bare hands."

Sal rubbed the scruff on his chin, the way he always did when he came up with his best strategies. "The meeting set with the Russians?"

"Yeah, some guy Max Novikov. At first, Nicky tells me I'm too junior to go. Now all of a sudden they can't hold it without me. Tony thinks they're planning a hit. If I go, I'm a dead man."

After a few moments of silence, a knowing expression washed over Sal's face. "I've met this guy. Novikov. Me and Patty Cuzmano a few years ago. Crazy as hell but a straight shooter...no pun intended," Sal said with a chuckle. "What I mean to say is, the man's all about the scharole. He's not loyal to people; he's loyal to profits. That's it." He paused again and flashed a cheese-eating grin. He had an idea. A good one. "Yeah, yeah. Listen. Go."

"To the meetin'? You gotta be kiddin' me."

"When you get your enemies and friends in one room, there's no better way to tell who's who. You understand what I'm sayin'?" Sal firmed his voice and poked his finger in Santino's chest. "But you've got to follow my instructions to the letter. Stay on the reservation, watch that fuckin' temper of yours, and you'll walk outta there no problem. First, we take care of business; then we take care of our enemies."

Santino's cell phone buzzed, and he scanned the screen. "It's from Nicky. It's on. Monday, the 23rd at 555 North 10th Street in Brooklyn."

"Good." Sal pulled out a cell phone he wasn't supposed to carry. "Get outta here. I'm gonna make some calls but remember what I'm telling you. Don't go off half-cocked."

Chapter 26

Saturday Night — U.S. Embassy, Moscow

After five days of hell, Six stole a few moments to catch some shuteye, but sleep would not come. He still had not devised an operation to get Vorobyev into the Embassy and out of harm's way. And while he had Mosin's netbook in his possession—perhaps the key to finding the intel—he couldn't turn it over to the CIA techs for examination. He didn't know any of the new cadre well enough to trust them with information so critical to his future. Everyone who'd supported his ops in the past had returned to Langley to await their next assignments. Furthermore, he still anguished over what to do with Mosin and was still on the clock with Ghost. With only five days left, he had to recover the intel before the only man on earth who knew its location was killed. He hadn't seen him in a couple of days. He'd begun to feel hopeless. And, for Six, there was one cure.

He dialed her number and prayed she'd answer. Even while in the midst of her own storms, she always found time to tend to his...at least before he made the mistake that ended their relationship—Kendell Phillips.

Gone from the world far too soon, Kendell never should've been part of his life. He'd intended her to be the classy stunner he passed one day on his way to grab a bite for lunch. But he tempted fate; his innocent flirtation went too far. The dinner at Old Ebbitt's went too far. Months of sneaking behind J.J.'s back went too far. The engagement and wedding went beyond the point of no return. His heart was always with J.J. but, unfortunately, parts further south too often did the leading.

Tepidly, he dialed her number hoping she would answer before he lost his nerve and hung up. He hated needing help, more than he loved her.

"Hey, J.J. it's me…I, uh," he began before falling silent. He let the void linger as he got his words together.

"Everything okay? I assume you didn't call for me to listen to you breathe."

"Oh…sorry," he replied. "I'm calling because I…I need your help. Operational issue…and a moral dilemma."

"Moral dilemma? Since when did you get morals? Did the CIA finally issue 'em to you?" J.J. cracked.

A heavy silence fell between them.

"Hey, not even a chuckle?" she continued. "We're wasting some of my best stuff here."

"Where do I begin?" he said, biting his nails. A nervous habit from childhood, one of the few he was unable to break. "We hired contractors—black bag—to help find our friend. He succeeded."

J.J. gasped, and her voice shifted an octave higher. "You've got him?"

"I would say yes if you me and the contractor weren't the only people on Earth with this information. It's an off-the-book transaction."

"Oh shit!" she said, before checking her excitement. "I-I-I don't understand…"

"The package he arrived with is still missing. Refuses to turn it over. And our contractor friend has a strong desire to follow orders contrary to mine. This has led the friend, a Marine, to use, shall we say, *creative means* to find out the location. Extremely creative."

J.J. exhaled and grumbled. "For crying out loud. When you get in trouble, you really do it in spectacular fashion."

"I've never been in a situation like this before, with this much at stake…a life and a missing package that is gravely damaging."

J.J.'s heavy sigh filled the phone. Took her a minute to absorb the shock. "In almost any other country, the FBI would make a formal request to detain and extradite, but we have no such agreement with Russia. Given the identity of the guest, they'd sooner crown him Emperor than turn him over to us."

"Yeah, Ghost said the same thing."

"Hate to agree, but he's right. The higher up the chain this goes, the more skittish folks become about bending the rules. And with the media circus, he'll morph into the political football no one will touch. What the contractor's done is give us the best chance of recovering the missing package."

"Yeah, but what about…I can't just stand by and let him…" Six stammered. "No one wants him dead more than me but there are rules."

"Six, you took an oath. I can't tell you what to do here, but on my watch, he gets only one chance to betray this country—no more. How will national security be served by the grave damage caused if it's leaked…or the entire station gets expelled? How is the U.S. made stronger? It isn't. It would be a major disservice. And if it takes a few bumps and bruises to spare us then let *him* be the sorry ass caught between a rock and a hard place. He put himself in that position; we didn't."

"Damn. Remind me never to cross you," Six said. "But I agree…which leads me to my next problem. Pocket litter…and a net-book. I need forensics but can't ask anyone here to do it. Everyone I trust is stateside."

J.J. paused. "Double wrap it. Address it to Sunnie at headquarters and give it to the Legat," J.J. said, referring to the Legal Attache, the FBI's embassy representative. "He'll pouch it to her, and I'll have CART examine it." The FBI's Computer Analysis and Response Team performed computer forensics. "We can handle it within the purview of the task force."

"Hmph. Beautiful and brilliant. Man, I owe you one."

"That's why they pay me that one really big buck." She chuckled.

J.J. always said the right thing in perfect time. Six loved her laugh, but it came to a sudden halt.

"Sheesh, I almost forgot," J.J. said. "You couldn't have timed this call better. I just received some troubling news from my good friend…the one at the embassy."

He did a quick calculation. She must be talking about *her* source.

"It seems the Center is filled with rumors and non-believers," J.J. said. "People doubt his status."

"Well, some rumors are true."

"Why don't you sound surprised?" J.J. said. "Did you hear the news from another source?"

"Let's just say I'm having trouble with both of our friends here. One won't talk. The other talks too much," Six replied.

"Don't I know it. He's stubborn and proud. The faster you end this, the better. You got a plan?"

Six belted out a facetious chuckle. "Do I have a plan? Ha! Do you follow rules?"

J.J. laughed.

"I've got nothing," he continued. "Security's tight. Checkpoints everywhere. Watchers on us like stink on shit. I couldn't get a stick of butter out of this country without ten FSB officers asking me to spread it on their toast. Getting our friend out without leaving the country in handcuffs for a spy trade would be nothing short of a miracle."

"Well, if my last two ops have taught me anything about Russian intelligence, it's this: What the ears hear, and the eyes see, the Russians believe."

Six took a moment to contemplate what she'd said; J.J. words resonated. Instead of trying to conceal Stan, show them what they want to see. Confirm what they think they know. She came through again. "That's the answer, damn it! Why didn't I think of this before? If you were standing in front of me right now, I'd kiss you."

"Yes, and five seconds later I'd lay you flat on your ass, but I'm glad I could be of service."

"Me too," Six said. "One problem down. Still one to go though. In a few days, I'm going to have to get someone out of the country who doesn't want to leave."

"See, that's where you and I differ, dear. You're exfil, one of the best there is. You focus on '*How do I get him out?*' Me? I'm counterintelligence. My focus would be on figuring out what I need to do to make him *want to leave*. In my experience, few things make men more skittish than angry enemies. And if he didn't have any enemies—I'd create one."

Six turned and glanced at the netbook. The answer may be sitting in his hands. He smiled. "You called me dear." For a moment, it was like old times.

J.J. sucked her tongue and fell silent. "It was a just figure of speech. Now I'm calling this conversation over. Goodnight."

Chapter 27

Early Sunday Morning — New York City

The phone's ring jarred J.J. awake. She rose still hung over from Dree's shot of reality the day before. Hardly slept two hours together, spent the night ignoring Tony's repeated calls and late-night texts. Their bloodlines had doomed their relationship, or misguided attempt at one, from day one. And then there was Six, an ever present reminder of a simpler life. He was easy…and not just in the gigolo sense. Once she got past his duplicitous lifestyle, constant lying, and inability to separate his life from his cover, loving him would've been as easy as breathing…through a thin tube. The swirling thoughts made her dizzy. Maybe she should answer Tony's calls.

She groped through the darkness for the handset and picked up. "This better be good."

"It's me, Six…again," the silky tenor said. "What are you wearing?"

"Morning breath and PMS." She fought back a smile and squinted at the clock. FIVE A.M. She grumbled. "Didn't I just get off the phone with you? What time is it there?"

"It's one o'clock in the afternoon. Haven't pulled an all-nighter like this one since grad school."

"What's going on?"

"Spent the night examining Mosin's netbook. Apparently, he never thought he'd get caught. The password hint was, in fact, the password. Tried to find something that might point me to where he stashed the intel."

"Any luck?"

"Most of his files are encrypted. Different password."

J.J. shrugged. "Not a problem for CART," she said. "WFO has one of the best teams. I'm gonna owe Hopper big for this favor. When are you pouching it?"

"It's already on the way," Six said. "But I found something else I need your help with. The one thing he failed to encrypt."

She scraped her scraggly hair from her eyes. "What's that?"

"A calendar. He's got some appointments, but there's no mention of what they're for, one at FIVE P.M. on the 9th of every month, and the other at TWO A.M. on the 23rd of every month."

J.J. bolted upright. The burst of adrenaline widened her eyes and her grin. "Did you say the 23rd?" she asked, her mind brimming with anticipation.

"Yeah? Mean something to you?"

The 5 – 9 and 2 – 23 had to be related to the Russian holidays Sunnie discussed in her briefing. The days the alleged babies were scheduled for delivery. With Mosin's involvement, she had an undisputable link to the sleeper network. The mob would conduct a drop on the 23rd but she still lacked a location.

"Sunnie…she briefed us yesterday. I'll have her send you the death by PowerPoint on the high side," J.J. said, referring to the most secure network. "Long story short, Troika's using legitimate operations to cover-up its role in a drug and arms trafficking network—laundering drug money to buy arms for drug cartels and the Russian mob. We believe a shipment's supposed to be transported tomorrow morning, but the SAC wouldn't authorize investigative resources because we don't have an address."

"Hmm. Then today is your lucky day…an address is listed on the calendar."

"What? Six, what is it?"

"Well, I have good news and bad news."

"Oh, Jesus. What'd you do?"

"Well, the bad news is, the notebook is on its way to FBI Headquarters via diplomatic pouch and the address inside."

"Ugh. Why me?"

"The good news is—I have a photographic memory and never forget anything I see."

"You mean pornographic?" J.J. quipped.

"That too."

"Is that so?" She rolled her eyes and smiled at the same time. "You haven't taken your crazy pills this morning, have you? Give me the address before I drive to your house, break into your garage, and key the Porsche…by accident."

"If you would stoop so low as to resort to a Porsche threat, you must need this," he said. "555 North 10th Street. Brooklyn."

J.J. couldn't contain her excitement. This was the lead they needed to get resources and make the bust. "I'm going to owe you big for this one, Six."

"No, if this pans out and you make an arrest, you'll already be paying me back. In a major way."

J.J.'s eyebrows scrunched. "What you talkin' 'bout, Willis?"

"Wasn't it *you* who suggested I needed to find Mosin some enemies?" Six paused to let J.J.'s thoughts catch up. "Make this bust. That should do the trick. But a better question is what the hell is he doing with the address to the drug shipment's location?"

J.J.'s mind churned. "Well, you've got him in custody. Sounds like a good question to ask."

"Good point."

"I'll bet since Lana's death they designated him to pay off the rest of the sleeper agents…until we blew his cover."

"I'll run this down and let you know what happens."

J.J. hung up the phone and flitted around the room in a panic, stumbling into her clothes and out of the door.

She ran to Tony's room giddy, the rush helping her remember the small things that excited her about the job. This was a break no one expected. She fired off successive knocks at his door and listened to feet scuttle across the floor.

When the door opened, she cracked her mouth open, prepared to share the news. She was frozen in shock when she saw who answered. "Gia? What the hell are you doing here?" she asked, the words fell out of her mouth before she could adjust the bitch-on-fire tone. J.J. looked over Gia's shoulder and scanned the room, but the bathroom door was closed. "Where's Tony?"

She smiled with a gloating contempt. "He's in the shower."

J.J. felt a surge of anger so powerful it almost thrust her hand into Gia's throat. But as she listened to the water shut off, Gia's expression turned from cocky to guilty. "He doesn't have any idea I'm here. The maid let me in."

Those words, as it turned out, saved Gia's life. J.J. jostled past her, knocking her into the wall. She took up a seat on the bed, crossed her legs, and folded her hands against her knee. Soon Tony walked out of the bathroom with a towel wrapped around his waist, his skin still glistening from the steam.

"Hey! Good…"—he turned and noticed Gia—"what are *you* doing here?"

"I just wanted to thank you for inviting me to dinner. That's all. I'll leave you to get dressed," she said, turning to make her exit.

After the door closed behind her, J.J. cleared her throat. "That bitch is going to get you cut one day."

"What the hell's goin' on?" he asked.

"She wanted to thank you for dinner all right—thank the hell out of you with her own special dessert. Probably told the maid she was your wife to get in here. Keep an eye on her before you make me catch a case."

"J.J., I had no idea she was here. I've been calling you all night. What's going on? Is everything okay?"

She shook her head no. "Hurry up and get dressed. We've got a shipment to seize."

"You serious? The odds of us seizing that shipment are equal or less than Godzilla's foot coming through this ceiling right now."

"If that's the case, you better move out of the way. A scaly foot should be coming through the window any second."

"How? You got a crystal ball?"

"No. I've got an address…and the justification we need to get resources and take down this network."

Chapter 28

Monday Afternoon — Moscow Safe House

Talking with J.J. invigorated Six's resolve to find the intel as well as to determine what his detainee knew about the drug and arms network linked to funding the sleeper network. Six hovered over Mosin's chair, his eyes burning like a desert brush fire from the stench of his body odor. He was in desperate need of a bar of soap and water. Animals in the woods smelled less offensive—at least they could lick themselves clean.

Before Ghost left the two alone, he told Six that he'd deprived Mosin of sleep. The obstinate detainee dozed for two hours after staying awake the last twenty-four hours, but Ghost also admitted he made no progress and was no closer to breaking Mosin than the day he arrived. In Six's eyes, Mosin's refusal to cooperate signaled one of two things: He was so confident they'd never find the intel, he had nothing to lose—or he believed he, in fact, had more to lose by revealing the location. Six's only hope of breaking him down before the mandatory stand down was to find out which case was true. His discussion with J.J. provided him with some leverage, enough facts to provoke a reaction. If he couldn't get Mosin to confess the intel's location, then the next best option was to create a scenario in which Mosin believed his life depended on him giving it up.

Mosin's head bobbled to the side in a jarring sweep, startling him awake. He jerked his head back and narrowed his eyes once they trained on Six. He sneered, "Back again, huh? You're wasting your time."

"I don't think so." Six grabbed a chair and placed it parallel to Mosin's. He faced the chair-back forward and sat down with his legs straddled across the seat. "I came to thank you…for the netbook. It has proven very helpful so far, the calendar in particular."

Mosin's eyes froze.

"Yeah…we know all about the shipment," Six said.

Mosin's mouth fell open, and he gasped. His eyes widened before he squeezed his lids shut.

"Mashkov's entire organized crime syndicate will be wondering how the FBI all of a sudden compromised an operation they've been running for years. One that'll cost them millions of dollars in drugs and cash. One thing about the mob, they don't like people responsible for fucking up their money, you understand? That's a hazardous occupation."

Mosin shook his head in disbelief, and a tenuous smile took over his face.

"I'm certain the netbook will be even more helpful when the FBI completes their forensics examination," Six said. "They've got a super-computer able to crack encrypted files in less time than it'll take you to get out of this chair. So, you've got a choice here, Hawk. Tell me where you stashed the intel, or I make sure the mafia finds out you're the reason their shipment got seized."

"I gave you nothing!" he snarled.

Six shrugged. "Well, you and I know that…but they don't."

"Heh," he said, his tone laden with condescension. "You are so full of shit. Think I can't hear what's going on between you two? Ghost, he schooled you like you were his child, and he was your daddy. You cower to him and bend to his will because you don't have the guts, the cold-blooded instinct it takes to turn my name over to the mob or even to your own government."

Six smirked and let out an uncomfortable chuckle.

"You should've brought that cunt bitch FBI agent you work with to handle your business. She's got bigger balls than you."

Six leaped out of his chair, which collided with a loud thud against the floor, and grabbed a fistful of Mosin's shirt and chest hair. He could feel the hair pull as he tightened his grip. "Let me tell you something," he rumbled through clenched teeth. "You keep that woman and everything about her out of your mouth, capiche? Keep talking shit, and I will fucking end you right here. The only thing they will find from your body is that tongue you keep wagging. "

"Careful," Mosin lashed back with a devious grin. "Your weakness is showing."

Six caught himself and released Hawk's shirt with a shove, rocking his chair backward. "You don't get it, do you? I'm the only person standing between you and a painful, torturous death. Ghost despises traitors and rats. He would've killed you on sight if it weren't for me so don't get it twisted. The only reason you're still sucking breath today is because I have honor…and I don't need to torture you in order to get what I want."

"Hmph. Then you're a fool, because I'm not saying shit to you or your daddy. And honor will get you nothing…except a gold watch, a plaque, and a useless thanks for your service."

"And what will you end up with? You think the Russians give a shit about you? Without the intelligence, you mean nothing to them. Zilch, nada, goose egg. You're risking your life to pass the FSB intel, and they haven't expended a single resource to locate you. I'm in and out of the embassy like a cleaning crew—nobody's following me. They can't miss intel they never had, so you are useless to them."

Mosin batted his eyes; Six realized he had hit a nerve, so he continued.

"You talk about my honor, what about yours? *You know* how this ends. Turn yourself over to the FSB. Get a party and a leased country house, a flat, an unlucky fall and a broken neck or a 'suicide', and a state-issued tombstone?" he said, reminding Mosin of the fate of other Russian defectors who led miserable lives to tragic ends, like Edward Lee Howard. "You look clueless enough to believe the tall tales about Howard dying in a slip-and-fall accident at his dacha. While his death could be characterized as a slip-and-fall. Accident? Yeah, okay."

Six wanted to ensure Mosin received his message loud and clear: If Americans are nothing else, they are relentless in settling scores. And the record reflected that the U.S. sowed seeds of vengeance until she reaped the justice she sought, no matter how long it took. "So, if you want to rot in this shack, knock yourself out. I guarantee you, confessing in here is better than the rude awakening waiting for you out there."

Six glared at Mosin and waited for a response. He had given him much food for thought. But he didn't eat for long.

"Your mind tricks will never work on me! Never. I will sooner die here than betray my country."

Six tightened his lips and grimaced. "And this is your final decision."

He shook his head. "No, but I'm sure about you—and you will never turn me over. So return to your embassy and push some paper. Your time is wasted here."

Six glanced at his watch; Bart would return soon. It was time to go. He slipped into his jacket and left, but not before saying, "As you wish…"

Six didn't need to stay a second longer. Mosin had given him the answer he sought. Mosin was so confident Six wouldn't find the intel he was willing to call Six's bluff.

Another day down—four to go.

Six's direction was clear now.

He only hoped he could live with his choice.

Chapter 29

Monday Morning — FBI New York Office

"This is some bullshit!" J.J. growled. Murphy's Law had further knotted an already impossible situation. She'd set herself up for failure believing Fitzpatrick was fair. Even with the additional intel, he still shut down their request. No surveillance team so nowhere near the number of cars they needed to cover Troika's executive team for the day. Manny, Tony, Scott and J.J. would have to run their own ops. No TAC team—they were supporting a higher priority op. If an arrest went down, they could call in for support, if required. No warrant—Fitzpatrick wouldn't seek one based on the available evidence. So now, they must have probable cause to stop and search the vehicle. With an hour before the bust, J.J.'s anger was flowing along with her creative juices. The team needed to devise a ruse to stop that car or the entire operation was screwed.

Two things worked in their favor: the element of surprise—no one was expecting them—and Tony's secret weapon, two NYPD officers in Brooklyn's narcotics squad. The high school chums were the only two people who hadn't turned against Tony for joining the FBI. They had wet dreams about running joint ops with the Feds; today their dreams would come true.

The op wouldn't be complex *if* they could identify the suspect vehicle. NYPD would stop them claiming a traffic violation. When officers asked for license and registration, they'd claim to smell a strange odor and ask the driver to step out of the car to conduct a search. Yes, the team was stretching the bounds of the law. The alternative was not an option.

The team got fitted with their operational radios and set up static surveillance along North 10th, a one-way street lined with brownstone warehouses and industrial buildings. Fresh gentrification abound, the neighborhood was in the midst of evolving from its dilapidating industrial roots to an artsy residential scene, with pristine brownstone apartments and boutique-style businesses sprawling up between graffiti-ridden, abandoned warehouses and old manufacturing strongholds. The difference was stark; Brooklyn's past juxtaposed against its future, uncoiling into the new Manhattan that everyone who knew anything about New York touted it to be.

J.J. perched herself just south of the meet location so she could serve as the lookout for the transport vehicle and warn the team when she spotted it coming.

She sat in her government-issued vehicle, an ancient Ford Taurus bound for the scrap heap, picking her fingernails and praying the op would draw to a trouble-free end.

When her stomach growled, she checked her operational backpack to ensure she'd brought the necessities. No cheese crackers but she did run her fingers across the compact .45 she copped from a perp years ago while on Major Crimes rotation. It was her first big take-down, had sentimental value and was a constant reminder of how close she came to death. It was a key reason she preferred operating against spies.

She sat inside the lemon that the New York office must've pulled from its final resting place to serve as loaners for this op.

The one-way road restricted her view to the rearview and side mirrors. Her senses were in overdrive as she trained her eyes on them and cracked the window to listen for the sound of a truck or van coming down the street. She figured it must be one of the two.

At last, TWO A.M. came and went. And still not much movement except a few stray cars cutting through to other destinations. She craned her neck looking around. No places were open for business on the block. The area appeared almost deserted, an industrial ghost town missing only tumbleweed flipping across the road.

As random thoughts buzzed around in her head, she received a text from Tony, who'd posted himself a few blocks ahead, adjacent to the target address—555 North 10th Street. He sent J.J. a picture. Max Novikov had arrived with three henchmen. Incredible Hulks if she ever saw them. Could've been the front line of any NFL defense, tall and solid, like human walls. J.J. Watts' bigger brothers. The picture showed them walking into the target location, an old industrial building with a fenced-in lot next to it. She figured they opened the gate to allow vehicles carrying shipments in and out. Once the vehicle was off the streets, they'd need a warrant to get to it—and with Fitzpatrick at the helm, they had no hope of getting authorization.

"Everyone in position?" J.J. asked. The FBI team responded in the affirmative. No NYPD.

"Farley? Fischer?" Scott said. "Hello?"

"Shit! Their radios must be jammed," Scott said. "We're out of time. Let me drive to their position and make sure everything's okay."

"Tony?" she called out. She was met with silence.

He responded to her with a second text. This time photos of Santino and an older Italian-looking man walking inside the warehouse.

Jesus! What the hell is going on? Does Santino have a death wish? Are they going to war right now?

Tony sent another text.

I don't believe what I'm seeing.
We might have another problem.

No sooner than she processed the gravity of the situation, a truck appeared at the corner behind her and stopped. She grabbed the binoculars and trained them on the truck's front bumper. Out-of-state plates.

"Guys. I've got a white van registered in Florida. This has got to be it," she said, waiting on a response. "Farley? Fischer? Tony?" Nothing. From anyone.

Stone silence. *Shit.* She gulped hard and scrambled to action.

She had to think fast. How in hell could she stop this truck? And who would be there to back her up if something went wrong? She watched it turn onto the block and approach her position. Time was short, and her choices were few. She glanced down at the ops bag and clenched her eyes shut.

She hated to do it, but she had no choice. She slipped on her gloves and went to work.

As the van crawled down the street, J.J. grabbed the .45 from the backpack, used her gloved hands to wipe off her prints, and shoved it in her jacket pocket. It would, at last, come in handy. After ripping the radio receiver from her ear and laying it on the seat so she didn't spook the driver, she took a deep breath and prepared to tap into her inner ghetto.

She prayed her NYPD reinforcements would be back online within a few moments, and this scene could end before it got out of hand.

"All right," she said to herself. "This is gonna hurt a little bit."

As the truck slow-rolled to within feet of her vehicle, J.J. mashed the gas, bolting into the single lane. The truck slammed into her driver-side door jarring her a bit. She emerged unhurt except where the door pressed against her arm.

Showtime.

Chapter 30

Santino crawled down North 10th Street in his Mustang, Nicky Mumbles at his side, scanning the brown-hued brick facades for the address numbers which were all but impossible to read from the car. His eyes flitted from side to side as he took in North Brooklyn's changing face. He glanced at his watch. They were still twenty minutes early. Frankie Z had told him Russians were always late, so time wasn't an issue.

Santino's heartbeat almost crushed his chest cavity, not so much from fear of the death sentence that awaited him, rather from the searing rage threatening to explode through his hands and squeeze the bones in Nicky's neck to powder. If thoughts could kill, Nicky would be slug food, lying six feet under with two hollow points in the back of his head. He wanted nothing more than to sink his soulless corpse in the East River. Instead, Santino forced his voice into its usual cordial tone, just as his Uncle Sal had ordered. Restraint was the opposite of every instinct his father had ingrained in him since he was a kid. The family silenced rats and traitors before they became cancers that subsumed everyone around them. Not this time. No. This time the plan was to sacrifice a *hen* to trap the *fox*.

And Santino was clucking like a motherfucker.

Nicky couldn't suspect for a second that Santino wanted to end him, but the task proved tougher than he ever conceived.

After eyeing Santino with a skeptical glare during the whole ride, Nicky paused before breaking the silence. "What the fuck's wrong with you? You on the rag? You've been acting like a little cunt all day."

Santino swallowed hard and growled inside; his gut knotted from forcing down the anger spilling from within. The split-second gave him an instant to conjure a lame excuse. "I went to that spot on 15th, the place where you got the Stromboli. I think they gave me some bad scampi." He patted his stomach and forced a belch.

"See, you don't listen. I told you not go there. Gave me food poising. I had the shits for two days."

"I hear you loud and clear, but Swifty said it was okay, so I thought I'd give it a shot," Santino responded.

"Swifty? Please. The man's got a stomach like an industrial storage tank. He could eat the torch off the fuckin' Statue of Liberty, and it wouldn't even give him gas."

Santino found it hard not to chuckle. "Yeah, yeah. I get the idea now. Too little, too late. I'll be all right. Just ready to get this meeting over with so I can go home and grab some Zs."

"You sure? 'Cause I can stop and get you a box of Midol and some Tampax. Gotta pick some up for the old lady while I'm at it."

"Which one? You got four of 'em, dontcha?" Santino stepped out of the car and looked up the street. All clear.

"Hey, hey. Watch ya mouth. My wife, she's got bionic hearing," Nicky said, trying to lighten the mood. "At least I'm doin' better than you. You couldn't get pussy at a cat convention." Nicky laughed hard at his own joke as he exited the car. He walked over to the warehouse and looked at the address. "555 North 10th Street in Brooklyn. This is it, right?"

Santino nodded as he checked the address on his phone. The location was perfect. On the corner of a one-way street with building construction on one side and a bunch of low-rise abandoned buildings in the surrounding area. It would be easy to spot the Feds if they showed up. On the right side of the building was a large fenced-in lot secured by a chain-link gate and padlock. Santino shot off a quick text and approached the door, knocking and peering inside the blacked-out windows, trying to get a heads-up on what awaited him.

"Somebody's coming," Nicky said from beside him.

When the door opened seconds later, the supersized Russians greeted him at the entrance, and Santino proceeded inside. It wasn't enough to call them big. They were chunks of flesh and blood carved out of Siberian mountains. The corners of their mouths turned downward, and their eyes hid under bushy uni-brows. Santino wanted to speak to them in their language. *Ugg.*

Each dressed from head to toe in black paramilitary cargo pants, tight shirts, and boots. Assault rifles were slung over their shoulders as if they were about to advance on a beachhead. Santino shoved his hands in his pockets, wrapped his fingers around his brass knuckle, and then clenched his eyes for a moment to feel the weight of his piece around his ankle. He was walking heavy, but not heavy enough to shoot his way out of this predicament.

Neither mountain spoke. Maybe they didn't understand English. But they nodded at him and jutted their heads toward a dark green metal door in the back of the room. It had three deadbolts which Santino took as a sign: When shit went down beyond the threshold, it was meant to stay there, like Vegas.

"This way?" Santino asked, pointing to the only door.

Both grunted in the affirmative.

Santino opened the door and allowed Nicky Mumbles to walk through first. Unlike Santino, he noticed there wasn't a hint of anxiousness in Nicky's demeanor, which he found odd given they'd just walked into the enemy's lair. Uncle Sal had told him to keep his eyes open, and it didn't take long for the revelations to begin. Nicky appeared comfortable, as if familiar with his surroundings. Santino trailed him down a narrow hall, four closed doors on either side. Nicky opened one at the end, without hesitation, without asking. And judging from the mumbles inside, he'd reached the correct one, confirming for Santino that Nicky was in bed with Russians and had plans to bump him off….right now.

In his mind, only one question remained: Was Frankie Z aligned against him or not. Once he got the answer, he'd walk away with all the information he needed—if indeed he walked away.

Trailing behind Nicky, Santino craned his neck to scan the room before entering. A dim light shone through the warehouse as they entered. On the wall facing him was a large blacked-out picture window that moonlight struggled to penetrate; it faced the empty lot. In the rear of the space, a large garage door also faced the adjacent fenced property.

His eyes then shifted to the dusty, wooden executive conference room table with about ten chairs positioned around it. Swifty sat next to some guy with strong Russian facial features—yellowish skin, thin lips, and a protruding nose—and testosterone bleeding through the pores. Santino figured the guy must be Max Novikov since no one else had entered except the mountains. Both Max and Swifty were dressed in tailored suits, and the smoke from their cigars clouded the air. As he moved forward, he drew a bead on bloody meat hooks swinging from the ceiling as if the carcasses had been removed moments before Santino's arrival, perhaps to make space for him.

"Santino, get ova here. Got somebody I want you to meet." Frankie greeted him with a handshake and fatherly pat on the back. "This is Max Novikov," Frankie said with a stogie smoking between the pudgy fingers of his other hand, gesturing for them to shake. Swifty turned to Nicky and shifted his glance from one to the other. "You two met?"

"I don't believe we have," Nicky said, extending his hand and a put-on grin. He avoided Max's gaze. The discomfort was unnatural.

Max was younger than Santino imagined, late 30's, early 40's. His stoic expression struck Santino as more business-like than mean-mugged. He and the mountains looked fresh from the same womb, like brothers, at least in the face. Not the build. Max was no mountain. More like a hill.

"Good to meet ya," Santino said. As a sign of respect, he gestured for permission to take a seat.

"Please," Max offered. Nicky followed suit.

As he bent down to sit, he identified a new threat. Two more mountainous brothers posted in darkened corners at the back of the room. Four of them total—strapped with heavy arms. Santino had a sudden urge to say a Hail Mary.

"You, uh, you sure got a lot of fire power. I thought this was a friendly meeting," Santino said as his phone sounded. He pulled it from his pocket and tapped out quick response.

"That's my intent," Max responded. "Let's call my brothers here an insurance policy, if you will, to ensure this is a pleasant visit for all involved."

Santino's eyebrows arched, and he let out a chuckle. "I see."

Nicky landed a condescending pat on Santino's back and belted out a fake laugh to break the tension. "It's okay, Santino. You can leave this conversation to the grown-ups from here." He turned to Frankie and gave him the stink eye.

"Look," Frankie said, taking the hint. "Whaddaya say we get down to business and dispense with the group grope, eh? We all understand why we're here."

"Do we?" Santino mumbled under his breath, drawing a wicked sneer from Nicky.

Frankie released his cigar to the ashtray, leaned back in his seat, and folded his hands across his rotund belly. He made eye-to-eye contact with everyone at the table before speaking.

"We've all got a lot at stake, right? I think we can agree the Feds have an extra stiff hard-on to take our organizations down right now. A war would bring a lot of unnecessary heat and lead to the demise of some critical business interests. So, reaching an agreement here is not optional; it's mandatory."

Santino hunkered down in his seat. His Beretta was still smoking from whacking Stevie Pics, and every fiber of his being wanted to pull it out, snap the trigger back, and set the barrel on fire, until every last one of them struck a dead-man pose. The Russian stumps standing in the shadows made him think better of taking action…except to say, "Somebody's got to pay for what they did to Dante."

The words fell out of his mouth without effort or thought. Zero consideration for Nicky's position which was a no-no. What else could he do? Sit by and let Nicky and this Russian prick play his family like a bad poker hand?

Uncle Sal's voice echoed in his mind. *Watch your temper.*

As expected, Nicky shot him a "shut the fuck up" glare to warn him he was talking out of school. "Despite the impetuousness of the Boss's nephew here," Nicky began, "I'm afraid he's right. My orders say we can't let your people skate on this one." Nicky eyed Max with a poker face.

Santino wondered if the rat bastard thought him both blind and stupid. Stevie Wonder could've seen the looks passing between them. Maybe the problem was less that they dismissed Santino, and more that they didn't give a damn what he noticed because they never planned for him to walk out alive.

"Stop right there," Max said. "The people who hit your cousin weren't my people—I'm with Levi Mashkov. Pavlov Mashkov, his brother in Moscow, ordered the hit. And he's untouchable; nobody gets to him. So, you've got to deal with me."

Santino made a mental note of the instigator's name. Pavlov Mashkov. If life in the mob had taught him anything, it was that nobody was untouchable. Anyone with a head could take two in the back of it.

He glanced at his escape route. A shadow appeared outside the window, breaking the beam flowing from the street light. No one else noticed. All eyes burned on him. Max shifted in his seat to face Santino and clasped his fingers together on the table. "You're the boss's nephew. What does he plan to do if we're unable to reach a meeting of the minds?" Max asked.

Santino shrugged. "To be truthful, I can't say," he replied, which in no way meant he didn't know. "I'm just a crew chief. *He* would be more knowledgeable than me about such matters," Santino said, gesturing toward his Captain.

Nicky hunched his shoulders in reply.

"So, this still leaves us with the question of who's gonna answer for Dante?" Santino said, still unable to restrain himself.

"Then I'm afraid we've reached an impasse, and it will do you well to remember one thing." Max's lips thinned; his nostrils flared, and the whites of his eyes cracked red. "We don't have to answer for shit!" He swept his hand in the air, signaling the mountains. With the precision of a color guard, their rifles crackled as they snapped into position—each barrel pointed at Santino's head.

Frankie turned to Santino and back to Max. "What the fuck is goin' on here? I told 'em you were a stand-up guy, and you go and pull this bullshit?"

Santino cocked his head to the side and smirked before leaning back in his seat. In a blazing fast move, he snatched the cold steel from his ankle holster and locked his aim on Max's head. A second later, the gun cocked. "Put your fucking guns down," he told the mountains. "Shoot me and nobody's walkin' out of here alive. Nobody."

Chapter 31

Monday Morning — New York City

J.J. had done it. Succeeded in stopping the truck that she hoped contained the Mashkov's shipment. With his front bumper now lodged firmly in her car door, and the driver annoyed, she needed to play her next step cool or her attempt to create probable cause might land her six feet under.

She threw up her hands in the air, feigning shock and frustration at the crash *she* caused. Then she turned down her driver side window and signaled for the driver to turn down the one on his passenger side.

The driver looked like the Russian missing link, one of the matched pair seen in Max Novikov's surveillance photo. Could've been a brother, equally wall-like. His nose beaked and his mouth curled into a hardened grit.

Once his window opened, he yelled, "What the hell are you doing?"

"What do you mean what am I doing? What the hell are *you* doing?" She yelled as though she'd missed a few doses of Prozac. "You can't see from under those eyebrows?"

He grumbled a bunch of expletives under his breath.

"You saw me pulling out," she continued. "You ever hear of a blind spot, douche bag. Back the truck up! I can't get out."

He reversed just far enough to allow her door to open. J.J. scanned the area, still looking for Tony's NYPD buddies. No one was in sight. She was beginning to understand why they weren't Feds.

She jumped out of the car and waited for the Russian to do the same. The moment he stepped out to confront her, she slipped the .45 into his passenger window and dropped it on the seat, hoping it landed in plain sight.

"Are you blind? What the fuck are you doing?" she said, continuing her rant in order to stall. Still no back up. Where were they?

"I had the right of way. You fly in front of me into the street. Are you blind, you stupid bitch!"

"Bitch? Yo' mama's a bitch, you stupid asshole." She planted her hands on her hips and twisted her neck in a ghetto frenzy. "I can't half understand you with that accent. You no speaka de English?"

"Better than you, you dumb cunt." He spat his words like venom.

J.J.'s eyes shifted waiting for NYPD to appear. She'd continued stalling but hoped Tony wouldn't swoop into intervene and blow the op too early if he feared the situation getting out of hand. Short of him shooting her, she could handle him.

The angry Russian walked over and scanned her door. "You call this a dent? This is nothing, a little nick."

"Are you kidding me? I could fit your head in there?" she said. "Where's my cell phone? I need the number for 9-1-1. And give me your license, registration, and insurance information."

He scanned left and right, surveying the area for potential witnesses. J.J. happened to know the only ones in the area were FBI agents and Russian Mafiya.

"Lady, I don't have time for this bullshit." He reached into his pocket, pulled out a wad of hundreds, looking down the street past her toward the warehouse. "Listen, I have an urgent appointment. Here," he said, handing her a wad of hundreds. "This should cover it."

She peered over his shoulder, feigning impatience. Then started counting the money. "One hundred, two-hundred…nine-hundred, a thousand…two thousand five-hundred, two-thousand five-hundred…wait? Did I just count that twice? Let me start over. One-hundred, two hundred…"

He snatched the money from her hand, snapped his finger around her throat, and slammed her against the car.

She couldn't breathe, taking life-and-death grasps at his fingers trying to pry the stumps from her neck. He leaned forward and growled, "You take this money and move this piece of shit out of the way or I will—"

Two sirens sounded. Out of the corner of her eye, the red and blue lights flashed in her peripheral vision. He released her and growled as he stepped back, unleashing a barrage of curse words in Russian. Then he spat toward J.J.'s face and fired the N-word at her like a hollow point.

As they stepped into the escalating scene, one officer checked on her as the other ordered the driver to strike the perp pose. "Sir, get on the ground and put your hands behind your back."

"Fuck that! I'm not getting on the ground. *She* pulled in front of *me*."

"Is it her fault you had your hand around her neck? I'm not going to ask you again," he said, raising his voice. He pulled out his Taser and yelled. "Get on the ground and get your hands behind your back! Now!"

The man conceded, grumbling all the while. The officer cuffed his wrists and went to retrieve the registration from the glove compartment.

J.J. eyed the cop's partner as he glanced inside the passenger window, and his head turned downward. "Fisch, there's a weapon on the floor. I'm going to search the rest of the car." Leaning against the car as she waited for them to find the loot, she felt a twinge of regret over crossing the line to make the bust, but defended her actions by blaming Fitzpatrick and his stone-walling. If he'd followed protocols and granted her requests, she wouldn't have had to resort to such extremes. A few moments later, Farley called out, "Holy shit! There must be millions in cash, thirty kilos, and enough Uzis to arm Brooklyn."

She suppressed a smile. The plan worked. Once again she'd bent the rules, but, in her mind, the end justified the means. Yes, she'd falsified the probable cause, but she hoped like hell the gamble would pay off once they made the bust.

"That belong to you, Mr. Jov Rakov?" Farley said.

J.J.'s ears perked up. She remembered the name. He was the former FSB officer and link between the drug and arms factions of the Mafiya network. The deal must've been major for him to travel to the states.

"I want my lawyer!"

"You'll need him. We're putting you under arrest," he said, just before they stuffed him into the back seat.

Rakov glared at J.J., baring his teeth. She crouched next to the squad car door, snarled through clenched teeth, and said, "Nigger? No. Bitch? Oh, yes. All day every day, you sorry son of a bitch." Then she returned his spit.

Once back at her car, J.J. retrieved her radio as Tony, Scott, and Manny ran to the scene after the action ended. As they approached her, she could see Novikov's henchmen step out the door of the warehouse and disappear inside as fast.

Rakov was off the streets. They were next.

Within in seconds, the street swarmed with press trucks. "How in hell did they know we were here?"

J.J. turned to the NYPD officers who both shrugged as if they had no clue.

Damn it, J.J. said. *This can't be good.*

•••

Back at FBI New York, J.J. and the crew returned to write their reports, hoping to get the right details to Fitzpatrick before the press got everything wrong.

"Donato, McCall, Lewis, Vasquez. My office—now!" Fitzpatrick yelled. She'd never worked for him before, but he was far from a happy camper. They all trudged inside exchanging guilty looks although none of them knew exactly why except J.J.

Once seated, he dropped the bomb, so to speak.

"Your arrest is a bust. We had to let the perp go."

"Why?" J.J. asked, thrusting forward to the edge of her seat.

"Seems in all the media excitement, NYPD failed to read him his rights."

"What about the drugs, guns, and money?"

"Oh, we keep the goodies. But the perp walks. And he's got a hard-on for you Agent McCall." She didn't have to guess why. There were a lot of things she could let slide.

Spit—no.

The N-word—hell no.

Fitzpatrick held back Manny and Scott as J.J. and Tony returned to their desks.

"Well, at least we've got the shipment off the streets and copies of the paperwork from the van."

"Yeah," Tony said. "But we've still got no direct link between Troika and the shipment and now we're on the radar. They'll probably start conducting damage control, and we'll never get access to the information we need to take them down."

J.J. closed her eyes, shook her head, and thought, Things couldn't possibly get worse. Then her cellphone buzzed. It was a message from Sunnie.

> Nixon got access to your mother's case file.
> It's gone.

Chapter 32

Tuesday Night — New York City

With his fingers tight to the grip, Santino's palm began to sweat as he waited for Nicky's reaction. Of course, the sorry fuck just sat there looking dazed and confused. Nicky glanced at Frankie, who stared at him as if he'd grown a second head. Then Nicky looked at Santino, who stared him down, wanting to fire a bullet into both of his faces.

Santino had to hand it to Max, who'd refused to budge or flinch despite the reversal of fortune. Max impressed and intimidated Santino; he wondered whether Max'd pull a rabbit out of the hat that he had not anticipated.

In a sluggish motion, Nicky pulled out his gun with a shaky hand and aimed it at Max's head, too, clearly second-guessing the wisdom of his move. His sorry performance had nothing to do with loyalty to Uncle Sal or to the family; it was for Frankie. If indeed the Russians took out Santino and Nicky lobbied to become boss, then Nicky needed a witness to vouch for the fact that he wasn't in cahoots with the Russians or they'd turn on him like rotten milk on a weak stomach.

Max signaled to the mountains to put their weapons down, but none of them moved. Neither did Max; his voice lacked the sincerity his request conveyed.

"C'mon," Frankie urged. "Stop this shit before it gets outta hand."

Santino didn't believe Frankie would support Nicky or this attempted trap but now his suspicions were confirmed.

His eyes still pressed on Max, Santino said, "Oh, I see what the problem is. My gun's too small. Why don't you have one of your brothers take a peek out the window over there?"

Mountain One walked over and rubbed his hand against an unpainted spot in the corner of the window. "Uhh, boss? Looks like he brought some members of his family with him."

Max bowed his head, feigning respect. "Is that so? That was not part of the agreement," he said to Santino. He glanced over his shoulder to the mountains and asked, "How many?"

"Judging from what I can see," the mountain began, "all of them. And they're all armed."

A slight miscalculation on everyone's part, including Nicky's. Santino had, on his Uncle Sal's orders, directed his earlier text to one of his Uncle's most loyal captains. Patrizio "Patty" Cuzmano, who made emergency phone calls to every soldier and associate he could contact; they stood guard outside Novikov's place. Without uttering a word, Santino sent a message. The Bonannos walked heavy and rolled deep. The family protected its own.

Santino narrowed his eyes and growled. "I might die tonight, but I won't die alone. Every motherfucker in the room will walk through the gates of hell beside me."

A stone silence permeated the room; every eye shifted in nervous beats, sweat beads dripped from every forehead—except for Max. Each man waited on the other's next move. At once, Max broke the silence with applause. Then a chuckle that evolved into an uproarious laugh, which he followed up with a standing ovation.

Max smiled wide at Santino. "Bravo, Mr. Castellano!" He wagged his finger and waved off the mountains who also laughed. Each released their weapons and leaned them on the walls in the back. "Heard you were crazy. Wanted to see for myself. I like my partners as mad as I am."

For Santino, the room spun because he was so filled with adrenaline. Took him a moment to return to his right mind.

"Partners?" Santino looked at Nicky and Frankie, who both shrugged. Nicky seemed more than content to put his gun away.

"Jesus, Mary, and Joseph, what's goin' on here?" Frankie said.

Max patted Frankie's hand to reassure him all was okay; then he looked over his shoulder and yelled, "Get the cases," to two of the mountains. They disappeared, and moments later their footsteps faded.

Santino lowered his weapon but didn't return it to his holster. The streets had taught him well, and the only thing more lethal than a dangerous man was a lunatic. Max was bat-shit crazy.

"Please, have a drink. Russky Standart Platinum. The best for my friend here," he said. The second pair of mountains brought glasses for the table and a fresh frosted white bottle with a black label. Santino's first drink disappeared as fast as they poured—the best Vodka, Russian or otherwise, he'd ever had in his life. Made Grey Goose taste like piss water.

Perhaps he and Max were friends after all.

Mountains one and two returned and dropped two large briefcases on the table, unlocking them without popping the latches open.

Max patted the tops of both, one with each hand, and said, "In these briefcases lay our agreement," he said. "But first I need you to understand something. The Mashkovs and I are at a crossroads in our relationship. I prefer a peaceful separation; they lean toward mayhem. The sooner I can break off my partnership with them the better. I'm here to tell you the order came from Moscow in retribution for Svetlana Mikhaylova's murder. To be frank, I hate those security service fucks. Our allegiance is an uneasy but necessary one…at least for now. That's where you come in."

He popped both cases open, one filled with at least ten kilos of cocaine and the other money. Piles of it. Five-hundred grand if there was a penny.

Nicky's hungry eyes devoured the case's contents. "So, what are you offering?"

Max turned to Santino. "We have some product we need to unload. I have a shipment of cash and cocaine my people are picking it up as we speak. You've already got distribution channels in ten cities. We'll cut in both of your families." His eyes shifted between Santino and Frankie Z. "An advance—say 1 million—and a percentage of the sales."

"Advance?" Frankie said. "Where I come from advance means you gotta pay it back from future earnings."

"Okay, fine. Let's call it a tax. In this briefcase is $500,000. I'll give you the rest of the supply and the money once our shipment is secured, which should be any moment."

The peace for one million dollars? Even Uncle Sal hadn't predicted they'd offer that much. Instead of getting himself killed, Santino's brand of crazy had helped secure a partner willing to bankroll a multimillion dollar operation. Santino waited a moment before speaking, but the pause gave Max concern.

"So, what's your decision?" he asked. "Will we thrive together…or die together. What's it going to be?"

Nicky gave Santino the side eye, no doubt because he'd hijacked the entire meeting.

"If we accept this deal, I want your word there will no more attacks on me or anyone in my family. Anyone."

Max looked at him with sincerity in his gaze. "Frankie knows me as a man of my word and you have it. If you set aside your desire for vengeance and don't seek retribution from *anyone* affiliated with me, I will not allow any attacks on you or your family…from anyone affiliated with my organization." He glanced at Nicky Mumbles. "But please don't mistake my kindness for weakness. Breach our contract, and I will rain down the fury of hell on each and every person responsible, I don't care what family they belong to. So, what do you say?"

"I say…we thrive."

As they stood up from their seats to shake on the deal, a mountain burst in the door and, in loud breathy words, whispered in Max's ear. Santino strained to listen, but he couldn't understand angry Russian.

The mountain stomped away, and Max turned to Santino and Frankie. "Please excuse me, you'll need to see yourselves out. There's been a slight…ahem…*problem* with my shipment. Nothing I can't handle but I must make a few calls. I'll reach out to you next week to arrange delivery of your other packages."

After the meeting concluded, and the family dispersed, Santino and a fire-spitting mad Nicky Mumbles stood outside waiting for Frankie to exit. He thought about the briefcases in the car and broke the uncomfortable silence.

"Listen, I'm sorry about how everything went down in the meeting. My temper got the best of me. After all is said and done, you have my utmost respect. And I mean that."

Nicky chuckled and shook his head. "You jackass. That was some crazy shit, heh? Thought we'd be forced to shoot our way outta there for a second. Max is *nuckin' futs*."

"Tell me about it, but this might turn into a lucrative partnership judging from the contents of those cases." Santino saw them sitting on his backseat. "I think you oughta hold onto 'em for the time being."

"Yeah, we'll ask the Boss how to split it later. I'll tell him to kick in a little extra for your crew. You showed some balls. It'd make Sal proud," Nicky said.

After Santino dropped off Nicky and arrived at his apartment, he made a phone call to Knuckles, the call he'd been waiting to place for weeks. He relayed the events of the meeting which left Knuckles speechless. "I got the name of the guy responsible for Dante. Pavlov Mashkov," Santino said. "Get your people on this and find out where he is. I don't care what this Novikov guy says. When we find Mashkov, he's dead."

●●●

Max saw the flicker of movement in his peripheral vision and the expression on his brother Igor's face. He realized the news couldn't be good. Igor leaned in his ear and half whispered, "The FBI seized today's shipment. The lead special agent, that bitch J.J. McCall from Washington, was trying to conceal her face during the press conference."

"Did they get everything?"

"Yes. Everything. Including Rakov. He's going to need help."

Max snarled, pointed his finger in Vasiliy's chest, and growled through clenched teeth. "Listen to me, and you listen closely. Make sure you hear every word I'm saying to you. No one is to respond without my order. Are we understood?"

"You know how he is. Whoever made the arrest…"

"I'll contain Rakov. You call The Duke and see if we can get him released."

Vasiliy nodded and disappeared.

Max would have to pay millions out of his own pockets to make good on his deal and pay his suppliers. That didn't worry him—but Rakov did. He was a vengeful son of a bitch. In Moscow, the last officer who arrested him was found hanging from a light pole days later; FBI agent J.J. McCall had awakened a sleeping giant that threatened the future of his operation. Max needed to keep the peace until Rakov returned to Moscow, and when he was released, they'd be assured of having anything but.

Chapter 33

Tuesday Morning — FBI New York Office

J.J. and the team dragged their worn, tired carcasses into the office Tuesday morning. Monday's TWO A.M. operation wasn't the epic failure Fitzpatrick touted it to be, but far from a success. They were still playing from behind. The press had splashed the operation across every headline. And Fitzpatrick was less than pleased, stomping around threatening to shut down the entire "goddamned field office" if anyone "fucked up again," which was extreme and yet understandable.

Tired and brow-beaten, the team scrambled to control the damage, find a way to regroup. Gia was off trading intel with Amie on the arms and Rakov angles while J.J. and the team sat in the squad conference room trying to come up with a Plan B. They had the money, drugs, guns, and a few documents but no perp. And they were no closer to getting on the inside of Troika than they were when she arrived in New York. In reality, the progress had turned into a setback.

She scanned the listless faces at the table, looking for signs of life, an idea, a stroke of genius, anything. Their expressions were as blank as their eyes.

"I dunno," Tony said. "Right now, our sole option is to put the squeeze on Misha. We've gotta ask his cousin Dani to go in for us."

"I don't—" J.J. hesitated, always squeamish about putting any source in danger, given Pavlov Mashkov had murdered two on her watch so far.

"J.J., I realize you don't want to endanger him but what choice do we have? We've got nothing else. The only way to neutralize Troika or to set up a meet with the accountant is to involve Misha."

J.J. took a deep breath and scanned the frustrated mugs glaring at her, a vote in every expression.

"I hate to say it," Scott said, "but Tony has a point. After yesterday's fiasco, the wire request is off the table. The phone records are as much as we're going to get without some miracle."

Manny nodded his head in agreement, as did Gia. Even though her opinion didn't mean anything to J.J.

Just as J.J. was about to capitulate and give in to the pressure another agent opened the door and interrupted with an announcement that floored them all.

"Zory Kozlov, the Troika accountant. He's downstairs getting booked. Just turned himself in."

"What?" the choir called out from around the table.

"Yeah. Confessed that heroin, coke, and cash belonged to him. Came in with a ledger claiming he's been laundering money he stole from Troika. Apparently, he can no longer live with the guilt," the agent said with an eye roll.

Turning himself in out of guilt? Zory's excuse had bullshit written all over it. The Mashkovs were in damage control mode, offering sacrifices to the FBI, which meant the team was now more than a step behind.

J.J. pursed her lips. "Yeah, if he's guilty, I'm Pocahontas. Let's go talk to him. Sounds like he has a lot he wants to get off of his chest."

The foursome took the stairwell down to the 22nd floor and walked to the interview room. Kozlov sat behind a table, no doubt cuffed to his chair by threats of brutality, providing his vitals to a duty agent until the interview team arrived; they looked at him through the two-way mirror.

He appeared nothing like the self-assured man in his surveillance photo. J.J. couldn't have pointed him out in a line-up except for the tattoo emerging from his shirt collar. The crucifix with a hand chained in manacles was hard to forget. The fact that he didn't attempt to conceal it meant something. He was sending a message to the world; she made a mental note to find out what.

He visibly sweated, wringing his hands with crackhead speed. His legs jittered beneath the table; the knocking of his heel against the floor would've grated on her nerves except for the carpeting.

"Who's going in first?" Manny asked.

"Oh, you gotta let J.J.—."

"Me and you!" Scott interrupted Tony and looked at Manny. "We're the lead New York agents, and we've been covering them longer and have more knowledge than Tony and J.J.," he said. Then he turned to them and said, "No offense."

"None taken," she said, conceding the lead to them. Russian criminal personnel emerged from the womb lying. Whatever Zory revealed during Nick and Manny's interrogation, she could do what neither of them could—detect his lies.

An hour later, the pair emerged from the interview room dejected. Kozlov slouched in his seat, silent as a stone, never revealing a word other than the rehearsed lines he'd been equipped to speak before he turned himself in.

"This guy," Scott said. "He's sealed as tight as a pickle jar. We couldn't get anything out of him."

J.J. pressed her lips together and in a reserved tone said, "Mind if I give it a go?"

Scott shrugged. "Whatever. I guarantee you if he won't talk to me, he's not gonna talk to you."

J.J. shrugged. "Hey. Nothing beats a failure but a try, right?" As she exited the room, she said, "Tony, why don't you come with me? Just in case I need a bad cop."

Moments later, J.J. and Tony slipped into the seats across from Kozlov. J.J. crossed her hands. The fact that he appeared ready to disintegrate into a massive puddle of fear and guilt eased her angst over the kind of personality she'd be dealing with.

J.J. scanned the form that was prepared by the original interviewer and then her eyes scrolled up to meet his. "I'm FBI Special Agent J.J. McCall and this is Agent Donato, Mr. Kozlov. Is it okay if we call you Zory?" She kept her voice soothing and matronly. Bad cop was unnecessary, might have sent him into cardiac arrest.

He nodded.

"A wife and three kids, I see," she said, reading from the sheet. "They're all in the U.S. I presume?"

He nodded again, but his voice creaked, "Yes, but my family— mother, father, and three brothers—they're still in Moscow."

"I understand," J.J. said, waiting for a sensation. None came. He was telling the truth...so far. She hadn't begun to delve into the difficult questions.

"So, you've come to confess a crime, I understand." She braced herself for a barrage of lies.

"Yes, please. Confess." His voice shook as much as his hands. "The shipment you seized yesterday. I'm responsible for it," he said.

J.J. waited for a reaction and felt only a slight tingle in her fingertips, but not as much as she'd expected.

"Define *responsible*," she replied.

He rolled his eyes to the ceiling and calculated his response. "I mean, I set up the logistics. The truck. The drugs. I arranged the meeting. I'm responsible."

The sensation moved into her arms and up to her neck. The revelation didn't surprise her. With a wife, children, and family in Russia, Mashkov's crew recognized how much Zory had at stake. He'd lie to save his family in a heartbeat.

J.J. turned her attention to the large ledger book on the table. "Can I look at that?"

He slid it over, and she scanned the entries. Several years' worth—all in the same exact ink. She ran her finger across one of the pages from three years ago and the ink smudged. Still fresh. She glanced at Tony with a skeptical smirk and turned back to Zory.

"You expect me to believe these are Troika's original records?"

"Yes."

J.J.'s leg jerked and the crawling sensation shot from the tips of her fingernails to the cracks between her toes. He was lying—big time.

Tony turned to her after she came close to squirming out of her seat. "You okay?"

"Yeah. Fine. It's just…the thing. You know…the thing. Could you please excuse us for a few minutes? I'd like to speak Zory alone."

"Sure. Sure," he said, the door closing behind him seconds later.

J.J. feigned exasperation. Paced around the table, muttering under her breath. Then she sat back down, her eyes wild; she glared at him. "Okay, Zory. Let me cut to the chase. If you're going to continue lying to me, we'll lie together. Maybe I'll call Troika and tell them instead of turning yourself in, you turned State's witness. I mean…since that's the kind of relationship we've established."

His eyes bulged, and he began to fidget. "You wouldn't."

She shrugged. "Hey, I have nothing to lose. Worst case scenario for *me* is we take you at your word, and you go to jail. Given your worst-case scenario, on the other hand, can you really afford to call my bluff? You've got thirty seconds to explain why you're doing this before I start making phone calls."

"I'm not—"

"Please, spare me, okay?"

"Agent McCall. I work for the Mashkovs," he said, his voice thin, urgent. "Why I'm saying this is no mystery. And one way or the other, I will say it to my grave."

"You want to spend the rest of your life never seeing your kids grow up, go to college, get married, bounce your grandchildren on your knee…all for a crime you didn't commit? C'mon. One ledger covering several years written in the same ink? This is an insult. Forget my interests, okay. Why would you do this to your family?"

"I'm doing this *for* them, not *to* them."

"If you want to do something for their future without looking over your shoulder for the rest of your life, you'll get us the records we need to shut down the bastards before they execute everyone you love, here and in Russia. You must know that's the plan no matter what tales you feed us today."

He dropped his chin to his chest. "You may be right, but…"

"But nothing. Get us access to the computer records. We'll offer you protection only the U.S. government can provide…if you give us what we need to take them out."

He shook his head no. "I can't," he said, hesitating to speak further but grimacing as if concealing the truth caused him physical pain.

"Fine. If that's how you want to play it." J.J. opened the door, asked Tony for his cell phone, and called information. "Yes, could you please connect me with Troika Technologies?" After a pause, she said, "Yes, that's the address."

"Please, stop!" he yelled.

She cut her eyes at him. "Why should I?" J.J. barked.

His mouth quivered before he spoke. "Don't see you? *I don't* have access. *I never* did."

J.J. waited for a reaction, an itch, a tingle, anything, but none came. He was telling the truth which sparked an entirely new round of questions. If *he* didn't have access to the financial records and never did, that meant…

"Wait a minute. Is…is there *another* accountant?"

Sitting with his chin to his chest, he peered up and pinched his lips but didn't speak.

"That's it, isn't it? They sent you here as bait…to take the rap so the FBI would cease the investigation. They didn't want us to find out the truth. They didn't want us to target the *real* accountant."

She stared in his face. His expression calmed as he shifted his body. He seemed grateful she'd figured out the truth without him speaking a word.

"Don't even answer that. Your body language is telling me everything I need to know…except the name of the real accountant. Listen, you don't have to give me his name. But understand I can't help you or your family without it."

She stood to leave and dawdled around on her way to the door, trying to give him a chance to come clean. She put her hand on the knob, and he yelled, "Wait!" She did an about-face and listened.

"Agent McCall, you've already got the information. If you examine the shipment, everything you need is there…in black and white. That's all I can offer."

She left the room and took a moment to consider his only admission.

Black and white? He was full of shit. She'd have been angry at the waste of time had he not appeared so pathetic. Then it dawned on her— no reaction. *He's telling the truth.*

"You heard him, right?" she said to Tony, who was posted outside the door. "I didn't see anything, except a few blank sheets of paper and a couple of fake invoices."

"Just because you can't see it," Zory called out from behind the door. "Doesn't mean nothing's there."

Chapter 34

Tuesday — U.S. Embassy, Moscow

Six sat on his bed feeling dejected after his fruitless visit with Mosin. He'd spent the better part of ten hours scouring Moscow, searching every place intelligence reporting had indicated Mosin visited to find the missing intel—and still came up empty-handed. He glanced at the calendar; they had only four days left before the stand-down, and he had only two days before Ghost and his crew collected Mosin. Resigned to give up questioning Mosin about the intel's location, he set out to find another path to the truth.

Wracking his brain, he'd convinced himself he had missed something. A clue somewhere that would help him achieve his mission—he'd never failed in one and refused to do so now. Perhaps the answer would arrive with the FBI's computer forensics report, but he couldn't depend on the findings with any certainty. He had no idea what contents were on the hard drive. Furthermore, despite his trash talking to Mosin, the Bureau might not even have the capability to break the encryption. And even if, by some miracle, they did accomplish that feat before Friday, he'd still need time to sift through the information and find the missing piece to the puzzle. He needed to identify another option.

Six reached into his nightstand drawer and pulled out the pocket litter he'd retrieved from Mosin's pants—a medical prescription and a receipt from a tattoo parlor. He read them both but never thought much of either before; his mind was bogged down in distractions. Thought perhaps Mosin needed to obtain medicine before traveling. People did it all the time. But as he studied the writing, he noticed the doctor prescribed antibiotics. He glanced at the doctor's name and location. *Odd*, he thought. The National Institute of Health Clinical Center in Bethesda? Why would a fugitive on the run from the FBI, and defecting to Russia no less, stop at NIH for some service requiring an antibiotic?

Six rushed to his laptop and Googled Dr. Dharmesh Badal, the prescribing physician. His eyes bulged when he read his specialty.

Are you kidding?

Six gazed at the wall, his vision blurring and refocusing in cycles as his thoughts materialized and congealed in his mind.

It all made sense now. Mark would think him out of his gourd without some hard evidence…and there was only one way to get the information yesterday, which was when he needed it. He'd skip the bureaucratic red tape and get some help to poke a proverbial a thumb in Dr. Badal's eye.

He started to call J.J. but contacting her three days in a row might start to appear suspicious. Yes, he wanted to hear her voice every day, but his request was business in the strictest terms. Besides, he wanted to tread carefully. After all, J.J. had a history of running when the pressure turned up too high…and not just in a literal sense. He sent a text to her instead containing Dr. Badal's address and office number. He asked if she could tap one of the agents at Washington Field to interview him.

She replied before he sat down his cell phone.

I'll get Hopper on this today!

He had a lot of work to do if this lead panned out. He'd need to contact the State Department pronto. His biggest problem was Ghost.

Will he go for it?

Six didn't know, but the power in Ghost's world was about to take a dramatic shift in Six's favor—whether he liked it or not.

First on his list—a come-to-Jesus meeting with Mark Levin, the Station Chief. Confessing they'd caught Mosin and held him in custody for days would choke down much easier with news of the intel's location.

When he stepped inside Mark's office with his report, the boss was head-down in paperwork. Intelligence reports as far as the eye could see from Reports Officers submitting their write-ups for final review. Six could tell by the typeface.

"What's going on? I'm pretty busy as you can see."

Six shut the door behind him and sat down, grim-faced. His head was bowed, and hands folded as if confessing his sins.

Mark sat back in his chair. "Uh-oh. What'd you do now?"

Six explained every event in excruciating detail, the pain emanating less from his physical being and more from the lack of transparency. Then he went on to detail his theory on the intel's location and present his findings in a report.

Mark scanned the pages. "I'm not even going to discuss the problematic way in which you and Ghost handled this op…but I'm not certain I'd have taken a different route under the circumstances." Mark spun his chair toward the window and looked outside. Six had given him a lot of food for thought. "You understand what this means, don't you? It's a significant risk."

"Yes, but a calculated one we've got to be willing to take. Otherwise, why are we here? Why do we wake up every day claiming we're defending our country and keeping it safe if we don't have the balls to man-up when it matters most? And right now, this matters. Take any other course of action, and we're not doing our jobs."

Mark turned to his desk and leaned forward with his elbows on the desk. Then he steepled his fingers and pressed the tips against his lips. After a few tense moments of silence, he said. "You've got authorization. I'll provide the top cover. Let's stick it to this son of a bitch once and for all."

Six smiled. Mark had made the right decision. Ghost might balk, but Six was running the op now.

"Hey," Mark said as Six turned to leave. "Not so fast. We've still got a problem on our hands. Another panicked phone call from Stan. The emergency line. Said he called from a payphone but I don't trust any unsecured Russian communications channel. I'm afraid if we don't devise a strategy to infiltrate him into the embassy within the next few days, the FSB will roll him up."

Six clenched his eyes shut for a moment and bit his bottom lip.

"You talk about keeping our country safe? All eyes are on Russia. Every press agency from here to Timbuktu has media in the region waiting to see what kind of crazy Putin will concoct next. How many sources do you think we'll recruit if we let Stan die with half the world watching? If you don't have any ideas, you better come up with one—fast!"

Six turned around and returned to his seat. "I've been wracking my brain. Never thought it'd be this hard to exfil a dead man."

Mark shook his head chuckled. "Yeah, somebody should've told him dead men must wear disguises…at all times."

"If we attempt a covert op and get caught, not only will we screw ourselves, we'll blow our NOC. Fifteen years down the shitter. We'll never get a cover that good again."

Mark stood up, walked to the office window, and stared at the embassy personnel pressing through the cold on the way to their morning grinds. "I suppose we could back channel it with the FSB. Tell them the truth. Make a spy trade in exchange for getting him out as part of a deal. There must be someone they want released."

Six shook his head. "Not a bad idea except they got everyone they wanted in the illegals trade. Who would we give them? The only person we're holding that even approaches Stan's level is Hanssen. The FBI would sooner blow up Supermax than turn him over."

Mark pursed his lips. "True…"

Six eyes widened, and his posture perked up. "But, what you said…you know, the truth may not be a bad idea." He remembered his conversation with J.J. *Show them what they want to see.*

Mark's face snapped toward him. "What are you talking about?"

Six stared at Mark in silence, examining every inch of his face, the gears in his mind spinning at breakneck speeds. "Come with me."

Six led him to the secure vault where the station kept the disguises. He placed a men's, short-cut brunette wig on Mark's head and looked at his face again. "No, the shape of your chin and jaw is all wrong. I need to find someone else."

He scanned the long line of file safe's lining the wall and walked to the one furthest from him. He spun the combination and pulled the latch to open the drawer. Inside, he found the album containing photos of all American personnel posted to the embassy. He rested the book on top of the safe and, in feverish sweeps, flipped the pages until he found the picture-perfect candidate.

"Come here," he said, waiting on Mark to join him. "Him. That's who I need to get this done."

Mark glared down at the book and then back at Six as if he'd grown a unicorn head with a bedazzled horn. "Slayton McCarthy? Have you taken your medication this morning?"

"Somebody once told me, 'what the eyes see, and the ears hear, the Russians believe."

"And?"

"Let's show them what they want to see, tell them what they want to hear—and then watch them squirm when they find out they're wrong," Six said, pointing at the dignified figure in the photo. He'd never noticed before, but with a little more gray in his hair and a shaved mustache….

Mark groaned under his breath. "This is either the stupidest idea that I've ever heard…or it'll earn you a medal."

"Time will tell…but I don't see any other way….not a *better* one, anyway."

"Keeping it real, I'm not sure whether this will work but it's brilliant. We've got to get Director and White House approval. Jesus. We've never attempted an operation of this magnitude before. Say a few Hail Marys," Mark said before turning away. Then he stopped in his tracks and turned back to Six. "My only question is…where in hell are we going to plant the information so the SVR can steal it?"

"Oh, that's the easy part," Six said. "In the White House."

Mark's eyebrows drew together.

"The hard part will be getting Slayton to agree…and making sure the timing is right."

Mark chuckled. "Oh, that's not hard. It's impossible."

Six set his mind to contact J.J. They needed help from within the Russian Embassy in Washington to make this operation work. And with J.J. in New York, there was only one way to task the source. He had to go through Washington Field—Hopper Mack.

Chapter 35

Tuesday Morning — New York City

Interviewing Zory Kozlov had revealed one key piece of information—he's not the official accountant and he had no access to the financial records. They'd been chasing a ghost for days and still didn't know the identity of the actual target. He revealed that the answer could be found in the evidence collected from the van. After examining each piece, they found—nothing.

"Well," J.J. said, turning to Tony. "Does your butt feel smoky? Because I'm beginning to suspect our friend, Zory, blew a bunch of it up our asses. Nothing's here…except *nothing*."

"Maybe he was dicking with us to get us to back off."

J.J. pressed her lips together. "Maybe. But seems like a ridiculous strategy…to piss off the people holding your future in their hands. There's gotta be something we're missing." She lifted the pages from the table with her gloved fingers and examined them front and back. "This is some bullshit, okay? I don't have time for —"

Tony peered up at her. "For what?"

J.J. snapped her back straight against the chair and held the page up to the light. "He said just because you can't see something doesn't mean it's not there."

"And?"

"If something is present, but you can't see it…"

"It's…*invisible?*" Tony piped in.

"Invisible, indeed. Such as ink? The tradecraft is old but simpler than using complicated codes and calculations. And if the Feds or the cops picked them up, the blank pages would appear to be little more than scraps of trash."

Tony glanced over her shoulder and locked his eyes on the paper. "How do we find out?"

"Invisible ink usually requires some type of agent, depending on the kind of ink. Sometimes, UV light works, but what drug courier drives around with a UV light on hand. Maybe heat will do it. Check with the evidence tech to see if we can get a desk lamp."

Moments later, Tony reappeared with one in hand. J.J. grabbed it from his grip and plugged it into the nearest wall. She held the paper over the light until the letters begin to form."

"Well, isn't this peachy? All written in Cyrillic."

"Great. Got to be a Russian speaker somewhere in this office. Let's check with Manny and see."

As they entered the squad bay doors, a voice called from a distance. "J.J., Devin Fitzpatrick needs to see you in his office. Right now. He's been trying to call. It's an emergency."

J.J. pulled out her cell phone and glanced at the screen. "Piece of crap phone. I haven't been able to keep a strong signal since I got here. Better go find out what this is about. Hope he's not ripping me a new one for the busted op...again."

"Oh, yeah," the agent called. "Tony, he said you should go, too. It affects both of you."

They exchanged uncomfortable glances and pressed forward to Fitzpatrick's office.

From the minute she set foot across the doorway and locked her eyes on his face, she could see *bad news* written all over it. Her mind raced. She feared Director Freeman had taken a turn for the worse. Maybe even her family. She braced herself and said a quick prayer.

He waved his hand, gesturing for them to come inside. "Shut the door behind you and have a seat."

"What's this about?" J.J. said, anxiousness permeating her voice. "Is my family okay?"

"Yes, yes. All is well on the home front, at least to my knowledge. No, this concerns *you*."

"Okay," she said, her curiosity piqued. She looked at Tony with a concerned expression and then back at Fitzpatrick. "What's going on?"

"One of our narcotics undercovers passed a message to me today. It's the Russians...they've put an open contract on your head."

"On me?" she said, bolting forward in her seat and gripping the chair arms. "And by *contract*, you mean—"

"Yes. They're hiring the first taker to kill you. Two million. And the word on the street is someone has accepted. I was afraid this might happen."

Her expression distressed, J.J. turned to Tony. Even when he saved her from Lana's bullet, she'd never seen genuine fear in his eyes the way she did at that moment. Maybe because he'd been born into a world where if someone put out a contract on your life, you died; she wasn't surprised, nor was she comforted.

"Do you think they're serious? I mean, do you believe they want me dead…or are they just trying to scare me into hiding?"

"Both. But make no mistake about it—two million qualifies as we-want-you-dead money. Generally, we might see $250K or a half mill. Not two million," he said.

He stood up, walked to the front of his desk and took a seat on the corner. "Italians won't take it. Killing an agent is bad for business. The Russians, though, they are the coldest, most ruthless sons of bitches I've ever worked against. When they have a vendetta, they become hell-bent on making their enemies pay. We're lucky the contract targeted you…and not your entire family."

"Shit," she said, running her fingers through her hair. She kept a calm exterior but felt dizzy, off-balance as if she had a case of vertigo. Her vision seemed to double. Her world had been unsteadied.

A contract.

While her aggressive investigations had landed her in hot water in the past, she never for a second believed they'd land her in a grave.

"I don't think it's going to be enough for you to lay low. My advice to you is to return to D.C. and take a few weeks off until this all blows over. Once you're out of New York, I think you'll be safer. Not safe, mind you, but better off than you are staying here."

All sound in the room disappeared. Tony, Fitzpatrick—they vanished. J.J. stood alone between her past and her future. What should she do? Return to D.C. Shrink and hide like a coward—or do her job. Fitzpatrick's opinion meant little to her. He'd been giving her grief since she arrived. Every time she attempted to make a move, he threw up more walls than the Chinese. He'd be thrilled to see her leave whimpering and wounded with her tail tucked between her legs.

As a sign of his misfortune, J.J. had never been one for shrinking.

She thought about her life, her family. Fighter's blood ran through her veins, deep red, hot, and valorous. Her mother, her father, they never backed down from a challenge. When she was in elementary school, fifth grade, a knuckleheaded boy named Ralph bullied J.J. for months. To her it seemed God put him on Earth to make her life miserable. Every day, jokes about her dark skin, her thin frame, the height which made her tower over most kids in her class. He pushed her, knocked her books out of her hand, pulled her hair. She took each denigrating act with grace. Then, one day, he went one Yo' Mamma joke too far. She snapped. Leaped across the desk and pulverized this boy, taller and bigger than she. Mrs. Campbell marched her down to the main office, her hair wild, her knuckles bruised and scraped. The principal made her call her mother at work and confess her sins. J.J.'s hands shook as she dialed the number. Her fingers and lips trembled like leaves in the fall wind. She explained the entire story to her mother…the bullying, the meanness, the constant picking away at her peace. After a moment of silence, her mother asked one question…and only one question.

"Did you win?"

J.J. smiled proudly and said, "Yes."

"That's my girl," she said. "We'll talk when you get home."

The Russians were welcomed to pick a fight with her if they wanted. At the end of the day, there'd be one man standing—a woman. FBI Special Agent J.J. McCall.

"I'm not going anywhere until I've accomplished what I came here to do. My mother always taught me never to pick a fight, but if someone brought one to my door, stomp the shit out of them. Make sure they walked away scared ever to bring another. I arrived in New York with my stomping boots on. So, if you'll excuse me…"

"J.J., wait!" Tony pleaded, asking her to listen with a level of reason she couldn't muster in that or any moment.

"Tony…" she said, trying to be understanding but firm. "I'll be careful…vigilant, but no one will ever make me run. The faster you help me wrap up this case, the faster we can return to headquarters—on our own terms."

Tony turned to the squad supervisor, his expression pained, and thanked him for his time before dragging J.J. into the hall.

"J.J., this isn't a game. It's serious, okay? I think you should reconsider your decision to stay. Go back to headquarters."

"You give me one good reason *I* should leave—and *you* shouldn't."

Tony stammered, trying to find the words to convince her. He no doubt believed the circumstances surrounding their contracts were different but not in her eyes. Besides, they were so close to wrapping up the case they'd be gone in a few days regardless.

"Let's find a Russian speaker. Once we get the translation, we'll visit Zory and end this thing once and for all. Oh, and I need to research Zory's tattoo. The meaning could help us figure out a way to get through to him." Her eyes fell upon his troubled expression. "Listen, you're worried about me, just like I worried about you. But I trusted you to handle yourself. Now, I'm asking you to do the same for me."

He pinched his lips together and grimaced. "Fine," he said. "But I'm not letting you out of my sight."

Chapter 36

Tuesday Morning — U.S. Embassy, Moscow

At a brisk pace, Six led Mark Levin to Slayton McCarthy's office. The op to rescue Stanislav Vorobyev was dead in the water if they couldn't get buy-in from him. They had no reason to believe he'd condone or back the operation, let alone serve as a key participant. Men in his position made friends, and the op they were about to propose was the deliberate and calculated act of an enemy—a provocation that, if ever discovered, could ignite a new Cold War and degrade Russian-American relations for decades to come.

There were reasons longstanding diplomatic protocols forbade true diplomats from crossing the murky line into intelligence, reasons why the two worlds coexisted in an uneasy yet necessary alliance. At a time when Russia was flexing its military might to the detriment of regional peace, Six and Mark proposed an op threatening to decimate the President's single-most important intelligence channel.

However, Slayton was a good friend of the President, one of his drinking buddies from law review; he served at the President's pleasure. If Six and Mark convinced him the op was low risk (at least in his role) and would strengthen the President's short-term political position and foreign policy image, his support would be reluctant but willing.

They rounded the corner past the conservatively decorated corridor, framed by rich mahogany and neutral Victorian seating, to Slayton's double-door office entrance straight ahead. His Secretary, a sharp-suited, middle-aged blonde with a librarian bun in her hair, greeted them with a smile. "Grayson Chance and Mark Levin here to see Slayton McCarthy," Mark said.

She nodded and smiled as if hiding a secret. They were part of the top-floor group—the spooks. Everyone *knew*…but didn't really *know*.

She escorted them inside and gestured for them to take seats in the burgundy leather executive chairs crowning his desk.

Slayton reached his hand out to Mark first and then Six. He and Mark were well acquainted, for the most part friendly. Slayton was more risk averse and Mark more risk prone; it was the nature of their jobs. They were always honest to a fault during daily briefings. Slayton smelled trouble in the unscheduled visit. Six could see the concern in his eyes.

"Good to see you again," Slayton said to Six. He volleyed his glance between the two. "What op from hell have you planned to make my life miserable today?"

"What do you mean?" Six replied.

"Don't play coy with me. My mother gave birth to me *at night*, not *last night*. The constipated looks on your faces tell me you're about to pitch an idea that's certain to get me canned. What's going on?"

"You may want to sit down for this," Mark replied.

"Perhaps I should call the President and resign right now."

Mark and Six took turns explaining Vorobyev's predicament and providing a detailed account of everything the U.S. stood to gain if they got their hands on Stan's intel. He understood the motivation and agreed, even if less than thrilled. The proposed operation, on the other hand, left him dumbfounded.

"Jesus. Do you believe, in your gut, we can get away with this?"

Mark shrugged. "Worst case—you get stopped and show them your credentials. You have diplomatic immunity so they can't arrest or detain you."

"But there's only one way they stop you. If they take the bait, we've got them by the balls."

"This all sounds too tidy for the Russians. If they find out what we're doing, it will set off a contest that'll leave a trail of piss from Moscow to D.C. It's always tit-for-tat with these guys. You, of all people, are well aware of that consequential fact," Slayton said to Mark, who rubbed his chin and grimaced.

"I've considered the possibility," Mark began, "but there isn't a country in the European Union not looking for Putin's head on a platter over the Ukraine," Mark continued. "What goodwill we lose with the Russians, we'll gain with our allies. Besides, they stand to lose as much as we do by escalating tensions. Whatever actions they take against the Station here, the FBI will serve right back to their residencies in the U.S. and our allies will follow. We have far more to gain than lose."

"So, why me?"

Six handed him a doctored photograph of Stanislav Vorobyev. He stared in stunned silence. "Wow."

"My thoughts as well," Six said. "What do you say?"

He walked to the window and stared out as if the right answer would fall from the sky. Six had always wondered whether he had any backbone.

"Let me talk to the President," Slayton said. "If he gives me the go ahead, I'm in."

Six and Mark smiled, shook his hand, stewing in disappointment as they walked to the door. Stall tactic if Six had ever seen one before. In politics, a slow no was equal to or greater than a fast one, just took longer to deliver and was buried in more bullshit. His hopes for Slayton were dashed.

"On second thought," Slayton said as they prepared to exit. "How often does a guy in my position get to help with something like this? I'll clear it with the President."

Chapter 37

J.J. and Tony stepped off the elevator, headed to the interview room and prepared once again to speak to Zory. She'd Googled the meaning of Zory's tattoo and realized she needed to devise a new strategy to question him about the documents. The tattoo of the crucifix at the neck meant he was true to the thieves' code. La Cosa Nostra called it omerta. He'd never admit to any information directly incriminating his colleagues. He'd never come straight out and tell her the truth. But she could depend on him to lie like a Persian rug. Armed with her strategy, she decided to use his lies to her advantage.

"Tony, I'm going to try something a little different during questioning. You may start to believe I've lost my mind, but please trust me."

"And this would be different from every other interview, how?"

J.J. smiled. "You got everything in the file?"

He held it up. "Just as you asked."

"Great, let's get to it."

When she entered the room, he appeared more relaxed than before but still on edge. His droopy eyes and the tenseness in his brow signaled he was both exhausted and apprehensive.

"Zory, I empathize with the fact that you must be pretty worn out, but I wanted to thank you for the lead. We found the documents. Account numbers for the various deposits. They don't use these accounts to launder money, right?"

J.J.'s question ran contrary to every class she took in Quantico on interviewing. Every question was leading…and in the opposite direction of where she really needed his answers to go. But with her ability, they would lead her to the truth.

Zory peered at her with a curious expression, surprised her questions had all but let him off the hook. He replied by shaking his head no.

"I need you to speak your responses, please," J.J. said. A nod wouldn't provoke a physical response.

"No," he said, his words shaky and timid. "Those aren't the money laundering accounts."

His response registered as a lie, a strong lie, but she'd braced herself anticipating it would.

"The letters next to each of the account numbers, do they represent the initials of Troika's leadership?"

"No," he said. "They do not. I mean…nobody ever told me what they stand for."

An itch again pulsed through her hand, and she clasped them together until the feeling dissipated. "Why don't I believe you?"

Now, knowing without question that the account numbers were indeed assigned to specific members of Troika, she found it interesting not a single one was noted with the letter "Z." This confirmed what she'd suspected since her first discussion with Zory—he was a cut-out. They'd used him as a scapegoat, a fall guy, and he'd played his part well.

"Based on all of the M's listed, my guess is Mashkov himself monitors these accounts?"

"As he is the president of a company, I imagine he'd control the money for his own business. Makes sense, wouldn't you say?"

Again, he sparked a reaction as the sensation moved through her. His response meant that Mashkov wasn't in control, at least not of every account. And if he wasn't, then who? Zory appeared strained to his limits, but she decided to attempt one more question on the topic. Max Novikov and Matvey Trifonov—one of them was the money man. Since Max ran the narcotics end, she went out on a limb and guessed Matvey was the real accountant, the reason why they'd written the letter "M" next to so many of the account numbers. That it was Matvey, not Zory, who had access to the records which could confirm Troika's funding of the illegals network. And finding the source of the funding meant they could end the case and take the network down.

"As I sift through the profiles we've developed regarding Troika's leadership, seems to me Matvey Trifonov is a nobody in the organization. No ties to the money or any critical activity, right?"

Zory nodded, "Yes. You are correct. Matvey has no connection to the money at all. He is as you say, a nobody." After he forced the words out, his eyes shifted in nervous twitches.

A crotch itch almost sent her crumbling into the floor. She experienced those when subjects told the worst lies. The excruciating sensation meant Zory had, without intent, identified the money man. They still had no way to get to him but at least now she knew who the hell he was.

J.J. drew in a long hard breath and leaned back in her seat. "This is the best you can do?" she asked, feigning disappointment at his answers that, to the unknowing, would sound as if he told her squat.

"I'm afraid so."

"Well, I won't accept this. You've told me nothing," J.J. said. "If you want my assistance then I'm giving one final chance to help me. I need to know if Troika's leadership has nicknames? Tell me this information, and I might lend you my support."

His contorted expression revealed his confusion. "Okay," he said, uncertainty coloring the tone in his voice. "Uhhh...I only know two. Levi Mashkov is called The Duke....and Matvey Trifonov—the Sparrow."

J.J. contained her excitement inside. There it was, confirmation she'd found The Sparrow. "I suppose we're done here, Tony. Let's go."

As they closed the door behind them, he asked, "Why'd you leave? And what's with all the leading questions? I could've Googled more information than he shared."

Now J.J.'s eyes were shifting as she searched for a lie of her own. "Are you kidding me? I asked you to trust me. He told us everything. Didn't you notice his expression when I asked whether Trifonov was a nobody? Matvey is our guy. He's the real accountant, not Zory. I'm certain of it."

Tony sucked in a deep breath and stuck his thumb in his belt. "Let's say you're right. We still don't have any way inside. If we could access their system records, accounting reports, some piece of evidence establishing a direct link between Troika and the illegals, we could make an arrest. With you interrogating, we might roll everyone up."

"Yeah, but—"she began when Tony's phone rang.

He glanced at the screen and batted his hand toward J.J. to get her attention. "For chrissakes. It's Misha."

"Hmph. He didn't lose the number," she said. "See what he wants."

Tony hit the button and placed the phone to his ear.

"Uh - huh."

Tony nodded his head.

"Pavlov Mashkov? In the U.S.?" Tony repeated so J.J. could hear. He couldn't suppress the concern in his eyes; they reflected the fear swelling in her belly.

Tony nodded again without speaking, leaving J.J. anxious to know what was next.

He shook his fist in the air, mouthed the word *Yes* and then whispered to J.J., "His cousin thinks he knows a way we can get into Troika. The cleaning service. They come in twice a week after hours."

She nodded.

"What days?" Tony asked, returning his attention to Misha.

He walked to a nearby desk and took down a note. "You just earned yourself a bonus."

After another pause he said, "We will."

J.J. glimpsed the smile emerging on Tony's face as she stood on the edge of anticipation waiting for him to spill the news. "Well?"

Tony looked at J.J. as she almost jumped out of her skin waiting on him to speak. "You heard about Pavlov Mashkov. He's flying into the U.S. Got to be using a fake passport. Turns out he's the one who accepted the contract to kill you."

A chill spiked through her. She, like few others, understood what Mashkov was capable of, given the brutal way he'd massacred her sources and carved them up for cooperating with American intelligence. For the first time, she was afraid. Didn't want her father receiving body parts in the mail. But she would not be deterred, either.

"Yeah, I caught that. What's the reason for the smile?"

"An all-female West Indian janitorial service cleans Troika's offices. Twice a week."

J.J.'s posture straightened. "Then that settles it. I'm going in."

Tony's anger bubbled to an instant boil. "Are you out of your fucking mind?" His face turned instant crimson, and his head nearly spun off into the ether. "These people want to kill you if you hadn't heard. And you think I'm gonna let you go undercover in their headquarters?"

"First of all…*let me?*" J.J. said, blinking her eyes. "Second of all, if you think about it, Troika is the last place they'll expect me to be. It's our only chance to get the intel. I'm going in, and that's the end of this discussion. Are you with me?"

Chapter 38

Wednesday Morning — Washington, D.C.

At Six's request, Hopper called Dr. Badal to set up an interview to discuss the medical services he provided Mosin before he defected to Russia. The appointment was scheduled for TWO P.M. Hopper's Spidey senses tingled because Badal's voice sounded tenuous; the call from an FBI agent shook him to the core. However, also in his voice was an undertone of expectation, as if Badal been waiting for Hopper's call, as if Hopper's voice had brought to life every nightmare he'd ever conceived. Hopper could hear the doom in Dr. Badal's voice when he agreed to the meeting, which is the precise reason Hopper went beyond the bounds of due diligence to prepare for the all-important interview. He conducted a full background check and called the doctor's nurse to verify his schedule before he ever picked up the phone to make the initial call.

That's how Hopper knew the true reason Dr. Badal had scheduled the meeting for TWO P.M. He'd months ago planned to be unavailable at that time…which is the exact reason he arrived at the NIH campus two hours early.

After parking his car, Hopper stepped his foot onto the frosted asphalt, and took in the expansive NIH campus; it was dense with low and high-rise research buildings over an area the size of one-hundred sixty football fields. The blue glass and cinnamon brick high-rise where Dr. Badal worked contrasted starkly against the stout white Neuroscience Research Center adjacent to it.

Hopper had neither the time nor energy to chase him down. So, instead of taking the elevator up to the doctor's suite, he rode down to the garage and paced the lot, scanning the license plates until he spotted the correct sequence. He found it on a late-model S-Class sandwiched between a Range Rover and Prius, barely enough room to open the doors on either side. He glanced over his shoulders to ensure no one was watching and retrieved the Slim Jim from his pocket, popped the lock, and disconnected the fuse to stop the alarm. Then he hunkered down in the back seat and waited for Dr. Badal to arrive. Hopper's Bureau uniform, a black suit beneath a navy all-weather coat would cloak him well.

While trying to conceal the light from his cell phone in the back seat, the locks opened—this time it was Dr. Badal—and the door handle clicked. Hopper could see Badal remove his top hat, toss it onto the passenger seat; he peered into the rearview mirror after sitting down and shut the door.

Hopper raised his FBI badge, and Dr. Badal noticed the gold glimmering in his periphery. He jerked his head around with a startled yelp.

"Imagine meeting you here," Hopper said, sitting upright. "You planning to skip out on our appointment?"

Dr. Badal's breath grew heavy as he scrambled to get out. He couldn't run forward—a wall blocked his getaway. The only way out was to pass by the back driver-side door where Hopper sat or jump over the hood. The podgy man didn't strike Hopper as an over-the-hood kind of guy.

When he stumbled out of the car trying to scamper away, Hopper slammed open the back door, and Dr. Badal's body bounced against it, forcing him backward.

"Ooooph!" he belted out, struggling to steady himself on his feet.

"Ouch," Hopper said. "Looked like that hurt, Dr. Badal. Much like my feelings. This is no way to treat a guest."

"What do you want?"

"The truth."

"I'm just a researcher. I don't know anything about anything."

Hopper chuckled. "All evidence to the contrary. I haven't asked you a single question. If you didn't know anything about the questions *I haven't asked,* you wouldn't bother to run. Now, you can continue to obstruct my investigation and lie to a Federal agent," Hopper said, using the buzzwords that spelled hefty charges. "Or we can sit down and have an honest discussion so you can get back to work. Which is it?"

Dr. Badal refused, shaking his head no. "I…I can't."

"Sorry to hear that. Care to offer a reason, just so I'll know what to say to Immigration when we discuss your visa…which, if I recall, is up for renewal?" Hopper glanced down at the date on his watch. "Next month, too! Man, you better tie up the loose ends on that research."

He stood motionless with his mouth gaping open, perhaps evaluating his options before he realized the truth of the moment—he had none. "Okay, okay. Just give me time to catch my breath, all right? I'll answer all of your questions. Just don't…not the visa. My family needs me. This job is our livelihood."

"Then let's get started. You know why I'm here."

•••

Dr. Badal appeared relieved to bare his soul and relieve his conscience. Hopper believed every word even though Mosin's extortion had reached a new level of low. He was as desperate as Dr. Badal.

Hopper offered a sheepish nod and ended the meeting on a handshake. Once he returned to his car, he scrolled through his cell phone until he came to her number. It rang.

"J.J., this is Hopper," he said after the beep. "Spoke to Dr. Badal today. Just make sure you're sitting down when you call. I've got some critical information for Six."

Chapter 39

Wednesday Morning — New York City

Santino walked out of Max Novikov's meeting with his life, a half million dollars for the family, and a name—Pavlov Mashkov. His next priority was eighty-sixing that son of a bitch as insurance that Pavlov would never threaten his family again. But to handle Step Two, he needed to accomplish Step One—collect thirty pieces of silver from Judas.

Uncle Sal had bought Santino and Knuckles a thirty-minute window. It'd take the guy at least a half hour to get over to Queens and back. By then they'd be gone. Good thing, too. Breaking into the house of a made guy was enough to get them both whacked.

"So, explain this to me again," Knuckles said to Santino as he shut off the headlights and slowed his speed to a crawl in the alleyway. "We just got half a million dollars from the Russians and you wanna boost a TV from some schmuck's house? I don't get it. Did Nicky give you the go-ahead on this?"

"You don't worry about who authorized it. Just stand watch and back me up. Trust me, this'll be worth your trouble, but don't ask questions you don't want the answer to."

The house, a vinyl-sided duplex that had been converted to a single family home, was familiar to Santino, but Knuckles had no idea what Santino had gotten him into. It was better that way. Santino knew the ins and outs well. The mobbed-up owner lived in a different house over in Dyker Heights from day to day. He used this place as a stash house when he received money from his dealers and packages from his drug runners. Sometimes as a place to bone his goomar…all of them. Didn't need an alarm or any type of security system. The neighborhood was borderline incestuous the way everyone was family, blood-related, or surrogate. Second, third, fourth, fifth… tenth cousins. Everybody was a cousin. So, anyone with half a brain had a clue about who lived there, and no one from outside the neighborhood could get close enough to break in. If a stranger dared to drive in the area, a gossip mill hotter than the TMZ hotline would alert every made guy in a five block radius…which was everyone. Between the barrage of foul-mouthed insults and the gun play, they'd never come back again.

In Santino's favor, he was a friend of sorts, not foe; his presence would not be news, and he knew the general layout. The guy kept the goods in similar locations in every stash house he owned. His only problem was getting in and out without drawing unwanted attention.

Cloaked in black from head-to-toe, from skull caps to sneakers and thick gloves, Santino jiggered the lock for what felt like forever before they made their way inside. He'd gotten slow in his old age. Ten years ago he could break inside in less than a minute. He considered sharpening up his skills but after he succeeded in his challenge, he might never have to return to his thievery roots again.

Once inside, he slipped a Maglite out of his pocket and held it low to his body, snaking through the almost bare living room. A few metal folding chairs, a card table, and a full mattress on the floor covered in dirty sheets served as the furnishings. Curtains covered every window, so the black of the darkness was pitch.

"You sure we got the right house?" Knuckles asked. "There can't be anything valuable in this old dump."

"On the contrary," Santino said. "Our future is in this house and we have less than thirty minutes to find it before we've gotta get outta here."

Knuckles cut his eyes at him and give him the side-eye. "Might help if you told me what we were looking for."

"A package," Santino lied. "You'll recognize it when you see it. Take a quick look around. If you don't see anything, stand lookout. I'll check around upstairs. And for godssakes don't yell, no matter what happens," he said in loud whispers.

Santino ascended the stairs and barreled in and out of each room, three bedrooms and one bath. His heart pounded in his ears, his breath heavy; his stomach curled with the surrounding smell of old socks, year-old garlic, and the pungent scent of cooked meth. Santino guessed that they used the room with the powder-coated tables to cut the cocaine before they distributed it.

The bathroom was disgusting. More brown than white. Rusted water flowing in the commode. A sheet of paper with an address lay next to the sink. He lifted it and panicked. It had a Queens address written on it.

"Fuuuuuuuuuuuck!" he yelled in a louder voice than he'd intended.

He returned it to its place, but not in its exact position, a mistake he feared he'd pay for soon. His eyes flitted around as he calculated his next step. If he was right, they needed to leave in a matter of minutes. He'd already made one pass through the rooms and found nothing even though he knew something was there. He had to check again. There was no other option. If he walked out empty handed, he, his cousin, and uncle were dead men walking.

He retraced his steps, examining the most minute of details from ceiling to floor to make certain he hadn't overlooked anything critical. By the time he reached the last bedroom, the one adjacent to the staircase, he'd almost given up hope. The sound of Knuckles' footsteps faded in louder, closer. Maybe he hadn't found anything either.

Santino opened the door and re-entered the last bedroom, shining the flashlight over every inch. The space was stone empty. He glanced down at his watch. He'd be out of time soon.

He opened the closet door and examined the walls. He found it odd they were paneled with laminate wood. Unusual feature in any house. Every closet he'd seen had been enclosed with drywall. At that moment, he realized—the choice was no accident.

Santino pressed the panes from top to bottom until one gave way. He squeezed his fingers behind the gap and gently pulled until a secret compartment was revealed.

The mother lode.

Piles of drugs, paraphernalia, a case of dime bags, a few stacks of cash, maybe a hundred large, a familiar briefcase—and a pile of handguns. He palmed the case handles and lifted them from the floor to ensure the weight reflected what he knew the contents to be, as opposed to empty. Then he slipped his hands into a pair of leather gloves, inspected the guns, ensuring he'd set the safeties. He pulled a plastic bag from his oversized jacket pocket and dropped a Sig inside. He grabbed a stack of cash before backing out of the closet and stepping out to return the panels to their original positions.

The briefcases could stay…for now.

Just as he stepped toward the door, Knuckles ran up to him panting like crazy. "I didn't find anything but somebody's coming."

Santino snatched Knuckles inside and whipped the door to a whisper-soft shut. He considered hiding behind the panel but noise echoed in the empty house, and the level of knocking around it would take to get inside might potentially spark a confrontation that would've landed him in the hot seat with more than just the owner. He held the flashlight to his face and pressed his index finger against his lips, warning Knuckles not to speak or budge.

Knuckles shot a quick look inside the compartment; his eyes bulged. Santino shut off the light.

Seconds later, footsteps, at least two sets, tapped toward the staircase. He could hear them getting closer, and his pulse made a loud pounding in his ear. Santino reached in his pocket and gripped the gun. The plastic was loose enough to allow him to fire a shot, if necessary. He prayed the situation would never come to that. A muffled crumple of the plastic was followed by the sound of a man's voice, the garbled rasp familiar to Santino. In a stroke of bad fortune, Knuckles would recognize it and no doubt begin shitting his pants. Santino had some explaining to do… if they made it out alive.

"I think I left the address in the bathroom when I was taking a leak. Gimme one sec," the man said in his indiscernible mutter.

The footsteps faded away, and the house went silent for a few moments that felt like a lifetime. Seconds later, the footsteps scurried again.

"Hey, Monty. Did you use the John up here? I found the address on the floor. Coulda swore I left it on the sink. Fuckin' Feds. Bet they've been wiring up the place. I want to do a sweep just in case."

Santino's eyes darted although he couldn't see anything but the floaters in his own vision from his eyes searching for light. His every sense heightened. He heard the shuffle of shoes against the hardwood floors. He smelled the musty scent of old dog and cigarettes in the air. Adrenaline ran his pulse high and temperature hot. Sweat began to seep from his between the cracks of his fingers.

"C'mon, you fuckin' kidding me? What do I look like, NSA? We gotta get Richie Rich or Gino to do it, but let's take care of this thing for Sal first."

"Just answer my fuckin' question. Did you move the paper?" he said, walking into the bedroom.

The man let out a hard sigh. "Yeah, I think so. Don't remember. It was sittin' there. I mighta moved it to wash my hands."

There was a long pause. "Quit lyin'. You don't wash your hands, you nasty bastard."

"Fuck you, I'm a nasty bastard. Can we finish the inquisition later and get outta here? We've got an appointment, and we're already late."

He moved forward a few steps and stopped. "I thought I closed this door too. I'm tellin' ya. Somebody's been in here."

Santino's heart collapsed in a colossal thump.

"How would you know? Ain't nothing in there. What? You can see the air now? Come on for chrissakes."

His feet tapped closer to the closet. The doorknob wiggled. Santino swallowed so hard he thought the sound was audible. He wanted to release the safety, ensure he could get off a shot if he needed to. But he stood paralyzed. Couldn't make a sound or the jig was up.

"Let's go, Nicky. We need to get outta here. With everything you're tryin' to do, you can't afford to piss off Sal, and we're already fifteen minutes too late for that."

A cellphone rang. Seconds later someone whispered, "Shit, it's Sal."

He paused again…and the doorknob stopped wiggling.

Santino held the breath he wanted to exhale.

"Yeah, let's get outta here. The Feds can wait. We gotta keep the boss happy…*for now*. Thanks to those useless Russian fucks our plan is gonna take a little longer than I thought."

Santino could feel his fingertips roll into his palm. He wanted to beat the Italian outta that asswipe, but he forced himself still. The door closed, and the sound of the car engine disappeared into the distance.

Knuckles' hand bumped against the door as he felt for the knob; he twisted it open while Santino flipped on the flashlight.

"Are you fucking out of you mind? You must be. This is Nicky Mumble's place. You tryin' to get us clipped?"

Santino reached into his pocket and handed Monty a wad of cash. "As a matter of fact, I'm tryin' to keep us alive. I'll explain later."

Knuckles fanned the cash and looked askance at Santino. "Why are we leaving all of that stuff?"

Santino patted his jacket pocket; the guns were secure. "Fughetabou-dit. We'll be back for it at a later date. I got the most important thing right here."

Knuckles shook his head as they made their way to the back door. "Nicky's tight on a dime; he's gonna notice it missing…and he's gonna hunt down whoever took it."

Santino chuckled. "I'm counting on it."

Chapter 40

Wednesday Afternoon — New York City

Tony seethed in a cloud of repressed fury as J.J. pitched her idea to infiltrate Troika. She agreed the operation required significant risk but the clock was winding down, and the time to debate had passed. She empathized with Tony but, in her view, he sounded like a whole lot of pot calling the kettle black.

"I'm in," J.J. said, looking around the table. While Manny and Scott and even Gia were cooperative, Tony, on the other hand, buttoned his lips tight and refused to offer a word in assistance. He remained adamant in his opposition to J.J.'s plan even though it was clear she was the only one within the team who could pull it off. The cleaning company, as they found out, was owned by a Jamaican and staffed by black West Indians, brown-skinned like she. Abigail Moncriefe had served as the most trusted nanny of Max Novikov's New York, white-bred socialite wife. Scott did some checking with his contact at Immigration and found out her status to compel her to cooperate. Turned out they didn't have to twist her arm too much. She hated the husband, who was abusive to his wife. Although she refused to participate in the op, she offered assistance and a plan to get J.J. inside. To get out, J.J. was on her own.

"I expended a lot of capital getting us in, so we better make sure this op pays dividends," Scott said.

"I agree," said J.J., anxious but ready to go. It'd been years since she'd gone undercover. The prospect gave her a rush better than any drug. "So, how are we going to play this? Based on what Misha said, once I get past security it should be a piece of cake. His cousin says the offices are always empty at night by the time the cleaning crew arrives. All I need to do is go in, copy the hard drives and files, and get out."

"You gotta get out clean or else run the risk of getting Abigail and her entire crew killed."

Manny handed her a high-capacity flash drive. "When you get inside the office, you stick this inside any USB slot and it'll clone the drive. Press this red button, the light will flash. That's how you confirm it's running. Once the cloning is complete, the light will shut off, and an audible beep will sound. Remove the drive and hit the next office until you get them all."

"Okay," J.J. said, walking through the process in her mind, visualizing helped her commit the steps to memory. "Misha's cousin said the shift lasts two hours, give or take thirty minutes. Should give me plenty of time to get in and out."

"Do we have a TAC team standing by…in case anything goes wrong?" Tony asked.

"Yeah," Manny said. "We've got them for two hours before they have to cover another operation. So, we don't have a second to waste."

After brooding in his feelings, Tony spoke up. "I foresee some problems here. J.J. may look Jamaican, but she sure as hell doesn't sound Jamaican … and in case you all didn't get the message, there's a brand new two million dollar bounty on her head. They know what she looks like. What if someone recognizes her?"

"Tony, trying to convince me not to do this pointless, okay? If I pull this off, do you understand what that means? The people responsible for Jim Cartwright's death, your brother's shooting…hell even this contract on my head—they will all pay.

"This network allows sleazy traitors to thrive. We take it down, and we can flush out the rest of the treasonous bastards and lock them up where they can spend the rest of their lives wishing they'd picked our side. Isn't that what we came here to do?"

"But the contract…"

"Tony, I'm going in wired. We've got a TAC team standing by a couple hundred feet away. If anything goes down, I'm covered."

"What if we're too late?"

"You won't be," J.J. said, barely getting the words out before Tony stormed out of the room and into the nearby stairwell. J.J. excused herself and followed closely on his heels. "Tony, Stop!" she said. "What the hell's with all this drama? We're FBI agents. This is our job."

"You're not doing this. I forbid it. And if you go through with it, you're making a choice—and your choice isn't me, it isn't our future, it isn't our life together or our future family—it's your job!"

J.J.'s eyes welled with tears too fast for her to stop them. She shook her head in disbelief stunned by the overdose of testosterone that took over her boyfriend. "I don't believe what I'm hearing. I would never ask you to make that choice."

"Yeah? Well, you wouldn't have to."

"Really? I wouldn't have to?" She twisted her neck ghetto style and waved her finger. "You're full of shit. Look around you, you hypocrite. Look at where we're standing…in New York City. You brought your ass here with a contract on your head, if my memory serves me correctly. Do you think I wanted you to come here? Don't you think I didn't want you to stay in D.C.?

"But, I pushed aside my fear and selfish desires and embraced my place in this relationship. Which, by the way, is *not* barefoot in a fucking kitchen knee-deep in red sauce or in bed with my ankles above my head. It's at your side when you want me and right behind your back if you need me."

"But—"

"No! You knew exactly who I was when we got involved. If my courage is too much for you to handle, if you don't want to have my back? Fine! You can take your place right next to Six—*in my past.* Now, I have an op to conduct."

She stormed away with tears washing down her cheeks, hoping Tony would come to his senses. When only silence filled the space behind her, she remembered a Nietzsche quote she'd heard a long time ago during another low point in her life.

In reality, hope is the worst of all evils because it prolongs man's torments.

Chapter 41

Hopper's request couldn't be more impossible. Aleksey Dmitriyev wondered how in hell he would convince the Resident to send the SIGINT officer to check the Situation Room listening device on the FBI's schedule. The op was almost out of his purview with the exception of the one time Komarov asked him to run countersurveillance. Any attempt to influence or interfere with the monitoring would be viewed with strong and immediate suspicion, especially with Filthchenko lurking around, breathing down his neck, and scrutinizing Aleksey's every move as if his life depended on it. This was one occasion Aleksey feared he couldn't deliver for J.J. but he would try to think of a way.

As he entered into his office, a voice called out from behind. "Aleksey Yegorovich, come to my office now," Komarov ordered. "It's urgent."

Aleksey rolled his eyes wondering what had gone wrong. Nothing was ever *urgent* if it had gone well. And Komarov had called him by his first and patronymic names which meant either Aleksey was already in trouble or soon to be. He stepped into Komarov's office as the resident gestured for him to close the door behind him.

Komarov squirmed in his seat, bit his lip, and his chin dipped to his chest.

"This cant' be good," Dmitriyev said. "I haven't seen you antsy since Golikov sent those two peons to watch over us like the bumbling snitches they are."

Komarov pulled back in his seat and kicked his feet up on the desk. "You mistake me, my friend. My discomfort comes not from what has happened to me, rather from what I must ask of you…again."

Aleksey braced himself. His gut told him why Komarov had called him into his office and what he'd be asked to do. The only question in his mind was why.

"As you know, Operation RAPTURE has been a key source of valuable intelligence for years. We've increased our monitoring schedule from weekly to daily, so we may stay well informed during this period before the stand-down."

"So, what's the problem?" Dmitriyev asked.

"The quality of the intelligence. We are certain the device is still in place and operating as normal. But the quality of the intelligence—it's diminishing. Not in an obvious way. The difference is subtle enough to be missed by someone less experienced. I want to find out why."

Dmitriyev's stomach plummeted. He was supposed to bring the problem to Komarov's attention before he figured it out on his own; he was too late. And probably now under suspicion. "What can I do? Do you want me to review the intelligence to determine its veracity?"

"No," Komarov said with a grimace. "I must once again order you to risk your cover. Run countersurveillance for Gusin. Look for any signs that the FBI compromised the operation. No other officer in the residency has the necessary experience or capability. And I cannot depend on that sorry excuse for a counterintelligence officer, Filchenko."

"You gave me your word," Aleksey said. "This could jeopardize my entire career. If I'm expelled, I'll never work overseas again."

"We don't believe the FBI compromised the operation. And the likelihood that you'll be caught is practically non-existent. But I'll warn you about what lies ahead. If we don't find a problem outside the residency, I must begin my search *inside*."

"So, the witch hunt begins."

"Let's call it a precautionary measure, ordered by a wise man who's worked in this business for too many years. Okay?"

Aleksey clenched his jaw and stiffened his posture. "This is an order, correct?"

"Complete this mission and I'll submit you for a commendation."

Aleksey grunted and stomped off without speaking.

He looked at his watch and calculated Moscow time. The President would be in the Sit Room by EIGHT A.M. delivering the report.

The Moscow operation would take place at FOUR P.M. Eastern time. Midnight in Moscow.

The timing couldn't be better…or worse.

Chapter 42

Wednesday Evening — New York City

New York nights were a different kind of cold from those in D.C. Maybe it was the proximity to the northern waters, but the chill set into her bones and locked her joints stiff, aging her thirty years in two minutes. J.J. hustled inside the service entrance at Troika past a half-drunken guard watching the door to the housekeeping storage area.

Rather than go undercover inside the cleaning company, they decided to keep the company's owner and Abigail out of harm's way. Eventually, the Russians would learn J.J. was an FBI agent posing as cleaning staff; she didn't want the company associated with her. So, she'd go in alone and claim she'd finished her previous job ahead of schedule and arrived before the rest of the crew. Abigail would have plausible deniability—the Russians had worked against the FBI long enough to recognize such a tactic was well within its bag of tricks.

But Abigail did offer a few words of advice. "Yuh listen to mi," she said, her accent as thick as buttermilk. "Windows, furniture, vacuum. Inna dat orda. They will step out when ah time to vacuum and yuh will 'ave a few minutes alone. Kip yuh eyes down. Don' speak. Do yuh job an' git de hell outta deh. De Novikov's don' leave nuh witnesses. Yuh understand?"

J.J. secured a gun into her ankle holster, just in case, fastened the ties on her smock, and tightened her wavy Chaka Khan wig on her head. Her stomach twisted in knots as she took the elevator up to the third floor of the four-level building; it was the location of Troika Technologies' executive suites. She patted her pockets to check for the flash drive. It was in place and ready to go.

When she pushed the cart into the lobby area, she was surprised the entire office area was so brightly lit, especially for a building Misha had told Tony would be empty. She suddenly wondered whether she'd chosen the wrong time to trust him. Something inside told her to reverse course, but she pressed on. The cleaning crew had done its job in keeping the spaces pristine. Not a speck of dust to be found on the contemporary office décor framed by bright walls, smoke-colored tinted glass and stainless steel. A smattering of beech wood shelves accented the furnishings. It wasn't as ornate as she expected except in the darkish marble tiles gilded with gold flecks.

As she jostled the cart through the glass doors and into the reception area, she was startled by the low rumble of Russian-accented basses and tenors emanating from the rear offices. The executives were still at work and the plan to clone the hard drives had gone to shit.

With her head down, she skipped cleaning the lobby and headed straight for the offices. She peered down the hall and spotted every door open. J.J. pushed the cart down to the first doorway. If anyone recognized her, she was dead on sight. A vision of some Andre the Giant looking guy dragging her to the garage in a headlock, throwing her to her knees, and firing a bullet into the back of her head stopped her heart. For a moment, the whisper of a second, she wished she'd listened to Tony. More than that, she wanted him to have her back the way she had his. A sense of loneliness overcame her, but she settled down and proceeded with the plan.

She entered the first office. It belonged Leonid Tenenbaum, Mr. Clean, the legit face of the company. They'd embossed his name on a gold nameplate outside the door, color coordinated with the flecks in the floors. She recognized his hardened mug from his surveillance photo. He had a grill that looked as if he ate steel with his teeth. She walked inside the expansive office, chin to chest, and swiped the duster across the furniture, keeping her distance as far as possible.

"They always start with the windows," he said, with a slight bark in his voice.

"Ahhh, yes," she said, drawing from her love of Bob Marley to produce some semblance of a Jamerican accent. Not perfect, but enough to be convincing and keep her alive. "Tanks," she said.

"You new?"

"Ah, mi first time here," she said, wiping the windows, leaving streaks. "De rest of de crew is runnin' behind."

"Fine," he grumbled. "Make sure you vacuum under the desk. Dropped my lunch on the floor today," he ordered before walking out.

J.J. quivered as she fumbled to remove the flash drive from her pocket. Just as she wrapped her fingers around it. He exploded back into the door. Her heart sank.

"Forgot my bathroom key," he said as he grabbed it from the drawer and paced out as if his bladder was about to burst.

She let out a long breath and shoved the flash drive in the CPU resting on the lower desk shelf. She pressed the button and continued dusting. Shifted her head back and forth as she waited for the light to turn on. Nothing. She waited a little longer. Still nothing. She pressed the button again. And again. Then glanced down at her watch. One more minute and she'd pull it. The light still hadn't come on. No sooner than the thought flitted through her mind, the door burst open again.

Leonid returned too soon.

If he sat down and noticed the flash drive, she was toast.

"You finished yet?"

She shook her head no, struggling to think of any excuse. As he stepped toward the desk, she looked at her savior and grabbed the vacuum. "Just one moment. I hafti run di vacuum cleaner unda di desk."

He stopped in his tracks and backed up.

She glanced down. The light sputtered and then disappeared again. Nothing. The fucking flash drive was a bust. Manny would die if she made it out alive.

J.J. found a plug for the vacuum cleaner, shoved it in, and turned it on. As she glared at him from outside the door, she raised her hand, gesturing with her index finger that she'd be one minute. When she closed the door to vacuum behind it, she yanked the empty drive and stuffed it into her smock pocket. The entire op had gone to shit, and now she needed to get out before she got killed.

She pushed the vacuum cleaner across the floor in rapid sweeps. Good thing she did.

"Okay, okay. I have business to do."

"Sorry, sir. 'ave a good evenin'."

She collected her equipment, exited out the door, and returned the vacuum cleaner to its spot. Then she turned to make her escape as fast as she arrived. Before she took a step, a voice called from behind her. "Hey, cleaning lady! I need you here. Now."

She cursed her misfortune, spun around, and followed the man into the office, pulling her cart in tow. It was Matvey Trifonov. He was a skinny, nervous looking man, with thick gray and black hair and had grown a thin mustache since his surveillance photo. He grabbed the phone, which was off the hook, and returned to his desk when J.J. appeared in the doorway.

"Mi dehyah to clean."

"Come in!" He waved her inside and spoke in an urgent hush. "Close the door behind you."

She paced to the windows and started to clean, listening to his whispers as she wiped the glass to a shine.

"He's here," he said. "And you damn well better bet he didn't come all this way to watch them light the tree at Rockefeller Center. You heard what they did to Zory, didn't you? If they could do that to him, who am I?"

J.J. pretended to clean as she leaned in close to listen.

"No, that Rakov son of a bitch is impulsive. Going off half-cocked because some bitch made him feel like the idiot he is. Max is pissed, but he'd never order that, he'd never support a contract. It's bad for business. He's all business."

Rakov—he was the narcotics courier who J.J. spat on after he fired the N-word. He's the one who wanted her dead. He must've been very convincing when he went crying to the Mashkovs.

Wimp.

J.J.'s eyes met his as he glanced at her. "I can't leave right now. But I have copies of everything. I'm going to send a courier. You put them into the safe deposit box. If anything happens, you follow the plan. I'll call you later with the details."

He paused again and she grabbed the vacuum cleaner handle, waiting for him to end his conversation. He scribbled a note on a pad and told her to plug the vacuum cleaner in the wall. When the motor droned, he leaned forward and whispered in her ear. "Please. I need you to make a delivery for me," he said, holding up the flash drive in his hand. "I'll pay you."

He reached into his pocket and counted out twenty hundred-dollar bills. She shook her head no, filling her expression with fear.

He counted out five-hundred dollars more. She still refused. He made one final offer, counting out ten more. She grabbed the money from his hand and tucked it inside her bra along with his flash drive. "All you need to do is deliver it to this address the second you leave here," he said, holding a slip of paper with a Brooklyn address. "And leave here as soon as you can."

"Okay, okay," she whispered. "I'll do it."

He nodded his head before she let herself out. Her mind was frenzied. The moment was surreal. Had what happened, in fact, happened? Had he handed the computer records to her on a silver platter? She promised to go to mass on Sunday and light a candle for a prayer answered. She snapped out of her thoughts and collected her equipment.

The second she pushed the vacuum into the hall, she bumped into an enormous mass of fat and muscle. Even at her 5-feet 10-inches, the man stood so tall she could practically press her nose into his belt buckle standing straight up. She couldn't see past him to the left or right.

She apologized, stepped back, and caught a glimpse of his face— Pavlov Mashkov. Golikov's henchman, flesh and evil, blocking her view. The man who had executed her sources, killed them like animals, and mailed their body parts to the American Embassy. The man who'd ordered Dante's shooting and who'd accepted the contract to carry out her own murder.

A wickedness emanated from his narrowed eyes and dark manner.

His gaze locked onto her face and hovered; he studied her like a scientist would a specimen, a moment too long for her comfort. The bad wig was her only cover.

"Who are you?" he barked in a deep hollow mutter.

She imagined snatching her gun from the ankle holster and unloading every round in his fat skull. Instead, she said, "Me done cleanin' now." She did an about-face and started up the hallway, sucking breath and swallowing hard the entire way.

"Wait, I know you."

"Me no tink so." She continued her pace up the hallway.

J.J. couldn't run. Not fast enough. She needed a way out…and she had to get out clean.

Just as she reached the reception area, her mind flitted, trying devise an escape. Her mind turned to Abigail. The cleaning crew was on the way, and she couldn't bolt without putting them under immediate suspicion.

If J.J. disappeared, there'd be questions Abby couldn't answer. No, J.J. needed a legitimate excuse, preferably within the next thirty seconds, before he connected the dots and put a name to her face. A distraction that would not only get her out of the office, but out of the building.

Then she spotted it. A razor. Judging from the pink goo on the blade, they used it to scrape gum. She pretended to return a cleaning cloth to the caddy and held her breath.

This is going to hurt a little bit.

She sliced the blade deep into her finger.

"Ahhh!" she screamed, holding her hand. "Oh no! Cut mi finger." The slice was deep and painful. His eyes shifted from her face to her finger, the blood dripping on the pristine floors.

"Wrap it….with that!" he said, thrusting his finger toward a white cleaning cloth. "You're getting blood everywhere."

She grabbed it and pressed it against the gash in her finger, squeezing tight as blood stains seeped through. "I needa go to duh bawtroom."

"You need a doctor."

"Mi car's outside. Be fasta to drive."

"Then go," he said. "Hurry. I'll have someone take care of the cart."

The closer J.J. got to the main entrance, the more her smile widened. Her eyes searched for the team, but no one was there. The radio reception must've cut off while she was inside. She headed toward the parking lot when a voice called from behind her. A familiar voice.

"J.J.… J.J.," the man called in a low tone.

She scanned the area until her eyes fixed on a figure in the passenger seat of a sparkling black Mercedes. It was Misha. He stepped out and rushed over to her.

"Misha, what are you doing here?"

"I figured you'd be here tonight. What happened to you?" he asked, looking at the bloody cloth.

"It's nothing. Just need a couple stitches," she said, clasping her bloody finger, trying to stifle the flow.

Misha moved close to her, as if trying to whisper in her ear, and in a lightning quick move, he jammed a gun into her gut.

"Give it to me," he growled through clenched teeth. "Give it to me now or I will kill you right here."

"Misha? Have you lost your mind?"

After a second of thought, he said, "I'm a businessman. If I return their intelligence and save them from prosecution, I can get enough money to save my family and disappear forever."

J.J.'s eyes narrowed. "I always knew you were a slithery, two-faced, snake in the grass. Thanks for proving me right you son of a bitch."

Her first instinct was to fight him with everything in her and make him wish he'd never seen a gun, let alone stuck the revolver into her stomach. But she thought better of it, decided to give him exactly what he asked for. She reached into the smock pocket and handed him the flash drive contained inside. "Here!" She shoved it toward him. "Why give him a flash drive when you could get much more money for turning me over. Sounds like bad business."

"You're FBI," he said. "I'm greedy, not crazy. Now don't move." He backed away, keeping the barrel trained on her as he ran inside the building. Her cover would be blown, but it didn't matter. As long as Matvey's drive contained the files from Troika's computers, she had everything needed to take down those bastards. The only question was whether she'd make the deadline.

Moments later a Ford that looked like a stock unmarked FBI vehicle skidded around the corner and stopped in front her with the precision of a race-car driver. She bent forward and peered inside, expecting Scott or Manny. Not *him*.

Chapter 43

Wednesday Morning — New York City

Slayton McCarthy exited his diplomatic-plated Lincoln Towncar and prepared to enter the Volga Siber driven by Bart, the desk officer in the CIA station. The nervous look on Bart's face gave Slayton little comfort. He'd never been in this situation…or this part of Moscow—a wooded area near the rail yard. The location, on the outskirts of Moscow's large migrant population, was desolate and dark except for a single lamp beaming down. It flickered in sporadic fits as if about to putter out. He took a deep breath and surveyed the scene before approaching Bart, who stood outside the car.

He rubbed his hands briskly and blew his fingers. "Jeez, it's cold out here. What are we waiting for?"

"The package. It's en route. We'll be leaving any minute."

Slayton nodded and slipped into the backseat after Bart opened the door.

Seconds after he was seated, a late-model BMW sedan pulled to screeching halt. Six exchanged a few words with the driver as the trunk hatch popped up; a gentleman dressed identical to Slayton emerged and slipped into the back seat of his Towncar, offering a salute before he disappeared.

Once belted in the driver seat, Bart announced, "It's time to go. This should be over in ten or fifteen minutes. So just hold tight, sir."

Six gave the thumbs up; the op commenced. Bart started the car and pulled onto M4 Highway, Moscow's I-95, heading back to the Embassy.

"Game on," Slayton said in a vain attempt to disguise his anxiety. "Bet you guys do things like this all of the time, huh?"

Bart shook his head as he maneuvered through the Moscow traffic. "No, this is a first. We've never attempted anything of this magnitude.

There's not another Station in the world insane enough to try this in such a hostile territory, let alone pull it off."

Slayton scrunched his eyebrows and tilted his head. "Word of advice, Bart. Don't ever volunteer for a suicide hotline."

Bart chuckled. "It'll be fine, sir. As long as you've got your passport and ID. Should be over in no time. If you're caught without papers, they consider you a terrorist."

Slayton froze with a bug-eyed stare, patted his jacket and pant pocket. "Oh, shit! They're in my Towncar. I forgot them on the seat."

"What!" Bart yelled. "Tell me you're kidding."

Slayton shook his head as his stomach plummeted.

"Jesus H. Christ!" Bart continued. "Well, I have mine. Let's hope that enou— do you hear that?"

They both quieted to listen to the choir of sirens. Slayton pulled out his cellphone and tapped out a text to Six. Then he studied the rearview mirror and waited for the signal that Six had delivered the package safe and sound inside the Embassy walls. Instead, a message he never expected came through.

> The package is not inside.
> Stopped at checkpoint.
> MVD and FSB.

Slayton fell back in his seat. Bart glanced over his shoulder and noticed Slayton's sullen expression. "Oh, God. What happened?"

"The package. The Russians stopped them. FSB and MVD."

The whir of flashing lights drew closer and closer. "This is it," Bart said. "They're coming for us, too. They're onto us."

Bart slowed until they forced him to a stop. Within seconds, a sea of security service cars and Russian press surrounded them. Black paddy wagons with windows blackened on all sides obstructed the road from behind. Police cars blocked them in front. Television vans emptied of pushy reporters, photographers. Cameramen swarmed the car and pressed against the windows. The Russian's planned to make a media spectacle of the arrest.

They were trapped in every direction. The militia dressed in black paramilitary uniforms and wielding semiautomatic weapons, circled the car and aimed them so he and Bart were literally staring down the barrels.

With the camera flashing in his face, Slayton braced himself for the moments ahead.

Bart put his hands in the air and advised Slayton to do the same. But Slayton shrouded his face behind his scarf first.

"Play dumb as long as possible. We need to give Six time to get out of that jam."

A gaunt gentleman in a starch-stiff military uniform approached the driver-side window. He wore no overcoat, just a dress jacket with three stars on each shoulder. His name tag read Golikov. "Identify yourself."

"I'm Bart Russell, an American diplomat returning to the Embassy."

"And your passenger?"

"What's going on?" Bart asked. "Why are we being stopped?"

"Who is your passenger?" Golikov barked louder.

Again and again, Bart refused to answer.

The general raised his hand, snatched the back door open, and two burly men dragged Slayton out by his coat, slamming his head into the ground with cameras rolling. A couple of Golikov's minions searched the car and patted him down for identification.

He never opened his mouth. Kept his face down and out of view until he saw the polished shoes and creased pant legs of a military uniform in his periphery. The man knelt, yanked the scarf off, and glared at Slayton's face before barking in Russian. "This is not, Stanislav Ivanovich. Stop the other car. Now!"

Slayton tilted his head upward and leered at the old man. "No, I'm not," Slayton said, the man's name etched in his mind. "General Golikov. I'm the United States Ambassador to Russia, Slayton McCarthy and you have just committed a flagrant violation of diplomatic protocol. Is this how your security services treat American Embassy personnel?"

Golikov tightened his lips; his cheeks reddened as a uniformed minion ran to him and said in Russian, "They released the other vehicle. It's already inside the embassy compound. He produced the passport for Slayton McCarthy and State Department credentials. We had to let them go."

Golikov shook in anger and yelled, "You idiots!"

Slayton revealed a cocky grin. "I claim diplomatic immunity. Expect a call from your Foreign Minister in the morning."

Slayton returned to the Siber. As Bart held the door open, his cell phone sounded. Six had sent a test message. Two simple words.

He's in.

Slayton and Bart smiled as they watched the parade of security cars clear the scene.

"Press headlines should be interesting tomorrow morning. *'Russian Security Services Arrest U.S. Ambassador in Colossal Diplomatic Blunder'*."

Bart laughed. "I'm sure the President will use this to his advantage."

"Oh, yes," Slayton said. "From what I understand, he's got some definite plans in mind."

Chapter 44

Wednesday Morning — New York City

Injured and robbed J.J. managed to walk out alive even though the operational flash drive was a blunder for which she'd jibe Manny for the rest of his career. However, the turn of events was the answer to her prayers; another answer was sitting in the car in front of her.

"You okay?" Tony asked, his window already down. "Your radio's not working. I couldn't hear anything until you got outside."

"I'm fine," she said, happy he showed up but not enough to show it. He stretched across the passenger seat to open the door. "But I need stitches before I bleed to death," she said as she slipped inside.

"Jesus, what happened?" he said, reaching to unwrap her finger and inspect it.

"I'm…I'm surprised to see you here."

"Yeah, well, I'm not," he said, looking into her eyes. "Whatever bullshit we go through, I'm always gonna have your back. I'm still not happy with you," he snapped.

"Is that right? Well, pay your membership fee and join the freakin' club because I'm not happy with you either."

Inside the car, she explained everything, including Misha's robbery. His emotions ranged from relieved to furious in a matter of seconds. "You kiddin' me? I knew that douche bag was dirty."

"Yeah, both our instincts were right about him."

"So, we're back to ground zero. You gave him the flash drive, right?"

"I gave him *a* flash drive…not *the* flash drive," she reached into her bra and pulled out the money along with the stick Trifonov gave her. "The crap Manny gave me didn't work. This is the real deal. Wonder what's going to happen to Misha when he hands them a blank drive."

"I wish I could be there to see it….on second thought…" Tony chuckled. "His stupidity does present a problem though—they'll know you were inside. They're gonna cover their tracks even more now, and then they'll be out for blood…your blood."

"If the evidence we need is on this, they'll be locked up and by the time we head back to D.C. and the gates of hell open."

Before J.J. had a moment to let the dramatic events sink in, Tony's phone signaled. It was a text message from Santino. He read it then showed it to J.J.

Dante's condition has improved. He's talking.
Get to the hospital right away!

•••

Santino stared at the ceiling as Nicky Mumbles roared in his ear over the phone, just moments after discovering someone broke into his stash house. Nicky's voice was somewhere between furious and suspicious. Although Santino had reached the stage where he didn't give two shits how Nicky felt about anything, he still needed to keep him close. Until he found out Mashkov's location, he couldn't make his next move.

"Had to be an inside job. Who would have a clue this shit's even here unless it's someone in the family did it?"

"You must be kiddin'?" Santino asked. "No way in hell anyone's gonna rob from you. I mean, best case scenario, they catch a beat down, if you're feeling charitable. And you don't have a rep for being charitable."

"I talked to a couple of people in the neighborhood. They said they saw a couple of guys from around the block. One of 'em sounded like you from the description."

Santino laughed. It was fake and strained. "Gimme a break. What do I look like breakin' into your place…to take, what a TV and an old couch?" he asked. "Did they clean you out?"

"No, they left the most valuable stuff there. Just twenty-five Gs in cash and one of my guns. That's a major concern. If the cocksucker uses it to rob, my prints are all over it; they could bring all kinds of heat from the Feds."

"Listen, I know what kind of shit you keep in those houses. If it was the Feds, you'd have been arrested already. A professional thief woulda cleaned you out. Probably some kids who didn't know what they were getting into. I'll get my people on it. If we see twelve-year-old kid driving a Mustang we'll have our man," he said, rolling his eyes and pursing his lips. "Right now, I'm at the hospital with Dante."

"Looks like he's gonna pull through, eh?" Nicky said, his voice falling flat.

"Yeah," Santino said. "Try not to sound so *disappointed.*"

"What the hell's that s'posed to mean?"

Uncle Sal's voice spoke to him, *Easy with the temper.*

"Forget what I said. I'm just exhausted. This has been the longest fuckin' week of my life," he offered.

"Well, rest up. Novikov wants to meet to deliver the rest of the cash Friday. Since you guys are bosom buddies now, he expects you to be there. I'll call you back with the time."

Santino turned around to enter Dante's room and noticed Tony pacing down the hall toward him. His mouth drew downward, and the tenseness in his face made him look more like his father than himself. He recognized the same brooding from their childhood when Tony worried about his pops, every day wondering if he'd return home alive. He lived in agony, feared for his father's safety more than any kid should have to. The reason he turned away from the life wasn't a mystery to anyone. But he'd feel better when he saw how much Dante's health improved.

"Hey!" Tony said, jutting his chin out. "My mother and sisters here yet?"

"Look what the cat drug in," Santino said. He looked over Tony's shoulder, with his eyebrows scrunched. "No, they're not here yet. Where's your better half?"

"She's in emergency gettin' stitches. Got injured in an op today."

"Jesus. She okay?"

"Yeah, better than I am. The stress of all this bullshit is killin' me."

"What stress?"

"Dante. The family…" Tony leaned in toward Santino and whispered, "The Russians put out a two-million dollar contract on her head."

His eyes bucked. "What Russians?"

"The Mashkovs. The brother arrived from Russia, the one that ordered the hit on Dante. Now he's got a hard-on for her because she recruited his people to help us out. So, he's gonna do it himself," Tony said. "I'd love the chance to take down that piece of shit myself. I'll never let him hurt her."

The news took Santino aback. Now that he and his cousin were again on speaking terms, his concerns had become Santino's concerns. And he'd never forget it was J.J. who convinced Tony to let him walk after he shot the Mikhaylova bitch.

His anger spiked. "The Mashkov's, huh? What are you gonna do? Risk you entire career, everything you sacrificed so much for, just to hit him? Stop talkin' crazy," he said. He kept his face serious for Tony's sake, but inside he smiled. Uncle Sal's plan could move into the final stage. Mashkov was in the U.S. now. Santino only needed to find out where the son of a bitch was staying.

"What? I'm gonna sit around and wait on him to clip her?"

"No, I'll tell you what you're gonna do. You're gonna stay close to her. Once word gets out you're back in your father's good graces, who's gonna touch her? Nobody. Okay? So fuhgedaboudit. Go inside and see your brother."

"How is he?" Tony asked.

"Better. He was up talkin' like old times."

Chapter 45

Wednesday Night — New York City

Tony crossed himself and thanked God. He felt relieved after talking to Santino. Now the time had come for him to make things right with Dante. They'd been estranged for so many years. They could never get back the wasted time, but he hoped, with all of his heart, they could begin again. Their decisions to take different career paths and Tony being falsely accused of being a rat had torn them apart, but with his reputation restored, he hoped they could pull the relationship back together now that Dante was on the mend.

Just as Tony turned to enter Dante's room, he heard the thunder of feet across the floor. Masked doctors and nurses with worried faces fled past Santino and Tony, and burst inside the door. Tony followed and Santino behind him.

Tony's eyes fell on Dante, and he watched as what little olive left in his brother's skin turned white and disappeared with his final breath. The flat line's tone seared through him as they yanked the defibrillators from the wall and slammed them into his chest. The nurses pushed them back into the hall, but he forced the door open, refusing to let it close.

"Clear!"

Dante's chest thrust upward as the nurses tried in desperation to resuscitate him.

"Clear!" the doctor yelled again, at least two times more. For Tony, the words didn't compute. The only sound that seeped through was the steady, monotonous beep signaling the end to his hopes—the cruel halting of an incomplete life.

Tony's body went cold as his knees folded beneath him. He collapsed to the floor, tears raining from his eyes. Not just for the brother he'd lost, but for the relationship he could never restore.

One name thundered through his mind and filled his every cell with acidic venom—Pavlov Mashkov.

He didn't pull the trigger, but his order was the shot that ended Dante's life. In an instant too short to measure, Tony snapped.

He hungered for revenge.

He'd transformed; his state altered. A warmth drained from his soul, leaving him hardened and numb. His life would never be the same. Dante's death left him shattered; he wondered whether he could ever be whole again.

His vision tunneled and vengeance was the bright light at the end of it. The darkness inside him drew toward it. He would not be satisfied until that light washed over him like torrential downpours…and he'd avenged his brother's murder.

•••

There were three things Tony would never forget in his life – the piercing scream his mother cried out on the news of Dante's death and watching his sisters dissolve into heartbreak; the moment he watched his brother draw his last breath; and the squeeze of his father's embrace after he exited the morgue.

It had been over a decade since Tony had felt the comfort of his father's arms around him, not since he graduated from college. He'd wondered whether his father would ever speak to him again, let alone hold him. It struck him that he was the last remaining son. The heir apparent to the Donato throne. He'd never witnessed Pop cry but as his father's eyes fell on Dante's lifeless body, he succumbed to the sorrow of a loss all too familiar in "the life," yet unbearable just the same.

He kissed his son goodbye and left the morgue, meeting Tony and Santino in the hall outside. As his mother and sisters grieved for their loss upstairs. The trio traded their pain for premeditation as they plotted their quest for vengeance.

Sal's voice cracked as he growled, "I want those fucking Mashkovs dead! You understand me? Dead!"

Santino nodded. "I'm on it…we can discuss it later." He minced his words and glanced at Tony. "Maybe you should go upstairs while we talk business. This isn't for your ears."

This was the part where Tony was supposed to remove himself from the conversation. See no evil and hear no evil, so he'd never have to speak of it, or testify to it. He'd stayed in D.C. and out of New York so he could avoid both playing witness and turning a blind eye…but the toxic rage percolating beneath his grieving exterior refused to let him. Instead, he found himself saying, "There's this rule."

Sal and Santino looked at him curiously. "Rule? What're you talkin' about, Ton'?"

"Well, as an FBI Special Agent, if I learn of a hit on another mobster, it's my obligation to meet with the potential victim and warn them," Tony said. "As a Fed, I just overheard a threat on their lives. Guess I've got to schedule a meeting with the Mashkovs. It's my duty."

They each exchanged knowing looks.

"You sure about this, Ton'?" Santino said. "I mean, if we do this, it changes everything…at least for you."

Tony turned to him, his eyes as empty and reddened as when Dante died. "Everything's changed. Nothing will ever be the same. Ever."

Chapter 46

Late Wednesday Night — New York City

J.J. allowed her mind to churn over the day's events as she rode the elevator to her Plaza hotel room, leaving the men to discuss funeral, or so they said. The sadness of grieving for his family, Misha robbing her at gunpoint, the contract on her head, it had begun to take a toll on her body and mind. For the first time, she was afraid, not just for Tony and his family but for herself. All of a sudden, she lost her breath, inhaling in long dramatic heaves. Her chest tightened, and head felt light. The distress was compounded by the fact that she was flanked by two armed "family guys" who escorted her back to the room—Tony, Sal, and Santino insisted for her own safety. Somehow she thought she'd feel safer without them. She wanted a drink. Needed a drink. Just a small one to soothe her nerves. She couldn't handle it, had almost forgotten her thirst for the taste until now.

"Calm down…you okay?" one of them said.

"I'm fine," J.J. said as she struggled to pull herself together and focus her thoughts. As she envisioned opening the minibar and twisting open the cap on the Smirnov, the doors opened on the fourth floor, and Gia stepped in, her face twisted in concern.

"I was just going to look for you…and Tony."

"Well…you found *me*." She forced herself not to roll her eyes and curse the heifer out. After all, Gia had lied her way into Tony's hotel room five minutes ago.

"Are you okay? I heard about what happened," Gia asked, her concern put-upon. She didn't give a rat's ass about how J.J. was feeling. Stevie Wonder could see it. Maybe after a stiff drink, J.J. could muster the strength to pretend, but absent a few shots she couldn't conjure up any award-winning performances after the horrible day she'd had.

"Gia, let's get real for a moment. I'm too drained to pretend to believe this bullshit you're shoveling right now. You don't give a shit about me, how I'm doing, whether I'm dead or alive. So, don't ask."

"I don't know what you're—"

"Gia, please," J.J. gave her the hand, resisting the urge to palm her face like a Spaulding. "Skip the doe-eyed innocent bit with me. Your feelings about me are clear…and I have no misconceptions regarding your affection for Tony. You want to find out how he's doing? Quit insulting my intelligence and grow a pair. Just ask."

Gia crossed her arms over her chest and tightened her lips, before saying. "Okay…how…is he okay?"

The elevator doors opened on the seventh floor.

"None of your fucking business. That's how he is," J.J. snapped. She held the doors open as she thanked the Donatos' people and then sent them all on their way. She didn't leave before saying, "Tony's a grown man; it's his job to put you in your place when you interact with him. As for me, the line is drawn. I promise, you don't want to cross it."

As J.J. undressed and settled in her room, her thoughts switched back to Tony's face as he cried for his brother's death; J.J. couldn't help but give into her tears. She didn't have to imagine his pain or anguish or sense of hopeless despair since she lived them daily…and had done so every single day since her mother died, a fate he was destined to suffer. He couldn't possibly comprehend how this void in his family would leave him just a little bit broken for the rest of his life. An ever-present sadness would bore a hole and hunker down just beneath his emotional surface, rearing its ugly head whenever he remembered the missing warmth, washing back the memories of his loss like a flood when he was least prepared to suppress it.

Her anguish mushroomed, not just for him, but for everyone connected with Dante. Spending the night helping to console them, it was clear to see the place each held in the family unit. Carla was the comforter. She was as much a motherer as Mrs. Donato, who possessed a dignified strength. Mrs. Donato and her mother were different and yet the same. Dree, on the other hand, she was the helpless child trapped in a devil's body. The news of Dante's death exposed a vulnerability J.J. didn't believe existed inside Dree. In her grief, she welcomed J.J.'s arms and eyed her as if she'd seen J.J.'s humanness for the first time.

Although under the worst of circumstances, J.J. felt like part of their family. She thought it odd the way death stirred those left behind, at once it served both as a dividing and unifying force, joining aching souls together. She worried most about Tony. He played the part of the strong son well, but there was an emptiness in his eyes never present before, as if the pain possessed him like a dark spirit. She hoped he'd scrape his way out of the abyss and back into her arms where he belonged. Their argument now felt petty. None of it mattered, not anymore.

Unblinking, she gazed at the minibar and shook her head. The thought of compounding Tony's distress with her drinking helped her resist. Instead, she opted for the distraction of her case, which was riding on whether Sunnie's analysis tied Troika to the spy rings. More than vodka, J.J. wanted warrants. She wanted to march into Troika and snatch every last one of them out of their shiny suits and into jail. She decided to get a progress report, and only one person would know. J.J. pulled out her cell and dialed.

"You must have read my mind!" Sunnie said at the sound of J.J.'s voice. "I was just getting ready to call you. I've got an update. But, first, how are you and Tony holding up?"

"Eh. We're here. We're survivors. What else can I say?"

"Well, I have news, but not about the flash drives. Damn near every file is encrypted. Walter says it's 128-bit encryption, which isn't the best, but still tough to break."

"Did you just use the 'd-word'? I don't think I've ever heard you curse."

"Well, this case is driving me past drinking and straight to vulgarity. Get used to it."

J.J. let out a strained chuckle. "Amen to that."

"NSA's system can break the code, but it takes time. They're hoping Trifonov used the same password on all of his files so when they break one, they break them all. Nobody can give me a hard estimate. Barring the minimal chance of Matvey volunteering the information there's nothing else to do except wait."

J.J.'s brow furrowed. "Fantastic. Then what's the news? "

"It's about the file…your mother's case file. You received my text, right? Nixon got it."

"Yes. It was the exclamation point at the end of a very shitty day." J.J. rubbed her temple to relieve the tension. Another setback was almost too much to bear. The minibar started looking better by the second. "What happened?"

"He waited for Wendell to leave for the day and strong-armed the night clerk who didn't know any better. He's acting director after all."

"Shit! I'll never find out the truth now."

"Ah, ah, ah…not so fast. I wouldn't go that far."

J.J. perked up. "What do you mean?"

"I mean, Wendell's got more cajones than either of us thought. That's for sure," Sunnie said. "When Nixon came into the Special File Room ordering him to turn over the file, Wendell found it suspicious to say the least. So he Xeroxed the entire file. As soon as he heard Nixon got his hands on it, he expressed the package to you in New York. You'll have it in the morning."

Finally!

She closed her eyes and pumped her fist in the air, relieved at Sunnie's words. Still she was apprehensive about what she'd find. After all the years of living in the darkness and deception surrounding her mother's case, the shroud would be removed. She could put her dogged curiosity to rest. But something told her, given the level of pain Nixon had gone through to keep the truth buried, she may very well have set in motion a tidal wave that threatened to reveal much more than a long-held bureau secret.

Chapter 47

Thursday Morning — New York City

Tony turned onto Beard Street, on the Columbia Waterfront, not far from Brooklyn's Red Hook. That's where he scheduled his meeting with the Mashkovs. The morning brought a bone-chilling frost that kept the streets surrounding the barren industrial complex lifeless and bare, just as he'd hoped. His emotions were still raw, the wounds on his soul still fresh, the pain of Dante's death still choleric fire burning through him. The thought of sitting in front of the mother-fuckers responsible and holding a conversation that didn't involve his Glock and two slugs to the backs of their heads sickened him. But the ends justified the means, made his course of action tolerable if discomforting. He stood on the brink of crossing lines he could never uncross. To Tony, his badge no longer mattered. Neither did his future. Only now.

He thought the Mashkovs would refuse to meet him, but they capitulated with little coercing. The task should've been more difficult which concerned him. But he didn't give them his true name, so they had no idea they were slated to meet with the brother of their latest victim.

When Tony called Levi, he identified himself as an FBI agent and told them he needed to speak to both on a life-and-death matter.

"I have no idea what you're speaking about," Levi said. "My brother, he is in Moscow. He's banned from traveling to the United States."

"Bullshit," Tony replied. "I saw him with own eyes. Last night at Troika. Trust me, if I wanted to arrest him I'd have done it already. I'm obligated to deliver an important message. But if you insist on blowing smoke up my ass, I'll show up with the cavalry. Our informal, off-the-record discussion will become an interrogation…at Federal Plaza."

"I don't know what you—"

"Listen, you and your brother can meet me at Red Hook tomorrow, or your offices and warehouses will be blanketed with so many FBI agents, looking into every crack and crevice, you'll wish the Orkin man had a spray for federal agents. You understand me?"

Tony had learned well from his lineage. If you give a man two shitty roads, he'll take the one that requires less toilet paper. It's human nature. Meeting with Tony was the lesser of two evils.

He found the perfect spot with a view of the river, abandoned buildings behind him, the East River trail ahead, and waited for them to arrive. Within moments, a car pulled up along the far curb, and the two brothers exited their cars and headed toward him. With Tony standing at six-foot-three, they were bigger than him in height and girth. The largest brother appeared to be the size of Tony and the smaller brother put together. Both were dressed in turtlenecks, black leather coats, and jeans.

Tony stood up from the hood of his car and greeted them with his badge and credentials which he flashed and, within seconds, returned to his jacket pocket. He introduced himself using his fake last name. Their faces were beet red from the cold and foggy air expelled from their noses and mouths like charging bulls.

"You wanted to meet us here," Pavlov said. "Now, we're here. What is so urgent for you to discuss?"

"The FBI has received information from a confidential informant that your lives are in danger. Members from the Bonanno family are planning a hit on both of you, in light of the shooting and recent death of Dante Donato." Tony choked the words out like rancid meat.

They glanced at each other, back at Tony, and then chuckled. Laughed as if Tony had told the joke of the day. "We had nothing to do with it. But that guy was a nobody. Nothing but a street thug. They will never attack us over him."

Tony's breathing grew more shallow. Rage spun through him like roaring tornadoes. He wanted them dead and had every intention of making it so.

"He was the son of a Bonanno Boss," Tony said, forcing the words from his lips. His hands shook with anger; his fury exploded. "And today's your unlucky day. So am I."

Before Tony could process his move, his gun was in his hand, aimed, and ready to fire. "That nobody you're talking about, he's my family. That agent you put a contract on, she's my family, too. Seems to me all of my family's troubles go away if I unload my Glock in you, you pieces of shit."

Tony's gun clicked as he loaded the first bullet in the chamber. He trained his eyes and locked his glare on the larger of the Mashkov's head. He smiled as their eyes bulged.

"My name isn't Tony DiCosta; it's Antonio Donato. And that nobody is my fucking brother. Welcome to Brooklyn."

Just as Tony pressed his finger against the trigger, a black Mustang skidded around the corner and screeched to a stop in front of them. Through the fog in his mind, Santino's voice screamed, "Get outta here. Put the gun away, Ton'. Get outta here!"

Tony's head heard what Santino said, but his heart wouldn't allow his feet to move. The taste of their deaths settled on his lips and satisfied him in a way walking away never would. Tony aimed at the knees, wanted them to die slow and painful deaths. Then he squeezed his finger to the trigger again.

"Think of J.J., Ton," Santino said.

Tony froze for a moment that seemed an eternity…and inched his arms down to his side. He glanced at Santino, who pointed his own gun at their heads. After another moment of thought, Tony turned his back on the scene and headed toward his car.

The first pop startled him.

But those that followed, at least ten more, satisfied him, edged the corners of his mouth upward in a sadistic smile. Those cocksucking killers were dead and the threat to his family a bad memory…save one.

Santino rolled up to him as he opened his car door to leave. "It's done."

"And the gun?" Tony asked.

"Left it at the scene of the crime, of course. Now get out of here. Our family needs you. J.J. needs you."

Santino was right. He needed to be with his family. But he had one stop to make first.

Chapter 48

Thursday — Moscow Safe House

Time was up. The deadline had fallen upon him like dirt in a grave, and Ghost and his crew were waiting to take Mosin away—for good. Six entered the shack for what would be the last time. He'd brought Stan to safety on the U.S. soil that is the embassy. Now to complete his final mission, he had some unfinished business with Mosin, and today was the day they'd settle up the score once and for all. It all made sense to him now. The scanners. The surgeon. The FSB. Although Mosin's plan was good, Six was more than convinced his was better.

He entered, and Ghost gave him a friendly salute. "You made it. Never thought I'd say this, but it's been a pleasure to working with you."

"Same here." Six scanned the room. Scattered boxes waiting for tape lay around the floor. "Looks like you've got this place about packed up."

"Yeah. One more day and I'm headed stateside. Think it's about time for me to move south and find somewhere to fish and drink all day," he said with a chuckle.

"Sounds like my kind of plan."

"You mind leaving me alone with him?" Six said, looking at Mosin, his arms and legs strapped to the chair rendering him all but immobile from the neck down. At least Ghost had allowed him to dress and clean up, but he still needed a haircut and shave. "I need about twenty minutes. Maybe less."

Ghost nodded and winked. "All right. Guess I'll go see a man about horse. Just keep in mind my orders are to release him when I leave here. You might want to make sure he can walk."

Six chuckled. "Yes, I will ensure we follow all orders to the letter. I'd just like to have a chat before we let him go. But, uh, why don't you and I meet for a drink later."

"Now that sounds like *my* kind of plan."

Six nodded in agreement as he watched Ghost and his cohorts disappear into the woods. Then he turned his attention to the man of the hour. Hawk.

Six moseyed over with a smug grin on his face while Hawk monitored his every movement. He pulled a roll of gauze from his pocket and sat it on an adjacent table. Then grabbed a chair and placed it parallel, facing the traitor. After straddling his legs across the seat, he pulled out a pristine jackknife and peeled open the blade. Six wanted nothing more than to carve his heart out, but he had another target today.

"Now, it's time for you to listen."

"W-w-w-what are you doing with that?" he asked, his voice jittery. "Y-y-you've been ordered to let me go. You heard Ghost."

"How about you shut the fuck up before I slit your neck from ear to ear?"

Mosin snapped his lips shut and breathed in heavy snorts through his nose, his chest heaving up and down with anger and fear.

Six leaned forward and glared at Mosin's hand, his eyes locked on the tattoo strategically placed in the space between his thumb and forefinger. It was a red hammer and sickle. How appropriate.

"Nice tattoo," Six said with a menacing glare as he spun the point of the knife's blade against the tip of his finger.

The sound of Mosin's heavy breaths ceased for a split second, then continued. "What's this about?"

"I'll tell you," Six began. "For days, I've chased my tail from one end of Moscow to the other, scouring every inch of every place you've stayed looking for the intel you stole." He ran his finger along the blade, staring at it as if he'd cracked up. The fluorescent light against the sharpened steel cast a blinding flash that made Mosin squint. "And I've come to a brilliant conclusion. But I'll get to that in a minute. First, you need a drink. Don't move," he joked, laughing out loud…as if Mosin could.

Six sauntered over to the cabinet drawer where Ghost kept the booze and pulled from its stores two shot glasses, a half-empty bottle of vodka, and a couple of plastic gloves. He returned to the table, filled the glasses, and held up one to Mosin's mouth. Hawk tightened his lips.

"Drink it."

Mosin looked at him with a confused expression.

"Trust me. In two minutes, you'll wish you had ten. I'm giving you two."

He hesitated but then opened his mouth to gulp back both. Six set the glass down and returned to his seat. "Good. Now back to my brilliant conclusion," he said. "You want me to tell you what it is, don't you?"

Mosin's facial features shifted, flashing with a knowing expression. His level of discomfort appeared to increase as the vodka kicked in. He nodded yes.

•••

Two Days Ago – NIH Campus

After Hopper confronted Dr. Badal in the garage and outlined his options, they strolled to a nearby park bench on campus as the brisk winds blew the auburn remnants of fall across the landscape. The timid man fixed his gaze on Hopper with a somber air and a wrinkled brow. "This is about Gary Mosin, isn't it?"

Hopper nodded. "He came to see you, didn't he?"

Dr. Badal gulped hard. "I've been in this country for five years and I never had an ounce of trouble until Gary Mosin darkened my doorstep…my life."

"How did you two meet?"

"My research. My department posted one of my articles on the Internet. He said he read it, but that was a lie, just as every word he spoke from his mouth was a lie."

"What's your field of study?"

"I specialize in biomedical engineering. Most of my recent work surrounded the study on the side effects of the VeriChip, a radio-frequency device injected beneath the skin with a syringe which holds medical records. They use similar technology to track dogs."

"Yeah," Hopper said. "Thought it sounded familiar. Did he say why he was interested in this particular subject matter?"

"No, not at first. His intentions became clear as time passed." Badal wiped his brow, which was now sweating despite the cold air. "He treated me to lunches. Gave me expensive bottles of vodka and scotch. Always asked for unclassified reports that seemed innocuous…at first. But soon his requests became more demanding."

Classic tradecraft, Hopper thought. Dr. Badal wouldn't be the first, nor the last to succumb to the enticement of Russian spies. Hopper kept nodding to assure the doctor his full attention had been captured.

"He started requesting more sensitive reports in exchange for small amounts of money. None of the research included classified information, but no matter how much I protested he refused to take no for an answer. Then one day he asked me about the program, and I knew…"

Hopper sat at attention. "What program?"

"The HITCH program."

"What's that?"

"The Human Intelligence Transport Chip. It's a Top Secret defense program studying the impact of high-capacity radio frequency data capture devices in soldiers of war. Whereas the VeriChip can carry only one or two kilobytes, the HITCH can carry up to ten gigabytes of data, in a small chip right inside your hand. It's bigger than a VeriChip so the implantation requires minor surgery and a couple of stitches. But there are few more secure or accessible ways to carry intelligence in a hostile territory."

A microchip in the hand. Hopper was floored by the implications for Six's case. He knew what was coming next but braced himself for it.

"About three weeks ago, he asked me to steal two HITCH proto-types. We had hundreds of them for testing purposes. I refused, and he threatened not only me but my family. At first he said he would out me as a spy for the Russians. When I remained unmoved, he said his people would kill us. I didn't take his word with any seriousness until one day my car wouldn't start. The mechanic checked under the hood and found a rudimentary bomb that failed to detonate."

"Jesus," Hopper said. "Did you report this to the authorities?"

He shook his head. "The local police, yes. They said whoever in-stalled the device hadn't armed it. If they planted it to scare me…well, the plan worked," he said, his hand now trembling. "Oh, when I think of my wife and children, I couldn't risk endangering their lives…or risk losing my visa. I had to give him what he wanted. I loaded many files onto two chips…I have no idea the number…then implanted them into his right hand."

"You didn't view the contents on the chip?"

He shook his head. "To be honest, given what he'd done…the bomb…I had no desire to know. Just wanted to get him out of my office and out my life as fast as possible. You're not going to take my visa, are you? What I did was wrong, but I believe we'd be dead now if I didn't comply."

"I understand. Once I verify the facts of the case, I'll be in touch. And the next time I set up an appointment—don't run."

•••

Six circled the room before he delivered the news. "The intel you stole. It isn't *out there*," he said pointing at the door with the knife in his hand. He shook his head. "It's been *in here* all along."

Mosin attempted to feign surprise and failed.

"Oh, give up, Hawk," Six said. "The secret's out. You see Maddix told J.J. about your doctor's appointment before you left the country. I saw the calendar on your netbook which noted your appointment and the receipt from the tattoo parlor…and I put two-and-two together after I got some information from Dr. Badal…well after the FBI did."

Mosin's expression was wide-eyed and glazed.

Six stood up, hulking over Mosin, then grabbed his arm just above the wrist and pressed his hand into the chair. "You had surgery. And what I had no clue about was the doctor you saw specializes in radio frequency chip implants. The intel is in your hand. And you got the tattoo to disguise the scar." He rested the knife on his leg and slipped his fingers into the gloves.

"You're crazy," Mosin exclaimed. "You have no idea what the hell you're talking about."

"Oh, I believe I do. And it's because Ghost concocted that explosion and brought you to this safe house that the Russians don't have the intel. With this chip, they could've passed you on the street with a scanner and taken possession of everything." Six pressed his finger along Mosin's hand until he touched two hard capsule-like forms the size of Tylenol caplets. "There they are."

Mosin shrugged. "So you found it. What makes you think they didn't already collect it."

"Because they're still looking for you. They wouldn't waste their time if they'd gotten what they needed."

"You said no one was looking for me."

Six shrugged. "I lied. Sue me."

"I'm a patriot," Mosin said. "My country will reward me for my valor, my service, and my bravery while you spend the rest of your shitty career pushing paper at some desk facing a hole in the wall. You'll never serve an overseas tour again after word of this debacle gets out."

"Your country, huh? Well, I too am a patriot…and not a surgeon. Brace yourself, this is gonna sting a bit." Six jabbed the knife into his skin until it broke and released blood, then carved into the stitches, prodding the flesh with the knife's tip until the small devices fell onto floor. Mosin screamed and clenched his teeth gurgling and growling to endure the pain.

Six put the bloody capsules in a plastic bag and shoved them in his pocket. Then he grabbed the bottle of vodka, opened the lid, and poured it on Mosin's hand, sending his screeching up another octave. After waiting for the noise to simmer down, Six pulled the gauze from his pocket and wrapped Mosin's hand. He shook his head as it struck him that Mosin was a pussy. "It's just a flesh wound and that's 80-proof, a perfect antiseptic. I warned you. Bet you wish you had ten shots now. Keep in mind I didn't have to give you anything."

Mosin spat in his direction. Still dehydrated and a little tipsy from the booze, his attempts were, for the most part, dry.

"Now what? What are you going to do with me?" he asked, watching Six go to the sink and rinse the blood from the knife. He folded the blade and returned it to his pocket.

"Oh, we'll be releasing you as scheduled. I've got the best part of you in this bag," he said. "Mission accomplished. My work is done. The exfil team will pick you up later and drop you off where we found you. I'm heading back to the embassy."

"It's about time," he said, his demeanor increasing in smugness by the second. He was a soulless bastard with no remorse. Always would be.

That's why it gave Six such pleasure to hold up his index finger and say, "One more thing before I go. As a courtesy, I should advise you of a few administrative procedures the State Department has undertaken on your behalf since we detained you."

Mosin looked at Six askance with a furrowed brow.

"First, at the request of the Justice Department, because you are a fugitive traitor, the State Department has revoked your U.S. Passport. It's all over the news today. I'm certain that'll blow over pretty fast when they find out your significance to my country is quite literally out of your hand and in my pocket."

"Fine," he said, his voice still colored with pain. "I'm Russian. I don't need a fucking U.S. passport or your citizenship. You can take that, too."

"Agreed. I told them you'd feel that way. So, the Citizen and Immigration Service determined that since it's clear you lied during your naturalization process, including your statements regarding your allegiance to another country and your work in their intelligence services, they had grounds to strip you of your citizenship on the spot. So, you are now, in fact, a man with no country."

"I'm Russian. I'm home."

"Well, I hope you enjoy your return…except…well, there's one little thing."

"What?"

"Mashkov's group? You know the most violent organized crime group in Moscow? Remember how you said I didn't have the balls to tell them you provided information to help the FBI seize a hundred-million-dollar shipment of heroin, arms and cash out of Brooklyn? Well, you were absolutely right about that. I couldn't do it."

Mosin's mouth curled into a sinister smile.

"Fortunately, Ghost had no problem with it at all. When you speak to them later today, they may claim the FBI told them you turned over the information so we'd release you."

"When they talk to me?"

"Yes. They somehow managed to intercept the details regarding the time and location of your release from U.S. custody. Ghost promised me not to say anything but…I'm not entirely certain he can be trusted."

Horror filled Mosin's eyes. "What did you do? They…they're gonna fucking slaughter me. I can't stay here. I can't…I have to leave. You can't take me to them. You have to take me back to America."

"Back to America? Why would I do that? You're Russian now."

"I'll turn myself over to the FBI. I will. Don't leave me here!"

"Sorry, the FBI gets involved with crimes involving U.S. citizens or, in your case, those possessing U.S. government information—but you no longer fit in either category. Seems you're no longer in their jurisdiction. Welcome to Moscow."

Six stood up, walked to the door, and spun around to glare at Mosin. "Who's your daddy, now?"

Chapter 49

Thursday Evening — New York City

A chill went through Nicky Mumbles' spine as he listened to the news report. He turned away and covered his mouth. Then blinked in rapid succession. He grabbed the remote control and flipped channels until he could find another.

There his name was again, scrolling across the blue banner along the bottom of the screen.

> *Bonanno family associate Nicolas "Nicky Mumbles" Muzzatto implicated in the double-slaying of Russian mob bosses, Pavlov and Lev Mashkov. Gun with his fingerprints found at the scene.*

His gaze blurred as he sat in disbelief. How could this happen, he asked himself in a repetitive cadence. He paced the bedroom and opened the closet door when it hit him. The money, the gun they robbed from his house.

It was a setup all along.

He reached under his bed, pulled out a black duffle bag, and thought about how he'd torture the motherfucker who did this. As he ran through the list of possibilities, two stuck out in his mind. Had to be them. Fucking Santino smiling in his face, pretending to be loyal. The son of a bitch had it in for him all along. The plan was smart. The Donatos wanted to get rid of him as much as he wanted to kill them. Now they could do so without causing a rift or turning half the family against them. They'd be united more than ever against the Russians. He wondered who thought of it first. Sal or Santino? Musta been Sal. He was one of the smartest bosses of any of the families, even if a pain the ass. Nicky forgot Sal's imprisonment reflected the stupidity of a few idiots in his family, not Sal himself.

Nicky loaded into his bag a few stacks of bills, his favorite Beretta, and a couple of clips. Then he covered them with underwear and T-shirts, a couple pairs of pants. He picked up his phone. Funny he'd not received a single call from anyone in light of the news reports.

Nobody called to ask him what was going on. The dead silence struck him as strange as seeing his name on the screen. If nobody was asking questions that meant everyone had answers. The traitor against him was in the family. All those backstabbing sons of bitches would pay.

For now, he'd go on the lam. If he knew anything about the Russians, they'd never let this ride. Killing the Mashkovs was like killing two bosses. Even if Max Novikov's people had no money tied to them, they wouldn't be happy with both being gunned down like animals in the street.

Nicky checked out the window. His neighborhood was dark and lifeless. Nothing out of the ordinary. Mrs. Cantrell walked her ugly mutt as usual in the front. He decided to go out the back door. Didn't want her seeing him leave in case the Feds came nosing around and asking questions.

He turned off the TV and the lights and crept outside, careful not to make a sound. He'd walk through the alley to the end of the block where he'd parked his Chrysler and sack out at his stash house in Jersey.

A few steps out of his yard, he heard a voice with a heavy Russian accent.

"Where the fuck do you think you're going?"

Nicky froze but didn't turn around. Just dropped his bag and put his hands up.

"You've got this all wrong. It wasn't me. I didn't kill 'em."

Nicky turned around in slow motion, quivering inside, but keeping a brave face. His weapons were in the bag. He couldn't pull them out. He looked to the left and right. There was nowhere to run, and he had the sprinting speed of a slug. He had no choice. Just closed his eyes and waited for the bullets to pierce him.

The first ones burned through his knees and legs. The next in his gut, his shirt soaked fast as he crumbled to the ground in anguished pain and cried out. One turned to the other and pulled out a small ax from his interior pocket.

"You know," one of the men said, his voice grainy and sinister. "In some Middle Eastern countries, when a man commits a crime they cut off the offending limbs. Which part offends you?"

His partner hoisted the axe over his head as Nicky pled for his life and said "All of them."

The next day they found Nicky. Headless and all of his fingers missing except one. That's how the NYPD identified him. The remains lying next to him belonged to Misha and Dani.

Chapter 50

Thursday Evening — New York City

North 10th Street was quiet when Santino arrived at the meeting. Max Novikov had summoned him despite the tit-for-tat attacks clogging the local news headlines. Law enforcement feared war but Santino knew—one way or the other—the conflict would end today.

He tightened his coat around his neck as he shut his car door. The last time he arrived at Max's warehouse offices, he was Nicky's sidekick. This time he was an equal. Nicky Mumbles was dead at the hands of a set of Russian executioners, just as Uncle Sal had planned. Now that his hands were clean, in relative terms, and his family more united than ever, it was time to solidify a deal that could ensure the Bonanno family prospered for years to come. Knuckles, his muscle, stood at his side, ready to help him deal with the devil.

The mountains met them at the door and escorted them inside the area where Max sat at the table waiting, his expression stoic. Judging from the look on Max's face, Santino began to question the true motivation for the gathering. He wondered whether the reason for the sit-down had anything to do with the Bonanno family future…and began to doubt whether he'd walk out alive. Max had told him that the Mashkovs were more liability than asset, that they'd cost him more money than they earned. But he didn't appear the least bit thankful.

He appeared ready to kill.

Walking heavy, Santino took a seat and leaned back with a cocksure attitude as if he'd done Max a favor. If Max disagreed with Santino when they started their discussions, he'd concede by the time Santino left through the front door…and on his feet.

"Well, well, well…the great Santino. Captain, right? You've been busy since we last met, yes?"

Santino nodded and looked him in the eye. "Bad news travels fast."

"Or good news," Max replied, "depending on which side of the ground you're on."

"True. True."

"Am I correct in assuming you've heard about the unfortunate demise of my former partners?"

"Yeah. I also heard they hit a top earner in my family, too. Funny how those nasty rumors get started, eh?"

"Funny? Perhaps," Max pulled a gun from the seat beside him and pointed the barrel at Santino. "A sign of misfortune for you, however. We Russians aren't famous for our senses of humor."

He snapped the trigger.

No shot fired.

The gun was empty…and Santino never flinched. Instead, he let out a strained chuckle and said, "And you say Russians don't have senses of humor."

Soon the entire room enveloped in depraved laughter. The mountains, Knuckles, and Max, who looked at his puppets and said, "You see? This is why I love this guy. Nerves of fucking steel. You, on the other hand, I say 'boo' and you jump. Leave us alone, please."

His people filed in line and exited the room, then Max pulled a briefcase from beneath the table and opened it on top. "Here's the other half of your money."

Santino scanned the contents, lifting several stacks and fanning them out to see the twenties and hundred-dollar bills. "This is beginning to smell a lot like business," he said, closing the case and sitting it on the floor. "We can discuss the details later."

They shook hands, and Santino left…with the family back in business. As they prepared to drive back to Bay Ridge, Santino's phone rang. It was Frankie Z.

"Hey, we got a problem," Frankie said, his voice lacking its usual upbeat tone. "We *all* got a problem."

Santino dismissed Swifty's attempt to start drama; he was full of it. "I'm carrying a briefcase heavy enough to wash all of our troubles away."

"Well, unless you're carrying immunity from prosecution, what you've got in that brief case don't mean jack!"

"Prosecution? What the hell are you talkin' about prosecution?"

"The fucking Feds. They picked up The Razor on racketeering and narcotics charges."

"What? I told his stupid ass to lay low."

"Cocksucker doesn't take instructions very well. They popped him while he was in the middle of boning his goomar. They followed her to the apartment where he was staying."

"Son of a bitch!"

"Well, it gets worse. He's turning state's witness. Rolled over like a fucking Labrador retriever begging for treats. Indictments are gonna be falling from the sky like rain. And, given all shit he's done, and the people he's whacked, there ain't a family from here to LA that ain't gettin' wet."

"Mother of God. Uncle Sal just got out. I gotta do something… and fast or he's goin' back in."

Chapter 51

Friday Morning — Scranton Half-Way House

Tony returned to the hotel room just past midnight after driving around for hours, too wired to sleep and too tired to function. Unable to settle down his mind, he took a two-hour drive to Scranton to visit his father. With his emotions swirling over Dante's death and his own life turning in circles, for the first time in decades he needed his father…and for the first time in decades his father would be there for him.

As they sat in the common area of the fifteen-room shelter developed from a duplex, Tony released his feelings to the person who'd give him the truth with brute honesty.

"I'm confused, Pop," he said. "What I did yesterday, I never thought I'd do. Now, I feel torn between two worlds and, for the first time in my life, I'm not sure which way to turn."

His father stood up, patted him on the shoulder, and took a seat in the chair adjacent to his. He leaned forward with his elbows on knees and clasped his fingers together. "Tony, my life is my life. I made my choices, and you made yours. You've been a lot of things in your life; indecisive's never been one of them. You know what you want."

Tony bit his bottom lip glanced away.

"Listen, whatever you think about this life, it allowed me to take care of my family, my kids. Fed you, kept you clothed, put you through five years of college. I have no shame about what I do or who I am. Did I want you to be a Fed? Hell no. But more than that I didn't want you to live without honor. I didn't want you to be a traitor to the life that sustained you for all those years."

"I have lived my life with honor, and I've stayed as far away the family business as I could."

Sal nodded. "Yep, and now the secret's out. You never were a rat. Anything else, I can live with…from a distance, of course. But I can live with it."

"So, what are you saying?"

"I'm saying you drove two hours for me to help you with a decision you've already made. Be a man. Honor your decisions. You're the warrior I raised you to be."

His father words soothed him like a balm. What he needed to do now, in his career, and in his life, seemed clearer than ever.

"Now that we've cleared the air, Santino tells me you're dating someone."

"I'm not dating her," Tony said. "I'm in love with her."

"Hmph," he said. "Is 'at right?"

"I know, right? Who woulda thought it. Me…in love with J.J. But she makes me happy. She's my choice—nothing indecisive about it."

"Well, I don't have to ask whether or not she loves you. From what I hear, she sounds a lot like your mother. But I'll tell you what I told Santino—in the dark and under the sheets, it's all pretty much the same. Courage? Loyalty? Protecting your family like her own? And taking shit from Dree without clockin' her? Women like that are hard to come by…in any color."

Tony chuckled. His father always had a way of putting things that hit straight to the heart with no chaser. Tony left Scranton with his mind made up to max his credit cards at Tiffany's and ask J.J. to be his wife. But first he needed sleep.

He had no medicine. No Tylenol PM or other sleep-inducing drugs to help settle his mind, which raced, spiraling into depressing thoughts of Dante. Giving up the struggle, he decided to raid the minibar, mixing a makeshift Long Island Iced tea from coke, vodka, gin, tequila, and rum, and downing it on an empty stomach, which he realized was a mistake as the heat surged through his belly. He was a relative lightweight when it came to hard liquor.

The booze warmed him to the point of sweating. He had begun stripping off his clothes when a knock came at the door. He blinked a few times to clear his blurring vision and stumbled over to answer it, each step less sure than the last.

"J.J.," he thought to himself. "My future wife."

He twisted the knob and pulled it open. "Gia?"

"Are you okay?" she asked. "I've been sick worrying about how you're doing."

"I'm okay," he said, looking down at his feet and noticing that he was standing in the door in his underwear with no shirt. He closed the door enough to conceal his body behind it.

"I'm fine," he said. The words didn't sound slurred in his head, but he could tell from Gia's expression something had not come out as intended. "Just had a drink so I could get some sleep. You better go. J.J. will be here in a minute."

"Please," she said, pressing her hand against the door to keep it from closing. Her eyes were innocent, her voice soothing and sweet. "Let me come in, just for a few minutes…to talk."

She's just a friend, he thought. J.J. would be his wife, and he was strong enough to resist her. He pursed his lips as he considered the choice he was about to make.

"Tony, you're over twice my weight and ten inches taller than me. What am I gonna do, rape you? I just want to talk. There's no harm in talking, right?"

He felt a pang in his stomach as he pulled the door open to allow her inside. "Okay…just let me throw on some clothes."

Chapter 52

Friday Morning — New York City

J.J. was borderline frantic all day and night until she received a text from Tony saying, "I'm okay. See you later." No mention of where he was or who he was with. Just some vague reassurance that he would live long enough to tell her about it later. She'd pulled the load for both of them at the office, finishing up paperwork so they could make a clean getaway back to D.C. after Sunnie completed the analysis. Now Devin Fitzpatrick, the squad supervisor, had called her into an emergency meeting, and she'd have to cover for Tony in his absence.

His brother's death had ripped him to the core, and it would be months before he found peace of mind enough to emotionally reattach himself to the world, to her, but with patience and time they'd muddle their way through together.

J.J. suited up and whizzed into the New York Office inside of a couple of hours. She was half awake and chomping on a bagel by the time the call came through. She rushed into Fitzpatrick's office to catch him in the middle of a phone call. He held up his index finger signaling he'd be ready to talk in a minute. In the meantime, she made her way to her temporary desk.

"J.J.! There you are," Manny's voice call from behind her. "How are you and Tony holding up?"

She flashed her bandaged finger. "Tony's having a rough time, but at least I have all my extremities which is a good thing, huh?"

"Yeah, that's more than we can say for Nicky Mumbles. At least they left one finger so we could identify him."

"Still no signs of his head?"

"No, not yet. They're still searching the area."

"If I know anything about the Russians, you'd have better luck checking with the Postal Service. It's probably in an express box on the way to his wife," she said. "Anyway, Fitzpatrick called me this morning. I'm gonna run and check my voicemail before he calls me in."

"Oh, yeah, before you go…a package came for you. Let me grab it."

He returned a few minutes later with two large inter-departmental envelopes no doubt containing the FBI files from her mother's case. "Here you go."

Her hands shook as she grabbed the packages from his hands. The answers to all of her questions were inside. She burned with anticipation ready to rip them open. "J.J.," Fitzpatrick called out. "I'm ready for you now."

"Shit!" she said to herself. She dropped the files in her bottom desk drawer and ran to him. Just as she reached his office door, he backed her out of it and said, "Follow me."

He led her downstairs to the twenty-second floor, the interview area where he she'd debriefed Zory Kozlov a day before. She hated to tell him, but Zory wouldn't be coughing up any more information. She'd bled him dry…and he'd lied to her. The only reason they had a snowball's chance in hell of using his debrief is because she could detect lies, another fact she couldn't share.

Once inside the secure area, he glanced over his shoulders to ensure the hall was empty before whispering, "This is between you, me, and the walls. You understand me?"

She nodded. "What's going on?"

"We had a new walk-in today, but we're keeping his identity secret for his own safety. His life is in danger, and he's scared shitless."

"Who is it?"

"Matvey Trifonov. Says he witnessed two murders, wants a plea deal. In exchange for the information we need to shut down Troika Technologies, he wants to go into the program."

"Witness protection?"

He nodded.

J.J. stood stunned. He must've been scared as hell to walk into the FBI, but the reason was no mystery, at least not to her. He had no inkling the cleaning woman was an FBI agent. He'd trusted the evidence to a stranger who had disappeared. In hindsight, going inside Troika was the best move she could've made. And now that he was in FBI custody, there'd be no turning back.

"Who got killed?"

"A chauffer…and his cousin."

"Jesus, Misha and Dani," she muttered. Now, Matvey's appearance at the FBI office made even more sense. When she disappeared with his flash drive and the money and Misha showed up with a blank drive, he had to wonder if she'd snitched on him to get more cash. "I warned Misha this would happen. A victim of his own greed. Where's Matvey?"

Fitzpatrick bowed his head toward the closed door next to them.

J.J. jutted her chin toward him and walked inside to see Matvey molting away in this seat. His face was ashen, and he'd turned his hands into his armpits, appearing almost doubled over in pain.

She pulled out her credentials and introduced herself. "I'm FBI Special Agent J.J. McCall."

He started to speak but froze and did a double take before his eyes narrowed and his mouth fell open. "It's you. You're the one who took my flash drive."

"No, you gave it to me," she said. "But, yes, I have it."

The realization that she was an FBI agent crystalized in his mind and his shoulders began to relax. He clasped his head with his hands and let out a long breath. "My God. When you didn't deliver it…I thought…I thought you turned me over to the Mashkovs. I've been walking around like death on a stick ever since."

"What happened? What brought you here?"

"Somebody I've never seen before, I heard him called Misha, handed over the flash drive; they checked it. When it turned out to be blank they killed them…slaughtered them both for not killing some agent…" his mind did a quick calculation, and he put the names together. "Wait, McCall. They wanted to kill you?"

"I'm afraid so," she said, "but who is they?"

"The Mashkovs. They told me they'd murder me if I said a word, but I had no doubt they'd do so no matter what."

"They're dead now, so why come here today?" J.J. said. So far, she had no reaction to anything he said. He'd been truthful. But the threat to his life had died with the Mashkovs…or so she thought.

"Yes, they're dead…but Max and Leonid are not. Together, they can be worse than both of the Mashkovs. If the Mashkov's told Max I was a threat to talk…I would've been dead all the same, just tortured for much longer."

"I see," J.J. replied.

"I want to go into witness protection. Me, my wife, my kids. I want a new identity. I want my family placed where they can be safe."

"And in exchange?"

"I'll tell you anything about Troika. The accounts. The people. Anything."

"You're willing to testify in open court?" she asked.

He offered a hesitant nod. "If you guarantee my protection…yes."

J.J. nodded. "Okay. I'll see what I can do. But I have a couple of key questions I need to ask you…and I need you to tell me the truth. If you even think about lying to me, I'll walk you outside and call Troika to tell them we're sending you back to work. Do you understand me?"

"Yes…try me. Ask anything."

"What can you share about the Svetlana Mikhaylova accounts?"

"They do exist. There's a definite connection. The Mashkovs transferred the money irregularly but a few times a month at a minimum. They set up the accounts as part of an agreement between Mashkov and General Golikov. You know him, yes?"

J.J. nodded. All too well.

"Mashkov gave me the cash and I deposited it into multiple accounts but this…it can all be traced if you're aware of what you're looking for. And I know what to search for."

His story aligned with her theory. Now she had one final issue to resolve—Gary Mosin. She needed to confirm that he was indeed responsible for maintaining the new accounts and paying the remaining agents after Svetlana's death.

"You heard of Gary Mosin?" she asked.

"Yes," he answered. "I watch the news. Everyone with a television must know who he is by now."

"Was his name linked to any of Svetlana's accounts? Was he linked to the new account after she died?"

"No," he answered without a second's hesitation…and she felt no reaction, which meant that he was telling the truth. The answer surprised her. She'd banked on the exact opposite response, and she was wrong.

"Are you sure?"

"One-hundred percent certain. The person responsible for the new account is an American. He lives in the Washington D.C. area; the name attached to the account is a false identity, but he has documentation."

"Do you have any other information?"

"Nothing but rumors. But from what I understand, the person is a male…and he is an officer in the military at the Pentagon."

J.J. gasped. "The Pentagon?"

* * *

Six couldn't pack his suitcases fast enough. He wanted more than anything in the world to get out of Moscow. He'd finished his business and accomplished two very difficult missions. Now, his only regret was that he couldn't get an earlier flight to Prague, the pit stop he'd have to make on behalf of Vorobeyev's family before returning stateside…to J.J.

A gnawing in his core told him J.J. and Tony were in the midst of some relationship upheaval. It was only a matter of time before the reality of its complications, in the stark light of these days and times, made it crumble under the weight of societal and familial pressures. Six would be there to lift her up, to remind her of the good in him, the love in him, before he turned into an egomaniacal Neanderthal…at least in her eyes. He needed to get home first, and he had one stop to make before he made his way to the airport.

After high-tailing it to Mark's office inside the secure vault, he knocked on his door.

"Take a load off and close the door behind you."

Six scanned the room and spotted an urn on the table next to Mark's desk. "Is that Stan?"

"Yeah. The cleaning crew emptied the contents from the vacuum cleaner. Mr. Vorobyev's ashes are ready for delivery to his family in Prague. There's a compartment under the false bottom with travel instructions."

"So, what's the plan?"

"When they get to Germany, we'll get them out on a military flight. Stan, too. If all goes well, they will be flying to the U.S. together," Mark said. "You catch the news this morning? The headline was very interesting."

"What's that?"

"The MVD found Gary Mosin's body. Fifteen rounds between his chest and head."

Six should've been happy; he should've celebrated. J.J. and the task force would. But instead, a pang of guilt overcame him. Perhaps, he could've dealt with Mosin in a different manner. The question lingering in his mind was whether he *should've*. "I gave him every chance to cooperate. He remained defiant until the end. At least we've got the intel."

"And your name is on the director's radar…again, in a good way. I see yet another commendation in your near future."

Six tried to force back the smile, but he couldn't. For what he'd accomplished, he deserved a commendation and more. "Speaking of future, I need to catch my flight. I'd tell you I look forward to working with you again…but I don't. Gonna settle myself down behind a desk at Langley for a while."

"Uh, uh. Not so fast. I'm not finished with you yet, Mr. Chance. I had an interesting visitor this morning. The FBI Legat. Imagine my surprise when he handed me a preliminary report from the CART team. Said you ordered it a few days ago."

Six swallowed hard and flashed a sheepish grin. "Oh, that. Yeah. I requested it before my confession. I thought it would take longer than that. Did you, by any chance, review the results?"

Mark handed the file across the table. "As a matter of fact, I did. Take a look. I think you'll find the initial findings as interesting as I did."

Six grabbed the file and scanned through the few pages in the folder. "They broke the encryption on one of the files." The contents almost made him lose his breath. "Jesus. These are Top Secret documents from the Joint Staff…and the J2 in Washington, no less," he said. The J2 was the Directorate of Intelligence, the Chairman of the Joint Chiefs intelligence representative. "What's this doing in Mosin's netbook?"

He locked eyes with Mark, who offered a nod. "You realize what this means, don't you?"

"Yeah," he replied, pinching his lips together. "It means we've got a problem."

•••

Five hours later, an exhausted J.J. neared collapse. Matvey's debriefing yielded more information than she ever expected—and every word he spoke was true. There was another mole in the network. During his endless droning about Troika politics, J.J. connected the dots between Matvey's information and that provided by the late Jim Cartwright after Svetlana murdered him weeks ago. Svetlana had suggested to him that a member of her network was burrowed deep inside the Pentagon, and now J.J. had confirmation. With J.J. about to shut down the money supply, the mole would be forced to reach out to the Washington-based Russian embassy or one of the consulates for his payments, most likely D.C. And with her source Aleksey Dmitriyev planted inside, he was positioned to help her identify the mole and get him off the streets. As long as Dmitriyev remained the Security Officer, the demise of Lana's network was near.

J.J. found comfort in that thought and could now turn her attention to her mother's case files. Back at her desk, she pulled the file from the drawer and took a deep breath before scanning through each sheet. Pages and pages detailing FBI Special Agent Naomi Jones' work inside the Black Panther Party. Clerks filed the most current documents at the front, so she started from the back so she could grasp how the case progressed from beginning to end.

Nothing appeared out of the norm at first. FD-302s. Operations reports outlining her activities. Very little suspicious activity, but it was clear in Jack Sabinski's reports that he hated her father, Max McCall, with a fervent passion. The visceral nature of his reporting bled through the page like Sharpie ink. At last, she reached it. The report filed on the day of her mother's shooting. J.J. read every word with microscopic focus and two familiar names were all over it—Jack Sabinski and John Nixon, the agent who drafted the report.

It was 1989. The FBI had received reports that members of the Nation of Islam had broken off to create the New Black Panther Party for Self Defense. One of Nixon's CIs told him the group had collected an arms cache in a Dallas warehouse containing armor piercing bullets that could cut through bullet proof vests. The CI reported that the cache would be used to target local law enforcement officers accused of brutality against the black community. The allegations indicated Max McCall set up a meeting between the arms supplier and the group; Naomi's supervisor sent her in to investigate. When the FBI and ATF raided the warehouse, her father pulled out a gun to fire on the agents, and the gun went off. In his attempt to kill the agents, the bullet severed Naomi in a major artery which eventually killed Agent Jones.

J.J. struggled to take in air.

My father … killed my mother?

Her stomach hardened, and she felt lightheaded as tears rushed down her face. Her entire body shook with confusion and shock.

It's not true. It's not true. My father would never…he would never, she repeated over and again in her mind. She lost her breath and carved her hands through her hair. Her heart thumped in her chest as her mind roiled. It didn't make sense.

Why had the Bureau never pressed charges? He never missed a day at home. It didn't make sense. She collapsed backward into her seat, her doubts about the veracity of the report growing by the second. It was clear why they didn't want her to view this file. Every word was bullshit. Somebody had something to hide, and J.J. made it her life's mission to expose the truth and bring down anyone and everyone involved in a coverup.

She wiped the tears from her eyes and returned the file to the locked space in her drawer. She looked down at her watch, and the entire day had flown by. Night fell, and the office was almost empty. At that moment, like never before, she wanted Tony. She needed Tony.

Chapter 53

Friday — FBI Headquarters

It was Russell Freeman's first day back to work after his "episode." He'd promised to take it easy, but today was a special day. He'd scheduled a meeting with Andrei Komarov. From Slayton McCarthy's brutal near-arrest and detainment (at least that's how it appeared in the photos with his face pressed against the asphalt) and the arrests of FBI and Secret Service agents, the Russians were reaping a mighty bitter harvest, especially with the President's announcement earlier that day. The Secret Service, in coordination with the FBI, had located a listening device inside the walls of the White House Situation Room, planted by an agent of the Russian intelligence services, found just one week after signing an agreement with the United States in which they promised to cease intelligence activity in exchange for counterterrorism cooperation.

The President couldn't have made the disclosure with more perfect timing, which is explains why he agreed to the stand-down in the first place—all along he knew he had the leverage to break the agreement…but not before getting the intelligence he needed to track the terrorist cell. While the outcome was a major public relations win for the U.S. government and would give the FBI and CIA the leverage they needed to resume offensive operations, he needed to receive one more concession from the Russians. One that would protect J.J.'s source, Aleksey Dmitriyev, from further scrutiny and pressure while he supported FBI ops.

Freeman fixed his tie as his secretary announced that his visitor had arrived. Andrei Komarov, destined for foreign service from birth it seemed, had a highly Westernized speech and dress. He could pull off an almost undetectable American accent, and his suits were a cut above Brooks Brothers, even on a public servant's salary. As Komarov entered the office, he flashed a half-friendly smile and Freeman greeted him likewise, with a handshake and then offered him a seat.

"I'll stand, thank you."

"Ohhh-kay," Freeman replied. "I'm going to have a seat if you don't mind. My wife will kill me if I die." Nothing from Komarov. He didn't even crack a smile. He intended to put on his hard ass mask so as not to appear that he was in a position of weakness. Freeman shrugged his shoulders inside. He would oblige given what he was about to request.

"If we could dispense with the pleasantries," Komarov growled. "I know what you believe we're here to do. And I will just warn you that Minister Lobanov is prepared to empty Moscow Station if you even attempt to take unfair advantage of what you perceive as our moment of weakness."

Freeman's neck warmed under his collar. He loosened his tie from his neck and rolled back his sleeves. Komarov had come to the wrong barnyard to shovel bullshit.

"Sounds like a threat to me. So, I'll feel free to inform you that the Secretary of State has authorized us to expel two of your people for every one of ours. And that's only the beginning. Let's not forget the world is watching your every move. You implanted a bug in the SitRoom after denying to an FBI Assistant Director of Counterintelligence that officers of your intelligence services engaged in any intel activity…after claiming we're now friends.

"Not to mention the fact that your security services arrested the U.S. Ambassador and the fact that we have hard evidence tying your intelligence services to organized crime and narcotics trafficking. Now, if we let this slip to the press, how do you think the story will play in the court of public opinion? Putin may not give a shit, but you're on the ground. You have to work and make friends in places he doesn't have to."

Komarov let out a long breath and took the seat Freeman originally offered.

Director Freeman continued. "You will you lose your residencies in the United States. And how many of our allies do you think we can persuade to follow our lead?"

Komarov swallowed hard and choked out a gruff, "What do you want?"

Freeman reached into a file on his desk and pulled out a sheet of paper.

"This is a list of people we want you to send home by week's end," he began, "if you agree, the State Department will allow you to refill those slots in a year. We'll put the entirety of the incidents to rest and get on with the important business of ensuring continued rela-tions…however, tenuous they may be at the moment."

Komarov scanned the list. "Boris Gusin, Yuriy Filchenko, Igor Sonin and Vasiliy Turov. Interesting."

Freeman's eyebrow raised. "Igor and Vasiliy were already scheduled to depart. Our surveillance operations suggest Filchenko and Gusin directly supported the SitRoom operation."

Komarov pinched his lips together and said, "Okay. We will agree to the names on this list…with one exception. We keep Igor Sonin…and send Aleksey Dmitriyev home."

Freeman held his poker face despite the shock. Expelling Dmitriyev would defeat the entire purpose of the move, but any reaction on Freeman's part might tip off Komarov, so he rubbed his chin as if he was considering the option and held his real reaction tight to the vest.

"Listen, I don't care who you select…as long as he's counterintelli-gence."

Komarov stood up and offered a handshake. "Fine. We have an agreement. Now, if you will excuse me, I must return to the Embassy."

"Glad we could reach a mutual understanding," Freeman said. "I'm certain both of our governments will be pleased. I'll expect to see the departures within the week. My secretary will escort you out."

After Komarov had left, Freeman collapsed into his desk and rubbed his temples. The move intended to remove any danger surrounding J.J.'s source may have resulted in his departure. He hoped Komarov was bluffing…but he'd never bluffed before. Freeman shook his head and fell back into his seat in frustration. His stress level went through the roof, but he didn't have to worry about his wife killing him…not if J.J. got to him first.

Chapter 54

Tony cracked open his eyes and looked at the clock. It was SEVEN P.M. and already dark outside. His head felt like lead bricks, and he sucked his tongue, smacking to remove the cotton mouth. His first thought was J.J. and why he hadn't heard from her. He picked up his cell phone and looked—five text messages in the past half hour. All from J.J., all unreturned. He was in trouble. As he pulled the sheets back to swing his feet over the edge of the bed, he felt movement on the other side.

He looked over his shoulder hoping it was J.J., praying it was J.J. but knowing inside that it wasn't. His memory of opening the door and allowing Gia inside came rushing back in the surge of a broken damn. His heart thumped when he saw just how naked she was.

He'd messed up in the worst way.

Although the sheet covered her midriff, her pertly formed, taut breasts and firm dark nipples were shielded only by her long flowing hair. Not an ounce of fat where it shouldn't be. Any other man would go for broke, slip his hardness inside her, so they could both walk away with an orgasm if not their lives. But at that moment he knew, like no other time—he was in love with J.J. All he wanted from Gia was her absence.

"What the hell?" he said, bolting upright. He held his head as if to keep his brain from exploding. "What happened?"

He scanned the room and noticed that the empty bottles of Jack and Vodka lay empty. "Shit! You gotta get outta here," he said, shaking her awake. Then he jumped out of bed and dressed at top speed. "I don't care what happened here. It doesn't mean anything. I'm in love with J.J."

Groggy, Gia pulled herself up and covered herself with a sheet as if he'd made her feel more naked than she already was. "Nothing happened," she said as he scrambled to put his socks and shoes on. "I wanted you…but you passed out."

Gia's words were still hanging in the air when the door flung open, and J.J. stormed in. With her mouth gaping open, she shook her head no, her eyes shifting back and forth between a not yet dressed Tony and a half-naked Gia. J.J.'s face crumbled, and Tony witnessed a heartbreaking for the first time in his life. His broke too.

He started toward her, saying, "J.J. it's not what you—"

She cut him off and growled through clenched teeth. "You lying son of a bitch! Stay the fuck out of my life. I never want to see your face again!" Then she charged down the hall toward her room.

Tony made sure Gia cleared out, and he finished getting dressed. He grabbed his badge and keys, holstered his gun, and slipped into his jacket. J.J. would run, and he had to stop her. Whatever drama they were going through right now, she had enemies out there, people who might still want her dead.

As he opened the door, he saw her fleeing down the hall with one suitcase in hand. She stepped onto the elevator before he could catch her, so he took the stairwell down to the garage level and listened for a car to start. The ex-agent and now Plaza security chief who got them the room rates had also managed to get them premium parking near the valet stand, so she didn't have far to run. The moment he turned the corner, he saw her taillights glow as she sped up the ramp.

He jumped in his car and followed her, trying to call her on the cell, but it went straight to voicemail; she'd turned off her phone. They sped down West 58th Avenue, blowing through light after light. His heart pounded through his chest as he feared she might be killed in an accident before he ever reached her.

At once, he heard the vroom of a black Range Rover with tinted glass zoom past him at twice his speed at least. It slowed as it reached J.J.'s car, and an arm emerged from the window wielding a gun.

He heard five pops before the truck disappeared, and J.J.'s car careened into a light pole.

"J.J.!" he yelled, screaming in a register he didn't know he could reach. "Nooooooooooo!" he cried out. He couldn't see through his tears, nor catch his breath. His body went into autopilot as he stopped, jumped out of his car and ran to hers, which was now a mass of mangled steel and broken glass.

Bystanders helped him pull the jammed door open as he caught himself saying over and again. "Please don't be dead. Don't you goddamned die on me, J.J.!"

He flung the door open and yelled. "Somebody call an ambulance," as he eyed her motionless body slumped over the wheel. His stomach jerked as the tears began to flow. Her seatbelt was unsecured. Her head was bloody, and her windshield shattered. He lifted her from the driver's seat, carried her to safety, and laid her on the ground. He checked her breathing; it was faint. She clung to life by a thread. He examined her body for gunshot wounds—one in the arm another in the thigh.

He wrapped her in his arms and held her limp hand in his as the siren, which sounded from a distance, grew closer. "Stay with me, babe. Don't you leave me, dammit. Don't leave me. I can't lose you…not this way."

Chapter 55

"MEMORIES ARE THE KEY NOT TO THE PAST, BUT TO THE FUTURE." CORRIE TEN BOOM

Monday Afternoon — New York City

The droning tone of ceaseless beeps snatched J.J. from her slumber. She emerged from her fog and strained to force her eyes open as the sun glared through the picturesque window. At the foot of her bed, her father and brother stood with their mouths dropping open as she struggled to move.

"J.J.?" her father said, tears of joy falling from his eyes. "You're awake?"

She groaned and blinked through her half-open eyes until the haze cleared from her vision, and her view sharpened. Her eyes scrolled up to the ceiling flinching at the glare from the fluorescent lights then shifted to the television perched on the wall mount in front her bed. Her eyes were sensitive to the light, and her head felt as if her brain had been squeezed in a vise grip. To her right, a blue and white checkered curtain hung between the divider.

"You've been in an accident, baby," her father said, grabbing her hand. "You're in the hospital. How do you fe—." He interrupted himself as he turned toward the footsteps approaching the door.

J.J.'s eyebrows scrunched in confusion when Tony burst past the curtain, his eyes wide and expression urgent. He rushed to her side, with heavy breaths. His cracked red eyes divulged his sleeplessness.

He snuggled her other hand against his cheek and pressed her fingers between his. In a loud whisper said, "You're awake! Those baby browns sure are a sight for my sore eyes. How you feelin'?"

J.J. was baffled beyond comprehension. *Why is Tony here?* she thought. *And why is he touching me?*

She tightened her lips, looked at her father and brother with a curious expression, and shifted her glance back to Tony. She pulled her hand from his and touched her head which was bandaged. "Tired. Confused," she said, attempting to sit up straight. "Where am I? What happened?"

Tony's eyes searched until they locked on the remote control for the bed; he handed it to her.

She pressed the button, and the head of the bed moved upright. Then she inspected the bandages on her arm and felt another tight one around her thigh. "Wha— I don't understand what's going on. How'd I get here?"

"You don't remember anything?" Tony asked.

J.J. stared off into the distance and sunk into her thoughts, searching her mind for any memory of what happened. The only thing she remembered would have landed her in church, perhaps, not the hospital. He reached up to touch her head; she pulled back.

"You were in an accident," Malcolm said. "Three days ago."

"Three days?" J.J. said, checking her wrist for her watch. Instead, she found the hospital bracelet with her name spelled across it. "Oh my God, was anybody hurt? Was it my fault?"

"Just you," her father said. "And a light pole. You were shot...in your arm and thigh. Flesh wounds. You'll be okay."

"Shot? Me? My god...what? I don't understand."

"No, see—," Tony began when the doctor interrupted him.

A white-coated gentleman strode in with a stethoscope dangling from his neck. "Ahhh, I see our patient's awake," he said as he scanned her chart.

Everyone eyed the doctor with awkward expressions.

He scanned each machine wired to J.J. and asked everyone to move aside so he could check her vitals. He pulled a skinny flashlight from his front pocket and shined it in both eyes; they watered from the glare.

J.J. examined his expression, looking for good news or bad, but she couldn't discern which.

"You took quite a blow to the head, young lady. How are you feeling?"

"Ugh, I don't know," she said. "I've got a killer headache. My back is killing me. Every muscle in my body aches like someone pulled them out of a blender."

The doctor looked around the room. "You had a pretty nasty accident. Your seatbelt wasn't secured, so you've sustained some pretty significant trauma to your head and chest."

"She suffered some memory loss…at least about what happened," Max McCall said.

The doctor slowly unloaded a barrage of questions, asking J.J. her name, birthdate, address, age, etc. She considered each one and answered those involving her past with accuracy. Still something was missing.

"What do you do for a living?"

"I'm an FBI agent," she said.

"Do you know the gentlemen standing in this room?" he asked.

She nodded, yes. "That's my father, Max McCall and my brother Malcolm."

"And?"

"Oh, That's—," she started, as a tall, hunk of chocolate entered the room bringing a bright smile to her face. "Six! Baby, I'm so glad you're here," she said, her voice full of joy. A far cry from the flat greeting she gave Tony. She reached out her arms to receive him, stoking Tony's ire. His expression soured. "Did you hear? I've been in an accident."

"I know," Six replied. He looked at her in complete and utter confusion, shrugging at Tony. But he returned her smile and entered her welcoming arms. "Uhhh, that's why I'm here."

Tony jumped to her side. "What's going on? I mean, I'm sorry about what happened, but—for chrissakes, J.J. You can't do this."

She shook her head. "What are you talking about, Tony? I don't understand," she said, increasing in agitation. "In my last memory…I was with Six. I'm not…why are you here?"

Moments later, a beautiful Italian-looking woman poked her head in the door. "Tony? Is everything okay?"

J.J.'s eyebrow crinkled in even more confusion. She volleyed her glance between Tony and the woman. "Wow, she's pretty. Don't I feel inadequate. This must be your girlfriend, Tony. Introduce us."

"You…you don't remember her? She's on the task force," he said. "Uhh…Gia, this is J.J. But Gia's *not* my girlfriend. We only work together."

Gia scrunched her eyebrows. "Pleasure…to, uhh…meet you?"

J.J. started to offer her hand when an itching sensation shot through her fingers. Her eyes began to water. "What task force?"

She turned toward the doctor who appeared to be alarmed but blew off his expression; it was the itching that bothered her most. She didn't know what brought it on all of a sudden. "Please, come in, Gia. Nice to meet you. I apologize but I'm still trying to figure out what's going on here."

"Uhhh, I'm just going to wait outside. Glad to see you're okay," Gia said.

A crawling sensation started from J.J.'s fingertips and up through her arms. She dug her fingernails into her skin and began to scratch until whelps rose like swelled track lines across her arm.

"God, my skin is itching me like crazy, doc," she said. "Do you think I could get some lotion… calamine lotion?"

"Uhhh, J.J. I think we need to—," Tony began.

"Oh. Forgive my manners. Six, have you met Tony?" J.J. asked. "Tony and I have been working together for a couple of months."

J.J. glanced down at her finger and scanned the room. "Umm, where's my purse? I need my engagement ring. I didn't lose it in the accident, did I?"

A collective "Huh?" emanated from every mouth in the room.

"I didn't tell you guys?" J.J. said, beaming from ear to ear. "Six proposed to me, and I said yes," she squealed. "I'm getting married!"

About the Author

S.D. Skye is a former FBI Counterintelligence Analyst in the Russia program and supported cases during her 12-year tenure at the Bureau. She has personally witnessed the blowback the Intelligence Community suffered due to the most significant compromises in U.S. history, including the arrests of former CIA Case Officer Aldrich Ames and two of the Bureau's own—FBI Agents Earl Pitts and Robert Hansen. She has spent 20 years in the U.S. Intelligence Community.

Skye is a member of the Maryland Writer's Association, Romance Writers of America, and International Thriller Writers. She's addicted to writing and chocolate—not necessarily in that order—and currently lives in the Washington D.C. area with her son. Skye is hard at work on several projects, including the next installment of the series.

For all the up-to-date news on S.D. Skye and the J.J. McCall Series visit:

Blog: www.authorsdskye.com
Facebook: www.facebook.com/authorsdskye
Twitter: www.twitter.com/sdskye1

www.ingramcontent.com/pod-product-compliance
Lightning Source LLC
Chambersburg PA
CBHW061016120726
47910CB00006B/1971